LOVE ON LEAVE

A HISTORICAL ROMANCE COLLECTION

JAYNE DAVIS

Verbena Books

CONTENTS

SAVING MEG

JAYNE DAVIS

A Regency Romance Novella

Copyright © 2023 by Jayne Davis

ACKNOWLEDGMENTS

Copyediting & proofreading: Sue Davison

Cover design: P Johnson

Thanks to my critique partners on Scribophile for comments and suggestions, particularly Jim, Lola, and Alex.

Thanks also to Beta readers Tina, Cilla, Dawn, Doris, Helen, Kristen, Leigh, Mary, Melissa, Patricia, Safina, Sarah, Sue, and Wendy.

CHAPTER 1

orcestershire, December 1812

Lieutenant Jonathan Lewis stopped by the finger-post at the edge of the trees, the breath of his hired horse making white clouds in the frigid air. Although snow blanketed the landscape, drifting against hedges and plastering over the lettering on the sign, he knew his way. He was almost home—if Upper Westley could still be called that—and weary to his core.

The road to his left led to the village, not half a mile away. It was only mid-afternoon, but the tiny flakes of snow drifting down turned anything more than a few hundred yards distant into grey shadows, fading into the gloom.

Upper Westley was his destination today, but he hesitated. To his right, the dark gap between the trees marked the entrance to a narrow path through the woods, as familiar as the road. It was the short cut to Oakdene House that he'd used in his youth. Oakdene had been a refuge at times—a home where the man of the house had never been in his cups, and spoke only kind words to his family. Then, the wood had been a magical land in which he and Fred Rymer had fought imaginary dragons and rescued maidens from towers. One maiden, to be precise. Meg, Fred's freckle-faced younger sister, had acted the helpless damsel only under protest, climbing unaided in and out of the oak trees that were their castle turrets.

Jon shifted in his saddle, the creak of leather drowned by the sound of the horse snorting and pawing the ground. Meg was no longer a playmate—not to him, at least. That first leave, after he and Fred had been eighteen months in the army, had changed everything. Fred had been happy to tell tales of derring-do in the taproom of the village inn, but Jon had revelled in the peace and calm of Oakdene, and Meg's company. Meg had matured into an attractive young woman—very attractive indeed. Or perhaps he'd only just noticed that her hair wasn't merely brown, but the rich colour of chestnuts, and that she had a smile that went straight to his heart. His feelings then had gone far beyond friendship. He'd said nothing, for an impecunious soldier about to go back to war was no fit husband for any woman.

The mare tossed her head and took a couple of steps forward. He patted her neck and brought his mind back to his destination. Oakdene was less than a mile away through the trees, but the branches were too low for a man on horseback. It was at least a couple of miles by the lane that looped around the edge of the woods, and then it would be the same distance back before he could head down the road to the village inn and a room for the night.

Waiting another day would make no difference, surely? He should turn here and let the poor animal get into a warm stable; she'd worked hard today, carrying him all the way from Cheltenham, the snow deepening as they got further north. He needed rest himself, too— preferably a hot bath and a meal, then several days' sleep.

But he'd come here before visiting his mother because he'd promised Fred to take care of Meg and Mrs Rymer. It was over two months since he'd made that vow, kneeling beside his friend in the medical tent. And then repeated it to himself the next day as the chaplain read the funeral service over the hastily dug mass grave. Two months—but he could not have got here any sooner.

Squinting up at the sky, there were only swirling flakes against the grey. Tiny flakes at the moment, but who was to say what would happen overnight? The roads might be impassable in the morning. But the feeling was more than that. He wanted to call at Oakdene tonight, to see Meg, no matter how exhausted or travel-stained he was. Being with Meg would help him forget the first, and she wouldn't care about the second, nor would her mother.

He urged the mare on—she would get a warm stable, but not just yet.

❧

Meg gripped the arms of her chair, resisting the impulse to pace the room. The cracking of the fire and the steady click of Mama's knitting needles only served to amplify her frustration. Everything appeared so peaceful—even the snow outside was only tiny, drifting flakes, floating gently downwards in the gathering dusk. Snow, isolating the house.

Isolating *her*—although that wasn't the snow, not really. Despite Mama's presence, and the others downstairs, she had never felt so alone. Papa was gone, Fred was gone, and even Pamela and Sarah—girlhood friends from the village—had married and moved away. There was Jon—a true friend, and more—but she'd heard nothing from him since that one, brief letter from Burgos. Shouldn't he be back by now, if he was still alive?

No. *Be sensible, Meg!* Letters would return to England much faster than men, particularly men who might not be released by their commanding officers merely for the asking. But newspaper reports told of the British army being harried by the French all the way to the Portuguese border, and of this retreat being as harsh as the one to Coruña four years ago. Fred and Jon had survived that, and much else since. She *had* to believe Jon had survived this, too.

Someone knocked at the door, and Meg jumped up to open it, hoping she was not about to have another confrontation with Cousin Rupert. But it was only the cook, bearing a tray with tea and biscuits.

"I've brought you some tea, Miss Meg."

"Thank you, Mrs Baines." Meg stood back to allow her into the room. "I would have come down for it."

"It's no trouble, Miss. I was wondering if you're going to eat dinner downstairs today?" She set the teapot on the little table by the window. "Mr Rupert said he hoped you would."

"That would be nice, dear," Mama said, before Meg could answer.

"No, Mama," Meg said firmly, then turned back to Mrs Baines. "We'll eat up here. I don't want to make extra work for you, so I'll come down to fetch it."

Mrs Baines shrugged. "It's no trouble, like I said. It seems a shame, though, Mr Rupert eating alone every day. So helpful as he's been, ever since…" She pressed her lips together and finished setting out the cups and plates.

Meg sat at the table as the door closed behind the cook and rubbed a hand across her forehead. Worrying over this was bringing on a headache. Since Fred had died, this was *her* house, not Rupert's.

Rupert appeared to be so *reasonable*; that was part of the problem. His motives had only become plain—to her, if to no-one else—three weeks ago, and by then everyone around had come to the conclusion that he was a caring young man. After all, he'd put his own affairs to one side to help his widowed aunt and his cousin.

"Don't fret so, dear." Mama put her knitting to one side and came to sit by Meg, pouring tea for them both. "It will be all right soon, you'll see. He'll help you. He's a good man."

"Then why are we sitting up here instead—?" Meg stopped talking as Mama's face crumpled and tears glistened in her eyes.

"It's my fault, isn't it? Ever since my accident—"

"Never think that." Meg reached across the table and took her mother's hands. Mama had fallen down the stairs only a few days before they'd heard of Fred's death. The bang to her head had made her more easily upset, as well as affecting her memory. "I'm sorry for snapping at you. I'm only worried about what Rupert will do."

Mama pulled a handkerchief from her sleeve and dabbed her eyes. "I've said before, dear—it will be all right when he comes home."

"Fred won't be coming back." Meg gripped her mother's hands

again. The words had come out more harshly than she'd intended. Her brother was dead, and no amount of wishing could change that. Sometimes Mama understood, but mostly she seemed to live in a world of her own, where everything would turn out right.

But Mama smiled. "Light another lamp, will you? It's time to shut out the night."

Meg sighed, and took a spill from the jar on the mantelpiece as Mama reached to close the curtains. She'd just lit one end in the fire when Mama spoke.

"There, I said he'd come."

Now Mama was seeing things! "Who has come?"

"Look, dear. I told you."

Meg cursed inwardly as she felt heat on her fingers, and threw the spill into the fire. She put her face close to the glass, rubbing to clear the mist from the cold panes. This window gave a view to one side of the house, and she made out the dark shape of a rider in the lane.

"It could be anyone." There were other houses further along the narrow road. "He will probably ride past."

Mama shook her head as she straightened and pulled the curtains together. "It was a soldier. I saw the shape of his shako. He said he'd look after us, and here he is. He wrote after he was killed, don't you remember?"

For a moment, Meg feared that Mama was talking of a ghost, but her sometimes addled wits had never taken her in that direction before. Not liking to display her forgetfulness about names, Mama had taken to never using names at all.

If she wasn't talking about Fred, who did she mean? Jon? He *had* promised to return as soon as he could. A tiny glimmer of hope started in Meg's chest as she peered out of the window again, but the rider had gone on.

Taking another spill, she lit the extra lamp with a hand that shook a little, and listened for the clop of hooves on the drive. A futile endeavour—the snow would muffle any such sound.

She opened the door and stepped onto the landing. From here she'd be able to hear what was said at the door—if Mama had been right. The feeling that someone might have come to help her—that *Jon* might be here—made her feel dizzy with relief.

As Jon approached the turning, Oakdene House became visible as a darker shadow in the gloom, a yellow glow showing from one of the upstairs windows. Then a hedge blocked his view until he reached the low stone gateposts that flanked the entrance to the drive. The snow was smooth here, unmarked by wheels or hooves. If it hadn't been for that glimpse of light, he might have thought the place deserted.

It felt wrong to ride this way alone, without Fred beside him. The last time had been almost exactly a year ago, both of them with a fortnight to spend in England while the battalion was in cantonments behind the Portuguese border. They'd arrived to find that Mr Rymer had died suddenly only the month before. A letter informing Fred of the fact had been awaiting them when they returned to the Peninsula.

The strength with which Meg had dealt with her father's illness and death while her mother grieved had drawn him towards her even more. But that had not been the time to declare himself, even if she had returned his regard. Instead, he'd kept in the background during those two short weeks, running errands when asked, removing himself from the family's grief when there was nothing for him to do. He'd grieved himself—Mr Rymer had been a better father to him than his own.

Now here he was again, in depressingly similar circumstances.

A glimmer of light showed through a gap between the curtains in the parlour as Jon dismounted and looped the reins over the mare's neck. He plied the knocker and stood back, waiting impatiently until he heard footsteps in the passageway.

The Rymers' manservant opened the door, wearing an apron over homespun breeches and waistcoat. He regarded Jon with round eyes, before a smile spread across his lined face.

"Mr Jon!"

He stood back, opening the door further, and Jon stepped over the threshold. "Farlow—good to see you. Is Miss Rymer at home?"

Before Farlow could answer, another voice spoke. "Miss Rymer is not receiving guests." A man came out of the parlour, clad in a well-fitting blue tailcoat over grey waistcoat and pale trousers. Jon was trying to place him when a sudden scuffle at the top of the stairs drew his attention. He thought he saw a swirl of a black skirt through the bannisters, but no-one came down.

"My cousin is indisposed," the newcomer said. "Farlow, you may return to your duties."

Cousin? Jon racked his brain as the manservant grimaced behind the newcomer's back and vanished through the kitchen door.

Rupert… Rupert Taylor; that was it. A connection on Mrs Rymer's side of the family.

"Mr Taylor." Jon nodded briefly.

"And you are…?" Taylor ran his eyes down Jon's greatcoat to his boots, both dripping into a spreading puddle on the floor. His eyes narrowed. "Lewis, isn't it? The drunken farmer's son? Margaret won't want to see you. Her brother would still be with us if you hadn't encouraged him to join the army."

What?

Taylor came closer, too close. Jon took a step back, into the flakes of snow beginning to drift in through the open door.

"Besides, she has other things to think about now, rather than reliving the past. A new future to look forward to." He smiled. "We are betrothed. On Tuesday, Miss Rymer will become Mrs Taylor."

CHAPTER 2

Meg's happiness at hearing Jon's voice turned to fright as a bony hand covered her mouth and another gripped her arm. Her nostrils filled with the smell of stale tobacco that always hung around Morrison, Rupert's manservant.

Heart racing, she twisted her head from side to side as he dragged her along the landing, but her struggles had no effect. She pulled against him again, but he didn't let go, his strength surprising for such a thin man. He did, though, stop moving—standing still enough for her to hear what was being said at the front door.

"...still be with us... reliving the past... betrothed... Tuesday..."

No! Meg turned her head and bit Morrison's hand, but although he muttered a curse, his grip on her only tightened. She kicked out—anything to let Jon know she was here—but Morrison grabbed her around the waist with his other arm and lifted her so her feet flailed above the floor.

And then it was too late. Jon's voice came, the words all too clear. "I wish you both well, Mr Taylor. Please give my regards to your cousin and aunt." And the door closed with a thump.

Jon mustn't leave without talking to her! Such a close friend surely wouldn't believe she wanted to marry Rupert?

She slumped in Morrison's grip. Why wouldn't he believe it? Everyone else did.

The rasp of bolts being shot home on the front door spurred her into another struggle. If she could get to a window and call...?

This time Morrison let her go, rubbing his bitten hand. Meg raced along the landing—her room looked over the drive.

Her hand was on the latch when hard fingers closed around her arm again. Morrison—and Rupert stood behind him.

"Tell your man to take his hands off me," she spat.

Rupert nodded, and Morrison let go. Rupert jerked his head, and with a poisonous look at Meg, Morrison clattered down the stairs.

"Is something wrong, dear?" Mama asked, coming out onto the landing. "Has he gone away?"

"All is well, Aunt Mary." Rupert's voice oozed reassurance and sincerity—the tone that had fooled Meg, too, at first. "It was only someone asking directions. Why don't you rest before dinner?"

Mama smiled as he led the way back to the bedroom and ushered her in.

"No need to upset your Mama," he said, coming back to Meg. "We wouldn't want to have to bring Mr Busby back, would we? You know he wishes to treat her in his sanatorium."

Meg turned and stalked down the stairs and into the parlour. She rounded on Rupert as he entered behind her. "Are you proud of yourself? Threatening women—blackmailing—to get your own way? And allowing your man to *assault* me?"

"Needs must, my dear." He sat in a chair by the fire and picked up a glass of wine. "And it's hardly a threat to wish for my father's sister to get the best medical treatment for her condition."

Meg's fingernails dug into her palms as she restrained the impulse to shout at him. Or throw things. They'd already had this argument several times. It was not even an argument, really—he just kept saying the same thing in a calm tone as if explaining something to a simpleton. So calm that, if any of the servants had been listening, they would have praised him for keeping his temper when faced with an unreasonable and hysterical woman.

"Have some wine, my dear Margaret. It might help to settle you." He held a glass out, but she ignored it. "I do begin to wonder if your mother's accident merely triggered some… some inherent weakness in her brain. It is to be hoped that such a weakness is not hereditary."

Meg stared at him and shook her head. Was he threatening her now? But she mustn't argue—that would only please him, and if the servants heard her raised voice, it would support his case.

"Why did you send… Lieutenant Lewis away?" It might be wise not to reveal how close their friendship was. Or had been. She pushed that thought aside.

"What good would it do you, or Aunt Mary, to hear the details of poor Fred's death? Aunt Mary is… fragile enough."

"I see." She took a deep breath. "How considerate of you, cousin."

"I trust you are not stupid enough to attempt to send a message to him?" He was examining his wine, as if this conversation were of minor importance. "The servants know on which side their bread is buttered."

They did. It wasn't that they were disloyal; more that Rupert had convinced Mrs Baines and Annie that he would be a good master to work for, and that Meg was being missish in her reluctance to marry him. And Farlow—she'd thought to send him with a message to the vicar, but he'd had no reason to go into the village since Rupert had come. No doubt everyone would say how helpful Rupert had been, seeing to all the ordering of food and paying of bills.

Meg shrugged. "How would a message to the Lieutenant help me? Besides, it is still snowing—I doubt Farlow could reach the village in this weather." That wasn't a terribly good reason—Jon had reached Oakdene, and not ten minutes ago. "You've never been here in winter, cousin, but the road to Upper Westley is notorious for getting blocked when it snows." That would be news to the villagers, but Rupert was unlikely to detect her lie.

"Good. I'm glad to see you're being sensible, Margaret." He waved a hand in dismissal and picked up a book. Seething, Meg bit down on her anger and controlled the impulse to slam the parlour door behind her.

It was Sunday—the banns would have been read for the third time this morning. Rupert had prevented her from going to the village these last few weeks, so she'd had no chance to talk to the vicar, or anyone else who might help her.

Her only option was what it had always been—to deny she was willing to wed when they got to the church. But she had a lowering feeling that it would merely delay the inevitable. Rupert would still pressure her to accept, and might well have the sympathy of everyone else. After all, only a hysterical woman would change her mind like that at the last moment.

It was Rupert's threat to Mama that worried her most. He could still send Mama to an asylum if she married him, of course, but she suspected he would not. That would use up some of the money he would gain from becoming the new owner of this house and the farms.

No!

Jon stepped back from the door as it shut in his face, his hands clenched into fists.

It could not be true. Could it?

He stared at the door as if it might answer him, then looked up. Above, the windows were dark—no-one was trying to call him back, saying there had been a mistake.

Swallowing against rising nausea, he took a deep breath and hunched his collar higher. Meg—the Meg he used to know—would have welcomed him in, sent Farlow to stable the horse, and produced a hot toddy and a meal. She would have done so even if she were betrothed to another man. They were still friends, and she knew Fred had persuaded him to join the army, not the other way around.

Did females find Rupert Taylor attractive in a way that he couldn't see? Certainly he was better dressed than Jon, whose greatcoat and faded red jacket bore the signs of the hard retreat across Spain and his travels since. But there had been something odd in Taylor's expression

—a gloating, self-satisfied look. Then there had been that movement at the top of the stairs. Had Taylor *prevented* Meg from seeing him? Did Meg really want to marry the man?

He would come back later to find out.

Feeling a little better with that decision made, Jon led the mare on around the house and past the small building where the Rymers kept their horse and gig. He turned beyond the hedge that separated the gardens from the surrounding fields and headed for the woods. He would return on foot later—he needed to speak to Meg without anyone else seeing him, and the horse would give him away. If he led the animal through the trees now, they would make a trail that would be easy to follow when he came back in the dark.

The white swan on the inn sign was invisible through its coating of snow, but welcoming light spilled out of the windows. Jon rode down the lane at the side of the building and dismounted in the small stable yard.

"Anyone there?"

He had to shout again before a door opened and a figure shuffled out, a sack keeping the snow from his head and shoulders.

Jon recognised the man's limp. "Harding—how are you?"

The figure straightened and squinted into his face. "Lewis? Bloody hell, man, what happened to you? You don't look at all well." He took the mare's reins and led her into the stables. "Come far?"

"Only from Cheltenham today." And all the way across Spain and Portugal before that, then the packet boat from Lisbon to Falmouth. The journey had seemed longer and harder because Fred wasn't with him.

"Bad business, Captain Rymer getting—" Harding broke off. "Get yourself inside. I'll hear all about it later, no doubt. No, go in the back way; it's nearer."

Jon did as he was told, slinging his saddle bags over his shoulder and pushing open the rear door into the scullery. Opening the kitchen door, a wall of warm air hit his chilled flesh, thick with the rich smell of fried onions and roasting meat.

"Jonny Lewis!" The landlady turned from the kitchen table to look him up and down. "Sam! Look who's arrived!"

Jon winced at her shout—Mrs Munnings was used to making herself heard above the babel of a busy taproom, but even his sergeant would have been proud of such a voice.

"Are you wanting a room? Of course you are. You look proper frozen, and half-starved as well. Get yourself into the taproom—I'll send some soup through while I sort out a bath and a room."

He'd had some idea of asking what she knew about Taylor, but her plan sounded exactly what he needed. A warm body and full stomach first, then information.

CHAPTER 3

*H*alf an hour later—thawed, clean, and shaved—Jon sat in the inn's parlour with a plate before him full of thick slices of beef and rich gravy, accompanied by roast potatoes and parsnips. He still wore his stained trousers, hastily dried in front of the fire, but Mr Munnings had lent him a clean shirt while one of the maids laundered his own linens. Apart from worrying about Meg, the only things stopping him from fully appreciating his dinner were his bone-weariness and the numerous pairs of eyes watching him.

Watching and waiting—at Mrs Munnings' insistence—before interrogating him about Spain and Portugal and what had happened to poor Fred Rymer. Things he didn't want to talk about, not yet. Fred's death, and the losses his battalion had taken on the long trek across Spain, were still too recent, too raw.

"Tell me what's happened here while I've been away," he said, to break the unnerving silence. He let the talk wash over him—someone's wife had run off, someone else had opened a new shop, the farm where Jon had grown up had been sold again…

It wasn't until someone mentioned Captain Rymer's name that he started to pay attention.

"Seems they're all set up." That was the clerk Mr Trythall had taken on when Jon decided that learning to be an attorney wasn't for him. "Miss Rymer's marrying that Taylor chap."

"Cousin, isn't he?" someone else said. "Good of him to come and help out when Mrs Rymer fell."

"…never been the same since…"

"…can't remember much, they say…"

Meg's mother was ill?

"Needs a man about the house, if you ask me."

Not Rupert, Jon thought savagely.

"Nice chap. Was ever so friendly when he came to get his horse re-shod. Said things have suffered there since Mr Rymer died…"

"…so sad…"

"…Taylor paid their bill for them…"

"…hard for two women to manage alone…"

"…bought extra sugar and tea—said they needed cheering up…"

"…woman has no business dealing with rents and leases…"

"Give the poor man some peace," the barmaid said, distributing another round of ale as the audience nodded and shrugged. "In fact, take yourselves off to the taproom and let him finish his meal."

Jon gave her a grateful smile. Becky had been doing this job since he could remember, and seemed to know everyone's business, but she always had a kind word. Amid good-natured grumbles, the others allowed her to usher them out. A few minutes later she returned with a dish of steaming apple pudding and a jug of cream, moved his empty plate to a nearby table and sat down opposite him.

"Did you call on your mother on the way, Jon?"

"Not this time. I came here first, straight from Falmouth. I promised Fred I'd look after his family. I'll visit Mother on my way back." He picked up the spoon she'd set beside the bowl, but didn't eat. "What happened to Mrs Rymer?" Poor Meg, having to deal with that as well as Fred's death.

"Fell down the stairs, she did, and banged her head. Never been quite right up here since." She tapped her temple. "That wasn't much before we heard about Captain Rymer. Good thing she'll have someone to help her with everything."

"I heard," Jon said, trying not to snap the words. Was he the only one who hadn't taken to Taylor? "From Taylor himself, before he shut the door in my face."

Becky's brows rose. "That don't sound nice. He was a pleasant enough bloke when he come in here. Come to look after them, he said, when Mrs Rymer didn't get better. But shutting the door in your face, and you come all this way…" She shook her head. "Funny thing, though—I don't remember seeing Miss Rymer in the village since the banns was called."

"Perhaps she's busy looking after her mother." For Meg's sake, he hoped that was the only reason.

Becky frowned, then went over to the door. "Charlie Allsup!" Her voice could rival Mrs Munnings'.

Allsup? The grocer? A couple of minutes later Charlie came in—a youth of sixteen or so.

"What did I hear you saying about delivering to the Rymers last week?" Becky asked, resuming her place opposite Jon.

"Last week?"

"You was complaining about cake."

His face cleared. "Oh, yes. I delivered their order last week, and that Taylor told me to leave the stuff and clear off, didn't even give me the time of day. No chance to get a word in edgeways, never mind the bit of cake their cook usually gives me."

Something was definitely wrong there.

"D'you think Miss Rymer wants to marry him?" Becky asked, once Charlie had left the parlour.

"That's what I want to know," Jon said. "I'm going back to find out later."

Becky gave a nod of approval. "You look dead to the world. Have you had enough to eat?"

"Enough for now, thank you." In truth, he wanted nothing more than to lie down somewhere. A full stomach, a pint of ale, and the warm room were conspiring with his fatigue to put him to sleep.

"Go to bed." Becky stood. "I'll come and wake you at… What time?"

"Eleven." If he set off then, everyone in the house should be asleep by the time he got there—including Meg, quite possibly. But if he went earlier and Taylor was still up, he would just be shown the door again. He knew which was Meg's window, and it wouldn't be the first time he'd thrown stones to wake someone.

Five hours. He felt as if only a full week in bed would ease him, but five hours would be a start.

"Don't forget, Becky, will you? No helpful ideas about me needing more rest!"

"I'll get you up, don't worry."

~

Meg lay awake in her bed, as she had done often in recent weeks. She'd eaten dinner with Mama in her room rather than have to sit with Rupert. Mama had retired to bed, sure that everything would be all right now Jon was back. Meg had expressed agreement and retreated to her own room. If only Mama could be right this time.

Downstairs, the clock in the hall chimed the half-hour. Or was it one o'clock? She'd heard the thing tolling midnight what seemed like hours ago.

Did Jon's return change anything? She felt as if it should, but if he'd taken Rupert's words at face value…

No—he could not have done. She turned onto her back, staring up into the darkness. Outside, everything was eerily still, only the wavering call of an owl breaking the silence. A thin sliver of moonlight coming through the curtains indicated that the clouds had cleared.

Another hoot. She loved the sound of tawny owls—so much more tuneful than the screech owls that normally called from the woods.

Owls? When Jon used to come to get Fred for a midnight adventure…

Meg flung back the covers, pulling a wrapper on as she crossed to the window and drew one curtain back. The world outside was patterned in black and white, moonlight bright on the snow and the shadows inky. Nothing moved.

There! As the owl sounded again, a figure stepped out of the shadow of a hedge.

Jon *had* come back!

Heart racing, she opened the window and waved, shivering as the chill air tumbled into the room. Jon raised a hand and pointed sideways, towards the small stable, then disappeared back into the blackness.

Clothes—never mind stays and chemise. The moon lit enough of the room for her to find the gown she'd worn earlier, and she dragged it on over her night rail. Easing open a drawer in the chest, she found her thickest pair of woollen stockings and pulled them on. That would have to do.

The landing outside her door was black, but moonlight lit the stairs. Meg crept along quietly, memories from her youth telling her which squeaky boards to avoid. She got down the stairs without a sound, and went into the kitchen.

A shape huddled in a chair by the stove spoke quietly. "Evening, Miss."

Meg thought her heart had stopped. She let out a shuddering breath as she realised it was Farlow, not Rupert's man. He opened the stove door and pushed something in, then stuck the lit candle into its holder and set it on the table.

"Why are you here, Farlow?"

"Not my choice, Miss. Mr Taylor said someone had to be awake to make sure 'that Lewis man' didn't try to get in. They were his words."

"Oh." Had Rupert told Farlow to stop her going out? "I... I was going to the stable to see if the cat's had her kittens yet." That was a stupid excuse. Farlow knew as well as she did that the cat wasn't expecting.

But Farlow nodded. "You'd be worried about her, yes." His lips curved. "If Mr Taylor or that bean pole that calls himself a valet find you went out there, neither of them would know whether the cat's about to have a litter. And they never told me to stop you going to the stable."

Meg closed her eyes for a moment and let out a breath of relief. "Farlow, why...?" Why was he helping her now when he'd seemed to approve of Rupert's presence?

"He fooled me, I'm afraid to say, Miss. Thought he meant well. But Annie was setting the fire in his room yesterday when Mr Jon called. She saw what Morrison did, and not a word of reprimand from Mr Taylor." He shook his head. "And I remember Mr Jon—he was a good lad. I remember the owls, too, and Mr Fred creeping out."

"Thank you, Farlow." If only he'd understood Rupert's true nature earlier—but that was irrelevant now. She pushed her feet into her old boots and, with a glance at Farlow for permission, took his thick coat off its hook and thrust her arms into the sleeves.

The latch on the back door made little noise, and she picked her way carefully across the moonlit yard. Farlow had cleared the snow in the afternoon, but the thin layer that had fallen since then had frozen into a treacherous sheet.

Jon let himself into the stable with relief, pleased that he didn't have to start digging in the snow to find stones to throw at Meg's window. He left the door open a little so he could see the kitchen door. He wasn't sure what he would do if Meg didn't come, but he should give her some time before starting to worry about that. He tucked his hands beneath his armpits in an attempt to thaw his fingers. At least in here, the horses provided a little warmth, and he was sheltered from the icy breeze. The animals shuffled in their stalls, dim shapes in the feeble light filtering through the windows. The dappled grey was Daisy, the Rymers' old mare; the other must belong to Taylor.

Finally, a dark shape picked its way across the yard, moonlight removing any colour. Meg. He pushed the door open further, then pulled it closed behind her.

"Jon?" Her voice wobbled. "Oh, Jon!"

Without thought, he reached out and drew her towards him,

holding her close. She rested her head on his shoulder, her body shaking.

"Meg?"

"I'm sorry." She lifted her head and sniffed, but her voice sounded no steadier than before.

"Don't be." He raised a hand to her head, pressing it gently against his shoulder again. "Have a good cry, then tell me." Leaning his cheek against her hair as he wrapped his arms around her, he breathed a faint scent of rosewater. Suddenly he didn't feel cold at all. He'd wanted this since that leave after Coruña—but not in these circumstances.

CHAPTER 4

Jon cursed Fred in his mind as he felt Meg's body gradually relax against his own. It wasn't as if Wellington were short of officers—there would have been plenty of others happy to buy his commission if he'd sold out last winter and come home to take his father's place. But Fred had always hankered after an army life, and had no desire to spend his time doing nothing more than overseeing a couple of tenant farms.

"Jon, I'm so happy to see you," she said at last, lifting her head from his shoulder.

He hugged her a little tighter. "It's good to see you, too." Better than good—as if he were home, and they belonged together.

About to ask if she really was going to marry her cousin, he thought better of it. She'd never clung to him like this before. Even if her trouble wasn't Taylor, she'd no business marrying a man she couldn't go to for comfort.

"Tell me about it, Meg." He looked around, straining to see in the gloom. There—a bench against the far wall, beneath pegs holding bridles and reins. "Come, sit down. I've a feeling it will be a long story."

"Not that long."

But she allowed him to lead her to the bench and they sat, shoulders and thighs pressed together. Was it wrong to regret the too-many layers of cloth between them?

"Rupert wants me to marry him."

"And you do not wish to." He needed to hear it.

"No."

Good. A little of the tension in him relaxed. "You could just tell him that." He made the suggestion tentatively—the Meg he knew would have no hesitation in doing so, and he did not wish to sound critical.

"I have, but he takes no notice. He says I'm being hysterical. He says the worry about Mama's fall and then Fred's death is affecting my mind, and he's only doing what's best for me and I should be happy about it."

"Fred did describe him as a lying weasel." He hadn't seen Taylor often when they were all boys, but he did remember Fred's antipathy.

"But I'm not afraid of weasels." Her voice was quiet, defeated.

Afraid of Taylor? He must have some hold over her for this situation to have arisen. Jon took a deep breath, suppressing the wish to break into the house and drag Taylor outside, to make *him* afraid. "I didn't mean to make light of things, Meg. Tell me from the beginning."

"When the letters came…" She stopped and shook her head. "No, not long before we heard about Fred, Mama tripped on the stairs. She seemed to recover, but she's… she's forgetful now. She can remember some things—like how to knit and sew—but not names. And sometimes she forgets things that happened in the past."

So Meg had had to deal with the news of Fred's death without her mother's support. "And Taylor?" he prompted, when she did not continue.

"I wrote to my uncle to let him know about Fred, and Rupert came here straight away. He took a room at the Swan, that time. I thought it was good of him to come to see if he could help. Everyone else did, too—even the vicar said what a helpful young man he was."

Wanting to hear Fred's will, more like, Jon thought savagely.

"He asked me to marry him. He sounded really kind, as if he did want to support me."

How else could he get his hands on the Rymer farms? The ones Meg had been dealing with perfectly well for a year, since the death of her father.

"I said no, and he went away—he seemed to accept my decision. But he came back a few weeks later. Mama… By then, Mama was up and about, but she was still forgetful, or doing silly things like putting salt in the sugar bowl. She gets upset more easily than before, too."

That might not be the result of the accident—Mrs Rymer had lost a husband and a son in a year. And Meg had lost a father and a brother. It wasn't surprising she didn't feel she could cope with her cousin's machinations.

"What did Doctor Curtis say?" He remembered the local doctor as a sensible man.

"There's nothing he can do. She manages perfectly well, mostly. He said time should help, and to try not to worry her. But Rupert… Rupert said a country physician wasn't good enough, and he paid for a man to come from London. He wants… Oh, Jon, he says he can cure her if she goes to his asylum. Mr Busby said that patients' minds become lazy, and have to be shocked into remembering. Rupert described the treatments—ice cold baths and a low diet. And he talked about keeping them calm by not allowing them to see their families until their memories came back."

"Sounds more like torture to me," Jon said, and regretted his words as Meg gave a little gulp. "Rupert thinks this is a way to *help* your mother?"

"He says so, yes. Sometimes I wonder if he's right, and I am harming Mama by not allowing this doctor to…" There were tears in her voice again.

With a muttered curse, Jon put his arm around her and hugged her close. "Never think that, Meg. Is your mother happy—can you tell?"

"I think so."

"Well, then."

"He says his father is Mama's brother, and has a right to ensure she has the best treatment."

Marriage wouldn't change that. "Let me guess, Meg. He says your Mama will be calmer with a man around the house, and if you will only marry him it might not be necessary for her to go to this asylum."

He felt a movement as she nodded. "Something like that, yes. But he could still send her away if we marry. The vicar called the banns without asking if I wanted the match."

The sudden change of subject threw him for a moment. "Did you not object when you heard them?"

"Rupert tried to stop me from finding out. It was a sunny morning, and Mama had a headache, so I walked through the woods to go to the service instead of taking the gig. I tried to stay behind afterwards to tell the vicar I didn't consent, but Rupert had arrived by then and took me away. He said Mama was ill and I was unwise to have left her alone."

"She wasn't ill," he guessed.

"No, she wasn't. But the vicar must have thought I wasn't looking after Mama properly. And Rupert has stopped me going into the village since then."

"You only have to say no in the church, Meg."

"I know. You must think I'm a weak fool."

"No, never that." Not when she'd had so much responsibility thrust upon her.

"I... I feel so alone, Jon. I know Rupert cannot make me say yes, but then I remember that the vicar read the banns without my permission. And Rupert... he's been talking to the magistrate. Farlow drove him there in the gig, and said he looked pleased when he came out. He is always saying things like a woman cannot manage the farms, and I worry that he's right. Or even if he's not, that everyone else will think so and they'll wear me down, and it will cause a huge fuss if I say no in the church..."

"Hush, now. A fuss doesn't matter, and you're not alone while I'm here." He'd start by talking to Mr Trythall tomorrow—the attorney had been a good friend to him in the past. "You have friends in the village." Becky, at least, and probably Mrs Munnings, too, once Becky had told her the situation. Not that two women would have much influence against the magistrate or the vicar, if the men took Taylor's side. No-one could *force* Meg, but he could see how continual pressure might wear her down.

"Mr Trythall will help you."

"But you'll go back to Spain, then I'll be alone again. And you might not come back this—"

"Don't worry, Meg. I'll make sure Rupert takes himself off—permanently—before I leave. Besides, the battalion's being sent to Jersey—not nearly as far away, and no Frenchmen there to fight." He rubbed her back gently, as he'd sometimes done when they were much younger and she'd been distressed about something.

Meg's next words were muffled, sitting as she was with her head on his shoulder. But he heard them clearly enough, for all that.

"Everything would be all right if I had you to help me," she said. "It's a pity I can't marry you."

Meg had said it without thinking, but it felt right. Jon was her best friend—and he'd never teased or pulled her hair like Fred sometimes had. He'd been the one who had backed her up when she wanted to join in their games. The one who'd comforted her when she fell out of a tree, while Fred was busy laughing at her clumsiness. And the one who'd spent hours talking to her when he came home with Fred after Coruña, sharing himself with her while Fred went off drinking with his other friends from childhood.

He had gone very still, his arm stiffening where it still encircled her.

She felt protected, sitting here beside him, his warmth comforting, the feel of his body next to hers reassuring. He would keep her safe.

But he still hadn't spoken. It had been forward of her to suggest it —was he shocked? Offended?

"I'm sorry, Jon. That was—"

"Don't be sorry. Unless you didn't mean it."

Was he agreeing? Oh, she hoped so, but she wished there were more light—she couldn't tell from his voice what he was thinking.

"People will think I'm a jilt." She straightened her spine. "But that's nothing if I escape Rupert."

"They won't believe that of you when they know the circumstances," Jon said, his voice curiously flat. "Shall I ask the vicar to call the banns for us?"

"Will… will he believe you if you say I will not marry Rupert?" He might—he'd known Jon since he was a boy. Then another thought struck and she leaned her head on his shoulder again. "Rupert will say it shows how unfit I am to look after Mama and the farms. And it would be another three weeks—what if he takes Mama? Once he has her… I mean, people will say he's looking after her, and I'm…"

She'd said it all before. Damn Rupert for getting her into this state. And her, for allowing herself to be worn down by him.

"I won't let him take her away. But Meg, I've only got three weeks before I have to return. If you want this, I'll have to get a licence."

"How long will that take?"

"I have to go to Worcester, I think—I'll check with the vicar, or with Mr Trythall. It cannot be above thirty miles, but in this weather… I can't promise to be back by Tuesday morning."

"If I can't find an excuse to delay things, I'll say no at the church." Jon's belief in her gave her heart—she would not let Rupert threaten Mama or herself and get away with it. "If I know you'll be coming back, I don't mind how much fuss it causes or what people say. Rupert cannot do anything in only a day or two."

"That's my girl." He gave her shoulder a quick squeeze and released her.

She felt bereft for a moment, and strangely disappointed at his hearty tone. "Jon, are you sure you're… willing to do this? I… if you are here to back me up, I might—"

"Of course I am." He stood, and pulled her to her feet. "Go in now, Meg; you must be freezing."

No more than he must be—he'd been out in the cold for much longer.

"I'll wait until you've gone in," he added. "The path to the woods is in view of the windows. If anyone sees me leaving, you'll already be safe back in your room."

Not safe. Not yet.

"I'll see you soon, Jon." She stood on tiptoe and kissed his cheek, then slipped out through the door.

Jon watched as Meg trod carefully back across the yard. How much had changed in half an hour! It didn't seem real.

During the last year, he'd spent many an evening in his tent, or in some tumbledown Spanish house where his company had taken shelter, dreaming of coming home to see Meg. Of courting her, in the hope that his feelings might be reciprocated. And dreading that every letter Fred received might bring the news that Meg was betrothed or married.

What he hadn't imagined was being asked to marry her like this—as a way to save her from her cousin. Was that all she wanted of him? Was he only a safer prospect than Taylor?

He shook his head. He was too tired to think clearly. Another few minutes and Meg should be safely back in her room, then he could set off through the snow again. The morning would be soon enough to go over what had been said here.

CHAPTER 5

Morning came all too soon. The smell of fresh coffee reached Jon before the knock on his door registered, then Becky was picking her way between his discarded garments to set a steaming mug on a small table near the bed.

"What time is it?" he mumbled, as Becky started to pick up stockings and trousers still sodden from the snowdrift he'd fallen into at the edge of the village.

"Nine o'clock. Mr Trythall's here for his breakfast, and asked if you would join him."

Trythall wanted to see him? His clerk must have told him that Jon was back.

"I'll bring up your clean shirt and stockings in a minute," Becky said. "You get that coffee inside you." She tutted as she picked up his trousers. "If you'd hung these up they'd be dryer. Have you got spares?"

"No." He'd replaced his lost shirts and undergarments in Lisbon, but had reserved the rest of his funds for the journey back to England.

"Ah, well. Be sure to sit near the fire in the parlour until you dry out."

"Yes, ma'am!"

Becky left with a laugh.

Trythall was halfway through a plate of ham and eggs when Jon arrived in the parlour. His hair appeared to have receded a little further since Jon saw him last, and his face had put on a little flesh, but he looked up with his usual welcoming expression.

"Glad to see you back safely, Jon," he said, and pointed with his fork to the plate Becky was carrying in. "Eat first; you look like you need it."

Blunt, as usual, but no-one ever took offence. Jon certainly didn't —Trythall had been the one to arrange the sale of the farm after Father had lost more at cards than he could pay. Trythall had done more than that, though—he'd tied up what was left after settling the debts so Father couldn't let that run through his fingers as well.

Jon took the chair indicated, and tucked in with a will. The ham was thick and juicy, the eggs fried to crispy edges but with the yolks still runny, and a second plate held slices of bread and butter to mop up the juices.

He couldn't help comparing it with most of his meals over the last few years, wondering if he'd made the right decision when he joined the army. Mother's sister—married to a rich merchant in Bristol—had helped them to find a house when the farm had been sold, and persuaded her husband to give Father a job. Trythall had offered to train Jon as a clerk—Jon had been grateful, but reluctant, not liking the idea of spending most of his time indoors poring over documents. Trythall had made little protest when Jon expressed a wish to join the army with Fred instead. Money from the farm had purchased his commission, but Jon knew it wouldn't have been possible without Trythall's help.

Jon finally emptied his plate and sat back in the chair, his third mug of coffee in front of him. "Best breakfast I've had in years."

Trythall smiled. "Certainly the best in the last few months, if what I've read in the papers is right. But I'm not here to ask you about that."

He tilted his head to one side. "Nor, I imagine, are you in the mood to talk about it."

"No."

"How is your mother?"

"I haven't heard from her for months—her last letter said she was going on well." Father had died early last year. The letter with the news reached Jon at the same time as one written a month later, saying that Mother was settled with her sister. It had seemed pointless to return to England when he'd be too late to be of any use. And the only grief he'd felt was for the years of unhappiness his mother had endured. Father had never lifted a hand against her, but that wasn't the only way a woman's life could be made miserable.

He brought himself back to the present—to his surprise, Trythall was frowning. He hadn't expected censure about that. "I wrote to her from Falmouth, so she knows I am well, and I will go to Bristol before I rejoin my battalion. However, I thought Meg's—Miss Rymer's—situation was more urgent, and it seems I was right."

Trythall's brows rose. "My clerk gave me only the news that you had returned. What's wrong?"

Jon started with Taylor closing the door in his face, and relayed everything Meg had told him, omitting only their proposed solution.

"A sorry tale," Trythall said, when Jon finished. "Now you've mentioned it, I don't remember seeing Miss Rymer or her mother in the village for weeks."

"*Could* Taylor get some kind of legal order to have Mrs Rymer taken away for treatment against the wishes of her daughter? I gathered that Mrs Rymer herself might be too easily influenced."

Trythall shook his head. "That would be most unusual. However, if he did take her without Miss Rymer's blessing, his claim that it would be for Mrs Rymer's own benefit would weigh with many. Miss Rymer could have great difficulty getting her back."

"By which time her mother would have already suffered from those… treatments."

"Indeed. I can see why the situation is worrying. A woman

managing alone—it's rarely easy. Your mother had to—" He broke off and shook his head.

"Meg... Miss Rymer thought... That is, I was intending to ask your advice this morning. Miss Rymer only needs to deny her wish to wed Taylor when he brings her to church, but she fears that will only induce him to take things further. She thought... that is, she and I discussed..." Good heavens, why could he not get it out? It wasn't as if he were reluctant to marry her—he only wished it were for a different reason. "She thought being married to someone else would provide the pair of them with protection."

"To you, in particular?"

Jon nodded.

"She does have a point. And I take it you are willing to go through with this—else you would be on your way to Bristol by now?"

"Yes. I wanted to ask what is involved in getting a marriage licence. I need to go to the bishop in Worcester, I think? But I cannot be back before the wedding is set to happen."

"I'm sure I can delay things for a day or two," Trythall said. "If Miss Rymer does not do so herself. You concentrate on getting yourself to Worcester and back."

"Thank you."

"I believe the licence will cost two or three pounds. There is also the matter of a bond for a hundred pounds."

"A *hundred*? I haven't got that much." He had barely ten pounds to his name at the moment.

"You don't need it. The money is forfeit only if you make a false statement about your, and Miss Rymer's, eligibility to marry."

Jon looked down at his shabby jacket with its frayed cuffs, inexpertly mended slash in one sleeve, and stains that would not wash out. "They'll never believe I have enough money for that."

"You have good excuse for your appearance, Jon—they might believe you. But it's of no matter. I will give you a signed and witnessed bond, and also a sealed letter of good character, in case further persuasion is needed."

"Thank you, sir. You're going to a lot of trouble."

"Not much trouble. I dislike seeing women mistreated, and it appears that this is happening to the Rymer ladies at the moment. Your mother…" He glanced out of the window. "Well, never mind that. I'll go and get this bond written for you. Have some more breakfast while you wait. The sky's clear now, but there's no guarantee it will stay that way. It'll be cold, whatever the clouds do. I'll send Becky in, and be back within an hour."

~

Meg carried Mama's breakfast tray into the kitchen, and paused at the sight of the long, central table covered in mixing bowls, flour jars, and dishes of eggs and butter. Mrs Baines had even unlocked the spice cupboard, and several of the little labelled pots were lined up at one end of the table. But she wasn't measuring or mixing—she was talking to their maid, arms folded across her narrow chest.

"Is something wrong, Mrs Baines?" Meg set the tray down near the edge of the table, pushing a couple of bowls out of the way to make room.

"That's what I'm wondering, Miss. I was going to start baking for a wedding breakfast, but you haven't said how many are coming."

Of course—a wedding was normally an occasion for celebrating.

"I thought I could—" Mrs Baines stopped at the sound of footsteps in the passage, and Morrison strode in.

"Master wants to see Miss Rymer right away." He glanced over the table. "You should be working, not gossiping."

"I'm busy." Meg turned her back on him and began scooping flour into the pan of the weighing scales. The way Morrison had restrained her yesterday had shocked her, but she might be able to take advantage of it. If she didn't meekly obey, would he grasp her arm again in front of Mrs Baines?

"Now, he said." Morrison came closer. At the other end of the room, young Annie was watching with her mouth open, Mrs Baines with narrowed eyes.

"No. This is *my* house, not his." Meg filled the scoop with flour, tempted to fling it into Morrison's face. Morrison grabbed her arm and the scoop flew out of her hand and covered both of them in flour anyway.

"You stupid bit—" He bit off the words as Rupert appeared in the doorway.

"This is your man's fault," she said to Rupert, indicating the flour covering her black gown. "And the second time he has laid hands on me."

If Mrs Baines didn't already know about what had happened yesterday, she did now.

"Cook wanted to know who is coming to the wedding breakfast," Meg went on, before Rupert could reply.

"I thought a celebration would be out of place, my dear, given your recent bereavement." He glanced at the laden table. "I'm sorry to disturb your plans, Mrs Baines. Of course, if you and the others wish to celebrate, by all means bake a cake or two." He smiled at Meg—it almost reached his eyes. "I'm sure, my dear, you may have a couple of friends from the village to join you in our happy occasion. Why don't you come to the parlour with me and let me know who you wish to invite? I can write a note or two, and Morrison can deliver them."

Damn him—he'd made the lack of celebration seem caring. Were Mrs Baines and Annie still convinced he was only concerned for her and Mama?

"Put this stuff away, Annie," Mrs Baines said. "Morrison, get a brush from the cupboard and clear up the mess you've made."

"Clear it up yourself. I've the master's clothes to see to." Morrison stamped out.

"Margaret, my dear?" Rupert said.

Meg sighed and followed him, brushing the flour off her gown as she went.

"I'll bring you tea shortly, Miss Meg," Mrs Baines called after her. "Anything else you want, just call."

Perhaps Rupert hadn't convinced the servants of his sincerity, after all.

Rupert shut the parlour door behind them. Meg felt a moment of unease, but if he were going to force his attentions on her, she thought he would have done it before this. Besides, she could make enough noise for Mrs Baines and Annie to hear, and they wouldn't stand for that happening, no matter how ingratiating Rupert had been.

Had he found out about Jon's return last night?

"I wished to warn you, my dear Margaret, to be ready by nine o'clock tomorrow morning."

Meg let out a silent breath.

"The vicar is not expecting us until eleven, but we don't want to risk the snow delaying our wedding, do we?"

Meg didn't deign to answer.

"Morrison will remain here with your mother. Such a shame she will miss the ceremony, but we wouldn't want to risk her fragile health in the cold."

That threat was clear, then. But could Rupert do anything in the next day or two? The snow would prevent him taking Mama away—but it would also delay Jon's return.

Rupert seated himself at the escritoire in one corner of the room. "Now, who do you wish to invite to witness our union?"

"Mr Trythall and Mrs Munnings." Trythall had worked for the Rymers for years, and had been good to Jon.

"Munnings?"

"The landlady of the Swan." A woman who took no nonsense from any man, not even her husband.

Rupert shook his head. "I don't think we want the lower orders present, my dear."

Meg shrugged—a number of curious villagers were likely to attend in any case. "Is that all, cousin?"

She waited until he nodded before leaving; she didn't want to antagonise him unnecessarily.

CHAPTER 6

Jon nudged the mare sideways at the fingerpost, and reached out to brush the snow from it, unmelted despite the sunny day.

Evesham 1

Still a mile to go, and it would be dark soon. His ride had started under blue skies, heading down from the higher ground of the Cotswolds. Yesterday's fall of snow had filled the lanes, drifting against hedges in impenetrable mounds. He'd had to let the mare pick her way along the edges of the lanes where the stuff was only hock-deep, but still tiring for the poor beast to get through.

It had been almost eleven by the time Jon set out. The landlord had produced a map, and they'd pored over it, concluding that although heading for Evesham first might add a few miles to his journey, from there to Worcester he would be on the turnpike where progress should be quicker. Jon wasn't entirely convinced, as the benefit of the mare not having to push her way through deeper drifts could be countered by previous traffic packing the snow down into uneven ice. But he would be less likely to lose his way on the busier route, and there would be more inns when the mare needed to rest.

Evesham was not half-way to Worcester, though. He hadn't been foolish enough to think he might get there in time to call at the bishop's office today, but he hadn't anticipated that the journey would take quite this long.

"Onwards, girl." He patted the mare's neck, and urged her into motion again. It would be fully dark by the time he reached the town —he would stop to rest the horse and let her eat. It was six or seven miles from Evesham to Pershore along the turnpike road—he should be able to get that far tonight. Possibly a little further, if the thin clouds did not thicken and block the moon.

For now, though, the setting sun painted the clouds in streaks of orange and pink. Smoke rose gently upwards from the farmhouses he passed—intact houses, their timbers not burned for cooking fires by passing armies. Farms with barns full of cows, the animals not slaughtered to feed half-starved soldiers.

This land was home. Perhaps he should stay here.

It was past ten o'clock when Jon rode into the yard of the Angel in Pershore. It seemed no more coaches were expected that night, for only a single lantern provided light in the yard. The moon shone palely through the high cloud, and the surrounding buildings cast impenetrable shadows across the cobbles, but a line of light was visible where the stable doors must be.

Jon dismounted and rubbed the mare's nose. "Some bran mash for you, girl, and a rest." He led her across the yard and knocked on the door. Then knocked again when his first attempt provoked no response.

"What the bloody hell do you want at this hour?" a voice grumbled as the door eased open. The speaker was a silhouette against the light. "It's bad enough with the stagecoaches coming through at all hours. Can't a body get—?"

"Coaches are getting through from Worcester?" Jon asked.

"Said so, didn't I?" A smell of ale and onions wafted out as the man spoke.

A newcomer appeared behind the man. Older, and a little bent, his face in the lantern light showed many lines. "Bugger off back to your ale, Jack, if you're going to be such a grouch." He lifted the lantern to look over the horse before returning his gaze to Jon. "Name's Ben. Come far?" He took the bridle and led the animal across the yard, opening a door that gave onto a row of stalls.

"Other side of Evesham," Jon said. "She needs to eat and drink." Ben grunted and hung the lantern on a hook before stumping off towards the end of the building.

She needed a rub down, too. Jon removed the saddle and picked up a handful of straw, wiping off the sweat so she didn't cool down too fast.

"Look like you've come further than that," Ben said, when he returned with a bucket of water and offered it to the horse. "Back from Spain?"

Jon grunted.

"Had a hard time of it, from what I heard. No need for Jack to be like that."

"I don't mind." Surliness at having to do some work was an improvement on Spanish peasants running off in fear, or desperately trying to protect their remaining food stores from hungry soldiers.

"Must be in a hurry, to travel this late." Ben took the bucket away and patted the mare's neck. "You can have more in a little while, old girl." He turned to Jon. "What's her name? Blackie?"

Number fourteen, the man in Cheltenham had called her. Jon looked at the weary way she stood. He was tired enough, and he'd only been sitting on her.

"Boadicea," he said, on a sudden impulse. She was helping him to eject an invading force.

"Good lass," the groom crooned. "You planning on getting further tonight?"

Jon nodded. "The going's been a little easier since I reached the turnpike. I'd like to get closer to Worcester, if I can."

Ben just stood there, as if waiting for the rest of the story.

"For a marriage licence," Jon added. It was no-one else's business, but Ben was being helpful and friendly.

"Come home to marry your woman, eh? Don't want to waste your leave on banns! She must be a stunner, your woman, to get you out in this weather." He laughed, and it turned into a cough.

"Worth the effort." And that was no exaggeration.

"Get yourself inside, lad," Ben said. "Have something to eat. I'll look after this girl for you for a couple of hours."

As he ate his way through a plate of cold meat and bread by the dying fire in the taproom, all Jon could think of was that Meg was due to marry tomorrow. But even that thought didn't keep him awake for long when they gave him a room and he took off his coat and boots and lay down.

He'd have a couple of hours' sleep—long enough for Boadicea to have a rest—then he'd press on while the moon still shone.

Jon's ability to wake when he wished to had deserted him, and he didn't return to consciousness until a hand shook his shoulder.

"Time to get up, lad."

"Wha…?" He opened his eyes, taking in the glow of a single candle and, on his other side, a faint line of grey between the curtains.

"Damn." He sat up, squinting against the light. "Ben?"

"Ay. I know you wanted to be on your way, but it clouded over—unless you wanted to carry a lantern, you'd not have got far. It's not dawn yet, but there's light enough for you to follow the road. You should be there before noon, if you're lucky."

Oh well, there was no help for it, and Ben might well be right. Jon stood and stretched, reaching for his coat before forcing his feet into his boots.

Out in the stable yard, Ben thrust a mug of over-sweet coffee into his hands, then led a strange horse out from the stables.

"Where's my horse?"

"You want to get home quick, right?" Ben asked.

Jon nodded.

"Take this one, then Boadie'll be fresh when you pick her up on the way back."

Boadie? Oh yes—the mare. Jon felt in his pocket for the little pouch of coins that Trythall had given him. He should have enough, and Boadie deserved the rest.

"Pay on the way back," Ben said, taking Jon's empty cup.

"Thank you, Ben."

"Bring her to see me some time. I like to see a pretty woman."

He would—if the plan succeeded. But he couldn't help thinking that if Rupert had his way, Meg might already be married by the time he reached Worcester.

"I'll see you later, Mama." Meg bent to kiss her mother's cheek. "Don't go anywhere, will you? No matter what Rupert or Morrison say."

"No, dear. Of course not." Mama frowned. "Where did you say you were going?"

"I'm going to the village."

"I'll sit with her a while," Mrs Baines said from the doorway. "I've some sewing to do."

Meg straightened. "Thank you." Although Mrs Baines most likely couldn't stop Morrison taking Mama away if he chose to, she'd feel happier if Mama had company.

"He's waiting for you downstairs." Mrs Baines jerked her head towards the door.

Meg grimaced, and went to fetch her coat.

"Just say no, Miss Meg," Mrs Baines whispered as Meg passed her again on her way downstairs.

Meg looked at her, surprised at this unexpected support.

"Showed his true colours yesterday," Mrs Baines said quietly, giving Meg a final nod before going to sit next to Mama with her basket of mending.

Meg stood taller as she descended the stairs—it made little practical difference, but somehow knowing she wasn't the only one who didn't trust Rupert made her feel more confident.

Rupert was standing in the hall, one foot tapping impatiently. He turned on his heel when she appeared, and opened the front door. Farlow was waiting outside, with Daisy harnessed to the gig.

Rupert climbed in without waiting for her, and took the reins. Farlow handed her up, and took his place on the backward-facing seat as the gig moved off.

The clear skies of the day before had given way to thick clouds, and the air felt damp. More snow to come, perhaps, although the air had lost its biting chill. As they bumped slowly down the lane, Meg saw that the snow on the bare twigs of the hedges was beginning to melt, but although Daisy still had to plod through a couple of feet of snow, there was not enough of it to prevent them reaching the village. Not reaching the church at all would have been an easier solution—for today—than denying her consent in front of the vicar. At least the melting snow would ease Jon's journey as well.

All too soon they were approaching the final bend before their narrow lane joined the wider road. Meg could see a couple of heads above the hedge—but having to find a gateway to squeeze past someone coming the other way would only take a few minutes.

"Damn!" Rupert's hands went slack on the reins and Daisy stopped.

Meg spirits lifted a little. It wasn't a matter of merely passing the other vehicle, but of getting the gig past a large farm cart with a broken wheel. One, moreover, that appeared to have spilled a load of turnips all over the lane.

Rupert swore again, and scrambled down. As he trudged through the snow, Meg heard exhortations to get that bloody cart moved. She squinted. That was the blacksmith's son, surely, and one of the grooms from the Swan.

Without prompting, Farlow came around to Daisy's head, his shoulders shaking suspiciously.

"Did you know about this, Farlow?"

"No, Miss." He grinned. "Looks like you've got more friends than you thought." He looked over his shoulder. "I'll go and give them a hand with those turnips."

Rupert was waving his arms at the blacksmith's son while Farlow joined the groom, who appeared to be doing little more than spreading the turnips more evenly across the snow. Meg sighed— although she was grateful for the delay, this lane wasn't the only way into Upper Westley. There was still plenty of time to take the longer way around.

CHAPTER 7

*J*on finally spotted the tower of Worcester Cathedral late in the morning. He'd been to the city once or twice in his youth, and recalled stopping at the King's Head, on the road in. When he reached it, he rode under the arch into the stable yard. A few coins changed hands, and an ostler led the horse away to be watered, fed, and rested. Jon went into the taproom for directions and something to eat.

"Bishop?" the barmaid said. "Lives out at Hartlebury most of the time. That's a few miles on the Kidderminster Road."

Hartlebury?

"Here, sit down, love."

She pushed him towards a table near the fire, and he sank onto the bench, resting his head against the wall behind. *Another few miles?*

The barmaid returned with a pint of ale and set it on the table, then drew up a chair and sat, leaning forward on her elbows. Jon took a long pull at his ale. She was a plump lass, with a face that looked as if she laughed a lot.

"You look a right mess, love. The bishop might be at the Palace here, but is it him you want, or his office?"

He could see only friendly concern in her expression, and his business wasn't a secret. Telling Ben in Pershore had done no harm—had helped, in fact. "Marriage licence," he said. "Don't want to waste my leave."

"Ah!" A beaming smile spread across her face. "It's the bishop's *office* you want. We get a few in here wanting one of them."

Thank God. A few miles less now was also less for the return journey.

"You want some food? You might have to wait a bit—it won't do to expire in the waiting room." She sniggered. "That'd put the cat amongst the pigeons right enough, with that stuffy lot."

Jon nodded, and she bustled off. She was accosted by other customers, but before too long a thin man enveloped in a huge apron brought a bowl of green soup, with hunks of fresh bread and a dish of butter. Pea soup had never been his favourite, but it was hot and he wolfed it down, accepting a slice of beef pie to follow when it was offered.

The bishop's office wasn't far, but the barmaid was right—he had to wait. The ante-room had only a meagre fire burning in the grate, but it was dry and he'd slept in worse places. He leaned back in the chair, stretching his legs out before him. If he did fall asleep, they'd surely wake him when it was his turn, if only to get his scruffy person and muddy boots out of the way.

Meg heard the church clock striking as the gig approached the first houses in the village. It was half an hour after the time arranged for their wedding, and also only half an hour before noon, when it would be too late to hold a wedding that day.

Would the vicar still be there?

It had taken some time to turn the gig in the lane, and Rupert's temper had been tested further by finding even deeper snow on the longer route, which made poor Daisy go more slowly still. Then they'd come across a herd of cows ambling along the road, accompanied by an uncommunicative yokel who refused to be hurried or divert them into a field to let the gig pass.

Meg didn't recognise the cows—who, apart from their owner, would? But she did recognise the man with them as the cowman of one of her tenants, and carefully avoided meeting his eyes. The cows should have been safe in their barn for the last couple of months, not being herded along snowy lanes, but Rupert wouldn't know that.

And now they were in Upper Westley, and Rupert's lips compressed as he saw the church doors closed.

"Go and see if anyone's there, Farlow," he ordered.

Farlow went through the lych gate and into the porch. He reappeared only a few moments later, another man beside him. Not a gentleman, by his clothing, Meg thought, although it was difficult to tell when everyone was muffled up in scarves and warm hats.

"Door's locked," Farlow announced when he returned. "This chap wants a word. Shall I see if Vicar's at home while he talks to you?"

"No. Get up behind," Rupert snapped, and flicked the reins to set Daisy into motion, leaving the unknown man staring after them.

The vicarage was only a few yards down the lane. "Wait here," Rupert commanded as he pulled up outside the gate and descended. He stalked up the path and banged on the door; the vicar's housekeeper opened it and Rupert was admitted. As they watched, the stranger skirted the gig and went to wait beside the vicarage door.

Meg wasn't sure whether to be relieved or dismayed when the door reopened and Rupert came out alone. She wanted to speak to the vicar, to explain her situation, but not with Rupert present. If she couldn't avoid Rupert, it was better to explain herself in church with other witnesses present—it did seem that at least some of the villagers would take her side.

Rupert and the stranger had a brief conversation in the vicarage garden before her cousin returned to the gig, his expression furious. They drove back to Oakdene in silence, the turnips and broken cart no longer in evidence.

Reprieve for another day—and Jon should be back tomorrow.

Boadicea carried Jon out of Evesham again in the grey dawn light, his surroundings becoming more familiar as the rising slopes ahead indicted the approaching end to their journey. Although he'd succeeded in his mission—the licence was safely stowed in an inner pocket—he didn't dare hope that he would actually be marrying Meg. Not until he learned whether or not he was too late.

No, Meg would refuse to marry Taylor.

She *must*.

The rain didn't help. It was beginning to melt the snow, but it soaked into his coat and trousers, and trickles ran down inside his collar when a gust blew in the wrong direction. The landscape was as bleak as the Spanish high plains, and he tried to imagine how it would look later in the year.

In a few months, these hedgerows would be sprinkled with green buds of hawthorn, white blackthorn flowers, and primroses in the banks. Cows would be grazing in the meadows beyond, and corn growing in the fields. Then, later, the summer sun would provide comfortable warmth, not the baking heat of a Spanish summer.

Somewhere across the fields, a church clock began to strike the hour. He didn't count the strokes—he would be in the village as soon as Boadie could carry him there, and Meg would already be married or she would not. Knowing the hour would not help.

He cursed himself again for taking the wrong road out of Evesham in the dark—he'd lost several hours by the time he'd realised his mistake and backtracked. But now the fingerposts had Upper Westley on them—only a few miles to go.

Meg hunched inside her coat as Rupert drove the gig into the village. There'd been no turnips this morning, no cows or even sheep. But Rupert had insisted they set off at eight o'clock, so they might have passed by too early for further attempts at delay. It was probably just as well. Rupert had been in a foul mood for the rest of yesterday, renewing his threats to her mother if she failed to marry him the next day.

Today, now.

And today Morrison was riding on the seat behind them, not Farlow. Rupert must have realised there was little any of the servants could to do to spirit Mama to safety without the gig.

When they came to a stop outside the church, Rupert ordered her down and took her arm to pull her towards the door. Morrison led Daisy and the gig on—towards the Swan, Meg hoped. There was no need for the animal to stand around in the cold and wet, even if Rupert seemed to be eschewing the warmth of a parlour at the inn.

The inner door of the church was locked, as it had been yesterday. Rupert sat on one of the stone benches that lined the sides of the porch, but Meg was cold from sitting still in the gig and paced up and down the small space.

After ten minutes or so the sexton appeared, brandishing a key. "Vicar's finishing his breakfast," he said as he unlocked the door. "He'll be along in half an hour or so."

"Thank you." Rupert looked as if he'd had to force the words out.

Cold seemed to radiate from the church walls as Rupert pushed her to sit in one of the front pews, but Meg didn't mind. She felt safer here than she would locked in a private parlour with him.

She felt even safer ten minutes later. The sound of the door latch echoed in the still air, and Rupert sprang up with an eager look on his face. His change of expression when he saw that it wasn't the vicar but Mrs Munnings would have been comical, had her nerves not been tying her stomach in knots.

"You can't come in here," Rupert protested. "This is a private—"

"No such thing as a private wedding in this village," Mrs Munnings asserted, folding her arms. "You going to assault me in God's house?" she added as Rupert moved towards her.

Rupert took a deep breath and returned to his seat, a muscle in his jaw working. He made no further move, keeping his eyes on the stained glass window above the altar as the blacksmith and his son appeared, along with the barmaid from the Swan, the grocer, the stranger from the day before, and the attorney.

Mr Trythall nodded at her as he sat down in the front pew across the aisle, and some of Meg's tension relaxed. He'd always been a good friend to her family—more so to Jon. Was he behind all this? She sensed that these people were on her side.

Then the vicar arrived, brushing drops of rain from the shoulders of his black cassock. He was a tall, stout man, his hair sprinkled with grey. He stopped beside their pew. "Miss Rymer, would you accompany me into the vestry, if you please?"

Meg stood, but Rupert did too, and placed her hand on his elbow as they followed the vicar.

"Is this really necessary?" Rupert asked as the vicar closed the vestry door behind them. "My dear Margaret has enough to put up with nursing her ailing mother, particularly after yesterday's unfortunate delays. We *did* arrive before noon yesterday, so our marriage then would have been perfectly legal."

The vicar removed his spectacles and began to polish them on a handkerchief. "That would not have allowed time for this little talk before the ceremony, Mr Taylor. I thought I made that clear yesterday."

"You did, sir. I'm sorry for my impatience."

Meg almost winced at the overdone penitence in Rupert's manner.

The vicar's brows rose. "Very good. As you know, marriage is a holy state ordained by God, and not to be taken lightly. Or…" He replaced his spectacles and focussed on Rupert. "Or to be undertaken without the full and free consent of both parties." He turned to Meg. "Do you freely consent to this marriage, Miss Rymer?"

Meg drew a deep breath. "No, I do not."

"My dear!" Rupert moved to take her hand, but she wrenched it from his grip.

"Mr Taylor has prevented me from coming into the village to let you know, and he has threatened to have my mother taken to an asylum."

"Is this true, Mr Taylor?"

Rupert gave a deprecating laugh. "I would argue with the phrasing, sir. My dear Margaret refuses to admit that her poor Mama is becoming worse. Mrs Rymer is my blood relative, my father's dear sister, and if Margaret will not follow my physician's advice, it behoves me to do so."

The vicar nodded, and Meg's heart sank. She would still refuse to say the words, but it would be so much easier if the vicar supported her.

"How is this relevant to the subject of Miss Rymer's consent?" the vicar asked. "The two matters appear unrelated."

"Only that Margaret herself is confused, sir."

"Indeed?"

"I am not!"

"Don't worry, my dear," the vicar said. "Mr Taylor's statement is sufficient. I will—" He broke off as a babble of voices sounded beyond the door.

CHAPTER 8

The first thing Jon saw when he rode into Upper Westley was Charlie Allsup, the grocer's son, waiting at the turning for the church, seemingly oblivious to the rain. Charlie beckoned, and Jon kicked Boadie into a canter.

"They're in the church! Hurry!"

Jon turned down the lane and dismounted outside the lych gate. He threw the reins over Boadie's head, leaving her to crop grass in the verge.

Heads of a dozen people inside the church turned as he pushed the door open. They were all in the pews—there was no-one standing before the altar.

Were they signing the register? Was he too late after all?

Then a babble of voices rose, and he saw Trythall walking towards him. The smile on his friend's face turned Jon limp with relief, and he grabbed the end of the back pew to stop himself falling.

"You've got it?" Trythall asked.

Jon nodded.

"Well done, lad! Things'll be easier with you back. Vicar's taken them into…"

Jon didn't hear the rest of Trythall's words, for the vestry door opened and the vicar came out. Behind him stood Meg, with Rupert's hand gripping one arm.

"Jon!"

She was beautiful to him, in spite of the black gown draining the colour from her skin and the anxiety on her face. An anxiety that did not dissipate now he had arrived.

"What are you doing here?" Rupert released Meg and stepped forward. "This is none of your business!"

The villagers turned their attention from Rupert back to Jon.

"I've come to marry Meg."

A ragged cheer broke out.

"Silence!" The vicar's voice thundered between the stone walls. "This is the house of God, and I will not have it made into a side show!"

"Sit down, lad, before you fall down." Trythall's voice was quiet, and he pulled Jon to sit beside him in the back pew.

The vicar glared at the congregation until the chatter died away and everyone resumed their seats. Then he turned to Meg. "Miss Rymer, do you consent to marry Mr Taylor?"

"I do not." Her voice was clear and firm.

She *wasn't* married. Trythall had implied as much, but now he believed it.

"Mr Taylor, you suggested that Miss Rymer is confused. Do you still maintain that?"

A murmur arose in the congregation but ceased at another glare from the vicar.

"She will not send her mother—"

"Yes or no?"

"I... er..." Rupert glanced around.

"I shall save you the bother." The vicar drew himself up to his full height. "Either Miss Rymer is in her right mind, in which case she refuses to marry you. Or she is mentally confused, in which case she is not *capable* of giving consent. In addition, you lied when you told me that Miss Rymer consented to the banns being called. Leave this church now!"

"Good man," Trythall said, low-voiced.

But Rupert still stood near the altar rail, now staring at the back of the church.

"What are you waiting for?" the vicar asked impatiently.

"Who's that?" Jon asked. A stranger was walking down the aisle, to whispers from the watching villagers.

"Don't know him," Trythall said, "but he's been hanging around the village for the last couple of days."

The man bowed to the vicar. He didn't raise his voice, but his words still carried clearly in the waiting silence.

"I apologise, sir, for raising this matter in a church, but I have a warrant for this man's arrest, for debt. A debt that he promised would be paid instantly in the event of his marriage."

"You two." The vicar pointed at two of the village men. "Escort Taylor from the church. What happens to him after that is none of my business. The rest of you may go as well. There will be no wedding here today. If you wish to discuss the matter, you may do so in the Swan."

Jon rested his head against the pew in front of him. Meg hadn't needed his help in the end. And with Rupert arrested, her cousin was no longer a threat to her or her mother.

She didn't need him, either.

He was back! Meg took in the water pooling on the floor at Jon's feet and the lines of fatigue around his eyes, visible even from this distance, and suddenly her flash of joy vanished. His face looked thinner than she remembered, too—this was the first time in a year that she'd seen him in daylight.

Rupert's grip on her arm tightened, then he swore under his breath before he headed towards Jon. Meg turned her attention to the vicar, managing a firm denial that she consented to marry her cousin. Then Rupert was escorted from the church and it seemed her problems were over. Mrs Munnings and Becky came to say how glad they were that things had turned out all right, and she managed to thank the blacksmith and the cowman for their efforts the day before.

But all she could think about was the weather Jon had endured on his trip to Worcester and back, all because she hadn't believed that saying no in church would be enough. And when the vicar dispersed the small crowd around her, Jon was no longer at the back of the church. She went out into the porch, but he was nowhere in sight.

Morrison—where was he?

"Miss Rymer!" Mr Trythall stood beside her, with a twinkle in his eye.

"I am sorry—did I ignore you?"

"You did, but understandably. Will you allow me to drive you home?" He opened a large umbrella. "Your gig is at the Swan."

"Is Morrison there?" If he was, he could not be threatening Mama.

"I advised the constable to lock him up until he can be questioned about his involvement."

That was one worry out of the way for now. She took his offered arm, and they set off.

"You will want to get back to your mama, I think?" Mr Trythall went on.

"Yes. I mean, no! Where is J— Lieutenant Lewis?"

"Mrs Munnings has taken him away to be dried off, warmed up, and fed."

"All that way, and for nothing..." He'd done it for her, willingly. She knew then that what she felt for him wasn't merely friendship, it was love. She didn't want to leave the village without thanking him, at the very least. "Thank you for your kind offer, sir, but I can drive the gig myself."

"Good heavens, not in this weather, and with snow still in the lanes! I will ride behind if you prefer to drive yourself. And I will be able to report back to Jon that you are home and safe."

"I must see him first, to..." To say that although her proposal to him had been made to help her escape, she *wanted* him in her life.

"If you wish, my dear, but pray do consider—your mama will be worried, and Jon... Well, I think you should both rest and put this nasty business with your cousin out of your minds before you talk. Now, here is the gig ready for you—do I ask for your horse to be unharnessed?"

Meg hesitated as Mr Trythall patiently held the umbrella over her. What he said made sense, although it seemed wrong to just leave.

"You will pass on my thanks to Jon, will you not, sir?"

"Indeed, I will. When I return." He shouted for his own horse, and had it tied to the gig, then handed Meg up. "If you hold the umbrella, my dear, we may both stay reasonably dry."

Meg looked back over her shoulder at the Swan, watching it grow smaller as Daisy plodded along, then turned her gaze resolutely ahead. If she knew Mrs Munnings, Jon would be in a hot bath now; then—if he had any sense—in bed. And she could always drive herself back into the village once she was sure Mama was all right.

Yesterday's delays—someone must have organised that. "Sir, do I have you to thank for the turnips and cows?"

"I did suggest to various people that a delay in the proceedings might be helpful."

Strange, she had never seen a twinkle in his eyes before—but then she had only had business with him after her father died, and when they heard that Fred had been killed.

"You said, Miss Rymer, that Jon had ridden to Worcester for nothing, but I do not agree. If not for your cousin's arrest, he might still have made life difficult for you, and none of us knew that would happen." He glanced at her. "If nothing else, the licence he has would have been an insurance policy."

What did Jon think—did he *want* to marry her or—?

No. She would not think of that now.

"You have been very good to me, Mr Trythall, but you hardly know me."

"To be frank, I did it for Jon as much as for you." Trythall's face reddened. "If... if things had gone differently... well, in short, at one time I courted his mother, but..." He sighed. "I sometimes think of him as the son I never had." He looked at her. "That is not to say I would not have done it all anyway—I do not like coercion and manipulation, not to mention lying to a man of God."

"I do thank you, sir, whatever your motivation."

"Yes, well…" He reddened again, but she thought she detected a pleased smile.

~

Jon pushed his plate away, shaking his head as Becky offered him more. He hadn't felt like eating, but knew he should have something before setting off for Oakdene. There would be time enough for food once his future was decided.

He'd refused the bath Mrs Munnings had suggested—a wash in front of a roaring fire had warmed him sufficiently before he donned one of Sam Munnings' shirts and a borrowed neckcloth. Mrs Munnings had done her best with the mud on his trousers, and someone had rinsed his boots for him. It didn't matter—he'd get wet again on the way. Meg deserved to be courted by someone clean, bearing flowers or other gifts, but he couldn't manage that.

"You want your horse?" Becky asked.

"She's called Boadicea," Jon said, while he considered. It was only a few miles, and the going this morning hadn't been too hard on the mare. There wasn't a spare stall in the stable at Oakdene, but there would be enough room for her to shelter for a while. "I'll go and saddle her myself."

"Good luck, love." Becky gave him a swift peck on the cheek before heading back to the kitchens.

Jon gaped after her for a moment, but he shouldn't have been surprised. He had announced his wish to wed Meg in the church, and any villagers not there would have heard by now.

He headed for the stables, where the mare eyed him with an air of weary resignation. The poor animal must be used to being taken out in all weathers, and probably ridden as hard as he had used her. As he mounted up and clattered out of the yard, he wondered how much it would cost to buy her from the coaching inn in Cheltenham, then shook his head. He needed to decide his own future first. Or at least, he needed Meg to decide his future.

When he came to the road junction with the fingerpost he stopped, as he had... was it really only three days ago? The woods were blacker now, melting snow revealing wet bark on trunks and twigs. Some impulse made him dismount and lead Boadie along the path, past places he remembered playing, and the overgrown side routes off to the best trees for climbing or the clearings where the sun shone in spring. Soon there would be snowdrops beneath the trees, then primroses and sweet violets, celandines, and wood anemones. As he walked, some of his thoughts from the journey to Worcester coalesced in his mind and he came to a decision. He was not going to Jersey to spend his days training up recalcitrant recruits, and watching boys still wet behind the ears promoted above him because their parents had money or influence.

No—whether or not Meg wanted him, he would sell his commission.

CHAPTER 9

Farlow, Mrs Baines, and Annie came running as Trythall pulled the gig to a stop outside the front door.

"Oh, Miss, you did give us a turn when we saw you being driven back!" Mrs Baines gasped.

"Not to worry, my dear," Trythall said, before Meg could speak. "Mr Taylor has been apprehended by the law for debt, and will bother Miss Rymer no more." He descended from the gig.

"Good news, Miss Rymer," Farlow said, more sedately. "Are you staying, Mr Trythall?"

"Do come in for some refreshment," Meg said.

"No, no, I must get back." He unhitched his horse as he spoke, and mounted it. "I will give your message to Lieutenant Lewis, Miss Rymer." He cantered off down the drive, and Meg turned to go into the house, leaving Farlow to unhitch Daisy.

"Make some tea, if you please, Mrs Baines," Meg said, removing her wet pelisse and handing it to Annie.

"Miss..." Mrs Baines remained where she was, hands clutched in front of her. "Miss, I'm sorry if I took Mr Taylor's part at any time. We didn't—"

"Don't worry, Mrs Baines—he was very plausible." So much so that he'd made her doubt herself—she could hardly blame the servants. "Is Mama upstairs?"

"Yes, Miss."

Mrs Baines hurried off, and Meg went upstairs. Mama sat by the window, knitting.

"Who was that with you?" she asked. "Is he back?"

"Mr Trythall drove me home," Meg said, not even trying to work out who Mama meant by 'he'. "Cousin Rupert has... has gone, and won't be back." There was little point in explaining further.

"Oh, good. I know you didn't like him, dear. Did you have a nice time in the village?"

Meg was saved from replying by the arrival of tea and a plate of biscuits. It was only as she sank into a chair and took a mouthful of tea that she realised how tired she was. She could relax now—all her troubles were over.

Apart from Jon. Not that he was a trouble, but he'd agreed to marry her because she asked him, and had convinced him she needed his help. But did he *want* to be with her the way she wanted to be with him?

"Oh, we have another caller," Mama said. "Someone is riding along the lane."

Jon was here already? Meg rushed to the window, but the rider was already out of sight.

She swallowed the rest of her tea, almost burning her throat, and hurried to her own room. A quick pull of a comb through her hair sorted out some of the tangles, and she swiftly pinned it into a simple knot. She could do nothing about the shadows under her eyes, or the drab mourning gown, but she smoothed her skirts as she descended the stairs.

Farlow had already answered the door. "A Mr Dutton to see you, Miss."

The Rymers' stable should have been a welcome sight as Jon emerged from the woods. Boadie, at least, would be comfortable for a while, even if there wasn't much space for three horses inside. But Jon felt as tense as he did before a battle; the next hour could decide his future happiness.

There were two strange horses outside the stable, both saddled. And Meg stood just inside the open door, talking to the bailiff who'd been at the church. Were Rupert's debts *still* causing her problems?

He dropped Boadie's reins and hurried towards them. "Meg, is everything all right?"

The smile she turned on him scattered his thoughts for a moment.

"Dutton." The bailiff held out a hand and Jon shook it automatically. "I've come for any of Mr Taylor's possessions that are here."

"Mr Trythall drove me back, Jon, and Mr Dutton met him on the road. He said there was no problem in releasing Rupert's things."

"He was so good as to provide me with a note to that effect," Dutton said.

Jon glanced at the proffered paper, torn from a notebook by the looks of it. As before, Meg hadn't needed his help.

"I'll be on my way, then, Miss. Someone will collect the trunk in a day or two." Dutton nodded to Jon and mounted one of the horses, leading the other away.

"Trunk?"

Meg smiled, although not the happy smile she'd greeted him with. "I left Farlow throwing—and I use the word deliberately—Rupert's belongings into the trunk he arrived with. There'll soon be no trace of him in the house."

"That's good."

"Jon, come in out of the rain. Now Dutton has taken Rupert's horse away, there's plenty of room for yours."

"This is Boadicea," Jon said as he followed her into the dim shelter of the stable. "She's worked hard for the last few days." Why was he babbling about the horse?

"Some oats for you, then, once we've dried you off." Meg rubbed the mare's nose. "Unsaddle her, Jon."

Meg went off to the end of the stable, returning with a bucket of water and two brushes. She handed one to Jon, and they stood on opposite sides of Boadie, brushing her down.

He took a deep breath. "Meg, I know you only asked me—"

"Jon, when I asked you—" Meg said at the same time.

There was an awkward silence.

"Meg, I didn't agree—"

"Jon, it wasn't—"

This time he met her eyes as they both stopped talking, and her face lit with the mischievous grin he remembered from their childhood. No—there was more than that in her eyes.

Much more.

It took only a moment for him to move around the horse and take her in his arms. The way she clung to him before turning her face up towards his said more than words ever could.

"Kiss me," she whispered, and his last shred of doubt vanished.

He bent his head towards hers and his fingers tangled in her hair. His tiredness seemed to drain away as her lips parted beneath his and she responded with all the enthusiasm he could have wished for.

Mrs Baines had only needed a look at Meg's face when she and Jon returned from the stable to see that celebrations were in order. By the time Meg came back to the kitchen after giving Mama the news, the cook was getting out flour, butter, and eggs, muttering something about Mr Jon needing to be fattened up. Meg hid her smile, and put the kettle on the range herself. She'd only had a few mouthfuls of tea before Mr Dutton called, and she hadn't managed to eat anything for breakfast this morning. She set out plates of biscuits and cake, and some slices of cold pigeon pie that Mrs Baines had in the larder.

This morning—such a short time for everything to have changed.

She carried the tray into the parlour. Mama was now installed in her proper place beside the fire, although she was still knitting. Jon…

Jon was sprawled in a chair, stockinged feet warming by the fire, asleep. Relaxed, his face looked years younger than it had in church this morning, and she felt a lump in her throat. That licence would not be wasted after all—they had only a few weeks before he had to return.

She set the tray down quietly, not wanting to wake him, but when she looked up again his eyes were open.

"Sorry." He looked so much like a boy about to be chastised that Meg laughed.

"Don't be silly, dear," Mama said. "There's nothing like a little nap when you're tired." She put her knitting to one side. "I said everything would be all right when he came back, didn't I?"

"You were right, Mama."

"When is the wedding?"

"As soon as the vicar will do it…" Meg paused—she should consider more than her own wishes. "No. Jon—your Mama will wish to come, will she not? You will have to go and see her. But how long do you have?"

Jon leaned forward, elbows resting on his knees. "I'm going to sell out, Meg. That is, if you have no objection to a husband with little knowledge about managing farms but a great desire to learn. Father would never teach me anything about it."

"Only if that husband is you, Jon." She wanted him to hold her close again, but Mama's presence prevented that. "Shall we call the banns? That will give you time to fetch your mother from Bristol, and we can marry in the middle of January." There was enough room here for Mrs Lewis to stay permanently, if she wanted to—at least, until babies arrived. Meg felt heat rising to her cheeks at the thought, and hurried on. "I suppose you will have to go to London to sell your commission."

"Yes. I need to get some new clothes, too. But three weeks gives me time enough for that."

She would gladly take him as he was, but he was eyeing the slices of pie, so she didn't say so. They could discuss all the details later. For now she would enjoy the anticipation, and assist Mrs Baines in feeding him up.

"Have some pigeon pie, Jon."

May 1813

Jon checked the harnesses on Daisy and Boadie. They made an odd couple—the shiny landau he had borrowed from the magistrate should rightly be drawn by a matched pair, but these two animals were almost family. Meg had woven ribbons into their manes, and they made a pretty sight in the spring sunshine. It was very different from the gentle snow that had fallen when he married Meg four months ago, but the weather then had not mattered to them.

Meg came out of the house, lifting her skirts to keep them well away from the dust in the cobbled yard. She'd bought a new gown for the occasion, but she was beautiful whatever she wore. Their mothers followed her out, also in new gowns.

He handed them into the landau and climbed in, and Farlow flicked the reins to set the horses in motion. Sitting beside Meg on the rear-facing seat, Jon watched the countryside unrolling behind them. The hedgerows in leaf and flower, bluebells colouring the woodland beneath the budding trees—all as he had imagined on that wet ride back from Worcester. He'd got one thing wrong though—this place was home, not for the countryside, but because he was with Meg. He reached for her hand, feeling the answering pressure of her fingers on his.

The whole village seemed to have turned out for the wedding. Meg and Mrs Rymer went in first, and Jon offered his arm to his mother. They walked together from the sunshine into the cool of the church, where Mr Trythall awaited them with an eager smile. Mother, too, would now have a loving husband.

Jon looked at Meg as the vicar read the opening words of the ceremony, and she met his eyes with the smile that still filled him with joy. If his mother and Mr Trythall could be even half as happy as he and Meg were, all would be well.

THE END

JAYNE DAVIS

Captain Kempton's *Christmas*

A Regency Romance

ACKNOWLEDGMENTS

Copyediting & proofreading: Sue Davison

Cover design: P Johnson

Thanks to my critique partners on Scribophile for comments and suggestions, particularly David N, Daphne, Jim, Kim, Lynden, Sharon, and Violetta.

Thanks also to Alpha readers Tina, Trudy, Helen, Mary G and Dane, and Beta readers Barbara, Cilla, Dawn, Doris, Fran, Leigh, Melanie, and Wendy.

CHAPTER 1

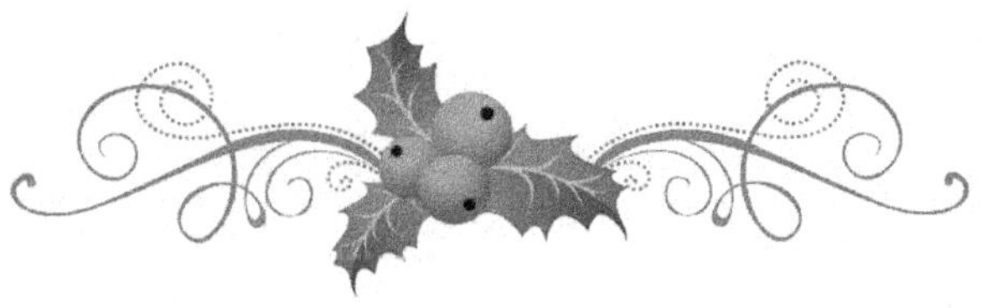

*D*ecember 23*rd*, 1814, Wiltshire

Captain Philip Kempton winced as he dismounted in front of the Blue Bell Inn. He'd been riding for hours and his back and legs ached. He shouldn't have been surprised—what had he expected after spending most of the last ten years at sea? It served him right, too. He'd barely mentioned the possibility of riding to Beechgrove when his mother launched into a lament about the cold weather, the state of the roads, and how he would be much more comfortable if he borrowed the chaise. Already irritated by the way she'd pressed him to accept the invitation from Aunt Beth and Uncle Thomas, he'd dug his heels in and insisted that his father's hunter would be the most comfortable way of making the journey. And he'd managed without a valet for a decade, thank you; his uncle's man could do anything needed over the festive season.

So here he was, still an hour's ride from his destination, with a backside that not even a hot bath would soothe, and fingers and toes numb from the chill air. The night would get colder still, he thought as he regarded the clear sky, its pale blue already turning a duskier shade. It would be dark by the time he arrived, but the moon was nearly full and would light his way. An hour spent thawing out in the inn would make little difference. The horse deserved a rest, too.

He walked into the inn, hoping his aching muscles didn't show in the way he moved. The stone-flagged passageway inside was dim, but a door stood ajar and Philip entered the heat and noise of the taproom. The air was thick with smells of woodsmoke, spilled ale, and unwashed bodies, the laughter raucous.

"What can I do for you, sir?" The landlord leaned in close and raised his voice to make himself heard above the hubbub.

Philip rubbed his face, the noise and smell almost making him regret his decision to halt here. But warming himself wasn't his only reason for stopping—he was still debating whether to just turn around and return home. He could think up some excuse and send Aunt Beth his regrets.

"Sir?"

He was here now, so he might as well eat. "Ale. And a hot meal."

"Very good, sir. We've a fish stew, or beef pie. Cook can do something else, if you wish, but you'd have to wait a bit."

"Beef pie will do nicely." It was too loud in here to think. "Do you have a private parlour that's warm?"

The man nodded. "Fire's lit in the room just across the hallway, sir. Send your food in there, shall I?"

"Yes, please do."

The parlour was furnished only with a couple of tables and chairs, and a high-backed settle near the fireplace. Philip threw a couple of extra logs onto the fire and stood with his back to the flames, hands behind him as if he was still on the quarterdeck of the *Penelope*. His fingers were warm and tingling by the time the landlord appeared, a maid with a laden tray behind him.

"Going far, sir?" the man said as the maid set out a plate with a huge slice of pie swimming in gravy, a dish of vegetables, and a mug of ale.

"Delfont Abbas," Philip said.

"Nice place; I come from there. Addison, at the Delfont Arms, brews a fine ale. Nearly as good as mine," he added, with a wink.

"I'm staying at Beechgrove, but no doubt I'll find time to test your recommendation."

"Friend of the family, sir?"

"Kempton's my uncle." Philip sat down, his stomach rumbling in anticipation.

"Ah, you'll be Captain Kempton, then. Addison and I have been following your actions in the papers. You've been making a splendid fight against the Frogs, sir."

"Yes, well..." Philip didn't know what to say—they'd all just been doing their duty.

"Enjoy your meal, Captain. It's on the house. Just shout if you want more ale."

Damn it—he was committed to spending Christmas at Beechgrove now. If the man was friendly with the landlord of the Delfont Arms, word would eventually reach his aunt and uncle that he'd been on his way.

It's been four years, he told himself—you should be over it by now. But flashes of that summer fortnight still came back to him when he couldn't sleep, or when he let his mind wander. Days of shared walks on the Downs or through the Beechgrove gardens. Days when he'd fallen in love with a woman who'd promised to wait for him.

And his thoughts always ended on the irony of being given command of a frigate named after a wife who *had* waited.

Lady Anna Radnor huddled into her pelisse, trying to ignore her discomfort as the post chaise rattled and bumped along the road. It wasn't the winter chill that troubled her, for her hands were warm inside her fur muff and the hot brick from the last posting inn kept the chill from her feet. No, the problem was the large pot of tea she'd drunk an hour before. She wriggled again, but it was no use. She couldn't wait until they reached Beechgrove.

She rapped on the glass to attract the attention of the Kemptons' groom, riding on the nearside horse. The icy air made her eyes water as she dropped the side window.

"Stop at the next inn, if you please. How far is it, do you know?"

"Only a mile or so, my lady."

Anna drew the window up, snuggling into the cushions with appreciation. It was good of Aunt Beth to have sent the chaise for her. She had enough funds now to keep a carriage of her own, but she had little use for one, and habits of economy were sometimes hard to discard. Beth Kempton was no relation to her, but she had been a close friend of her mother and treated her like a niece.

Anna wasn't as happy about the prospect of seeing Philip again, but it was something she had to do. As Aunt Beth had written, a final meeting might allow Anna to dismiss him from her mind even if it achieved little else. What had concerned Anna, though, was Aunt Beth saying that Philip didn't know she was to be one of the party.

What must he think of her if Aunt Beth thought that her presence might keep him away?

"Do you wish for some refreshment, my lady?" the maid asked, as Anna emerged from the small room set aside for ladies' use.

Anna hesitated. The groom had said they were only an hour from Beechgrove, but it hardly seemed fair to the inn to leave without buying something.

"The private parlour's occupied, my lady, but it's only a gentleman. I'm sure he won't mind sharing. Captain Kempton, it is. He's known in these parts, so you needn't worry."

Philip? Here?

Her heart fluttered—she had not expected to see him so soon.

It shouldn't be so surprising; they were both on their way to the same place, after all. But although it was a fortnight since she'd received Aunt Beth's letter, she still had not decided what she should say to him. She'd thought she would have a little more time to consider, but perhaps a first meeting here would be best. If he ignored her or just walked away, there would be no witnesses.

"A glass of wine, if you please."

Anna took a deep breath. She had until the maid returned to compose herself. She smoothed her skirts—she looked smart enough. Knowing she was dressed well helped to stoke her confidence.

It wasn't the maid who returned, but the landlord, with a glass of wine on a small tray. "This way, my lady."

Anna followed him down the dimly lit passage, hesitating by the parlour door as the landlord entered.

"There's a lady here, Captain. I hoped you won't mind her sharing the parlour while she drinks her wine."

The landlord blocked her view of the room.

"By all means."

Anna's breath caught. The sound of his voice was still familiar after all this time, and her hands clenched until the nails bit into her palms. Then the landlord moved into the room to set her wine on an empty table, and she was looking directly at Philip.

He'd changed, and he hadn't. The same hazel eyes, but with more creases at their corners. The same brown hair, a little lighter than she remembered, perhaps bleached by the tropical sun. The smile was cool, a smile for a stranger.

Had he forgotten her so completely? Was that why he'd never answered her letters?

Philip saw only a dark red pelisse beyond the landlord as he agreed to share the parlour. He hadn't paid for the privilege of having it to himself, after all. As he stood, the woman's face came into view and his polite smile froze.

How could *she* be here?

For a moment he wondered if his thoughts had conjured up a vision, then she moved and the spell was broken.

"Captain Kempton." She inclined her head and turned to the land-lord. "Thank you. Can you ask my groom to be ready in ten minutes?"

The landlord bowed and left, leaving the door ajar. Anna, his Anna, sat down at the table and sipped her wine. He dragged his eyes away from her face, dismayed to find he was still attracted to her in spite of what she had done.

'Please, Captain, do finish your meal."

Her voice sounded different than it did in his dreams—cooler, more confident. He sat down but ignored the food. "You look well, Anna. My lady, I should say." What was her name now? He'd destroyed the letter—all he could remember was that the man had a title.

"I am Lady Radnor now," she said. "You seem to be none the worse for your sojourn in the tropics, Captain. I should congratulate you on being made post."

"And I should congratulate you on your marriage." Despite his efforts, bitterness coloured his tone. She had done well for herself; he could see that from her garments. Edgings and trim of deep pink turned what might have been a drab pelisse into one of understated elegance, an effect that was unlikely to have come cheap. Her hair was dressed plainly, as it had been that summer, twisted into a knot with only a few tendrils to frame her face.

"Thank you. But my husband died two years ago."

"Commiserations, my lady." He tried to sound sincere, and was ashamed of himself for the effort it took.

"It was not unexpected," she said, a shadow crossing her face. "But it is always sad when a good man dies."

Good man? Taking a wife young enough to have been his granddaughter?

Anna—Lady Radnor—drank more of her wine, her fingers cradling the glass. He wanted to reach out and touch them, to caress her cheek, feel if her skin was as smooth as before. She had more poise now than when they first met, but to his dismay the new maturity this gave her only added to the need filling him.

"I was sorry you did not reply to my letter, Captain. I wrote again, in case the first one did not reach you."

Philip felt the heat rise to his face.

"So either several letters went astray, or you decided not to reply." She paused for a moment. "Or perhaps you did not even read them."

He lowered his eyes, one hand toying with his knife. He had received a letter from her after he'd already learned of her marriage. He'd read only enough to realise who the letter was from, then held it in a candle flame, watching the paper char and burn until there was nothing left but ash. After what she had done, writing to him had seemed like an insult.

Her chair scraped on the floor as she stood. "Thank you for allowing me to share the parlour. I bid you good day, Captain."

She left without waiting for an answer, although he had no idea what he could have said. He pushed the plate away and went to the window. A chaise stood ready. A groom put up the steps behind her and closed the door. It pulled away, taking the road to the north—the same way he was travelling.

Could she be going to Beechgrove too? She must be—why else would she be on this road, today?

The desire to turn back was stronger than ever, but so were the reasons to carry on. If he went home now, *she* would know he'd cried craven, as well as Aunt Beth and any others who remembered that summer house party.

His legs and backside protested as he finally pulled himself up into the saddle, having drunk perhaps one mug of mulled ale too many. It was just as well the way from here had few turnings.

In no rush to arrive, he let the horse amble on through a landscape of black shadows and silhouettes, the only sounds the clop of the horse's hooves on stone and frozen mud. The cold was no worse than many a night at sea in the Channel, and here, at least, he was dry.

He'd last ridden this road four years ago, on a sunny July afternoon. Aunt Beth had greeted him and directed him to where her younger guests were picnicking beyond the woods on the lower slopes of Delfont Down. That was where he'd first met Anna.

· · ·

He hadn't noticed her at first. Half a dozen adults sat on blankets spread on the grass, with as many children of varying ages chattering around them and poring over sheets of paper. His cousin Toby had risen as he approached, and clapped him on the shoulder in welcome. He recognised Thalia, Aunt Beth's younger daughter—she must be fifteen or so now. A quick glance showed that most of the others present were cousins on Aunt Beth's side of the family and their offspring—cousins he didn't know well.

A heap of sticks, string and spades lay nearby. Further up the slope, a few patches of white showed where someone had dug up the turf to reveal the chalk beneath. Mystified, Philip asked what they were doing.

"Designing a horse to go on the hillside," one of the boys piped up.

"Or a giant," another added, looking up from his drawing.

"Someone told them about schoolboys at Marlborough making a white horse on land near the town," Toby explained. "Mama said they could make one here, but they'd have to dig the turf out themselves." He nodded to the patches of white further up the hill. "They dug a couple of holes to check the chalk isn't too far down here."

"There is a recent figure at Weymouth, too, with King George on it." The woman who spoke had a soft voice, and grey eyes set in an oval face. A young girl sat on the blanket beside her, holding a sketch pad and pencil. "It was made about two years ago."

"And Uncle Toby has been telling us about the giant at Cerne."

Philip suppressed a smile. Uncle Thomas had a booklet about the chalk figures of England, and he and Toby had sniggered over the drawing of the giant when they were boys. The naked figure was… 'well endowed' might be a polite way of putting it. "How big is his weapon, Toby, can you remember?"

Toby smirked, resuming his recumbent position on the blanket. "You read the same book as I did, Phil. You tell them."

The woman's lips compressed, as if she were suppressing a smile. She gazed up at Philip with wide, innocent eyes—too innocent. "His club, do you mean?" Her cheeks dimpled, and he felt a flush of embarrassment that she'd understood his indelicate allusion.

"Anna's been there," the first boy said. "She said we could go to see it when we're older. Uncle Edward says Emily mustn't—"

"Let the gentleman speak, James," Anna admonished, and the lad subsided.

"His club must be a hundred feet long, I think," Philip said. He made a bow. "Lieutenant Philip Kempton, at your service."

"Anna Tremayne." She smiled, those dimples appearing again. "These are my cousins, James and Emily." Both children had the same dark brown hair, but their faces bore little resemblance to hers. The boy looked to be around ten years old, the girl a little younger.

Miss or Mrs Tremayne, he wondered, then shook his head. It mattered not—he was here for only a few weeks.

"I don't think Aunt Beth would approve of a copy of the giant here," Philip said.

"Why not?" James asked.

"I…" Too late, Philip realised the impossibility of explaining why not in front of young girls and women.

Anna Tremayne watched him with interest as he foundered for words, then one corner of her mouth curved upwards before she turned to her cousin.

"Well, James, if his club is a hundred feet long, he must be about twice as tall as that. How long do you think it would take you boys to cut lines in the grass to make a giant that big?"

"We could have a smaller giant," another boy suggested.

"Remember Aunt Beth said you had to dig the figure yourselves?" Anna said. "You could only make a very small giant, then he wouldn't be a giant at all."

The boys' faces fell.

"You could have a horse, or a dog," Philip suggested, relieved to be let off the hook.

"Horses are too common," one of the boys objected. "We want ours to be different."

"What kind of dog? Like Aunt Beth's spaniel?" James could hardly have shown less enthusiasm.

"Cerberus, perhaps?" Anna suggested.

James' brow creased in thought, before he dredged the knowledge from his memory. "The dog that guards the underworld—"

"With three heads!" the other lad added.

"You could ask Emily to draw it for you," Anna suggested.

"Then it will be time for the picnic," one of the other women announced.

Philip wandered away; Toby got to his feet and followed him. Wildflowers grew amongst the grass, and Philip bent to pick purple scabious and knapweed, white umbels of wild carrot and trembling harebells. These were some of the things he missed while at sea.

"Who is Miss Tremayne?" he asked.

"Daughter of Mama's best friend from her schooldays," Toby said. "The friend died some years ago, though, and Anna lives with her uncle and those two children. Mama invites Anna quite often—I'm surprised you've never met her."

He hadn't—he would have remembered. In repose, her face was pleasing: a clear skin, touched by the summer sun, a mouth that looked as if it smiled a lot. The way she'd laughed at him before coming to his aid had been entrancing.

She was not married—Toby had not contradicted his use of 'Miss'.

"Wooing her with flowers?" Toby asked.

"Thanking her, rather."

"Ha! That served you right for trying to embarrass me."

But, looking back, the flowers *had* been the first stage in courting her; that had become plain soon enough. He'd thought the attraction that had grown during those weeks—love, even—had faded, but their brief meeting at the inn had been sufficient to show he'd been mistaken. His want for her was as strong as ever, despite her betrayal.

He wrenched his mind away from his memories, gazing up at the infinity of stars. Ursa Minor hung above the lane he rode, guiding his way north. He turned his thoughts to the decision he had to make soon. What was he going to do with himself now the war was over? The *Penelope* had already been broken up—she'd been old and time-worn before he'd been given command. With no ship, and a surfeit of officers on half-pay, it was time he gave serious consideration to what he would do with the rest of his life.

If he had to avoid Anna—Lady Radnor—while he was at Beech-grove, perhaps that would give him time to consider Admiral Lord Harpenden's suggestion.

CHAPTER 2

*A*nna clasped her hands inside her muff as the chaise moved off, dismayed to find they were shaking. It had been more than four years since she'd seen him, and over three since she'd given up hope that he would reply to her letter. She should not be having this reaction.

Thank goodness she'd stopped at the inn—now, at least, she had some time in the chaise to try to regain her calm.

What had he thought of her? She could not tell. His cool, initial, smile had indeed been for a stranger, but when he'd recognised her his face had become unreadable, blank. The faint hope of his being pleased to see her had vanished.

The way he'd avoided her eyes when she wondered if he had read her letters had been telling—she guessed he had received them but had not looked at her explanation. If he'd cared for her, why wouldn't he have read them?

If he felt nothing for her, why hadn't he just said so?

She rested her head against the squabs. It was going to be difficult to maintain a cheerful front for the few days she would be at Beech-grove, but she must do her best. It might be too late to mend the misunderstandings between them, but she would at least like to know if he had meant those words of love when he'd said them.

Anna's spirits lifted as the carriage turned into the drive. Although the house was just a black shadow against the starry sky, she'd visited it so often that she could see it in her mind. Originally a small Jacobean manor, Beechgrove had been extended by different owners and was now a hodgepodge of different styles. No one could call it elegant, but it looked comfortable, settled in its surrounding gardens and woodland at the foot of a grassy hillside.

As she hurried up the steps the front door opened, spilling light into the dark. Aunt Beth stood in the doorway, the usual wisps of greying hair escaping their pins.

"Welcome, my dear!" Beth gave Anna a quick hug and a peck on the cheek, and drew her into the hall. "It seems an age since I've seen you!"

"Less than six months." Anna removed her bonnet and gloves. "But yes—too long. It is good to be here." Apart from her young cousins, the Kemptons were the nearest thing she had to family, and it was comforting to be with them over Christmastide. "You should come to Weymouth more often, Beth. There is plenty of room to put you up."

"Perhaps I will, but only when James is away at school." Beth shook her head. "I find I'm getting too old to keep up with energetic schoolboys, even though you've brought James up to be well-mannered. My brood are here for the whole twelve days; luckily the grandchildren are still young enough to be confined to the nursery most of the time. But come in and warm yourself. Bates will have your trunk taken to your room."

The parlour was light and cheerful, the cream coloured wallpaper and yellow upholstery reflecting the lamplight. Books and papers strewn across a table near the window showed recent occupation.

"They're all dressing for dinner," Beth explained as Anna crossed to the blazing fire and held her hands to its warmth. "What have you done with James and Emily? Your note said only that you would be coming alone."

"I thought it best under the circumstances. They were both invited to spend a few days with school friends, but I do need to return the day after Boxing Day. I had hoped to be here earlier, but it took longer to see them off than I'd thought." Her hands now fully thawed, she took a seat near Beth.

"As is always the way with children. It is a pity you could not stay longer. Perhaps they could come here instead for the last days of Christmas?"

"No, not with Philip—" Anna took a deep breath. "I stopped at the Blue Bell on the way. I met Captain Kempton there. He..." She swallowed.

Beth leaned over and patted her knee. "No need to tell me if you do not wish to, my dear. I hope it was not a mistake to invite the two of you. I'm afraid it is to be only a small party for Christmastide. Apart from my children and their families, Philip is the only other guest."

Anna tried to maintain her polite smile, but Aunt Beth was too perceptive.

"Don't worry about being forced together, Anna. I have lots of activities planned. There will be no need to be paired off into couples, and no need to participate at all unless you wish to. Now, do you need to change for dinner, or would you prefer a tray in your room for this evening? If so, I'll look in on you after dinner and you can tell me what James and Emily have been up to. I'll not have you brooding alone *all* evening."

"I'd be happy to have a tray, thank you." Philip could arrive at any moment, and she didn't want to face him again in front of the whole Kempton family. Not yet.

Aunt Beth left Anna alone after their exchange of family news. Now she could either spend a dull evening alone in her room or she could venture downstairs and explain that she'd missed dinner because she'd been tired from her journey. Talking to Beth's children and their spouses would take her mind off her memories, but she would also be likely to encounter Philip. He must have arrived by now, unless he had changed his mind about coming. Would he take the coward's way out to avoid her?

That thought decided her. What was she doing but behaving like a coward herself? Downstairs, she would be able to get used to seeing him in company without having to talk to him directly.

Inspecting the evening gowns she had brought with her, she chose a simple one in cream satin with a yellow sash and small knots of matching ribbon around the hem. She looked well in it, but no one would assume she had dressed to impress. It didn't take her long to arrange the usual simple knot in her hair.

Fate was against her, it seemed. As she reached the foot of the stairs a knock sounded on the front door, and Bates opened it.

"Welcome, Captain. You are later than we expected—have you had some mishap?"

Encountering Philip alone in the hall was not what she had in mind.

"No, Bates. I merely..." The rest of Philip's words faded as she slipped into Uncle Thomas' small library and closed the door behind her.

The room was empty, only the flickering light from the fire illuminating the bookcases and furniture. This was a quiet retreat for anyone who found the hubbub of Kempton life fatiguing. That was often the case at Beechgrove, with many cousins on both sides of the family welcome to visit whenever it took their fancy.

It had been a retreat for her four years ago, too. Although Anna loved her little cousins dearly, the chance to leave them playing with the other youngsters had been a welcome relief at times. Lieutenant Kempton, understandably, had also wanted to escape, and she'd found him in here the first evening of his stay. They had been in this room together several times after that, but one time in particular stood out in her memory.

They had enjoyed several days of sunshine, a time in which Lieutenant Kempton had enthusiastically joined the two boys in the creation of the chalk Cerberus, leaving her free to lounge on a blanket nearby and read a novel while Emily and Thalia sketched. And the lieutenant had helped her to organise the ceremonial unveiling when the thing was finished.

Then the weather turned. A day of patchy drizzle still allowed the houseful of children to release some of their energy in the gardens, and the adults had amused themselves acting selected scenes from Shakespeare. But when the following morning dawned too wet for anyone to wish to be out of doors most of the menfolk cravenly retreated to the Delfont Arms, leaving their wives to keep the children entertained. Lieutenant Kempton, for reasons unknown to her, had opted to stay, and soon a game of hide and go seek was suggested. Thalia, the younger Kempton daughter, declared the entertainment childish and retreated to her room with a book, while Aunt Beth declared she needed to consult the housekeeper.

James was delighted to draw the short straw as the first seeker.

"Do you want me to come with you?" Anna asked Emily.

Emily shook her head, her dark ringlets bobbing. "I'm eight now," she protested. "I can hide by myself!"

Anna tried not to laugh. "So you can. Very well then. Mary is but five, do you think I should help her instead?"

"Oh, yes. Five is only little." Emily laughed and ran off as Mary's mother mouthed her thanks, taking the hand of her even younger son.

"I'm counting up to fifty!" James called, his hands over his eyes. "One, two, three…"

The hall full of people emptied.

"James, don't find the young ones first," Anna whispered. "Let them think they're hidden well."

James nodded without removing his hands. "…fifteen, sixteen, seventeen…"

Anna hadn't seen which directions the others had taken. Mary would still be climbing the stairs when James finished counting, so they had to conceal themselves somewhere on this floor.

"…twenty-nine, thirty, thirty-one…"

Uncle Thomas' library was close. The door stood slightly ajar, and Anna led Mary in, a finger to her lips.

Perhaps this was not a good choice after all, Anna thought. A desk stood in one corner, there was a cloth-covered table near the window, and a couple of armchairs were arranged either side of the fire.

The table it would have to be. Mary giggled as Anna tip-toed exaggeratedly towards the table, then shrieked as a hand appeared at the bottom of the cloth and lifted it up.

"Sshhh," Anna whispered, her own heart racing with the surprise.

"Coming!" James' shout echoed in the hallway.

The hand beckoned. "Hurry up!" Lieutenant Kempton's head popped out. "He'll find you if you don't hide."

Mary scurried under the table, but Anna hesitated. She could just sit and pretend to read; after all, she was helping Mary, not playing the game herself.

"Come on, Anna!" Mary whispered. "Please!"

Anna sighed and crawled under the cloth, sitting with her knees drawn up under the centre of the table. It was not a large space, but at least the legs were at the corners so they all fitted—just. Not much of the day's grey light made its way through the cloth, but she could make out the lieutenant's smile.

"Welcome to my lair, Miss Tremayne," he said, his sepulchral tone belied by the laughter in his expression.

Beside her, Mary giggled, then the three of them sat still with only the sound of their breathing breaking the silence. The air held a hint of lemon and spices mingled with the lavender water she was wearing —his cologne? Anna felt strangely breathless, her pulse still beating fast and a strange feeling in her stomach. How ridiculous to feel that way about a game of hide and go seek.

"Found you!"

Mary grabbed Anna's arm as they heard James' call, even though he was not in the library. The little hand gripped tighter as footsteps sounded.

"Someone's bound to be in here—come on." James must have joined forces with the first hider he'd found.

"We're about to be discovered, I think," Lieutenant Kempton whispered. "What do you say to giving young James a scare?"

Mary's giggle was sufficient answer. The lieutenant leaned against Anna in the tight space as he brought his feet up under him, lifting the edge of the tablecloth with one hand. In the extra light, she could see the grin on his face.

"There's no one under the desk."

The footsteps came closer, and the lieutenant's thigh brushed against her arm as he leapt out with a roar. Mary's hand tightened on hers at the sudden movement, then she giggled as the two boys shrieked.

"That frightened them," Anna said to Mary, crawling out after her. The lieutenant held a hand out to help her up, his shoulders shaking with laughter.

She got to her feet, his hand warm on hers, and brushed dust from her gown. The two boys were convulsed with laughter; Lieutenant Kempton just stood there with a grin on his face.

"I've still found you, sir," James gasped.

"So you have. Why don't you take Mary along to help look for the others?"

The nervous fluttering of her heart had not abated; the look in his eyes as they met hers made her breath catch. She'd never felt this way before, but she knew it was nothing to do with the childish game.

"Yes, that's a good idea," she said, not looking at her cousin.

"Come on, Mary." James took the girl's hand and the boys led her out of the room. "Let's look in the billiards room."

"How old are you, lieutenant?" she asked, pleased that her voice sounded fairly normal.

He smiled down at her. "Oh, I don't know. About ten?"

She laughed, and the odd feelings turned into a warm glow.

"Please, won't you call me Philip?"

She felt her cheeks warm, although there was no reason why she shouldn't. She was not related to the Kemptons, but she'd been calling Toby by his Christian name for years as if he really were a cousin. Why should doing the same with this man feel different?

"Very well, Philip." It felt right, somehow, to call him that. "What do you intend to do now you have excused us from the game?"

"I think those lads should have cleared the billiards room by now. Do you play?"

Recalling that day now, Anna wrapped her arms around herself in the warm glow of the fire. They'd spent some time in the billiards room, most of it with the table between them. The feelings his presence induced had been interesting—enjoyable, even—but she'd been wary of encouraging them too quickly.

She'd soundly beaten him, having spent many a wet day at Beechgrove playing with Toby, and with Lizzie too. Back then Thalia had been too young to wield a cue. Philip had taken it in good part, claiming the inability to practise while at sea as his excuse.

Aunt Beth had said all her children had come for Christmas. They would be here somewhere, together with the spouses of the older two. It was time for her to stop hiding and go to greet the company.

"The ladies are in the parlour, sir," Bates said as he closed the front door behind Philip and took his hat and gloves. "The gentlemen are still with their port in the dining room. Your room is ready if you wish to change, and cook can provide a meal if you require it."

"No, thank you, Bates. I ate on the way." Guiltily conscious of the time he'd spent at the Blue Bell after Anna had left, Philip shed his coat and handed it to the butler. Aunt Beth had probably been expecting him for dinner.

He looked down at his clothing. Although the dry, cold weather meant he didn't have the usual spattering of mud on his breeches and boots, his clothing still bore the marks of travel. Joining the ladies was out of the question unless he changed, but Uncle Thomas and his cousins wouldn't mind. That was just an excuse, though, he admitted to himself.

"The dining room, I think, but I don't need food."

The butler handed Philip's garments to a footman and opened the dining room door. "Captain Kempton."

"Philip!" Toby called, getting to his feet. "We expected you long since—is all well?"

"Yes." Philip forced a smile. "It's good to be here. Uncle Thomas. Anthony."

"It must be six years since we've seen you, Philip," Anthony said. "Since I wed Lizzie?"

"Indeed." He remembered cousin Lizzie's wedding, a couple of years before he'd met Anna, but he'd been at sea when Toby married Catherine. "How are things with you?" He pulled out a chair and sat down, accepting a glass of port. His mother and sisters had written long letters full of family news over the years, but he welcomed any opportunity to avoid the reason for his late arrival.

'Where's everyone else?" he asked, when the recitals of family history came to an end.

"You're the last," Uncle Thomas said. "There's only these two, with their wives and brats, and Thalia, of course. And Anna arrived a couple of hours ago—you've met Anna, haven't you? Anna Tremayne, as was."

"Of course he has, father. Anna was here when Phil came on leave before going off to the Caribbean."

"Yes, I remember Anna." There was no knowing look from Toby— if he'd worn his heart too much on his sleeve that summer, at least his cousin and uncle didn't appear to remember. Cousin Lizzie, likely to be more observant about such things, had been visiting friends then. He'd been expecting a much larger party. With so few guests, he'd find it difficult to keep his feelings hidden and avoid Anna.

Was Aunt Beth trying to throw them together?

Unless… What if Anna wasn't the reason he'd been invited?

"Is Thalia not wed yet?" She must be old enough now. All he remembered was a pretty girl who seemed to always be attaching herself to the adults in the party rather than playing with the children.

Not that he could blame her for that—what girl of that age wanted to spend time with cousins still in the nursery?

"She spent some time in Town this spring," Toby said. "I gather she had a few offers, but rejected them all. Some nonsense about her heart already being given. Catherine was increasing at the time, so we weren't there. Thalia's to go again next year."

"That'll be her last chance in London," Uncle Thomas muttered. "Too expensive."

"But that's women's stuff, Phil," Toby added. "Tell us about that action off Guadalupe. The papers never give enough detail on such things."

Quite willing to spin out his time away from Aunt Beth's probable questions, Philip moved the dishes of cheese and sweetmeats around to represent islands, and pressed glasses and knives into service as frigates. He could make this story last for some time, then claim he was tired from his long ride.

"We had good luck in our sailing master," he started. "Knew all the shoals and reefs..."

CHAPTER 3

Philip did not wake until first light the following morning, in spite of the turmoil of his thoughts. He threw back the covers and went to the window. The sky was clear, a few stars still visible as black turned to grey. A pale line on the south-eastern horizon showed where the sun would rise. It would be cold out, but perhaps a walk would help to loosen the sore muscles in his legs and backside. And perhaps also help him think what he would say to Anna, for he couldn't avoid meeting her today.

He dressed in the clothes he'd arrived in, leaving his clean sets for Uncle Thomas' valet to press. A couple of maids were about in the corridors, carrying scuttles of coal to set fires in the bedrooms. He told one not to bother with his room, and made his way to the kitchens. He'd stayed here often as a child, and important details of the house—such as where to wheedle food from Cook—had stuck in his memory.

With a cup of coffee inside him, he set off through the gardens. At sea, dawn had always been one of his favourite times, a period of calm before the routines of the day began. Now he crossed the lawns, frosted grass crisp beneath his boots and his breath making puffs of mist in the still air. Beyond the hedge was a small belt of woodland, bare branches stark against the lightening sky, and then he was on the grassy slope of the downs. He pushed himself hard until he reached the top, then paused to take in the view stretching around him.

He stood and watched the rising sun turn the sky to pastel blue. He'd walked up here with Anna several times during that summer fortnight—sometimes with others, later just the two of them. Now, as always, he enjoyed the beauty of the changing colours, but he couldn't help thinking that it would be even better with Anna beside him. The Anna he'd fallen in love with.

Freezing fingers and toes finally forced him to move. He made his way down by a different route, heading for the place where the chalk dog had been.

It was still there, the white lines sharp against the grass—someone must have weeded the gaps in the turf a few times since it was created. He'd initially helped with the making of it as an excuse to be near Anna as she kept an eye on her young cousins, but he'd been surprised to find he enjoyed working with the boys. Was it because he'd stayed here so often as a youth that he reverted so easily to enjoying children's games?

That had been the first time he'd seriously contemplated what it might be like to have children of his own. The idea of a family had become more concrete, rather than merely a vague expectation. Had he sensed, even in those first few days, that Anna might be a woman he could enjoy being with for the rest of his life?

He set off back to the house. Above, long wisps of high cloud were drifting in from the west. Perhaps there was snow on the way.

Ready to help Aunt Beth with preparations inside the house, Anna was surprised when Lizzie appeared and handed her a basket and a large pair of scissors. "Catherine's staying in, so I need you to come and gather holly, ivy, and mistletoe. Thalia will be along in a minute, and Anthony."

"Our official tree-climber?"

"Indeed." Lizzie laughed. "He likes the excuse to behave like a schoolboy now and then. The others have gone out to look for a Yule log."

Anna liked Lizzie and her husband—both had easy-going personalities with a sense of fun. Anna suspected that Lizzie would turn out very like her mother, with Beth's liking for being surrounded with friends and family. She'd probably turn plump like Beth, too, with her fondness for sweetmeats, but plumpness seemed to suit the Kempton women.

Anthony had joined Lizzie by the time Anna returned in her pelisse and half boots, Thalia trailing behind her down the stairs. Since she reached an age to attend balls and assemblies, Thalia had become more particular about her clothing than her sister had ever been. Today she wore a pale green pelisse trimmed with white fur around the neck. A matching bonnet and a huge fur muff completed the ensemble.

"Very practical, Thalia!" Lizzie said. "Are you sure you want to wear that? You're bound to get mud on it."

"It's a stupid idea to send me out for ivy." Thalia's pretty mouth pursed in what could only be called a scowl. "There are plenty of servants to do it."

"The fun is in finding it ourselves," Lizzie said. She picked up her own basket and shears and led the way across the gardens. Anna didn't comment, wondering at the change in the girl. She had never been particularly friendly towards Anna, but this morning at breakfast she had been almost rude.

The narrow belt of trees behind the house widened to the east, and Uncle Thomas' gardeners kept the paths free of brambles and nettles. The frost had not reached far into the wood, and the paths were indeed soft with mud. Lizzie and Anna wandered happily along, inspecting the closer trees for the greenery they were seeking.

Anna pointed to an ancient trunk sheathed in ivy. "Here's a good one."

"Anthony, come and employ your stick on these brambles," Lizzie called. They stood back while Anthony set to with a will. Anna approached the tree, carefully holding in her pelisse to keep it away from the thorns on the battered stems. She began to pull on the strands of ivy, prising them away from the trunk with her scissors, cutting off lengths and passing them to Lizzie.

"I'm bored," Thalia muttered. "And cold. My nose is turning red."

"Well, walk on and look for mistletoe," Lizzie suggested. "Or holly. Anna, can you reach that long piece just above you?"

"It's too muddy," Thalia whined.

"Oh, for heaven's sake, Thalia!" Lizzie exclaimed. "Take your long face back to the house if you don't want to be here."

"I can't go by myself."

"You've been playing in these woods—"

"Allow me to escort you, Thalia," Anthony interrupted. "It would be a shame to dirty such a beautiful garment, especially when it suits you so well."

Thalia hesitated, then laid a hand on his bent arm. Anna suppressed a smile as Lizzie shook her head, and chuckled aloud as the departing Anthony grimaced over his shoulder.

"I'm sorry, Anna. I don't know what's got into her. Now, have we taken all we can from that tree?"

"I think so." Anna made her way back to the path. They would have to harvest what they could from trees that didn't need Anthony's assistance to get through the surrounding brambles.

Philip, having managed to avoid the breakfast room while the women were present, was relieved to find that Anna would be helping Aunt Beth in the house, while the men of the family were to locate and bring home a Yule log.

"We'll look in the woods to the west," Uncle Thomas announced. "It'll take several hours to find something suitable, I'm sure," he added, as they entered the woods. "Small enough to fit our fireplace, but big enough to stay alight for at least a few days." He paused at a log lying close to the path, tilted his head to one side, then strode on.

"What's wrong with that one?" Philip asked. Surely his uncle couldn't judge it too big by eye alone?

"Not a thing," Toby said with a laugh. "You've not been here at Christmas before, have you?"

Philip shook his head.

"We're heading for a few pints in the Delfont Arms. Father got the gardener to find that log weeks ago." He lowered his voice. "He thinks Mama doesn't know."

"Does she?"

"Of course. She prefers the men out from under her feet while she's making the final preparations."

"I say, wait a moment."

The call came from behind, and they all stopped and turned. Anthony waved at them, just visible through the bare trunks. He had a woman with him—not Anna, Philip was relieved to see. Thalia, now a pretty young woman. They waited while Anthony made his slow way towards them.

"Thalia, what are you doing here?" Uncle Thomas asked.

"I wanted to help find the Yule log, Papa," she said, casting a quick glance towards Philip as she spoke. "It's no fun cutting ivy with Lizzie."

"You said you wanted to return to the house to prevent your pelisse getting muddy." Anthony was clearly struggling to keep exasperation from his voice.

"This is just as muddy as the east woods," Uncle Thomas said. "Go back, Thalia."

Philip moved a few steps away, not wanting to witness a family argument.

"Come on, Thalia," Anthony said. "Lizzie'll have my head if I don't get back to help her."

"But I want to come with—"

"No, Thalia." Uncle Thomas was beginning to sound uncharacteristically curt. "I'll take you back." He turned to the rest of them. "I'll see you in the pub later."

Thalia pouted, but said nothing further. She looked at Philip again, a tentative smile on her lips.

"I'll escort her, Uncle," Philip offered, and Thalia's smile widened. "And, Anthony, I can give Lizzie a hand, if you wish." He didn't feel like drinking the day away, and Lizzie was always pleasant company.

"Thanks Philip. I owe you a favour."

The men trooped off, and Thalia smiled up at him as she took his arm.

"It is such a long time since I've seen you, Captain."

"Yes, indeed." What else could he say, particularly as she must have been the fourth or fifth person to say so since he arrived? "That happens when one is in the Navy."

"Papa read out the reports of your actions in the Gazette."

"That must have made for poor entertainment." Please, not the 'brave sailors' speech again.

"I do so admire the courageous men who fight for our country."

Philip grunted.

"Anna says you must have earned lots of prize money."

"Oh." The fact that Anna had thought about him enough to follow his career shouldn't lift his spirits.

"She must be looking for another rich husband by now," Thalia went on. "She's been out of mourning for nearly a year."

The lift to his spirits vanished. "You have had a season in London, I understand?" He was not going to discuss Anna with Thalia.

"Oh yes. I was a great success, and much admired."

He glanced at her as he spoke. Was she fluttering her eyelashes at him? Surely not. "You have a suitor, then?"

She gazed up at him, a coy smile on her lips. "Oh, no. I did have several offers, but I did not care for any of them."

Thalia *was* flirting with him. He increased his pace, hoping that the speed would not leave her enough breath to talk. Fortunately they soon emerged from the woods.

"Here we are," he said, unnecessarily. "I'm sure you can make your own way back across the gardens." He lifted her hand from his arm as he spoke. There was no need for him to escort her all the way to the house.

"I will come with you."

She reached out to take his arm again, but he clasped his hands behind his back. The expression that reduced errant midshipmen to quavering excuses didn't have quite the same effect on her, but she did take a step away.

"It will still be as muddy as it was when you left." Philip spoke firmly.

"I shan't mind if—"

"Excuse me." How transparent could she be? He strode off without waiting for a reply.

One advantage of being on active service had been the absence of marriage-minded females. He hadn't expected to find one here. At least Cousin Lizzie's chatter would be innocuous, and she was safely married. He wasn't sure exactly where to find her, but he was not going to go back and ask Thalia for directions.

He headed for the east woods. Once in the trees he chose a path at random and slowed his pace. Flattened brambles and a criss-cross pattern in the mud where someone had set down a basket indicated that he was going the right way. Finally, he heard a murmur of voices. Lizzie must be with Toby's wife.

Or Anna—that sounded like Anna's voice.

He stopped, but he was too late; Lizzie had heard his approach. "Anthony? Come and help! You've been an age!"

He had no choice but to join them. Lizzie stood alone beneath a tree, pulling strands of ivy from its trunk. A basket of the stuff rested on the path nearby. She turned her head as he trod through the undergrowth.

"Anthony went with the others to the Delfont Arms."

"Typical!" Lizzie shook her head. "Still, he did escort Thalia back for us."

"It's no use, Lizzie, we'll have to wait until— Oh!" Anna rounded a bend in the path ahead, coming to an abrupt halt as she saw him.

"Captain Kempton." She nodded briefly; nothing in her expression said she was pleased to see him.

"Lady Radnor," he said. Cold or exertion had reddened her face, but did nothing to reduce the attraction he felt.

Lizzie's gaze flicked from Anna to himself and back again. "Oh, don't be so stuffy, you two. Phil, Anna was trying to reach some mistletoe, but neither of us are tall enough." She held out a pair of scissors. "Show him the way, Anna."

He pocketed the scissors and followed Anna along the path. She turned, walking a little way into the undergrowth, and pointed to a ball of mistletoe clinging to a thick branch above her head.

It was too far for him to reach, despite his greater height. "How did you think you could reach that?" Off balance at finding her here, his words came out harshly.

Her lips turned down at the corners for a second, then she shrugged. "I tried to climb up, but the branches are too far apart. At least, for someone wearing a dress."

"Allow me," he said, trying to dismiss an image of her wearing breeches to attempt the task. Jumping to get his hands around the branch, he pulled himself up until he could get one leg over it.

"Oh, very impressive, Phil!" Lizzie clapped, and he felt his face redden. He could easily have climbed up using stumps of old branches but no, he had to show off by doing it the hard way.

"Just cut off some pieces," his cousin ordered. "We don't need the whole thing. Throw them down."

He did as she said, and waited until the two women had gathered them up and returned to the path before letting himself down.

As he reached the path himself, Lizzie disappeared around a bend with a basket on each arm.

"You sent her back?" Philip asked, wondering if Anna was about to behave like Thalia.

Her lips compressed, and her eyes met his briefly before she looked away again. "No, I did not. She just said the baskets were full and she'd be back soon."

"Ah, I see." Her expression was far from flirtatious and, irrationally, he felt a slight pang of regret. "I was surprised to find you here at Beechgrove. Why have you come?"

"I was invited." Her chin lifted. "But if I had known my presence would be so distasteful to you, I would not have accepted the invitation."

It wasn't what she said, but what she hadn't that made him pause. "Did you know I would be here?" Was Thalia right?

"Yes. Aunt Beth—"

"You thought a Captain with prize money might do now you are free to find another rich husband? One, this time, less than twice your age."

Her body stiffened. The hurt in her expression showed his assumption about her motive was wrong, but it was too late to unsay the words.

"You are mistaken, Captain. My late husband was at least three times my age." There was a faint tremor to her voice. "I came because I hoped to get a chance to explain why I married when I had promised to wait for you."

"Anna, I didn't—"

"But there seems little point," she went on. "I think we do not know each other as well as we once supposed. Good day, Captain Kempton."

She turned and stalked away.

CHAPTER 4

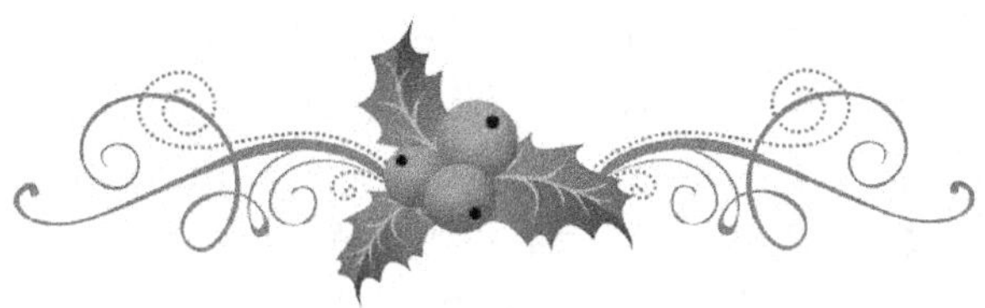

*A*nna took deep breaths as she walked, clenching her fists. She would not cry; the time for that had long gone. It was foolish to have come here, raking up past emotions, past hopes.

He'd assumed that she'd married only for money, and that she now wanted more. That breaking her promise had been easy. And he'd not even read her letter when she'd tried to explain.

She had believed he'd loved and respected her. And no matter what he did or didn't feel for her, she hadn't thought he was a man to leap to hasty judgements.

The path forked, and she turned away from the house, heading north out of the woods and onto the rising grassland. Thin clouds veiled the sky, the sun showing through only as a white disc. The pale light leached colour from the landscape, matching her mood as she climbed.

She was trapped here for the next few days—she could not ask Beth to lend her the chaise again at this busy time. All she could do was to stay away from Philip as much as possible.

Reaching the rounded ridge, she turned east. She'd walked this way several times with Philip, usually with James running around them and Emily looking for flowers. On other visits to Beechgrove she'd come here with Lizzie and Anthony when they were courting, and occasionally with Aunt Beth and Uncle Thomas. Beth would wonder why she wasn't back at the house helping to arrange the evergreens she and Lizzie had gathered.

Let Philip explain, she thought. Aunt Beth would guess their meeting hadn't gone well.

Half an hour later, when she set off down the hill to loop through the fields and back to Beechgrove, she realised she'd made a mistake coming this way. There were too many memories up here. Watching as Philip helped James to fly his kite, both of them dashing up and down on the grass. Philip—surprisingly—telling Emily the names of all the flowers she'd collected and helping her to draw them. Amongst it all, little touches and exchanged glances, the warmth of his hand on the small of her back, the support of his arm when crossing rough ground, shared enjoyment of the glorious weather and the countryside.

Well, he'd given up on her quickly enough. He hadn't written, even before the events that led to her hasty marriage. She tried to stoke her anger against him as she strode on, but it didn't come. Instead, she felt regret for things that might have been, and a deep loneliness. Nothing had changed, really, with today's confrontation; it had merely reinforced the feeling that everything was over between them.

Her return route took her through the woods, and brought back the most vivid memory of all. She was *not* going to look for the clearing with a stream running through it. It would be too painful to see the last place they'd been together that summer.

Philip had come to her as she was helping Beth to cut flowers for the house, snipping dahlias and phlox, long stems of delphiniums and veronica.

"Walk with me?" he asked, his usual smile absent.

Anna hesitated, but Beth flapped a hand at her. "Go. I can manage this."

Philip had led her into the woods, arm in arm as had become their custom. The bubble of happiness that had been inside her for days began to evaporate as she took in the way his lips were pressed together.

"Daniels has just brought the post," he said.

"Orders?" What else would have removed the smile from his face?

"I'm afraid so. I'm wanted in Portsmouth immediately."

"Oh." She looked away, swallowing hard against a lump in her throat. "I thought you had another week." Even that had not seemed long enough.

"So did I, but it appears the *Garnet*'s first lieutenant has been taken ill, so I'm needed to supervise loading stores. I must leave this afternoon."

"That is a shame. I will miss our walks together." And the warm feeling when they were in contact as they were now. Without intending to, she found herself walking closer, so their arms touched as well. He put his hand on hers, where it rested on his arm, and gave a gentle squeeze.

"I will miss you too." There was sincerity in his deep voice.

They walked on in silence, still close, until they came to the glade. The stream burbled in the dappled shade, the cool air welcome after the sunshine in the gardens.

"Anna."

She turned to face him.

"Anna, I've never talked with a woman as I have with you here. Never shared my thoughts and wishes."

He raised his hand, as if he were about to touch her cheek, but let it drop again.

"I could be away for two years, or even longer. I don't think I'm giving away any secrets by telling you we're bound for the Caribbean. That's better than the East Indies, I suppose. Not quite as far away."

"So long?" She'd known he would have to go to sea, of course, but hadn't thought it would be so soon and for such a time. Or that the news would produce this hollow pit in her stomach. "I wish you well, Philip." She wanted to say more, but suddenly wondered if the time they'd spent together was just Philip's way of passing his leave pleasantly.

"Anna, we have only known each other a fortnight." He looked away, rubbing one hand through his hair.

It seemed as if she'd known him forever, the way they talked easily about everything and nothing, yet the feeling that had been growing inside her was something new. A heady emotion she'd thought she was going to have a little more time to explore.

"Anna..."

She waited, but rather than speaking he reached up and tugged gently on the ribbons beneath her chin, slowly pulling the bow loose. She could have stopped him had she wished to, but as her heart began to race she knew she did not. The knot fell undone, and she reached up and removed her bonnet, laying it on the grass.

"That's better," he said, his voice so quiet it was almost a whisper. He ran his fingers down her cheek and her breath caught as she raised her eyes to his. He took a step closer, until their bodies were almost touching. No man had stood close to her in this way before, but it felt right. Then he bent his head until their lips touched.

Anna put a hand to her cold face, recalling the heat of his mouth on hers, the thrill that shot right down to her toes as her lips parted and their tongues met.

She still wanted him, wanted to discover what came next. What it felt like to touch a man's bare flesh and have him touch her. How it felt to have the final joining. And with him—not with anyone else.

Mama had explained what happened in a marriage when Anna turned seventeen, just before her final illness. At the time, Anna had thought it sounded most unpleasant, but there had been a wistful look in Mama's eyes that told her there was more to it than a simple joining of bodies.

"Wait for me?" Philip had asked, when the kiss finally ended. She could still remember the sadness in his voice. "I should speak to your uncle before..." He gazed into her eyes. "There was so much we could have said, with only a little more time. Promise me you'll wait, Anna? Please?"

And she had promised.

~

Philip sat on a fallen log, gazing after Anna as she disappeared into the trees. What had possessed him to say such a thing? Thalia's suggestion had prompted it, but he hadn't really believed Anna would pursue him for his money. No, already irritated with himself for still wanting her, he'd lashed out with the most hurtful thing he could say.

Her words to him had hurt, too. They didn't know each other. There was no way in which he could twist that into something complimentary. She was disappointed in him. Yet it was *she* who had broken her promise.

The sound of female voices alerted him to Lizzie's return, with company. He got to his feet and walked deeper into the woods, moving quietly. If Lizzie didn't spot him leaving, there would be no awkward questions later about why he was avoiding her.

He could loop around the house and make his way to the pub. The idea of drinking his sorrows away was beginning to seem more appealing, and the others would leave him in peace while he did so. But he would still have to face Aunt Beth and Anna later, and probably with a sore head.

Better just to walk. He wouldn't get lost while the rise of the downs behind the house showed his direction. Walk, and think.

He'd felt wronged for nearly four years. She'd promised to wait for him, and she hadn't.

The letter had reached him at a bad time.

He was leaning against the railing surrounding the quarterdeck of the *Garnet*, his hands gripping the wood to help him balance without putting weight on his injured leg. The graze caused by the flying splinter had stopped bleeding, but it hurt like the devil still.

He'd posted lookouts, but he scanned the horizon himself as well. It was unlikely there were any more enemy privateers this close to Antigua, but the ship couldn't survive another encounter. The captured vessel kept pace astern, now commanded by the *Garnet's* third lieutenant.

In spite of his efforts not to dwell on the recent engagement, his every gaze over the far side of the ship paused on the row of canvas-wrapped bodies. One of the large ones was Gadstone, the first lieutenant and a good friend. The smaller bundles held the youngest midshipman and two of the powder monkeys.

So young.

The tree-clad hills above English Harbour loomed higher now; it would not be long before they could drop anchor. Thank God for that. He called to one of the seamen sweeping debris from the deck. "Leave that now, Tanner. Tell the captain we should be at anchor within the hour."

"Aye aye, sir." The man dashed off, down the companionway to where Captain Jerrick lay in his bunk. Informing him was merely a courtesy—with the loss of his leg, he was in no state to take charge.

You're turning soft, Philip told himself, glancing at those sad bundles of canvas again. He'd seen death at sea before—who had not? Perhaps it was that time he'd spent at Aunt Beth's last summer that made the loss of the youngest members of the crew so distressing. At that moment, he wanted nothing more than to be back on the sunlit downs, hand in hand with Anna. Hers was a different world—civilised, kind, happy. He allowed his mind to wander for a moment, imagining more—Anna in his arms, in his bed. Waking beside her each morning.

He was still on duty that evening as the sun neared the horizon, the *Garnet* safely moored in the shelter of Fort Berkeley. Three dockyard men were filling their notebooks with lists of repairs. The longboat, remarkably undamaged, was pulling towards them. The purser sat in the stern, having escorted the dead to the cemetery. They would be buried tomorrow.

He watched as Venner climbed aboard and mounted the steps to the quarterdeck.

"Got some post, sir."

"Very good. Hand it out when the men have dinner, if you please."

"Aye, sir. There's one for you." Venner took several letters from his satchel, sorting through them and picking one out.

Impatient, Philip held his hand out for it. Instead of just the single letter, Venner gave him several.

"The others are for Lieutenant Gadstone and Samuelson, sir."

Two of the canvas bundles the purser had taken ashore. Their correspondence would have to be returned to the senders, with an explanation.

"I'll deal with them," he said. It wasn't something he'd had to do before, but he'd helped Gadstone to write a few letters to next of kin. Now he'd have to do the same for Gadstone's wife.

He put those in his pocket as the purser left. A pang of disappointment struck as he examined the handwriting on the one addressed to him—it was not Anna's hand. Breaking the seal, he turned first to the signature. Aunt Beth.

Anna—married? The words *titled* and *rich* swam before his eyes. *Old enough to be her grandfather...so sorry to have to tell you...could not dissuade her.*

With an oath, he crumpled the letter and flung it over the side where it turned to pulp, tendrils of ink briefly visible as the words disappeared.

Philip picked at the bark on the log, remembering the days and weeks that had followed. He'd worked longer hours than he needed to, supervising the repair of the *Garnet*. Too much work was better than having too much time to think.

The woman who had become so precious to him had broken her word within a few months of giving it. And with the contents of that letter in mind, he'd destroyed hers without reading it when it arrived a few weeks later.

Had that been unfair? He hadn't thought so at the time, or even yesterday. What explanation could there be, after all? She'd chosen money and rank over a lowly naval lieutenant.

At least Aunt Beth had told him—better to know than to wait for letters from Anna that would never come.

Aunt Beth?

Although he couldn't remember the exact words of the letter, it had definitely been critical of Anna's choice. Almost spiteful, but that was not like his aunt. And Anna would not be here at Beechgrove without an invitation from Beth. Something must have made Beth change her mind.

He must apologise to Anna for his words today, and for his lack of faith, but perhaps he should talk to Beth first.

"It's about Anna," Philip started, as soon as he was alone in the library with his aunt. Beth sat in one of the worn leather armchairs by the fire, but he could not be still.

"Go on."

"Why did you invite her here?" he asked, pacing over to the window and back. "And why didn't you tell me?"

"Anna has a standing invitation to come here at any time she can get away. She spent last Christmas with us, although she brought her cousins then. I didn't tell you because I thought you might not come if you knew."

She was right. "Why did you want us to meet?"

"I thought it might help Anna's peace of mind if she could learn why you never responded to her letters. It might help you, too. Your mama writes that you have not been happy since you returned."

So his mother had conspired with Aunt Beth to get him here; that was why she'd been insistent that he accept the invitation. He ran a hand through his hair, wondering how much to tell Beth.

"I talked to Anna yesterday evening," Beth went on. "It must have been about the time you arrived. She thought you hadn't read the explanation she sent you."

Aunt Beth had kept any accusation from her voice, but Philip felt his face reddening again. "That is correct."

"Why?"

"Because of your letter."

"A letter from me? Philip, I don't write to you, any more than you do to me. Your mama lets you have all the news, and passes on what you tell her."

Aunt Beth hadn't written it? He felt his mind numb.

"Philip, what did the letter say?"

"That Anna had married only for title and rank."

Beth's eyes narrowed. "I can see how the fact of Anna's marriage could be presented in an uncomplimentary way, if the writer didn't know the reasons behind it. But I didn't write to you."

Philip gazed at her—there was no guile in his aunt's face, only puzzlement. If she hadn't written the letter, who had? He put that question to one side—mending things with Anna was more important at the moment.

"Philip?"

"The tone of the letter...the one that had your name on it..." He took a deep breath. "That was still in my mind when Anna's letter arrived. I didn't even open it."

Whoever *had* written it had poisoned his mind against a woman he'd loved—and still did, if the turmoil within him was any indication. And his own faith in her hadn't been strong enough to question it. He crossed to the window again, shame washing through him.

"What do you know about Anna's family?" Beth asked.

What had that to do with it?

"Philip? Do sit down, please. This may take a little time."

Obeying reluctantly, he sighed. "She was here with her young cousins, James and Emily," he recalled. "And she lives with their father, her uncle... Edward?"

Beth shook her head. "She did live with Edward, yes, but he never married."

Who were James and Emily, then? There had been so many other things to talk about at the time. Books and music, birds and flowers, art and history. It was Anna he had loved, and he liked her little cousins because she did.

"The Tremaynes had a lot of tragedy—I suppose she did not wish to dwell on such things," Beth said.

"I didn't give her chapter and verse on my own family, either."

"Well, it's time you knew something of her circumstances. Her father was the oldest of four children. He died when Anna was... around eleven, if I recall correctly. I never cared for him, but Susan—his wife, and my friend—seemed happy enough. Anna being an only child, the house went to Edward, the next brother. They might have lived with him but Pamela, the youngest sibling, invited Susan to bring Anna to live with her. She was married to a naval captain, and she welcomed the companionship while her husband was away at sea. James and Emily are their children."

Philip frowned, trying to keep track of the names.

"Don't worry about remembering all the details," Aunt Beth added, as if she'd read his mind. "I'm just giving you the overall picture."

Philip nodded; he was following so far. "If Anna went to her aunt, why was she living with Edward Tremayne four years ago?"

"The children's father was killed in the East Indies a couple of years after Anna's father died, then her aunt and mother both succumbed to the influenza. About eight years ago now."

Four years before they'd met.

"Anna did go to Edward then, with the children. The poor mites needed someone they knew, losing both parents so close together. She's been the nearest thing to a mother they've had ever since."

"Good heavens." She'd lost her father, then her mother and aunt. Eight years ago? She must have been young then, only around seventeen. "You said her father was one of four children."

"Yes. The third brother is dead, too, but he left a son and a couple of daughters. Josiah, the son, is married. He and Diana have three or four brats—and I use that term advisedly."

"So she was living with Edward when she married?"

Aunt Beth stood. "No. He died not long after you went to the Caribbean. But you should ask her to tell you the rest of the story. She married in a hurry. I also know that the lack of communication from you distressed her greatly."

He would normally consider a married woman pining for a letter from another man as unfaithful, in wish if not in deed. Perhaps the poison of that letter was leaving him, for his first thought was not that, but to wonder about the circumstances of her marriage.

He closed his eyes against the thought that she had been forced into it. "Did you meet her husband?" He asked the question, although he wasn't sure he wanted to hear the answer.

"Yes, I did. He was a good man, Philip…"

That's what Anna had said, at the inn.

"…but again, you must ask her if you want to know more. I will consider who might have written that letter to you, but now I really must get back to Cook."

Philip continued to sit there after his aunt left, gazing into the fire. Anna must be a stronger woman than he'd ever suspected, with all those changes in her young life. And although Aunt Beth hadn't said so directly, she clearly believed that there had been a good reason for her marriage.

He bent his head down until it rested in his hands. His lack of trust had probably destroyed whatever might have been between them.

Could it be mended? He hoped so, but he should, at the very least, apologise.

He would find her and do that.

CHAPTER 5

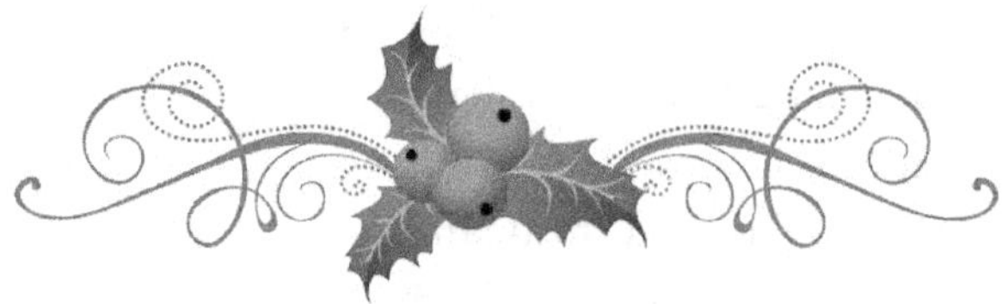

*P*hilip found Lizzie adorning mantelpieces and pictures in the parlour with the evergreens they'd gathered that morning. Anna was not with them, nor was she helping Catherine and Thalia weave kissing balls in the dining room. Becoming concerned, for it was cold outside, Philip questioned the butler and footman. Neither of them had seen Anna return, and the maid sent to look in her room reported that she was not there.

He had a little more luck in the stables—one of the grooms thought he'd seen a female figure walking along the hill, heading east. He remembered a route they'd taken together several times, and hurried back to his room to collect his greatcoat and hat. Dusk would fall early with the thickening clouds, and the faint yellow tinge to the light spoke of snow to come. It would not do for her to be out alone as darkness fell, and who knew how far she might have walked. And it was his fault that she had gone off as she had.

Rather than follow her, he set off to walk the route in reverse. Tiny flakes fell from the sky, drifting around in the still air and melting when they touched the ground.

The path divided not far into the trees. He hesitated, unsure which to take, and wondering whether he was making too much of her absence. She was a sensible woman, probably more so than he'd realised, and would return before dark. On the other hand, even sensible women could have mishaps. But as those considerations went through his mind he caught a glimpse of movement through the trees.

He knew the moment Anna spotted him. She hesitated, then put her chin up and carried on walking.

"Captain." She nodded, her expression polite and as cold as the winter air. She stepped sideways to walk around him.

His heart sank. "Anna, please wait a moment."

She stopped, but did not turn to face him.

"Anna, I'm sorry for what I said earlier—it was totally unjustified."

"Thank you." Her tone was flat, as if his apology didn't really matter.

"Are you returning to the house? May I walk with you?"

She hesitated. "If you wish."

It was not an enthusiastic acceptance, but she *had* agreed. He moved beside her and held his arm out, but she ignored him and walked on. That hurt, but after what he'd said he couldn't blame her.

"Anna, may we talk?"

"We are talking now, are we not?" She didn't pause, or look at him. "If you only came to apologise for your slur on my character, you have done so."

"I didn't. I mean, that was not the only reason. I wanted to explain my actions."

They were out of the trees now, fatter white flakes swirling around them in a rising breeze. She stopped and faced him, her lips set in a hard line. "You denied me an opportunity to explain, yet expect me to listen to you?"

"Not expect, no. Hope. Hope that you will give me another chance."

Anna finally looked away as his gaze did not waver. If she refused, she would be as much to blame for the end of their friendship as he. For the end of any possibility of more.

"Very well, I will listen. But not here—after dinner, perhaps. Or tomorrow."

"Thank you." He held his arm out again, and this time she took it.

"I wrote to you from Antigua, as soon as the *Garnet* arrived. Did you receive that?"

"No." She remembered how she'd calculated the length of the *Garnet*'s Atlantic voyage, the time it would take for mail to return, schooling herself not to look for a letter until there was a reasonable possibility of its arriving. Then Uncle Edward had died and she'd had to put it to the back of her mind. "At least, not unless Diana took it. It's just the kind of thing she might do."

"Diana?"

"That's part of my explanation, Captain. Now is not the time for that, either."

But he was not to be put off, it seemed. "Anna, when we met at the inn, you said you'd sent me two letters. Am I recalling correctly?"

Why did that matter?

"Yes. I sent the first via the Admiralty, as you said. When there was no reply I wrote again, but sent it to Aunt Beth to forward, in case your situation had changed." She preferred not to remember those anxious months of waiting.

"Ah."

"What do you mean?"

His lips curved a little, a hint of the teasing smile she remembered —the one that said he knew she would be amused too. "The 'ah' is part of *my* explanation, which you do not want to hear yet."

"Philip! You are just as annoying as ever!" She still wanted to be angry with him, but instead was irritated at the feelings his smile could still arouse.

"It is a very short explanation, Anna. Will you not hear it now?"

A sudden gust blew snow into their faces. "Inside," she said.

"Come on, then." He took her hand and hurried her along until they arrived, breathless, at the back of the house. Smells of roasting meat and gingerbread filled the air as he looked into rooms along the servants' corridor, finally pulling her into the stillroom and closing the door. "We may be private here for a few minutes."

She stripped off her gloves and pulled her bonnet ribbons undone, seeing from the sudden intensity in his expression that he, too, was remembering that day when they'd kissed.

Would he do it again, now? She shouldn't want him to.

He took a step back.

"Anna." He appeared to be bracing himself. "Before your letter arrived, I received one from Aunt Beth. One I *thought* was from Aunt Beth. It described your marriage in the most unflattering terms possible. I know now that Beth did not write it." He glanced away, before meeting her gaze again. "Anna, I should not have accepted that correspondence at face value, and I am ashamed of myself for doing so. It was not long after that when your first letter arrived."

What would she have thought, if she'd received such a letter about him? Doubted her judgement of his character, probably.

"It doesn't excuse me," he said, "but I hope it explains a little."

"It does, yes." It also went a long way to excusing him, but she wasn't quite ready to admit that yet.

Philip let out a breath. "Thank you."

"What was the 'ah' for, Philip?"

"My note of your address got wet and the ink ran, so rather than risk misdirecting it I sent my letter from Antigua here for Beth to forward. Your second letter to me also came here."

She frowned. "Someone here kept them?"

"It seems likely."

She nodded. "I sent a short note to Aunt Beth before my marriage. I wonder if someone read that before Aunt Beth received it, and wrote to you pretending to be her."

"Probably. I find it hard to believe that any of my cousins could do such a thing, but someone did. Aunt Beth is thinking about who the culprit might be."

"Good." It was too late to change the past, but it might help if they knew why someone had tried to make trouble between them.

Philip stepped forwards, reaching out and touching her arm.

"Anna, you said we did not know each other well. That is true, but may we try to get to know each other better? We have twelve days here."

"I can't stay until Twelfth Night, Philip. I have to go back to Weymouth."

"Why? Oh, your cousins?"

"Yes."

"Aunt Beth told me something of your background. Will you tell me the rest? We have a few days, at least."

"If you still wish to know." She did owe him an explanation for her actions.

"I do. Thank you."

She held her hand out, but instead of shaking it he raised it to his lips. Her cheeks heated as she pulled her hand away, fumbling to unlatch the door before hurrying upstairs to her room. Being in the same house with Philip was no longer something to be avoided, but she already felt guilty about not spending Christmas Day with James and Emily. She could not stay longer.

Even if she could, she wasn't sure that she should.

It seemed Aunt Beth's supervisory activities were over, for Philip found her in the parlour with her feet up on a stool and a cup of tea in one hand. The mistletoe ball that Catherine and Thalia had been making hung from the small chandelier in the centre of the room, and swags of holly and ivy decorated the mantelpiece and picture frames.

"The girls have done well, don't you think, Philip?" She cocked her head to one side at the sound of over-loud male voices in the hall. "Ah, the Yule log finally arrives. Well, we'll have a few minutes peace while they get it into the drawing room fireplace. Do sit down."

He took a chair facing her, unsure how to begin.

"Have you made your peace with Anna yet?"

He should have known she'd ask that. "I've started," he said. "But I came to ask you about a letter."

"Another letter?" Her brows rose and she took a sip of tea.

"Yes. Anna said she sent a second letter to me via you, but I only received one."

"That would be Thalia, I expect." Her brow creased, a mix of annoyance and sorrow.

Philip gaped for a moment at her instant conclusion. "Are you sure? Have you spoken to her?"

Beth shook her head. "No, and I do not intend to raise the subject until Anna has left."

"How do you know Thalia kept it back?"

"I only suspect at the moment, after what you told me earlier. But I have been thinking about it, and I don't see who else it could have been. I doubt that Anna confided in anyone at home about her feelings for you, let alone details of your posting. It has to be someone in this house, and most likely the same person who wrote that unpleasant letter to you. I don't want to believe there are two members of my family acting in such an underhand way."

She set her cup down and swung her feet to the floor, sitting up straight. "Philip, did you flirt with Thalia that summer? Or say anything that might make her think you particularly liked her?"

"Good grief, no. She was just a child."

"Fifteen is old enough for her to have started thinking about potential suitors."

Philip tried to recall. "She did come with us sometimes, when we took Anna's cousins up on the downs. I just assumed the other children here at the time were too young for her."

Beth sat back. "A natural assumption. I'm guessing she was jealous of the attention you paid to Anna."

That could also explain her sulks and flirting today. And that comment about prize money that he'd been stupid enough to repeat to Anna.

"Philip, I cannot say how sorry I am for the distress those letters have caused the pair of you. If it was Thalia, it's possible she may try to stir up more trouble, but I will keep a close eye on her. If I confront her now, there'll be tantrums that could spoil everyone's

Christmas and make things very uncomfortable for Anna, and for you."

She had a point. "Aunt Beth, may I tell Anna what you suspect?"

"By all means. Part of Thalia's punishment, if she is the one, should be to see that her stratagem has failed. Now go and change for dinner while I finish my tea."

Philip gave her his best salute, and she laughed as she shooed him away.

Sitting before the mirror as Aunt Beth's maid arranged her hair, Anna found that she was looking forward to dinner. At least Philip had agreed to hear her explanation—had even asked her to explain. Whether he would accept her reasons for breaking her promise to him remained to be seen, but she would face that tomorrow.

Aunt Beth's children had been almost as close as brother and sisters to her on the visits she'd made during her childhood. Now she could enjoy a family Christmas Eve dinner with them all.

She smoothed her gown as she walked downstairs, knowing its gold silk with a paler net overdress became her well. The maid had woven matching ribbons into her hair, and added a small sprig of holly to acknowledge the season.

A hubbub of chatter already filled the drawing room when she entered, and the air held the spicy scent of mulled wine. Uncle Thomas handed her a glass and she sipped it, feeling the warmth spreading through her. She admired the huge log blazing in the fireplace, still amused by everyone's pretence that it had taken the menfolk all day to find it. Only a few minutes later, Bates announced that dinner was served.

"Let me escort you in, my dear Anna," Uncle Thomas said, holding his arm so she could lay her hand upon it. "Beth has decreed that you shall keep me company and tell me all about young James and how he is enjoying school."

Uncle Thomas took the seat at the head of the table, with Anna beside him. Aunt Beth and Philip had the equivalent positions at the far end of the dining table. Anna wasn't sorry—although she had made her peace with him, it was too soon in their mending relationship to be thrown together.

"Bless me, Cook has done us proud again," Uncle Thomas said, regarding the array of dishes spread before them. "Although I'll warrant this is nothing to our Christmas feast tomorrow. Now, what can I help you to, my dear? A slice of pheasant? Some of these excellent beans?"

Anna allowed Uncle Thomas to serve her. "Not too much, Uncle. I'm sure there are some tasty desserts to come." As they ate the first course their talk turned to how James and Emily were getting on, and the doings of the various Kempton grandchildren then took them through the rest of the meal.

Bursts of laughter came from the other end of the table, where a cheerful-looking Philip seemed to be keeping his neighbours entertained. Thalia, in particular, was regarding him with a coy expression, although Anna could not see that he was returning the attention. Then his gaze met her own and the warm smile that spread across his face could have been one from four years ago.

The Kemptons never stood on ceremony, regularly talking across the table, so Anna wasn't surprised when Uncle Thomas raised his voice a little and asked Philip what he intended to do with himself now the war was over.

"For there'll be less call for naval men, I should think. Will they give you another frigate?"

"They might, Uncle, but there are captains senior to me, and more experienced, wanting ships as well."

"We've been following your exploits in the papers, Phil," Toby said. "You must have made a fair bit of prize money. Enough to live on?"

Anna listened with interest. For her own sanity, she had stopped reading naval reports from the Caribbean, trusting that Aunt Beth would tell her if Philip had been badly injured or killed.

"I could buy a small estate with it," Philip said. "And put some in the five percents. I'd get by tolerably well."

"You, a farmer?" Toby laughed. "I can't see you being happy in one place."

Anna thought he might do very well as a landowner. From what she remembered so vividly of their time together, he loved being in the countryside. But Toby had known Philip from their childhoods—he must understand him much better than she did.

"I'd miss the sea, certainly," Philip admitted. "I haven't decided yet—there is no pressing need to do so, after all."

It sounded as if he'd take another command if one were to be offered. Anna turned her gaze to the plate before her, her appetite for the trifle fading. She stabbed her spoon in, annoyed with herself for wishing that Philip would find a way to stay in the country. All she had hoped for from this visit was to clear up the misunderstanding between them.

"How about standing for parliament?" Uncle Thomas suggested. "They could do with some men of sense in the Commons."

Entering politics was an idea that Philip had toyed with, but it didn't appeal to him.

"I could help you if you decide to go that route, Philip," Anthony put in. "I know a few people with influence."

"Thanks, Tony, but—"

'Well, if you men are going to talk politics, I think it's time we retired to the drawing room." Aunt Beth stood as she spoke. "Don't be too long now, or I will have to come and fetch you." She wagged a finger at her husband. Uncle Thomas laughed.

Thank goodness for that—at last he would be free of Thalia's flirtatious comments and fluttering eyelashes. He studiously ignored her parting smile as she followed her mother out of the room, watching Anna instead. Their eyes had met a few times during the meal and, to his delight, his smiles had elicited answering ones, and even a blush. Now, though, she did not look at him as she left the room.

Damn. Something had upset her, but he had no idea what it could be.

"Philip?"

"What?" He looked up from his plate to find all eyes on him. "My apologies, I was distracted."

"Have some more wine," Anthony said, passing the decanter. Philip poured a little into his glass, but did not drink.

"So, might you stand for a seat in parliament, Philip?" Uncle Thomas persisted.

"It doesn't appeal to me, Uncle. Too much corruption involved at the ballot."

"Fair point," Anthony said.

"It has been suggested I could join the diplomatic service," Philip said, recalling the letter from Lord Harpenden that he still hadn't given much consideration to.

Toby snorted. "Diplomacy, Phil? Really?"

"Don't judge him by yourself, my boy," Uncle Thomas said, and Toby gave a wry smile.

"What prompted that idea?" Anthony asked, his face serious. "I've heard of admirals having to deal with political matters, but a captain? Not that I'm impugning your abilities in any way, you understand."

"I'm not sure," Philip replied. There had been several incidents when he'd become involved in dealings with the governors of Caribbean islands, but he didn't want to start lengthy explanations at the moment.

"Are you going to join the Boxing Day hunt?" Toby asked Anthony. "I've a new hunter…"

Philip stopped listening as the others embarked on a detailed discussion of the merits of their own mounts. He was hoping to get Anna to himself after dinner, and perhaps hear her explanation.

Finally losing patience, he pushed his chair back. "If you will excuse me, gentlemen, I will join the ladies."

"We all will," Uncle Thomas said, getting to his feet.

Good. He just hoped Anna had not yet retired to her room.

CHAPTER 6

In the drawing room, Lizzie was arranging chairs around the circular table, a deck of cards ready in its centre. Philip's spirits sank as he realised that Anna was not here—but then neither was Aunt Beth.

Uncle Thomas paused beside him as the others entered the room. "Anna and Beth will be in the parlour," he said quietly.

"We thought we'd play Speculation," Lizzie said, "but I can get the Pope Joan board out if you prefer?"

"Speculation will do nicely." Anthony sat down at the table and rubbed his hands. "Prepare to lose money to me, wife!"

"Ha!" Lizzie replied with a grin.

"I'm for the parlour." Uncle Thomas patted his stomach. "Takes time to digest at my age, you know."

"I'll join you, if I may?" Philip said. Hopefully Anna would be there, but if not it might be useful to have a serious discussion with Uncle Thomas about his possible futures.

"I'll come as well, Papa." Thalia had approached them without Philip noticing. "Speculation is a childish game."

Uncle Thomas regarded her with raised brows. "You've always enjoyed it before, Thalia. Are you feeling quite well?"

Thalia's eyelashes fluttered as she glanced at Philip before facing her father. "Of course I am well, Papa."

Philip tried not to show his irritation. He'd retire to his room if necessary—he was not going to sit through yet more flirting.

"I'm sure you must be unwell, Thalia," Uncle Thomas said, his voice devoid of sympathy. "If you aren't feeling up to a game, perhaps you should retire to your room."

At another time, the chagrin in Thalia's face might have been amusing.

"I'll ask Bates to get some hot milk sent up," Uncle Thomas added. "It's what your mama has when she's indisposed."

Thalia's mouth fell open for a moment. "Oh, very well, I'll play, but I shan't enjoy it!"

"Come, Philip." Uncle Thomas clapped him on the shoulder and headed for the parlour without waiting to see what his daughter did. "She can sulk to her heart's content—the others will take no notice." He opened the parlour door, Philip letting out a breath of relief as he saw Anna sitting with Aunt Beth near the fire.

"You were right about what Thalia would do, my dear," Uncle Thomas said as he sat down near his wife.

Aunt Beth nodded, her lips pursing briefly before she smiled at Philip. "You are welcome to join us." She glanced at Anna. "Unless the two of you wish for private conversation."

"I would, if that suits Anna," Philip said, still concerned by Anna's lack of a smile.

Anna stood. "Very well, Captain. Shall we go to the library?"

Captain? She had called him Philip this afternoon.

The library was dim, its fire burning low. Anna lit more lamps while Philip added logs to the fire. She took a seat, declining Philip's offer of a glass of port. She'd had enough wine at dinner, and wanted to keep a clear head now—both to explain things properly, and to guard her own emotions. She did not want to rekindle all the feelings she'd had for him.

"Will you tell me about your husband, Anna?" Philip sat down. "You said he was a good man."

"And that he was three times my age. In fact, he was older still." Anna gazed at him, her eyes narrowed. The difference in their ages was one of the things he'd thrown at her in the woods this morning.

"Go on."

There was nothing in his expression beyond polite enquiry; the tension in her shoulders relaxed.

"You said he was a good man," he prompted again.

"He was. I met him just after my mother died and I went to live with my Uncle Edward, but I'd known of him for a couple of years before that. This was all a few years before you and I met."

"Aunt Beth gave me some of your family history," Philip said. "But she told me nothing about Lord Radnor."

Anna shook her head. "Not Lord Radnor. Admiral Sir Alastair Radnor."

"Admiral Radnor?"

"You've heard of him?"

"Indeed, yes. He's—he *was*—well-respected in naval circles."

"Well, Captain Severin, the children's father, had come to Alastair's notice when he was but a midshipman. Alastair acted as a kind of sponsor, I think. Later, when he married, Severin asked if Alastair would see that his family were looked after if anything should happen to him."

"A guardian?"

"Not formally, no. Unfortunately. Alastair wrote regularly after Captain Severin died," she went on, "although he never came to see us. I was living with Mama and Aunt Pamela then, in Plymouth."

"Then your mother and aunt died."

"Yes. I went back to live with my uncle in Yeovil, with the children. James was six then, and Emily only four. That was where I grew up, but Papa willed it to Uncle Edward, rather than to my mother."

"Your uncle treated you well?"

"Oh, yes. That is to say, he meant well, but he was a confirmed bachelor and spent most of his time shut up in his study. He had no idea what to do with small children."

"I understand you live in Weymouth now. Was that where Radnor lived?"

"Yes—Yeovil is but thirty miles from it, much closer than Plymouth. I wrote to inform him of our change of circumstances. I was hoping he might visit, but I heard nothing for nearly a month."

The letters Alastair had written to Pamela after Severin's death had been friendly, showing what Anna felt to be genuine concern for the wellbeing of the children and their mother. Still distraught at the deaths of her mother and aunt, Anna had longed for someone to confide in and consult.

"That must have been a difficult time for you."

Anna looked up to find Philip's gaze fixed on her face. His tone was gentle, full of sympathy.

"It was." She rubbed her temple—it didn't seem right to speak ill of the dead, but her family's failings were pertinent to her story. "Mama always said the Tremaynes were hopeless with money—Uncle Edward certainly was. I had a little from what Papa had left to Mama, but he had made no specific provision for me. Captain Severin was more sensible—he set up a trust for his children. A solicitor in London arranged for funds to be paid to my uncle, but I discovered the housekeeper was diverting some of it into her own pocket."

"Your uncle did not object?"

"He only wanted a quiet life, and doubted what I was telling him. Besides which, the woman appeared to have Uncle Edward pretty well under her thumb. That money was intended for the children, so I wrote to Sir Alastair again."

That second letter had produced results.

Uncle Edward's manservant knocked on the door. Anna looked up from the account book she was trying to decipher.

"There's a Mr Donaldson to see you, Miss. Says he's come from Admiral Radnor."

Anna felt a mixture of relief that the admiral had finally responded to her letters, and dread in case something had happened to him.

"Please show him into the parlour." Anna closed the account book and checked that her hair was tidy before going to meet her visitor.

Donaldson stood and made a small bow as Anna entered the parlour. He was nearly as old as Uncle Edward, and much thinner, with black hair just beginning to grey at the temples and a weather-beaten face. "Miss Tremayne, Admiral Radnor has sent me in answer to your second letter."

"Is he well, Mr Donaldson? Do, please, sit down."

Donaldson shrugged as he resumed his seat. "He is never entirely well, Miss Tremayne, but he is much as usual. Shortly after your first communication, the admiral sent you an invitation to visit him in Weymouth. From your recent letter, it appears you never received it."

"No, I did not."

"Sir Alastair asked me to repeat the invitation in person. Unfortunately he is not fit to travel himself."

"I'm sorry to hear it." That would explain why he had never suggested visiting them at Plymouth.

"Would it be possible for you and the children to accompany me to Weymouth for the day tomorrow? We will return you here tomorrow evening."

That would be a long day, but it would be better than having to stay somewhere overnight.

"I will be happy to accept the admiral's invitation, as long as my uncle has no objection."

"Thank you, Miss Tremayne. If Mr Tremayne cannot spare you, a note to the Mermaid will reach me." He stood as he spoke, and made another small bow before leaving.

Uncle Edward's study door stood open; Anna could see him sitting near the window, his spectacles balanced on the end of his nose. He looked up at her knock, and placed a finger in his book to keep his place.

"Anna, what is it? Who was that caller?"

Taking this as permission to enter, Anna made her way past the desk piled with dusty books and letters, and the stack of newspapers on the floor.

"It was a Mr Donaldson, Uncle, come from Admiral Radnor. He stands sponsor to James and Emily, you recall."

"Radnor? Oh, yes." He gazed at her over his spectacles, one brow raised in enquiry.

"The admiral invites me and the children to visit him tomorrow." She briefly explained the arrangements before her uncle could protest that there was no carriage to take her.

"Very well, I see no objection." Uncle Edward nodded, and turned back to his book.

"Uncle." Anna waited until he looked up again—it hadn't taken her long to realise that he heard nothing unless she had his full attention.

"What is it? I've said you—"

"Uncle, Mr Donaldson said the admiral wrote to me a month ago, but I did not receive a letter."

"A letter? A month... Ah!" This time Uncle Edward put a marker in his book and closed it with a sigh. He heaved himself out of the chair and crossed to the desk. After much moving of books and papers, and several sneezes, he finally held out a sealed letter to Anna. "There, I knew it would be here somewhere. I must have forgotten to give it to you."

He looked so pleased to have found it that Anna didn't have the heart to ask him to be more careful in future. She thanked him, and went to ensure that in future the manservant would deliver all the post to her.

James and Emily were still missing their mother, and even new sights along the road to Weymouth the next morning did little to divert them. James, at least, cheered up when they came in sight of the sea and they could smell the salt in the air.

The coach halted on a road between the sands and a terraced row of houses. Anna noted three floors, and windows for servants' quarters in the roof. The brass knocker on the front door shone, and the two windows beside it were spotless.

"Welcome, Miss Tremayne." A stately butler bowed in the open doorway, and stood to one side to usher her in. "Master James, Miss Emily."

James chuckled as the butler bowed to him as well but Emily just clutched Anna's hand more tightly. The furnishings in the hall were sparse and functional, but as spic and span as the outside.

"My name is Bradley, Miss Tremayne. Sir Alastair asked me to show you to his parlour. He would like to see you first, while Donaldson takes the children upstairs."

"Sir Alastair has a telescope set up to look at ships," Donaldson said, and James's doubtful expression cleared.

"Look after your sister, James," Anna added as she followed Bradley into a bright and airy parlour.

Sir Alastair sat in a wheeled chair near the window, a blanket draped over his legs. He had a full head of white hair, tied neatly back. Anna thought at first that he wore a wig, as would have been the fashion when he was younger, but there were no rolls above his ears. His face was gaunt and lined, nearly as pale as his hair and with shadows beneath his eyes.

She crossed the room and made her curtsey.

"Welcome, my dear. I am glad to meet you at last." His voice was stronger than Anna expected, but the hand he waved trembled slightly. "Your aunt thought highly of you, from what she wrote in her letters. And now you have charge of her children."

"Yes, sir. In a manner of speaking." Anna took the seat indicated.

Sir Alastair gestured towards the blanket. "You will see why I have not been able to visit. Now, tell me how things are, and why I received no reply to my invitation a month ago."

Anna haltingly described Uncle Edward's household, and her worries about the children's trust fund. Sir Alastair nodded and asked pertinent questions; his physical frailty did not appear to have affected his mind.

"Do you think your uncle intends to make his own use of the children's trust fund?" he asked.

Anna had considered that question over the last few weeks. She shook her head. "No. He is well intentioned, but too..." Lazy or selfish sounded very harsh. "To be plain, sir, I think my uncle is far too disorganised to manage any fraudulent scheme, even if he wished to."

"Ha, yes, he sounds that way. Let me think about it, my dear. In the meantime, please ask Bradley to have the children brought down."

A maid with a tea tray followed the children into the room, and Anna poured while James enthused about the telescope Donaldson had shown him, and the ships 'just like Papa's' that he'd seen moored in the bay. Emily was more interested in a portrait of the admiral over the fireplace, asking if Papa's uniform had looked like that. She moved on to examine a model ship in a glass case and demanded to know why there weren't any people on it. Sir Alastair conversed easily with them, and they seemed to like him.

Philip listened as much to Anna's tone as to the words she spoke. Her great affection for the admiral was clear, but her description of his age and frail health removed most of the jealousy he felt.

"We stayed the whole day," she continued. "We went to see him often after that, usually once a month. He even came out with us a few times, for a carriage ride to the Isle of Portland or to Chesil Bank." She chuckled. "James was not impressed by the beach there—he complained that he couldn't make castles out of pebbles."

That reminded Philip of the ten-year-old James he'd helped with the chalk dog. The lad would be fourteen now. "Did Sir Alastair help you sort out the problem with the housekeeper?"

Anna smiled, a wry curve of her lips. "In a way. Donaldson was his man of business; he came several times to go through Uncle Edward's accounts with me. We didn't accuse her of theft, but I showed Uncle the books and explained how the housekeeper could save a great deal of money by changing suppliers."

"She was making her own profits?"

"Clearly, yes. It's quite common where there is no one to supervise. This time Uncle Edward listened to me, and when he told her to change she resigned in a fit of pique. The only problem with that was that my uncle decided I knew enough to become the housekeeper myself."

Edward Tremayne was long dead, but Philip still felt anger growing at the man for taking advantage of his niece. Something must have shown on his face.

"Oh, I didn't mind, Philip. It kept me busy, and I learned a lot. I had very little money of my own, and running his household meant I could save it for the future instead of contributing for my keep."

From what Aunt Beth had told him, Edward had died shortly after Philip had received his urgent summons back to Portsmouth. That must have been the event that led to her marriage, although surely Aunt Beth would have offered her a home if her uncle had not left her enough to support herself.

Anna was gazing into the fire, a soft smile on her face as if she was remembering pleasant times. She looked up, and her smile took his breath away. He just hoped some of it was for him, and not all for her late husband.

"Uncle Edward…" Her voice broke off as they heard voices in the hallway, then Toby burst in.

"What are you two doing here? We need you to make up the numbers for cards."

Philip glanced at Anna, wanting to hear the rest of her explanation. But tomorrow would be soon enough—he knew now that there must have been a good reason for the marriage.

"Do you feel like joining the others?" he asked.

She smiled, and took his arm as she stood.

CHAPTER 7

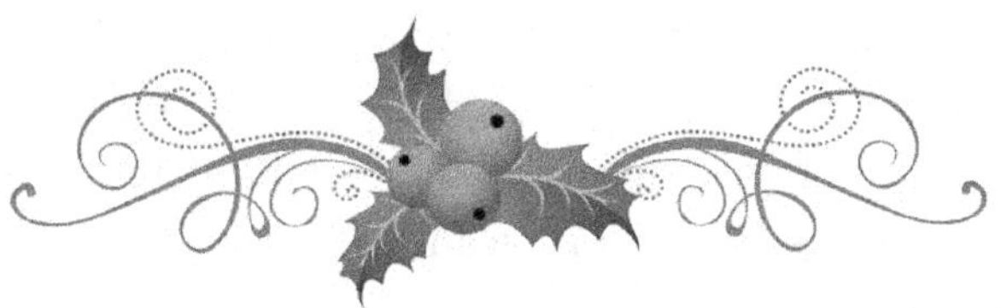

hilip did not manage to get Anna alone until the next afternoon. Snow had fallen overnight, and everyone had been ferried to the village church in their carriages for the Christmas Day service. Then he had to sit through the feast that Aunt Beth had arranged. At any other time he would have enjoyed the roast goose and venison, vegetables, jellies, creams, and plum pudding; now, he just wanted the chance to talk to Anna alone again.

The meal finally over, Aunt Beth and Uncle Thomas retired to the parlour to doze the afternoon away, and his cousins headed for the billiards room or the nursery to play with their children. Philip followed Anna to the library.

She sat near the window, watching as snow started to drift down again, pale against the grey clouds. A small crease between her brows gave her a pensive, almost worried, look.

He drew up a chair to sit close to her. "Is something troubling you?"

She looked at him, smoothing her expression. "I promised to return home the day after tomorrow, so I could spend some of the festive season with the children. It looks as if that may not be possible."

So soon? She'd said she couldn't stay until Twelfth Night, but he'd hoped to have a few more days. "It's no deeper than it was this morning," he said. "And it isn't freezing—the snow may not lie for long."

"I hope you're right." She did look a little more cheerful. Her gaze turned to the window again, although approaching dusk meant that little was visible through the reflections in the glass. "I wish I'd brought them along. They would have enjoyed the gardens and downs, even in this weather. Emily would love Aunt Beth's decorations. But under the circumstances…"

Guilt over his past behaviour stabbed him again. She'd come expecting that she might be upset and hadn't wanted to show it in front of her cousins.

"We have a little time before we're expected to eat again," he said. He glanced around, although he would have heard if anyone else had come into the room. "Will you tell me the rest of your story?"

Anna looked at her hands for a moment, then drew a deep breath. "Uncle Edward died at the end of October, only a few months after we met."

He nodded. "Aunt Beth told me that. I suppose the house went to your remaining uncle?" He frowned, trying to recall exactly what Beth had said. "No, his son?"

"Yes. Cousin Josiah. For, naturally, Uncle Edward considered that women are not mentally equipped to hold property themselves."

He couldn't make out if her tone was one of bitterness or sarcasm —whichever it was, he sympathised. "In spite of the fact that you'd been managing his household accounts far better than he ever had."

Something in her relaxed, and she smiled. "Indeed. Cousin Josiah chose to live there and sell his previous dwelling, and was quite happy for me to continue my duties as housekeeper."

"Without pay, naturally."

The corners of her mouth turned down as she nodded. "That wouldn't have been so bad, except for Diana—his wife. Everything had to be done her way, even things that had been running perfectly well before, and nothing was ever good enough for her or her children."

"Aunt Beth referred to them as brats," he put in, remembering Beth's expression as she said it.

"I would describe them as spoiled bullies," Anna said bluntly. "Within a day, Emily had her hair pulled and her favourite doll taken. James had been punished for trying to defend her."

An unenviable situation to have been left in. "Aunt Beth would have been happy to have you live here," he suggested.

"She would, yes. She said as much, after… after my marriage. But I couldn't leave the children. I couldn't protect them if I stayed, either, not when Diana believed everything her offspring told her, even the most obvious lies."

That made sense—but she could have brought them here with her. Aunt Beth loved having family around her, the more the better. "Why didn't you ask…?" His voice tailed off as something nudged at his memory. "The trust fund?"

"Yes. They—Josiah and Diana—decided that their sons should share James' tutor, at no cost to themselves, and that James didn't really need to start attending the school Donaldson had helped to arrange for him."

Her lips compressed as she spoke, and Philip guessed there were other ways in which her relatives had made life unpleasant for her and her charges. He clenched a fist, wishing he could plant it in the face of this Cousin Josiah.

"If the children were not living with them, there would be no reason for the solicitor to pay money from their trust fund to Josiah. Although I'd been acting as their guardian, it was not a formal arrangement. If I'd tried to move them here—or anywhere else— Josiah would have had little difficulty in convincing others that he should remain in charge of them."

"Uncle Thomas…" He knew as he said it that it was not a possible solution. "Josiah is a relative, and Thomas is not."

"Exactly."

"But Admiral Radnor was not a relative, either."

"Ah, but he had money, a title, and influence. So, you see, I did marry for a title and money, just as that letter said."

. . .

Anna waited while Philip considered her words, her stomach fluttering.

"The motive makes all the difference," he said, although he spoke slowly. As if he were thinking of something else.

"It was not an easy decision to make, Philip," she added, but he appeared abstracted still.

She did not want to sit and wait for his verdict. "I will see you later," she said, rising from her chair and smoothing her skirts. She hoped they had made enough progress that he would still speak to her, even if he did not accept her reasons for breaking her promise.

"Anna."

She turned to face him.

"Thank you for telling me." There was little indication in his face about what he thought, what he felt.

Anna retreated to her bedroom and sat on the window seat, watching the snow again. In spite of what Philip had said, she did think it was settling. The lines of the clipped hedges in the formal gardens below had blurred as snow collected on their tops.

The friends that James and Emily were staying with lived not far from Weymouth, and Anna had arranged to send word when she had returned. No harm would come to them if she was a day or two late, but they were expecting her and she did not want to disappoint them.

There was no reason for her to stay here beyond Boxing Day. Philip would either accept her explanation or not, and she would discover which next time they encountered each other—this evening, probably. She wished his approbation didn't matter so much to her, but it did. The heaviness in her stomach was nothing to do with the Christmas feast she'd merely picked at.

Her decision to marry hadn't been taken lightly. Sir Alastair, seated in his usual chair overlooking the bay, had explained how he could apply to the Court of Chancery to become the children's guardian—he could easily afford the necessary expenses.

"But I have no legal remit from Severin," he finished. "Your cousin could contest the case on the grounds that he is kin. But if we were married, that argument would be largely negated. It would be a marriage in name only, my dear."

She stared out to sea, trying to think through the practical implications of his suggestion. It was a way out of her predicament, and she believed his assurance that it would work, but her mind kept returning to the promise she'd given to Philip in the woodland glade.

Sir Alastair finally broke the long silence. "Anna, you know how sorry I am that you have been put in this situation. It was a dereliction of duty on your uncle's part not to have provided for you adequately, particularly as what he had came from your father."

"You are too kind, sir." As her memories of Papa had faded with time, she had come to resent his lack of forethought. "The original fault was my father's. He made no provision for a dowry for me, only the small income he left Mama that came to me on her death."

"A marriage between us would benefit me as well, you know," he said gently. "Who, in my situation, would not wish to have a beautiful young woman at his beck and call?"

The twinkle in his eye made her smile. She thought he would enjoy having all three of them in the house, as long as she ensured the children did not tire him. But she was still reluctant to break her promise, to obliterate the hope of a happy future with Philip.

Something of that must have shown in her face.

"Is there a young man involved?"

She felt her cheeks heat, and nodded. "Yes, but there is no formal arrangement."

"Can he not help you?"

"He is the second lieutenant in the *Garnet*, bound for the Caribbean. He expects to be away for at least a couple of years."

"Ah." He gazed out of the window, to where the sun sparkled on the sea. "It is not easy, being a naval wife."

Her face grew even hotter. "We had not discussed that, sir. We did not get that far." She almost told him that she had promised to wait, but the decision whether to keep her word should be hers alone.

"I was thinking of my own late wife."

The kindly, middle-aged lady in a miniature portrait the admiral kept on the mantelpiece.

"I did not see as much of her as I wished, nor did I know my children well, to my great regret. I did my duty to my country, and got great satisfaction from doing so, but that can come at a high price for one's family."

He appeared lost in reminiscence for a moment. Anna didn't speak.

"But that is just my experience, my dear, and not relevant to your decision. Do bear in mind that even the most optimistic of my physicians give me no more than a couple of years. You are likely to be a widow by the time your young man returns."

She swallowed against a sudden lump in her throat. She knew he was ill, that was obvious, but he seemed not to mind that he was dying.

"No, do not look so upset, Anna. I've had a long life, and a useful one. Apart from not knowing my family better, my only regret in leaving this Earth would be that I hadn't done better to keep my word to Severin. He was a promising officer when I met him, and a good man."

Anna sat up straighter in her chair. "Sir, that is tantamount to…" She bit her lips against further words.

"Blackmail?" He had that twinkle in his eye again. "Manipulation? Perhaps it is. But tell me, if you explained all the circumstances to your young man, do you think he would understand?"

Would he? She hoped so, but she didn't know. Philip could not help her himself—even if he were here and willing to take on both her and the children, he might not be able to obtain guardianship. He was away doing his duty for the country. Looking after James and Emily was her duty. It was not as if Sir Alastair had proposed a full marriage, after all. There would be no consummation.

"Very well. Thank you, Sir Alastair."

. . .

There had been repercussions at home, of course. Josiah and Diana had ranted about her lack of family feeling, and were even less inclined to control their children's behaviour towards James and Emily. But all that was more bearable now they knew it would end soon, and it had taken Donaldson little more than a week to arrange for a special licence and for their removal to Weymouth.

Looking out at the snow still falling, she thought that she could not regret her marriage to Alastair, even if Philip did not accept her explanation. Alastair had provided the help she needed to keep James and Emily safe and happy, but he'd been a good friend, too, in many ways. If she had not been blissfully happy with him, she had been content.

But she wanted more than just contentment.

She got to her feet abruptly. It was nearly time for supper, and to perhaps discover what Philip now thought about her.

Philip considered what Anna had said. She'd had no legal duty towards her young cousins, but the duty was there, nevertheless.

If he'd been in England at the time, he would have helped if he could, but there was no changing the past. The thought that she hadn't even asked him stung for a moment, until he put his emotions aside and considered the situation rationally. It would have taken many months for a letter to arrive and for him to reach England again. He couldn't even be sure that he would have returned—his own duty at the time had been to the Navy, and her need might not have persuaded his commanding officer to allow him leave.

Still trying to ignore his emotions, he wondered if it had been fair of him to ask for that promise. He'd been expecting to be away for a couple of years, but he knew full well that plans could change and some Navy men were away for much longer than that.

It was a lot to ask of a young woman, to wait for years without the security of a formal engagement. Even had he proposed marriage after only two weeks' acquaintance, it would still have been a lot to ask for. And she would then have been faced with the dilemma of breaking a formal engagement or allowing her cousins to be exploited and bullied.

There was nothing else she could have done. And if she could forgive his crediting that spiteful letter, he could surely forgive her justifiable breaking of her word.

Perhaps they could start again.

Aunt Beth had arranged a cold collation for their evening meal, to allow the servants to have their own feast below stairs. Anna had little appetite; she contemplated excusing herself, but she had to face Philip again at some time.

"Come, sit by me, Anna," Lizzie said as they entered the dining room. Philip had not yet arrived, so Anna took the seat between Lizzie and Toby. She was toying with a slice of ham when Philip spoke close behind her, making her jump.

"I don't see that you could have made any other decision," was all he said, his voice low enough that only she could hear it. There was no chance for more, as Anthony called him over with a question about horses and he took a seat further down the table.

He caught her eye, and his smile brought heat to her face. Taken with that, those few words were enough. The leaden feeling in her stomach dissipated, and she accepted an offer of chicken pie from Toby.

"So who's for the hunt tomorrow?" Anthony asked. "Anna, you don't care for it, I think?"

"No, thank you." She shook her head in emphasis. She could ride, but had no wish to jump hedges and gates.

"Philip? That was a fine hunter you arrived on."

"I'm not used to long hours in the saddle," Philip replied. "I'll have to decline this time." His eyes met Anna's again. "Although I'll enjoy a ride out on the downs if anyone is interested."

She gave the smallest of nods—with any luck it would just be the two of them, and they would have more chance to talk. Then Lizzie spoke to her, and the rest of the meal passed quickly as Lizzie gave her all the news about her children.

"Think of something to do that doesn't involve moving," Toby groaned, sprawling in his chair an hour later. Looking around the parlour, Anna could see that everyone else felt much the same.

"You could read to us," Lizzie suggested. Anna suppressed a grimace—that would preclude any private conversation with Philip.

"Good idea," Toby said. "But not me, sister dear. I'd make a mull of it—that was very good Burgundy that Papa provided."

"We could read scenes from Shakespeare," Thalia suggested, "like we did last time Philip was here."

"I've no need to show off, Thally, but I don't mind if you do." Toby leaned his head on the back of the chair and closed his eyes.

Thalia sniffed, and turned her shoulder to her brother. "We could do Romeo and Juliet again, perhaps."

"I've always liked Much Ado About Nothing," Aunt Beth put in. "If read well, the banter between Beatrice and Benedick is most amusing."

"Oh, if we must do that play, I prefer the scenes between Claudio and Hero," Thalia said. She looked at Philip as she spoke, a coy smile on her face. Anna's eyes narrowed—the new understanding between her and Philip had put the deceitful letter-writer out of her head, but now she thought about it, Thalia was the obvious culprit. She'd cast other flirtatious looks at Philip these few days past.

"I'll read Hero, shall I?" Thalia's eyelashes fluttered again in Philip's direction.

"What, 'Leonato's short daughter'?" Toby sniggered.

Thalia's expression slipped for a moment. "A wronged maiden," she said. "There is no need to be rude, Toby. Philip, you should read Claudio."

Yes, it must have been Thalia. Anna sighed. She'd never been as close to Thalia as she was to Lizzie, because of the difference in their ages, but she hadn't expected such spite. What would Philip do at this blatant attempt at pairing the two of them off?

"If you wish," he said, sitting straighter in his chair. A happy smile spread across Thalia's face. Philip looked at her, his expression stern. "That seems most appropriate," he said. "I am, after all, a fool who believed a malicious fabrication against the woman I love."

Anna's breath caught as heat rose to her face. There had been an unmistakable note of sincerity in his voice. The silence in the room was almost palpable, all eyes on Philip.

Thalia lifted her chin. "Whatever do you mean, cousin?" But she didn't look puzzled, and her gaze slid away from Philip's face.

"I think you're more suited to Don John, Thalia. The architect of the lie."

Thalia's lips set in a hard line. "I didn't write anything that wasn't true."

"You lied about—"

"Philip, please." Anna's voice was quiet, but Philip stopped talking.

"Thalia, go to your bedroom," Aunt Beth ordered.

"But I didn't—"

"Now, Thalia!" Anna had never heard such command in Aunt Beth's voice. It appeared that Thalia hadn't either, for her mouth fell open.

Uncle Thomas stood. "Come with me, Thalia."

Thalia scowled at him, unmoving. He put one hand on her shoulder, waiting patiently until she turned and stalked out of the room. Anna didn't envy her the reckoning to come from Aunt Beth, but Thalia had brought it on herself, after all.

The air was thick with unasked questions. Anna decided it was best to give a straightforward explanation.

"Someone tried to make trouble between Philip and me four years ago," she said, her voice remarkably calm. "Through a letter that purported to come from Aunt Beth." From the silence, the others were reaching the same conclusion that she had come to.

"Cards, anyone?" Aunt Beth said. There was an instant murmur of agreement. "There are enough of us for two whist tables, when

Thomas returns. Toby, rouse yourself and bring the small table over here."

Philip moved over to Anna's seat. She looked up at him with a smile and a shrug. "It seems we have been commanded," she said.

"Anna, I did not mean to distress you."

Warmth spread through her at the concern on his face. "You did not." Quite the opposite, in fact. "We are among friends, Philip," she added. "We have spent enough time alone together these few days that no one should be surprised there is something between us."

"Philip, Anna, come and join this table." Aunt Beth summoned them to one of the card tables.

"Can we talk tomorrow?" Philip asked as she stood up.

"Of course." She would look forward to it.

CHAPTER 8

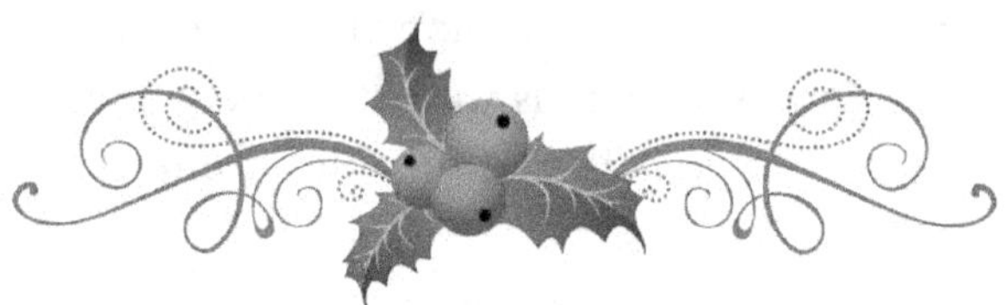

$\mathcal{A}$nna reined in Aunt Beth's docile mare as they reached the crest of the downs. Philip came to a halt beside her, close enough that their knees were almost touching. Below, the white land-scape was intersected by the lines of hedges, black squares marking bare woodland. Thin lines of smoke rose from houses into the blue skies, and the horses' breath made frosty clouds in the still air. The faint sound of a hunting horn reached them, along with the baying of hounds.

"It will be melting by tomorrow," Philip said, his gaze to the south where a thin sheet of cloud was beginning to whiten the sky.

"How do you know?"

"You don't spend years at sea without learning something about the weather. Clouds like that often bring warmer air." He glanced at her, a wry smile on his face. "It will probably also bring rain, but if you must go tomorrow you should get home without too much difficulty."

"That's good." Except it didn't seem so, not now.

The whist last night had been a disaster; it was just as well they'd been playing for penny points. She'd done her best to concentrate on the game, to forget that he'd just announced that he loved her in front of everyone, but with little success. His smiles, the look in his eyes, were like those from four years ago. He laid down cards, and she'd looked at his hands, remembering how they had felt on hers. When he took a sip from his glass, her attention was on his lips, not which suit she should be playing. From the odd mutter of disgust from Toby or Lizzie, Philip's own play had been little better.

The party did not break up until late, and there'd been time only for him to quickly ask if she would walk or ride with him today before Aunt Beth shooed them all upstairs. She'd said goodnight to him in the parlour—after what she had been thinking, talking alone in a darkened corridor would not have been wise.

They had said little this morning as they mounted up; it hadn't seemed necessary. Just a few words as he'd adjusted the stirrup leather for her, then they'd set off towards the high ground.

The shapes of the landscape were the same as they'd been four years ago, the glitter of sun on snow as glorious as the greens and golds of summer had been. She was tempted to revel in the beauty, and the joy of having someone to share it with. These few days had demonstrated that those feelings were still present in both of them, but today there was a small voice of caution.

Two weeks was not long to get to know a person.

"Tell me about your life at sea, Philip," she said, urging the horse into a walk along the broad ridge. He'd spent over half his life in the Navy.

"What do you want to know?" His expression was wary, as if she'd asked about something she shouldn't.

"Oh, not the battles." What she could imagine of those was quite sufficient. "You were not fighting all the time, I think?"

"Hah, no. Most of life at sea is uncomfortable boredom. Damp and too hot in the tropics, wet and freezing in northern seas."

"Yet you enjoyed the life."

Alastair had talked of the satisfaction of doing his duty, but there must be many different reasons why men were drawn to the sea.

He allowed the horses to walk on, appearing to consider his words. "Part of it was the comradeship of men working together for a common purpose," he said. "But it was not only that. There is something majestic in looking out over rolling water, knowing that it stretches on for thousands of miles."

Anna shivered—that seemed frightening to her, rather than majestic.

"Too much, you think?" Philip was smiling at her, understanding mixed with amusement, and something else. "You learn to trust in the ship and its crew. But there's beauty in the vast emptiness."

Anna watched his face as he talked about the sun sinking towards the horizon, making a glittering track of gold towards the ship; the bows creating white foam on blue water, schools of dolphins surfing on the ship's wave; flying fish, bright tropical birds, the shadows of spars and rigging against the stars.

"You miss it," she stated.

"I missed you," he replied. "Many times I wished you'd been beside me to share the moment."

She felt a rush of pleasure at his words, but it was tinged with melancholy. What she longed for was someone to share her life with, someone to love and to love her. She wanted more than just shared moments.

With Alastair she'd had companionship, someone to confide in. They'd had long discussions about art and literature, politics and history. She'd learned a lot from him, without ever feeling as though he was talking down to her.

She wanted that with Philip, if he was to be the one, as well as the intimacies and children that would come with a proper marriage.

"Have you decided yet what to do, Philip? Will you wait until they give you a new ship?"

Philip detected a wistful note in Anna's voice. She'd smiled when he said how he'd missed her, but then her expression had become more solemn.

"I'm not sure," he said. "I have been recommended to the diplomatic service." He'd talked about that with the menfolk at dinner after the ladies had left. "It is an offer I am seriously considering."

"Aren't most of the diplomats in Vienna?" she asked.

"There's always a need for competent men." He noted one corner of her mouth lift. "And yes, madam, some *do* consider me competent!"

She smiled then, her face lightening. "I'm sorry, Philip, I should not tease."

No apology was needed—he rather liked it. He knew she intended no malice.

"That will allow to you to travel, still, I suppose," she added.

"That's true. But there are other considerations as well." Such as how well he was really suited to long negotiations or remaining polite with people he disliked and disagreed with.

"I'm sure you'll make a success of anything you decide to turn your hand to."

That sounded like a compliment, but also final, as if she didn't want to discuss it further. Philip allowed the horse to walk on further, wondering if he'd said something wrong.

"Should we turn back, do you think?"

Her question made him take note of his surroundings. The advancing clouds would soon cover the sun, and the air would turn even colder.

"We can take that ridge down towards the village." He pointed with his whip. "The going should be easy on the lane from there."

She nodded, and they turned their horses. There would be other times to talk about his future—a discussion he wanted her to be part of.

"How is your life now, Anna?" he asked. Was she happy as a widow? He tried to suppress the hope that she wasn't, ashamed for even thinking it.

"Not at all exciting, compared to yours." She glanced at him and shrugged. "There isn't much to tell, Philip. There are balls in the assembly rooms twice a week, if I care to pay the subscription. Libraries, shops, a theatre. I come here several times a year."

"Is James away at school?" he asked, dredging up memories of things she'd told him.

"Yes, he boards at a school in Dorchester, but comes home most weekends, or goes to a friend's home."

"And Emily? I remember her enjoying drawing."

Anna laughed. "She does, and I am still hopeless at it. I teach her some things, but she shares tutors for drawing and music with some other girls in the town."

Emily was a little younger than James, he thought. Perhaps twelve? Anna would be responsible for her for some years yet. James, too.

He followed her into a belt of woodland, reining the hunter back to follow her along the narrow path, ducking beneath the occasional low branch.

He'd not considered her young cousins when asking her to wait for him, but at that time she had not been solely responsible for them. That had changed—could he take on two half-grown children? Looking at Anna's form, moving easily on the horse ahead of him, remembering their shared discussions and laughter, that kiss, he thought he could. He would do his best to be a good stepfather.

They emerged from the woods to find the hunting party filling the lane, and his chance for private conversation was over.

No matter—he would call on her in Weymouth, where they would not have to continually try to find a place to be alone.

He did manage to have a private moment after dinner. She'd joined him, Toby and Anthony in the billiards room, and lingered behind when the other two decided they'd played enough.

"I return home tomorrow morning, Philip. I intend to leave at first light, before the roads become too muddy with melting snow." She looked away, her fingers fiddling with the fringe on her shawl. "I'm glad we have cleared the air between us."

Cleared the air? He'd hoped they had done more than that.

"Anna." He wanted to draw her to him, but something about her stillness gave him pause. He'd hoped for a repeat of that kiss, for an indication that her hopes for the future were similar to his.

She held her hand out, but made no move towards him. He raised it to his lips—that was not what he wanted, but he'd take it if that was all she was offering. Her hand was warm on his, but removed too soon.

"Anna, may I call on you in Weymouth?" He'd been going to ask so much more before she left, but now he dared not. He wasn't sure what had changed, but he didn't want to risk an outright refusal. That could be the end of all his hopes.

"I…" She took a deep breath, and Philip feared she was about to deny him even that. "Yes, if you wish."

"Thank you. Goodnight, Anna."

"Goodnight."

Anna gazed out of the chaise window, watching drops of rain dribble down the glass. The weather was as miserable as her mood.

Aunt Beth and her family had gathered to say their goodbyes in the hall, some still yawning. The hurt on Philip's face when her farewell to him had been a brief handshake had cut right to her heart.

The Anna of four years ago would not have done that, but she was a different person now, with different responsibilities.

Had she made a mistake last night, with that cool goodnight to Philip? It had taken a great effort not to step closer to him and accept the embrace that he clearly wanted. That she wanted too, now that the misunderstandings between them were no more.

That would be her heart ruling her head, and she was wary of allowing that. Sitting back against the squabs, she rubbed her temples.

Seeing Aunt Beth's family together had shown her what she was missing by living as a widow. The easy companionship between Beth and Thomas, and between her children and their spouses—that was what she wanted.

She could have that with Philip, she was sure.

For a while, at least. Until he started to pine for the sea or was given a new command. Then she'd turn into Aunt Pamela, waiting endlessly for letters, scanning the Gazette for news of actions in which her husband might have been involved. Might have been wounded or killed. The country was now at peace, true, but more naval men died from shipwreck and disease than in battle.

Better not to be close to him at all, than to have happiness for a short while and then lose it again.

There were her cousins to think of, too. They'd lost so many adults in their short lives. Anna suspected that the loss of Captain Severin had made little impact, as they'd hardly known him. But their mother had died, then Uncle Edward, and then the admiral. Could she introduce another man into their life who would be there for a while and then leave again?

Take a risk, her heart said, but she had more to think of than just herself.

Philip hesitated outside the open door of the breakfast parlour, not wanting to face possible questions from his aunt or cousins. He turned away—he'd have to face them at some time today, but not just yet.

"Philip."

Damn—Aunt Beth had seen him.

"Philip, wait a moment." She stood behind him, a cup of tea still in her hand.

He sighed. There was no help for it—he could not be rude to Aunt Beth.

"Come into the library." He did as he was bid, and they sat by the fire. "Now, tell me what troubles you," Beth went on, when they had settled themselves.

Aunt Beth waited. He hated laying out his feelings before another person, but he needed some advice. Badly.

"I think you know, Aunt. What I don't understand is why, or if I've said or done something wrong."

"Hmm." Beth took a sip of her tea. "What, exactly, do you want?"

"To marry her." He'd begun to want that even before Anna had finished her explanation.

"Did you ask her?"

"No." He ran a hand through his hair; Aunt Beth couldn't advise him unless he was honest. "I thought things were going well, that she might still feel for me what she did before. Then yesterday she seemed to change, to pull away."

"She wasn't happy when she left, Philip. That was clear."

"Then why did she go?"

"Why don't you ask her?"

He leaned forward and put his head in his hands. She'd given him permission to call, reluctantly. Would calling on her too soon turn her further against him?

"Have courage, Philip. I suspect she wants you as much as you want her, but I can see why she may not wish to wed you."

"Why?" He clenched his fists in frustration as Aunt Beth drank more tea, her brow creased in thought.

"When you are fighting an enemy ship, Philip, do you put yourself in the other captain's position and think about what they might do?"

"Of course."

"Well, then. It might be more difficult here, but try to think of this from Anna's point of view. What her life has been, and what it is now. And perhaps think about what you were talking of when she stopped being happy with you."

She set her cup down and stood up. "I could suggest what you should do but, to be frank, if you cannot work out at least some of it for yourself, you do not deserve to win her."

CHAPTER 9

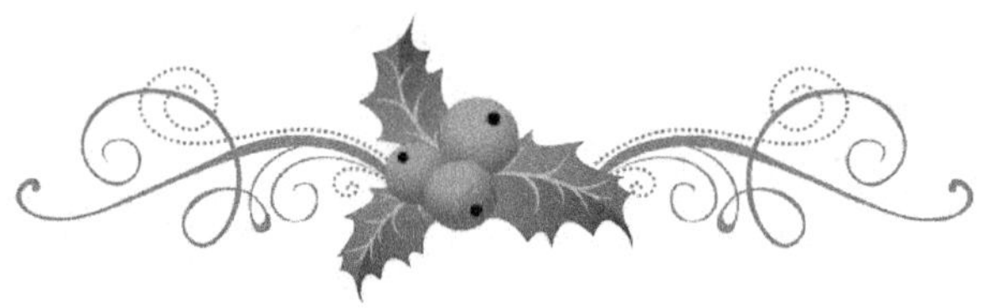

Anna descended from the carriage and walked up the steps. The house looked as unwelcoming as the grey drizzle on the dull sea, and the damp air was filled with the mournful cries of gulls. She turned the key in the lock and pushed the door open.

"Excuse me, my lady." Aunt Beth's groom stood on the steps behind her, holding her trunk. She hurriedly got out of his way, and fished in her reticule for some coin. He'd got her here in record time, and now had a miserable journey back to Beechgrove.

"Thank you, my lady. I'll be off now, if there's nothing else?" He cast a doubtful glance into the empty hall.

"That is all, thank you."

Anna watched him toss a farthing at the lad holding the horses, then stepped into her house and closed the door. A faint smell of baking bread reached her—Mrs Tennant must have returned. The kitchens, at least, would be warm.

The cook was chopping onions when Anna walked in. She put the knife down and wiped her hands on her apron. "My lady, I wasn't expecting you back so early. Joss is just lighting some fires."

"Don't worry, Mrs Tennant, I set off early." She pulled out a chair near the end of the long table and sat down. She felt drained from the jolting ride in the chaise. The same thoughts had repeated themselves throughout the journey; her head still said she'd made the right decision, but it didn't *feel* right.

"Tea, my lady?"

"Please." Anna sat while Mrs Tennant made tea and then returned to her cooking. A clatter of buckets heralded the return of Joss Tennant.

"Fire's lit in the parlour, my lady, but it's still a bit cold. I've done your bedroom as well."

"Thank you." She didn't move. It was warmer here, and the staff were used to her presence in the kitchen. She sat watching the bustle as the maids and the butler returned from their short holiday and set about their usual tasks, trying to keep her thoughts of Philip at bay.

But she could not hide from herself in the kitchen forever, and she finally asked for another tray of tea in the parlour. Settling at her escritoire, she wrote a note to the Framptons, asking them to send James and Emily home tomorrow, and sent Joss off with it. She would have to be more cheerful when the children returned.

The parlour felt bare compared to Aunt Beth's cheery rooms. The day before she left for Beechgrove she'd found some ivy to drape along the mantel, but there was not enough of it and it looked sad rather than festive. Even lighting all the candles and lamps made little difference.

It wasn't the parlour, though, it was her own feelings. Regret, and guilt, she realised, warming herself before the fire. She gazed up at Alastair's portrait, which still hung on the chimney breast. Recalling his words about the satisfaction he'd gained from his life at sea, she'd assumed that Philip felt the same. That might be true, but she should at least have asked him more about it. And explained why she'd suddenly turned cold towards him—trying to protect herself from wanting him was no excuse for hurting his feelings.

And it hadn't worked.

She couldn't go back to Beechgrove, not with James and Emily due back, but she could send someone with a letter. The irony of trying to explain herself again this way struck her as she picked up her pen, but what else could she do?

Writing the letter took some time, and involved much staring into space and several fresh starts. In the end, she said only that she regretted the way she had said goodbye, and she would be happy to see him if he would call. Dusk had fallen by the time she finished. She wrote a covering note to Aunt Beth, asking her to forward the letter if Philip had already left Beechgrove.

She drew the curtains against the night and picked up the letter. She would put it on the hall table ready to be taken to the post office in the morning. As she stepped into the hall, the knocker sounded.

Bradley walked to the door with his usual measured tread, and opened it. The man on the step wore his hat low over his face, and had a sack slung over one shoulder, but she recognised him just the same.

"Captain Kempton to see Lady Radnor."

She stared at the letter in her hand, as if writing it had conjured him up. Then Bradley stood aside and Philip entered, swinging the sack to the floor. A small pool of water gathered around him on the chequered tiles, dripping from his sodden coat and hat.

"Philip!"

Philip didn't notice Anna in the hallway until she said his name. She stood with one hand on her chest, eyes wide. Surprised, certainly, but he couldn't tell whether or not she was pleased to see him.

Assume that she is, he told himself. She looked lovely, although anxiety for the outcome of this call outweighed his pleasure in seeing her again.

He removed his hat and knocked it against his leg to dislodge the raindrops clinging to it. "May I come in? I have to say how nice it is to be coming into a warm house after such a wet journey, rather than a cold and damp ship's cabin."

She smiled, although she still appeared dazed.

"Your coat, sir?" The butler must have taken her silence for assent, and Philip readily handed over coat, hat, and gloves. His shoes had not become too wet or dirty in the short walk from the inn where he'd changed and left his saddle bags.

The butler eyed the sack dubiously. It, too, was dripping water onto the floor.

"Leave that for now," Philip said. "Lady Radnor might not want it."

The butler nodded, and bore his wet things away.

"Philip. I wasn't expecting to see you so soon."

"I hope you don't mind. You did say I could call," he added, trying to keep the uncertainty from his voice.

"I… No, of course I don't mind." She glanced at something in her hand, then back at him, her smile broadening.

That sounded promising. He picked up the sack and emptied it onto a dry patch of floor. The sprigs of holly and mistletoe, strands of ivy, spilled out across the tiles.

"What…? Where did you get all that at short notice?"

"I stole it from the library at Beechgrove," he admitted. "You may already have decorated, in which case I will gather it all up and take it away."

"Stole it…?" She chuckled, a sound that warmed his heart. "I have a little, but not enough."

Good. "We should leave it here to dry." He bent to spread the greenery out on the floor at one side of the hallway.

"Please, come into the parlour, Philip. I've asked Bradley for tea, but you may have ale or brandy if you wish."

"Tea will be perfect, thank you."

Philip paused in the parlour doorway, confronted with a portrait of an admiral in a powdered wig. The optimism he'd persuaded himself into faded a little—was the portrait still there because she missed her late husband?

She took a seat by the fire. He moved to add another log, then paused. This was her house, not his.

"Please." She gestured to the log basket. "You must be cold—your coat was very wet."

He shrugged, poking the log into place then sitting down. "I've been far wetter at sea."

There was an awkward pause. Anna wasn't even looking at him, but fiddling with whatever she had in her hand. Finally, she looked up, and held out a folded paper.

"Philip, I had just finished writing this. You can see why I was surprised to see you."

He let out a breath of relief as he read it. She *did* want to see him again.

"Why have you come? So soon, I mean."

He wanted to tell her he'd come to ask her to marry him, but that was too precipitate.

"To continue the conversation we had on the downs yesterday." He leaned forward, arms resting on his knees. "Anna, you asked me to tell you about my life at sea, and I described some of the things I enjoyed."

She nodded, her hands folded in her lap.

"I could have described other things: being in wet clothes for days at a time, the taste of water gone green from being too long in a barrel, rarely getting a full night's sleep." He sat back. "I could have said how I enjoy being ashore so I can sleep in a bed that does not move, and have a fire like this to lounge beside. That I don't mind riding through the pouring rain because I know I can get dry and warm at the end of my journey. I can have a whole—"

He broke off with a mental curse as a knock on the door heralded the arrival of the tea tray.

"I took the liberty of providing sandwiches, my lady," the butler said. Philip, eyeing the plate of food, instantly forgave the interruption.

Anna busied herself pouring the tea, her face thoughtful. Philip took a sandwich and bit into it hungrily.

"A butler worth his weight in gold," he said. "I've not eaten since breakfast."

"Philip, what was so urgent that you had to ride here in this weather?"

He put the rest of the sandwich down. This was more important than appeasing his hunger. "You were," he said. "You are. Anna, when we were riding yesterday, you seemed to withdraw from me. It was after I'd been talking about the sea."

She nodded.

"I wanted you to know that I am not wedded to a career at sea." That was possibly an unfortunate choice of words. "It is not all enjoyable, by any means."

She considered his words for a moment, her cup of tea untouched on the table beside her. "Yet that was your chosen career. The advantages must outweigh the disadvantages."

"They did." He was tempted to stop there, but he had to be honest with her. "They do still, if there is nothing else to be considered. I joined the Navy because my older brother would inherit Father's lands, and the only time I've regretted that choice was four years ago, when duty took me away from you."

She looked down at her hands, a blush rising to her cheeks. Then she met his gaze again. "You would miss the sea if you took up a different occupation."

"I would, yes."

Her mouth turned down a little at the corners; a small movement, quickly erased, but it gave him hope. He had suspected that was one of the problems.

"I wish I had my sketchbook with me," he said. "I thought of going back to my parents' house for it, but I wanted to make sure you got the greenery before the children returned."

"Sketchbook?"

"I wanted to show you some of the things I drew at sea. My box of watercolours has managed to survive all battles so far."

"Sunsets and dolphins?" A small crease of puzzlement formed between her brows. "I'm sure they are very good, Philip, but—"

"Not those. I did paint those things, of course, but I also painted from memory: the sun rising through trees on a misty morning, roses around the arch in Mama's garden, wind making waves in a field of wheat." That last attempt hadn't been too successful. Neither had his attempts to draw Anna—he could depict her features, but not the essence of her, the expressions that animated her face. "All things about the land that I miss when I'm at sea."

Anna gazed at him for a moment without speaking, wondering if she was reading too much into his words. "You miss the land?"

Philip shrugged, a wry smile curving his lips. "It sounds as if I'm never satisfied, doesn't it? What I'm making a mull of trying to say is that I'm going to resign my commission."

He stood. Her breath caught as he knelt in front of her chair, taking her hand in his.

"Anna, I love you, and I want you to be my wife. I think… I hope, that you feel the same way too."

She nodded, unable to speak.

"But there is more than love to a marriage, I think. That is why I came, to make sure there are no more misunderstandings between us."

"Philip, I'm so sorry for how I behaved last night and this morning. For saying goodbye to you in such a way."

"Don't be. You had every reason."

She hadn't, but it was lovely of him to say so. Sudden tears pricked her eyes; she could have spoiled things between them, but thankfully she had not.

"Anna." He stood, and pulled her to her feet, holding her close to his chest. She wound her arms around his waist and laid her head on his shoulder, the warmth of his embrace spreading peace through her body.

"Anna," he said again, softly, his breath tickling her ear. "You've had so many people leave your life, and you've had to be strong. You don't have to do it alone any longer."

She tightened her hold around his waist, and felt his hand stroking her back.

Anna wanted nothing more at this moment than to say yes, and let him take care of everything, but she had others to think of.

"Many of my fellow officers were married," he went on. "I always thought long absences were hard on the wives, more so than the men —at least we had our job to occupy our thoughts."

She tried to concentrate on what he was saying, not on the way she could feel his heart beating against her own.

"What if you don't like life on land?" she asked, her voiced muffled against his coat. Would he come to regret their marriage?

"I won't regret leaving the Navy. Anna, this isn't a sudden decision; it's something I've been thinking about since Boney abdicated." He released his hold and moved her away a little, gazing into her eyes. "The timing, however, is because of… of us."

She nodded.

"When you withdrew from me yesterday, was it because you want a husband who will not be away for years at a time?"

"In part, yes. But there are the children to consider, too," she added, taking a step back. The joy his words had produced would be a false one if he was expecting her to abandon James and Emily.

"I know. Anna, we have known each other such a short time. You said yourself that we don't know each other very well, so—"

"Well enough," she interrupted.

He put out a hand to stroke her cheek. "Nevertheless, if we married, I would effectively be a father to James and Emily. Don't give me an answer now, but let us spend some time together this week— you, me, and the children. I liked them when I met them at Beech-grove; I'm sure we'll rub along together well. I've taken a room at the Black Dog, and can stay in Weymouth as long as you wish."

She took a deep breath. He was right.

"That's an excellent idea."

"If we have a future together, Anna, it will always include James and Emily. They have lost enough people in their short lives."

"Thank you, Philip." She found it hard to talk past the lump in her throat. They still had much to say to each other, but there would be time for that. "Will you help me to arrange the greenery? The children will be returning tomorrow morning."

"I am yours to command."

They drank the almost cold tea, then brought in the greenery from the hall. Anna moved a stool towards the fireplace. "I'm not tall enough, Philip. Can you drape some of the ivy over the picture frame?"

He stepped up and placed ivy and sprigs of holly as she directed, but she saw his frequent glances at the painted face of her late husband.

"It didn't seem right to remove that portrait," she said, handing him another sprig of holly. "This house, all that I have, is because of him."

She stood back, regarding his handiwork critically, then placed more holly beside the clock on the mantelpiece. Working together, even on such a simple task, felt good. "That will do nicely, thank you. The rest will make a lovely table decoration."

He stepped down and moved the stool back to its place.

"He was like a father to me," Anna went on. "And a friend, but no more." She thought Philip already knew that, but she wanted him to be sure.

"Thank you for telling me." He looked into her eyes, one hand on her cheek. "It should not matter, but it does."

There was an intensity in his gaze that sent liquid heat through her body, and she stepped forward into his arms. The kiss felt as good as she remembered—no, better, for now there was also the knowledge that this was just a beginning.

Philip finally raised his head, his breathing as ragged as her own. She wanted more, but it was not yet the time for that.

"Will you stay to dinner?"

"Need you ask?"

The wind from the sea was cold, in spite of the pale sunshine. After several days of rain, Philip had hired a carriage and brought them all the few miles to Chesil Bank for a walk and a change of scenery. Anna and Emily had, sensibly, now retreated to the nearby inn, but James was still enjoying his new spyglass.

"Come, James. Anna and Emily will be waiting for us."

James took one last look at the frigate sailing eastwards past the end of Portland Bill, then reluctantly closed the spyglass. "Thank you for my present, sir."

"Do you really like it? It's not as powerful as the one at home." The one mounted in an upstairs room that James used to examine vessels moored in Weymouth Roads. Over the last week he'd spent some time talking to James about ships and the sea, and helping Emily with her drawing and painting.

James grinned up at him. "I know, but I can carry it around, and it's my own. Can I take it back to school with me?"

"If you wish."

They set off back towards the inn. Over the last week, he and Anna had talked of many things in the evenings when the children had gone to bed. Of his prize money, and how he might enjoy running an estate. How she and the children could visit London, or live there if they chose. Of the diplomatic service, and whether they might all live abroad. It didn't matter what they talked of—their shared glances and touches were promises for the future, and they would talk through any decisions between them, and then with the children. All of those things depended on whether she accepted his offer, of course.

Anna looked up as they walked into the inn's parlour, her lovely smile going right to his heart, as it always did.

"Sir, are you going to be our new father?" James asked.

"Do you think that's a good idea?" he asked, looking from James to Emily. If either of them said no, he'd do his best to change their minds.

"Of course it is!" James sounded almost indignant. Emily, still shy, smiled at him and bobbed her head in agreement.

But it was for Anna to answer.

"Yes, he is."

That promise of a future with Anna was the best Christmas gift he could have imagined.

THE END

A
QUESTION
OF DUTY
The Marstone Series
Prequel Novella
JAYNE
DAVIS

ACKNOWLEDGMENTS

Copyediting & proofreading: Sue Davison

Cover design: P Johnson

Thanks to my critique partners on Scribophile for comments and suggestions, particularly Kim and Jim.

Thanks also to Alpha reader Tina, and Beta readers Cilla, Dawn, Doris, Helen, Leigh, Mary G, Mary R, Melissa, Patricia, Safina, Sarah, and Sue.

CHAPTER 1

ort Frederick, Albany, August 1760
"Captain Stanlake to see Colonel Harper."

The clerk in Harper's outer office looked up as Jack spoke, and laid a ruler across the ledger he was examining before getting to his feet.

"I think the colonel is available, sir. I will go and check."

Jack dropped his saddlebags over a chair as the clerk left through a door at the back of the office. He'd sent Booth ahead with his trunks to find rooms in the town and get settled in, and he was looking forward to a bath after days in the saddle.

Rather than take one of the seats against the wall, he paced the room, impatient to know why he'd been ordered here while his battalion was still stationed in Fort Niagara. He'd only had time to take in some framed prints of what appeared to be a mansion in England before the clerk returned to show him through to the inner office.

Colonel Harper was somewhere in his mid-forties, running a little to fat—unsurprising for someone who spent most of his days behind a desk. He stood as Jack entered, holding out a hand in greeting.

"Pleased to see you here, Captain," he said, shaking hands then indicating a chair beside the desk.

"I was ordered to report to you, sir," Jack said, dispensing with the formalities. He'd never met Harper and had heard of him only as a man who knew a great deal about their native allies.

"Indeed." Appearing unoffended, Harper resumed his seat and took a sealed letter from a drawer. "This was forwarded to me from the Secretary at War's office, with instructions to hand it to you in person. You are to return to England with all despatch—I understand that this letter will explain why."

Jack maintained a neutral expression during this explanation, as was usually wise when listening to unknown superior officers.

"Perhaps you should read it before I explain the travel arrangements I have taken the liberty of making for you," Harper went on.

Jack frowned—the direction was in his brother's hand. Breaking the seal, he scanned the contents—Father was ill, and wished him to return before he died.

"Bad news?" Harper's expression showed sympathy, and Jack wondered how much the man knew.

"On the face of it, yes. My father is unwell."

Harper leaned forward. "Forgive me for prying, Stanlake, but you appear to be annoyed rather than distressed by it."

"I received a letter like this two years ago," Jack explained. "When I reached home, Father had fully recovered."

"Two years...?"

"At least I missed Abercrombie's fiasco at Carillon." He shouldn't complain too much—the French were just about beaten now, and his regiment was only manning a fort, not taking part in Amherst's attack on Montreal. If this letter had come last year he'd have missed the taking of Quebec. "You said I'd been ordered home?" That wasn't usual—last time he'd had to ask his commanding officer for leave.

"Your father's an earl. Connections in high places, I expect." Harper shrugged.

That was the way the world worked—it was a pity, though, that Father had never used his influence, or his money, to get Jack promoted further than captain. Particularly in view of the incompetence of some of his senior colleagues.

"I've arranged a berth on the *Pegasus*, a packet ship sailing from Boston in a week. Lucky, really—I'd arranged for Lieutenant Ffynes to escort my family on the voyage, but he's—"

Family? Escort?

"—been taken ill and won't get there before the *Pegasus* is due to sail. You've got his cabin, and you will make an excellent replacement for him."

"Family, sir?"

Harper nodded with a fond smile. "Yes. My wife and daughters are returning to London, to stay with my wife's brother. Time for the two girls to find husbands; more choice there. They're all eagerly anticipating access to better mantua-makers and so on. Women's things." He waved a dismissive hand.

Good grief—it was bad enough being dragged away from his duty on what would probably be another false alarm. But accompanying three women...?

Harper pushed a packet of papers towards Jack. "Here are the details. I've recompensed Ffynes for the ticket."

Damn—he hadn't enough cash to pay his way across the Atlantic.

"I'm afraid—"

"No, no," Harper interrupted. "Pay my bankers in London, Captain. All the details are there."

Well, Father would have to give him the money first. Most of his meagre allowance for this quarter was already spent, and he needed to keep something back to pay for the rest of his journey.

"If that is all, sir...?"

"Yes, Captain. I hope you do not return to bad news. Enjoy your voyage."

"Thank you, sir."

As Jack strode back into town, his feelings veered between worry that his father really was dying this time, and irritation at the escort duty Harper had just foisted upon him. It could have been worse, he supposed—there was less chance of foul weather at this time of year, so he might not spend too much of the voyage being sick.

Booth was in the room he'd arranged for Jack, removing clothing from one of his trunks.

"Don't unpack too much, Booth. We're off to Boston tomorrow, taking ship within the week."

"Back to England, sir?" Booth scowled.

"Is there a problem?" Jack was surprised at this reaction from his usually imperturbable batman.

"No, sir." Booth's expression was wooden.

"Out with it, man!" Jack said, then suppressed a smile as he noticed a dull redness creeping up Booth's neck. "A woman?"

Booth cleared his throat. "Yes, sir. Was hoping to get permission to marry, sir."

They'd be away for three months, most likely, even if Jack didn't linger at home. And if there was one thing worse than no servant, it was a servant in the sulks. He wouldn't have much need of Booth on board ship, and leaving him behind would conserve some of his meagre funds.

"Just unpack what I need for tonight," he said. "I'll see what I can do."

A note to Harper might help. If the colonel was going to impose his wife and daughters on Jack, the least he could do would be to put in a word with Jack's commanding officer to give his servant leave to marry.

Jack watched the wharves and warehouses grow smaller as the oarsmen pulled out into the choppy water of Boston harbour, and resentment swelled again at being ordered home in this way. He suppressed the feeling—if his father really was so seriously ill, he hoped he would be home in time to see him once more.

He turned his attention to the *Pegasus*, moored out in the bay, and squinted as the wind blew drops of water from the oars into his face. To his landlubberly eyes, the ship looked more like a wallowing whale than a flying horse. They reached the lee of the ship and the oarsmen grabbed the trailing ropes. Jack stood and accepted a steadying hand from above as he scrambled up the ladder and onto the deck.

"Welcome aboard, sir." The greeting was from a young man with a weather-beaten complexion. "I'm Sessions, the first mate. You must be Captain Stanlake?"

"I am." Jack shook hands and turned to watch his trunks being hauled up.

"Jenkins is the steward; he'll show you to your cabin." Sessions indicated a short, round man waiting several paces behind him. "We do not carry many passengers, but we generally manage to keep you comfortable. The last few passengers haven't arrived yet, I'm afraid. We will be ready to sail within the hour, if they are aboard by then." He cast a glance at the overcast sky. "We've a fair wind; it would be a shame to waste it."

As the mate moved away to speak to the boat's crew, Jenkins stepped forward. "The cabins are not very big, sir. Which of your trunks do you require on the voyage?"

"The small one," Jack said. He'd arrived yesterday in time to buy a few volumes from a bookshop and the latest newspapers from England—nearly a month out of date. He'd packed everything he needed for the next few weeks into the smaller of his two trunks.

"If you will come this way, sir?"

Jenkins led the way below, into a dining saloon with a large central table, lit at present by a large skylight above, and a few comfortable chairs bolted to the floor at one end. The passenger cabins opened off the saloon—the one he'd been allocated was tiny, and there was barely room to stand beside the bunk while the seaman carrying his trunk squeezed in behind him and placed it on the floor, then brought him a lantern. A table at one end of the narrow space held a bowl and ewer —empty—and had a small chair tucked under it. There were hooks on the wall, and a couple of shelves with bars across the fronts.

Jack threw his hat on the blankets and scrubbed a hand through his hair. Unpacking took only a few minutes—his new books on the shelves, together with a pack of cards and his shaving things and comb, his coat and spare jacket on the hooks. The rest would stay in the trunk, which just fitted beneath the bunk.

What to do now? Not wanting to get through his books too quickly, he settled on finding a place on deck to watch the preparations for their departure. He should enjoy a surface that stayed in one place beneath his feet while he could. There was no sign of the women he was supposed to be escorting, but they were probably settling in to their cabins.

He hadn't been above decks long when Sessions approached him. "I'm sorry to bother you, Captain, but I understand from Jenkins that you have the cabin originally allocated to a Lieutenant Ffynes, who was to be travelling with Mrs Harper and her daughters."

"I believe so." Jack suppressed rising irritation—he could guess what was coming. "Colonel Harper asked me to look out for them. I take it they are the missing passengers?"

A look of relief crossed Sessions' face. "Yes. They were to stay at the Royal George."

"They set off from Albany well ahead of me, I think, and I came across no ladies in distress on the way. Do you wish me to go and enquire?"

"I would be in your debt, sir. The captain… Well, suffice it to say he is irascible enough at the start of a voyage, without, er…"

"I understand perfectly." Even the best of superior officers could be trying at times.

"Mama, we were supposed to board the ship this morning!" Clara tried hard to keep the exasperation from her voice as her mother removed a gown from one of the large trunks yet again.

"I know, dear, but they will not leave without us," Mrs Harper said, her gaze not moving from the garment she was holding. "Kitty, do you think this will become Clara better than her blue—?"

"Mama, it's a packet boat," Clara said. "They have sailing dates to keep to!"

"Yes, dear, but we are not yet late, are we? Kitty, what about this one?"

Clara rolled her eyes, hoping her sister could talk some sense into Mama. She'd packed her own trunks for the voyage this morning. The small one held her lap desk and books, and Papa's manuscript; the larger one contained the few garments she would need at sea. They didn't have time for Mama to repack everything.

"You must both look your best on the ship," Mama said, for what must be the fifth time today. "I trust Kitty to have chosen her best gowns, but you take so little trouble with your appearance—"

"Mama, I helped Clara to choose," Kitty said, her fingers crossed behind her back at the lie. "What she has packed will do perfectly well. And it is only a small vessel—there will not be many people to see what we wear."

"But this is the most becoming one." Mama held up Clara's burgundy silk brocade embroidered with ivory flowers.

"Then it should not be exposed to the damp, and possibly salt spray," Kitty said, taking the garment from their mother's hands and carefully folding it back into one of the trunks that would be stowed in the hold. "Besides, you do not want us to marry sailors, do you?"

"No, of course not dear. But Clara has got out of the habit of associating with young gentlemen, and—"

"Mama," Clara interrupted ruthlessly. "We have not even sent a message to the ship. For all they know, we have been delayed on the journey and may not arrive for days."

"Don't be silly, Clara. Captain Stanlake will not let them go without us. How lucky that Lieutenant Ffynes was ill; a captain is—"

"When we left Albany, Papa had only just sent for the captain. He may not get here in time." Clara wished she felt her mother's confidence that things would turn out for the best. But Mama had always been like that, despite frequent evidence to the contrary.

"I'm nearly ready," Mama protested. "You must tidy your hair, Clara. For heaven's sake, why do you insist on wearing it in such a plain knot? Mary did Kitty's very nicely this morning. Why aren't you more like your sister?"

Clara glanced at Kitty's glossy black curls dressed around her head, with a few long ringlets draped over one shoulder. Kitty mouthed 'sorry' with a quick grimace.

"Where *is* Mary?"

"You sent her to ask for tea, Mama." Kitty had far more patience with her mother than Clara had at the moment, but then Kitty was happy to be on her way to London.

Clara bit her lips against the temptation to ask why, if her mother was so concerned about the choice of gowns to wear on board, she hadn't decided during the week or more they'd been travelling. She had, of course, but then changed her mind numerous times.

"Well, never mind now. But Clara, this captain is the son of the Earl of Marstone. It would be a good connection for either of you—"

"I thought we were returning to England for us to make titled matches?" Clara said. The captain must be a second or third son, otherwise he'd be Captain Lord something-or-other. She had hoped she'd have the weeks at sea to herself before having to be polite to a succession of undoubtedly tedious and self-important young men. Men, moreover, who would be attracted to her only in the hope of her uncle giving her a large dowry. A little like the young officers in Albany, many of whom seemed to be motivated more by her father's rank than her appearance or personality. Only Ensign Blake had seemed to have a genuine liking for her company, and he had been killed three years ago.

"You can never have too many suitors, Clara." Mrs Harper finally shut the trunk, leaving the straps for their maid to fasten when she returned from ordering tea. "Your father was quite the catch at the time; it's a pity…"

Her voice trailed off, and she shrugged.

A pity that he was a good administrator who the higher command had the sense to keep well away from action, Clara thought. Marriage to the third son of a baron had been a step upwards, socially, for a woman from the merchant classes, but Anne Morton's hope that her future husband would go on to achieve fame and glory, and possibly a title of his own, had come to nothing.

And now she had transferred her ambitions to her daughters.

"Well, we'll see," Mama said. "We'll go to the ship as soon as we've had our tea."

CHAPTER 2

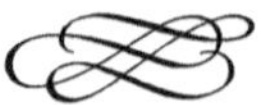

"At last," Clara muttered, as someone knocked at the door and entered. It would be Mary, with the tea.

It was Mary, but she was empty handed, and appeared rather flustered, with one strand of her grey hair coming loose from beneath her cap. "Begging your pardon, mum, but there's a gen'leman come to fetch you to the ship."

"We had better go down, Mama," Kitty said.

"He's in the parlour, mum." Mary started to fasten the straps on the trunks. Clara picked up their coats and followed Kitty and Mama downstairs.

The man awaiting them was tall and lean, with startlingly blue eyes and wide shoulders in his faded red coat. He wore his brown hair unpowdered, tied back with a black ribbon. He could be upwards of thirty, although his weathered complexion and stern expression might give a false impression of his age.

"Captain Stanlake." He bowed briefly in Mama's direction. "You are Mrs Harper?"

"Indeed, sir. May I present my daughters? Clara, my elder, and Catherine. How good of you to escort us home."

Clara, watching the captain rather than her mother, saw his brows crease for a moment. An unwilling escort? Their being late would not have helped matters.

"I trust you are all well?" he said.

"Yes, thank you, Captain." Mama sat at a table. "Will you sit and share a dish of tea with us? I have already ordered refreshments." She looked around. "Mary? Where is that woman?"

"No tea, thank you, ma'am." The captain made no move to sit. "Your maid said you were packed, so I asked her to supervise the removal of your luggage. The first mate informs me that you are the last passengers to board, and the captain wishes to weigh anchor within the hour as the wind is currently set fair."

Even as he spoke, Clara heard the thumps of heavy trunks being manoeuvred down the narrow staircase. He was very sure of himself, ordering their luggage removed on only Mary's say-so. But they *were* late, thanks to Mama's dithering, so she should not really resent it.

"Oh, so soon!" Mama exclaimed. "I must go and check that Mary has packed everything. Come upstairs with me, girls."

That brief frown crossed Captain Stanlake's face again, and Clara took her mother's arm as she moved towards the door. "Mary will have made sure nothing is left behind." They would be in close company with the few passengers on the *Pegasus* for weeks; it would not do to annoy their escort now. Behind her, Kitty was making a pretty apology for the delay as she followed with the captain.

In the hallway, Clara steered her mother towards the outer door, thankful that she had managed to persuade her to settle their bill after breakfast. If there was a further charge for the tea they'd not had time to drink, the inn had Papa's address.

Outside, the trunks were already loaded on a handcart and being taken down the street, Mary following behind.

"The walk will do us good, Mama." There would be fresh air aplenty in the coming weeks, but little chance for exercise. Kitty moved to Mama's other side and started to talk about the voyage, preventing any more dithering. The captain followed, Clara aware of his silent presence behind them.

The sky was a dull grey, with a hint of rain in the air. Clara shivered, glad she had insisted on packing her old winter calico jacket and petticoat—not fashionable, but much warmer than her other clothes, and its dark green more practical for shipboard life. The cries of seagulls and the salt air had been with them since they arrived in Boston two days ago, but as they neared the water, Clara heard the slap of waves against the jetties. A sea voyage was an adventure, but she was not looking forward to Mama attempting to marry her to a title. The relative freedom of her life as an army daughter in the Colonies was about to change.

Snatches of the women's conversation drifted back as Jack followed them down the street. Mrs Harper's exclamations about being rushed away were soon replaced by the younger daughter's quieter chatter. A pretty thing, Miss Catherine, with her black curls and alabaster skin. It would be no hardship to face her across the dinner table. Miss Harper, too, looked well enough, although her scraped-back hair was a nondescript brown above a rounder face, and she appeared to take less effort with her appearance. The same could be said for him, he thought, glancing down at his coat; he was looking distinctly shabby.

Mrs Harper said something about an earl's son, but was quickly hushed by her elder daughter. He scowled, wondering if Miss Harper had interrupted out of embarrassment, or from a desire not to warn their quarry. If they thought he was a fine matrimonial catch, they didn't have their sights set high enough. He barely scraped by on his allowance and army pay as it was, and he had no desire to encumber himself with a wife.

Once on board, Mrs Harper started to discuss which items would be needed on the voyage, so Jack left Jenkins to deal with her. Already men were climbing the rigging and moving out along the yards ready to set the sails. He found an out-of-the-way place from which to observe the final preparations for sea.

At last the anchor was weighed and the shouted orders lessened as the ship gathered way. Jack walked to the rail, gazing back as Boston and its surrounding hills shrank behind them. The Harper daughters came on deck and stood nearby, also watching the land they were leaving. The colours and shapes of the buildings gradually blended until the town could not be made out at all against the land behind.

Miss Catherine glanced at him over her shoulder and smiled. Jack decided to accept the implied invitation and joined them. "Are you glad to be leaving?"

"In some ways. This place has been our home for five years—I was only twelve when we came. But it's exciting to be going to London; there will be so many more shops, and the theatre, and pleasure gardens. Mama has told us all about it. And it will be good to see Uncle George again."

Jack didn't enquire about Uncle George; one of them was bound to tell him at some point in the coming weeks.

"Clara didn't want to come back," Miss Catherine added.

"Kitty!" Miss Clara protested.

"Well, you didn't, did you?"

Miss Clara sighed and shook her head, casting a rueful smile in Jack's direction. "I've enjoyed my time here," she explained. "The country is so... so big and untamed. I'm sorry I never managed to persuade Papa to take us any further than Albany."

"You are not looking forward to shopping?"

"Bookshops, yes."

Miss Kitty tutted. "You will make Captain Stanlake think you are bookish."

"I am." Miss Clara kept her gaze on the distant land, her tone matter of fact.

Her sister rolled her eyes heavenwards, but with a little curl to her lips that made Jack think this might be a common, affectionate disagreement between them.

The land was now only a dark line on the horizon, and Miss Kitty turned away from the rail. "Come below, Clara, there is nothing more to see."

Miss Clara looked as if she were about to object, but then nodded and took her sister's arm.

"We will see you at dinner, Captain," Miss Kitty said.

Jack said something non-committal and turned his attention back to the rolling waves as the young women left. The gentle pitching of the deck wasn't too disturbing. If his stomach had not protested at the motion by the time dinner was served, he might risk eating with the company.

Mary knocked on their cabin door an hour later, with the news that dinner was ready for them in the saloon.

"Are you eating with us?" Clara asked. Their maid had taken meals with them at the inns where they'd stopped on the journey from Albany, but had clearly been uncomfortable sharing their table.

"No, miss. I'll be eating with Jenkins and the cook separately, and there's a manservant with the other passengers. You two go on, now. I'll brush down your coats while you're at dinner."

In the saloon, Clara took her place with her mother and sister on one side of the long table. Two other passengers, both men, sat opposite—the older one was rotund, his face lined beneath a grey full-bottomed wig, and his clothing well-fitting, with ornate embroidered trim on his coat and waistcoat. His companion was much younger and slimmer; he had regular features and wore a dark coat with much more restrained embellishments. Some similarity in their features suggested that the two men might be related. Captain Stanlake arrived to take the final place opposite Kitty.

This was a much smaller vessel than the one they had sailed on when they came to the Colonies, and with so few other passengers, Clara thought she might have time for reading after all. And for dealing with Papa's notes.

Jenkins carried in a steaming tureen, its savoury smell filling the air and making Clara's stomach rumble. A crewman followed with platters of buttered bread.

"Broth tonight, ladies and gentlemen," the steward said, swaying gently with the motion of the ship. "While the sea is still flat enough to allow us to serve such things."

Clara tried not to laugh, imagining soup sloshing everywhere as the ship rolled. Glancing at Jenkins, she thought she saw a quick wink before the steward started setting out bowls.

"The captain and mate send their apologies," he added. "The mate will normally dine with you, but both are busy with the business of departure."

"Do excuse me for not introducing myself," the younger passenger said, once Jenkins had left. "I am Jonas Nolan, and this is my uncle, Sir Cedric Nolan."

Sir Cedric nodded, but concentrated on his soup.

Mama made the introductions. "I am Mrs Anne Harper, and these are my daughters. We are travelling home so that they may enter society. My husband, Colonel Harper, remains in Albany."

Mr Nolan's gaze passed over Clara and fixed on Kitty, a gleam of appreciation quickly suppressed. "I'm sure they will be ornaments to society. My uncle and I have been in Boston on business, making new trading connections."

Clara wondered how Sir Cedric had come by his title, if he was in trade. A large loan on favourable terms to someone with the King's ear, perhaps?

"And you, sir?" Mr Nolan turned towards Captain Stanlake, who gave his rank and name but said nothing more.

"Eat up, boy," Sir Cedric muttered, reaching for another piece of bread. "Make a good meal while you can—the smooth seas won't last long."

"Oh, dear, yes." Mama glanced at Clara. "If you remember, eating became quite difficult at times on the way over."

The soup tasted as good as it smelled, and was followed by dishes of poached fish, roast turkey, and vegetables, and they all ate in silence for a while.

"Have you been in the Colonies long, Mrs Harper?" Mr Nolan asked.

"Five years," Mama said. "Before then, my husband was posted to Dublin, and we lived with him there."

"And have you enjoyed your time here? In Albany, I mean." Mr Nolan was looking at Kitty as he spoke, and Clara saw a brief crease of his forehead as her mother replied. But his interest in the conversation appeared to quicken when Mama mentioned Uncle George's surname.

"Morton?"

"Do you know my brother?" Mama asked.

Sir Cedric raised his head. "We do a little business with him. Decent chap, good head for investments."

"He will enjoy entertaining the three of you, I'm sure," Mr Nolan said.

"He is a good brother. Tell me, Mr Nolan, where in England do you live?"

Clara couldn't help but be amused at the adroit way Mama kept the following conversation focussed on generalities and away from business. Papa had discouraged such talk—not that he was ashamed of the connection to Uncle George, but he held that business was not a suitable topic for womenfolk. Mr Nolan's apparent interest in Kitty had not escaped Mama's notice, and she had far higher ambitions for her daughters than a mere merchant's nephew.

"Anyone for cards?" Sir Cedric asked, when sweetmeats and pastries had been cleared away, and a bottle of port placed on the table. "Stanlake?"

"Don't mind if I do." The captain had hardly spoken during the meal, and Clara wondered if his aristocratic background made him look down on people in trade, or if he was merely taciturn by nature. He had been friendly enough when they talked on deck, but that was before he knew about their connection to George Morton. He seemed happy to play cards with them, but there was little else to do.

"I'm rather fond of a game of whist," Mama said. "If you three gentlemen don't mind playing for penny points?"

Whether they did or not, they were all too polite to object, and Clara went to fetch a book and Kitty's embroidery from the cabin she shared with her sister. They retired while the whist players were still engrossed, but a knock on the door interrupted them as they were settling into their berths.

"It's only me," their mother called.

Clara pulled the bolt back and Mama came in and sat on the single chair. "Mr Nolan seems a very pleasant young man," she started.

"Do you think he's a fortune hunter, Mama?"

Mama sighed. "He might be—he did show a great interest once my brother's name was mentioned. Captain Stanlake is far more suitable, but he had very little to say all evening. You should talk to both of them, girls. You have not been in society much."

"I have been, Mama," Kitty said.

"I don't count those young subalterns you had flocking around you, Kitty. Being able to converse easily with people in all walks of life will stand you in good stead once we are in London."

"Yes, Mama." Kitty gave an exaggerated yawn. "Sorry, Mama, but it won't do for us to have dark circles under our eyes from lack of sleep."

"Oh, no, indeed. Good night then, dears."

CHAPTER 3

Jack tucked his scarf more tightly into the neck of his greatcoat and breathed deep of the salt air. The wind had strengthened overnight, and he'd woken to find himself being rolled from side to side in his bunk. He'd enjoyed the coffee that Jenkins brought him, but decided to see how his stomach reacted to the new motion before risking putting more into it.

Yesterday's clouds had cleared, and white foam on the waves glittered in the sunshine. Jack sat on a bench on the windward side of the low structure that supported the skylight to the passenger cabin. Tilting his head back, he closed his eyes, enjoying the feel of the sun warming his face.

"Good morning, Captain."

He opened his eyes to see Miss Kitty facing him.

"May I join you?"

"If you wish." He sat up straighter, looking around for her mother.

"It is not improper, I think, for me to sit with you on the open deck with the crew all around."

"No, I imagine not." He moved down the bench, allowing plenty of space for her to sit at the other end.

"It is lovely to have sunshine, is it not?" she said, sitting half-turned towards him. "The waves sparkle so. Such a welcome change from yesterday's grey weather."

"If one must be flung about, it is more pleasant for it to happen in sunshine, certainly."

She gave a pretty pout at his churlish response, then smiled, her eyes twinkling. "Does the motion upset your digestion, sir? I'm sure it will pass. We Harpers seem to be blessed with strong stomachs."

"Thank you for your sympathy, Miss Kitty." He returned his gaze to the horizon—his incipient nausea receded a little when he could see the movement his insides were feeling.

She chuckled. "Did you enjoy cards last evening?"

"I did, although a better partner would have been preferable." He wasn't sorry to have been playing for small stakes, as he had drawn Sir Cedric as a partner, who had a better opinion of his abilities than Jack did, and Mrs Harper had proved to be an unexpectedly astute player.

"I hope you did not lose too much, Captain. Men often assume Mama will dither over her cards as she does with other decisions."

"Not too much," he admitted, with a wry twist of his lips at his own expense; he had thought that himself. But he had enjoyed the game. If his stomach settled enough to allow him to spend the evenings at cards, this voyage might not turn out to be too tedious, after all.

Jonas Nolan crossed his line of vision, coming to a momentary halt as his gaze flicked from Jack to his companion. His lips compressed as he gave a quick nod and walked on.

"You would be more comfortable out of the wind," Jack said. "There is another bench on the other side—I believe this skylight contraption is just high enough to shelter you from the wind there."

"I'll survive a little breeze, Captain. Besides, we learned a lot about Mr Nolan at dinner yesterday, and very little about you."

Startled at this blatant approach, Jack's eyes turned to her face. She fluttered her eyelashes with an innocent expression, but she had that little curl to her mouth that he'd seen the day before.

"Are you flirting with me, Miss Kitty?"

"I am attempting to, but you are not making it very easy."

"Hmph." He resumed his inspection of the horizon.

"I have only had the chance to practise on some of the younger officers in Albany," she said, with an expression of regret. "They are not the kind of husband I want."

"That is being very direct. Am I to assume that I *am* the kind of husband you require?" If so, she was going about it the wrong way.

"Oh, no. You would not do at all."

Jack was startled into a laugh. "That certainly puts me in my place."

"May I be honest, sir?"

"By all means. Why stop now?"

"Truly, sir, I did not mean to offend you. It's just that Mama…" She looked down at her hands, as if unsure how to go on.

"I did overhear a comment about my being the son of an earl."

"Mama wants us to be happy, but she thinks that means having titled husbands, or someone with such connections."

"And you do not?"

"Not necessarily. I wouldn't turn someone down because of the title if he met my other requirements."

"That is very open-minded of you." Jack couldn't help smiling—he wondered if she had written a list. "What are these requirements, if I may ask?"

"I want a comfortable, *settled* home where I can grow roses, and a husband who holds me in some affection, at least."

"Roses? That seems very… specific." This was the strangest conversation Jack had ever had with a young lady. Although as they tended to be in short supply in remote forts like Niagara, he hadn't conversed with many recently. He generally preferred the company of his fellow officers, or amenable camp followers for more intimate companionship.

"It doesn't have to be roses," she admitted. "But we have never lived in one house for more than a few years together. I want to be able to make a garden that I won't have to leave before it's developed."

"To put down roots." Jack nodded, keeping his expression serious. "Like a tree. Or a rose bush—lovely, but with thorns." He wondered if that last had offended her, but she giggled.

"I suppose I deserved that."

A movement along the deck turned out to be Miss Clara approaching, book in hand.

"Clara, have you come to join us?" Miss Kitty asked. "Captain Stanlake said I am prickly."

Miss Clara raised one brow. "I wonder what you said to him, then. Good day, Captain."

"Miss Clara." She didn't seem to mind that he'd dropped the formality of addressing her by her surname. "Your sister said only that she wishes to become a tree, and that I am not suitable husband material."

Miss Clara shook her head, but her expression was one of resignation, not censure. "One day, Kitty, you must learn to curb your tongue."

"I thought it would be best to clear the air. Captain Stanlake will be in our company for several weeks, and it would not do for the poor man to feel… hunted… all that time." She turned her head to face him. "Clara does not wish to marry at all."

Clara felt her face heat with embarrassment. Could Kitty be any more direct? Luckily the captain appeared to be amused rather than offended, his smile lightening his normally serious expression into something friendly.

"What are you doing here on the windy side of the ship?" she asked her sister. "It will do nothing for your complexion."

"My complexion will recover before we reach England."

Clara regarded the space between Kitty and the captain—the bench was not quite long enough for three people to sit comfortably.

The captain stood. "If you wish to join your sister, Miss Clara, I can find—"

"No, Captain, pray do not disturb yourself. I fear I would become cold too quickly, sitting here."

Kitty stood. "Thank you for your company, Captain. I will leave you in peace. Please, do not get up."

The captain bowed his head as they left.

"I've been following Mama's instructions," Kitty said, when they had settled themselves on a sheltered bench. "You should, too."

"There's plenty of time for that," Clara pointed out. "Although now you've so subtly announced that I don't want to wed, there seems little point."

"Oh, Clara—I suspect the captain wants to get married as little as you do. You cannot spend the whole voyage avoiding him. He is amusing." Her gaze slid sideways. "But here is Mr Nolan."

Clara looked around to see that young man approaching.

"Good day, ladies," Mr Nolan said, coming to a halt in front of them. "May I join you?"

Clara dropped her book in her lap and slid along the bench until her hip met Kitty's. She gestured to the remaining space. Mr Nolan stepped forward, then paused.

"It will be too difficult for you to talk to both of us," Kitty said, from Clara's other side. "I will leave you together."

"You must be anticipating the delights of London," Mr Nolan said, once Kitty had gone and he was settled beside Clara.

"Yes. Mama has told us much about it, although when we last lived there I was too young to be taken to theatres and other entertainments."

"You have not seen Vauxhall Gardens, then, or Ranelagh. The latter is considered more genteel, I know, as the higher price of admission keeps out many of the lower orders."

"Mama has described them to us, although it is some time since she has been in London." Fifteen years, more or less, when Clara had been but seven years old.

"The Rotunda at Ranelagh is a splendid sight, and means that entertainments need not be limited by the weather..."

Clara supposed he meant well, and she might have been interested had he described anything that she had not already learned from Mama. Out of politeness, she said a few words in the right places, but didn't bother to pay much attention. A theatre was a theatre, after all, even if the London ones were larger than any she'd been to. But when Mr Nolan started to describe the style of houses in London—as if Boston and Dublin were not civilised—she had finally had enough.

"This has been a most interesting conversation, Mr Nolan, but it is rather cold on deck. If you will excuse me, I should go below and check that Mama has all she needs."

Mr Nolan stood. "Enjoyable indeed, Miss Harper. Do let me know if there is anything I can do to make your voyage more comfortable."

Clara inclined her head as she stood, a sudden roll almost making her lose her balance. She ignored the steadying hand Mr Nolan held out as she headed for the companionway leading down to the saloon.

Jack stayed on deck most of the afternoon, reading some of the time, looking up now and then to see streaks of high cloud gathering and then thickening in the western sky. By late afternoon his stomach felt more settled—so much better that he decided to eat dinner with the other passengers.

The first mate joined them at the table, and Miss Clara and Miss Kitty kept him busy answering questions about the ship and the countries he'd visited. Sessions told a story well, and had a fund of amusing incidents to draw upon. Sir Cedric was concentrating on his food, but Mrs Harper and the younger Nolan were also listening with interest.

Whist was once more proposed, but this time Sessions joined Mrs Harper, Miss Kitty and Sir Cedric. Jack, still not entirely sure his dinner would stay where it should, nevertheless accepted a glass of port from the steward and sat back in his chair to watch the game from the other end of the table. Jonas Nolan began a conversation with Miss Clara. He caught snippets of their words, eavesdropping shamelessly while keeping his eyes on the card players.

"...working on this afternoon?" Nolan asked.

"...father's manuscript... fair copy... publishers in London."

Jack shifted in his chair, turning to face them so he could hear better.

"That is a big task for a young lady such as yourself."

"I have plenty of time," Miss Clara replied. "And I find the subject matter fascinating."

When had Colonel Harper found the time to write a book?

"Military tactics, I suppose," Nolan said.

"Oh, no. He's interested in the customs of our native allies."

Nolan's eyebrows rose towards his wig. "Their customs must be very different from our own civilised practices."

Miss Clara's lips curved, although the smile did not reach her eyes. "Indeed they are. My father is naturally most familiar with the Mohawk people, as he has been based in their lands, but the other tribes in the Six Nations have similar customs."

"What do you find most interesting, Miss Harper?"

She gazed at Nolan for a moment, as if considering what to say, then gave a tiny nod before speaking. "Day-to-day duties are divided between men and women, with the men as hunters and the women responsible for—"

"Which is the natural order of things."

"I was going to say that the women are responsible for farming." Miss Clara didn't seem annoyed at Nolan's interjection.

"Oh, well. But women are better suited to more domestic responsibilities, are they not?"

"That is the custom in Britain, to be sure. However, in the tribes my father has studied, the women are stewards of the land. Although only male leaders take part in negotiations between tribes…"

Nolan nodded—in approval, Jack suspected.

"…those leaders are appointed by the Clan Mothers, and can be removed by them."

Nolan's brows drew together. "It is no wonder, Miss Harper, that our civilisation is so much superior. Such duties are clearly best given to those with the aptitude for them."

Miss Clara smiled—a thin smile, the way his schoolmasters had looked when Jack answered a difficult question correctly. Odd. And strange that she did not appear offended by his patronising manner.

"I'm sure you must be correct, sir."

"Men have more logical brains, after all, and a greater understanding of the world."

Miss Clara had a little curl to her lips, just like her sister's, but Jack couldn't work out what she found amusing. Miss Kitty sounded like the kind of woman Nolan had described, happy to confine her responsibilities to the home. He was beginning to suspect that Miss Clara was not.

"I saw Mr Sessions on deck today," she went on. "He had an instrument, and was looking at the sun. Do you know what he was doing?"

"Ah, yes, finding the longitude." Nolan smiled at her. "That's the distance north or south of the equator, you know."

"How does it work, sir? It seemed very complicated."

To Jack, her expression was too innocent—was she teasing Nolan in some way?

"I... er... It is complicated, Miss Harper. It is to do with the angle of the sun above the horizon, but there is a great deal of mathematics involved."

"Oh, my woman's brain would not understand, then. Never mind."

Nolan appeared to be oblivious to the sarcasm. Miss Clara put a hand to her mouth and coughed, then stood up. "Excuse me, Mr Nolan. I'm afraid I need a drink of water."

Not long after Miss Clara left, her sister got up from the card game. "I must see if my sister is well, Mr Nolan. Please, would you take my place?"

Jack opened his mouth to volunteer, but Miss Kitty caught his eye and shook her head as she left the saloon. It was such a small movement that he wondered whether he'd imagined it. But when the two sisters returned a few minutes later, armed with a book and an embroidery hoop, he had to suppress a laugh. Nolan was now safely trapped in the card game where neither of them had to talk to him.

He debated joining them, even though Miss Clara appeared intent on reading, but the deck suddenly lurched beneath him. An accompanying protest from his stomach made him think he would be wiser to lie down in his cabin. His seasickness usually wore off after a few days at sea—unless the weather was particularly rough—but it clearly hadn't quite reached that stage yet.

The sisters loosened each other's laces, then Kitty sat out of the way on the end of the bottom bunk to give Clara room to undress. She didn't move when Clara got under the covers.

"So what did Mr Nolan do to make you interrupt my card game? Mama and I were winning."

Clara drew up her knees and wrapped her arms around them. "Women are not capable of making important decisions. And whatever the topic, he's certain he has more knowledge than me because I am a woman."

"He said that?"

"Not in so many words, but his meaning was perfectly clear."

"That's what most men would say."

"I know." Clara sighed. "I think I'd rather spend the voyage in silence than have to listen to him instructing me. The Nolans do not appear to be in need of money—they have fine clothes."

"That may be why he wants to marry money," Kitty suggested.

"It's possible, I suppose. Captain Stanlake appears more in need of funds. That, or he hasn't managed to find a tailor recently." To be fair, it must be difficult to keep a uniform in good condition in the forested wilderness.

"But his father's an earl; he must be rich."

"If he is, why is he still a captain? I'm sure Papa was a colonel by his age."

"Perhaps he's been cast off by his father, left to fend for himself amidst the wild natives and the horrors of war?" Kitty assumed a dramatic pose, tilting her head back and putting one hand to her forehead, wincing as her elbow hit the cabin wall.

"Serves you right," Clara said, as Kitty rubbed her elbow. "It's none of our business, anyway."

"Mama would like it to be."

"Mama would like many things to be. Now get undressed and go to sleep."

Kitty donned her night shift and climbed into the top bunk, dousing the lantern hanging from the ceiling. Clara listened as Kitty's breathing became slow and regular, envying the ready way her sister could fall asleep at any time. Her mind was full of the tales Mr Sessions had told at dinner—stories of foreign lands that she was unlikely to ever see. Women did travel, but generally only those with wealth of their own.

Captain Stanlake probably had many tales, too. Although he had said very little to her so far, he hadn't had much opportunity, and he'd taken Kitty's flirting and frank comments with good humour. She preferred his more rugged features to Mr Nolan's smoother looks— perhaps she would do as Mama wished and spend some time talking to him.

CHAPTER 4

When Jack emerged from his cabin for breakfast the next morning, only the Nolans were present. He sat beside them and made polite conversation over the bread rolls and cold meats—the usual platitudes about the current weather, and uninformed guesses about their arrival date in Falmouth.

His food eaten, and a fresh cup of coffee before him, he turned to the newspapers he'd bought in Boston. A fire in the Portsmouth dockyard was the most interesting happening; most of the parliamentary reports were about funding for the war with France.

"Take an interest in politics, do you, Captain?" Sir Cedric asked, as the Harper women arrived and Jenkins set them places further down the table.

Jack put the paper down without regret. "I try, but reports such as these..." He flicked the paper with a finger. "They are written assuming the reader knows what has gone before—it is hard to make sense of some of it when the papers only reach Fort Niagara intermittently, and months old."

"Hmm, it must be. It's not so bad in Boston. Need to follow events, you know. So many happenings can affect the price of goods, and the government could always do more to protect trading vessels.

However, there are opportunities aplenty, despite these troubled times, for those with an eye for mutual profit."

Jack wondered if Sir Cedric was about to invite him to join in some trade venture. "My family mostly has income from farming," he said. That wasn't a lie, although Father doubtless had investments in addition to revenues from land rents.

Sir Cedric seemed to lose interest, merely giving Jack a nod and resuming his breakfast. Jack picked up his paper again.

"You should get some fresh air, Clara." Mrs Harper's voice interrupted his reading only a few minutes later. "Perhaps Captain Stanlake would be good enough to escort you?"

"Mama!" Miss Clara's protest, although quiet, was clearly audible, her face reddening.

Nolan had heard, too. "I would be happy to escort Miss Harper, if—"

"No need, Nolan," Jack broke in. He was curious about that conversation between Nolan and Miss Clara at dinner last night. "I'd be very happy to take a turn about the deck."

She glanced at him, then got to her feet. "Thank you, sir. I will see you up there shortly."

He fetched his greatcoat and scarf, and awaited her at the entrance to the companionway. Thin clouds covered the sky, turning the sun to a mere bright patch. The wind was stronger than the previous day, blowing from directly aft and filling the sails.

When Miss Clara appeared, he led the way to the sheltered bench. She did not sit, but stood facing him with her hands clasped together.

"I must apologise, Captain. I would not wish to be foisted on you like this." She met his eyes briefly, clearly still embarrassed by her mother's action. He couldn't tell if the rosy blush on her cheeks was due to that or the cold wind; whatever the reason, it gave her face an attractive colour.

"I would enjoy your company, Miss Clara. However, we may just sit here, if you prefer. I can fetch a book from my cabin, and we need not—"

"No, no, Captain. I have no objection to conversing with you, but Mama…" She took a deep breath. "May I be frank, sir?"

"By all means."

"We are returning to England so that I might meet more people—men, to be precise. Mama has decided that it is time I found a husband."

"That is not unusual, Miss Clara. But your sister has already informed me of this, as well as my peripatetic occupation making me unsuitable as a candidate for her." Or for anyone else, really. He could not imagine himself permanently settled—with or without a rose garden—and what woman would be happy to be left at home when he was posted abroad, often for years at a time?

"Unfortunately, Captain, you are still a potential…"

"Target?"

"Indeed. A potential target in Mama's eyes, due to your connections."

"Ah. My father's title."

"That is *her* opinion." Her gaze met his firmly this time. "I try not to judge a man merely by who his parents are, but on what *he* is."

"That will put me on my mettle," Jack said, hoping to put her more at ease.

"I… I did not mean—"

"Miss Clara, I spoke in jest. Please do not be uneasy about this. If you prefer to talk to young Nolan, you have only to say so."

"No."

He couldn't help smiling at the decisiveness of her denial. "You appeared amused by his conversation at dinner last night. I'm afraid I was eavesdropping for some of it, but it did not seem to be a private discussion."

She sat on the bench, half-turned towards him, but did not speak.

"I found his explanation of navigation particularly illuminating," Jack prompted.

Miss Clara gave a wry smile. "Even I, a woman not suited to the comprehension of complex matters, know that longitude is the distance east or west of Greenwich, not a north-south measurement as Mr Nolan said."

"We should be grateful, then, that he is not in charge of the vessel. And that I am not, either. I wouldn't have the first idea about finding our position."

"At least you do not pretend that you do, sir."

"Or *assume* that I know better because I think I'm superior." Like Major De Lacy. "That can be dangerous."

"Is that the voice of experience?"

Clara wished she hadn't asked as Captain Stanlake frowned. Scowled would be a better word, really. "I apologise if—"

He shook his head, his expression smoothing. "No need. I was remembering an incident when I was a raw lieutenant, fresh from England. Our Indian allies have been fighting in their forests for centuries, and it requires quite different tactics from those suited to the more open terrain the British army is accustomed to."

"Papa says the local militia fight better than the regular battalions sometimes."

"I have found it so, certainly. A lot depends on the attitudes of the officers. When I arrived in the Colonies, I served under a major who thought that no Indian or militiaman could possibly know better than he how to use his men to fight off a greater number of Frenchmen. He didn't live to regret ignoring their advice, but neither did a fair number of the men. The rest of us were lucky to escape." He met her eyes. "It was a salutary lesson not to pass judgement on others' opinions or knowledge without thought."

"As Mr Nolan did to me, although without such dire consequences. His assumption that women are not capable of taking part in the governance of a tribe was both annoying and predictable. Most men—most people, even—think the same." She wondered if he did, and was only being polite.

"About the superiority of our civilisation? Or the superiority of men?"

"Both. Does the fact that the people in another land do things differently mean we are better than they are?"

He appeared to be seriously considering her question. "Not necessarily, no. But their society doesn't have the same material comforts we do."

"Must that make their society worse than ours? That was Mr Nolan's immediate assumption." Clara awaited Captain Stanlake's response with interest—and some trepidation. He had fought alongside the natives, and she would be interested in learning about his experiences, but not if he had the same disdain for the traditions of others as Mr Nolan. Strangely, she felt that it mattered to her that he did not.

"Their society appears to work well enough, by their standards," he said, after giving it some thought. "I don't know a great deal about the way their tribes are organised, but if they are governed by the gentler… what we call the gentler sex, it doesn't appear to make them any less warlike." He regarded her with a slightly wary expression, as if he were afraid of offending her.

"I do not mind being referred to as the gentler sex, Captain. I am not going to bite your head off if I disagree with something."

"Hmm, no." One corner of his mouth curled up in a lopsided smile. A very attractive expression, particularly when combined with the humour in his blue eyes. "You will be quietly amused, and likely go away and abuse me to your sister."

She denied it, although she had done just that after Mr Nolan's conversation.

"I do regard our society as more civilised, in many ways," he went on. "In our treatment of prisoners, for example."

She had to agree. Papa had told her that prisoners were often put to death in agonising ways, and she'd been grateful to have been spared too many details so far.

"Clara, there you are!"

Clara bit back a word of protest as Kitty approached. She had been enjoying the discussion. It was a novelty to have an attract— to have any man agree with her ideas.

Kitty was well wrapped up in a coat and scarf, and so had not merely come to summon her below decks. Captain Stanlake stood. "I will leave the sheltered seat for you, Miss Kitty. Miss Clara, it was a pleasure talking to you." He bowed and headed towards the stern. Clara couldn't tell from his expression whether he was relieved or disappointed that their discussion had come to an end.

"Your quarry escaped, Kitty."

Kitty shrugged as she sat beside Clara. "Never mind. He's fun to flirt with because he knows I'm not serious."

And enjoyable to talk to because he knew she was, Clara thought.

The wind rose throughout the afternoon and changed direction, blowing from one quarter and tearing foam from the white tops of the waves. The thickening clouds blocked the sun, and the *Pegasus* heeled over, rising and swooping down as the waves passed. Sessions finally called for men to go aloft to reduce sail.

Jack steadied himself with one hand on the rail, watching the activity. He was fascinated, as always, by the dexterity with which the men swarmed out along the yards with only a rope to support their feet, and wrestled the billowing sails into submission.

About to retreat to the saloon, he changed his mind when Miss Clara came to stand beside him. The sisters had not stayed long on deck this morning after he left them, but here she was again, and in worse weather.

"Miss Clara, is something wrong?"

She met his gaze with a grin, the wind whipping tendrils of hair across her face. "I heard orders being shouted, so I came to see what was happening."

Jack tilted his head towards the west, where the dark clouds were lit occasionally with a flicker of lightning. "A storm."

A sudden lurch made her stagger, and he put out a hand to steady her. She nodded thanks, and peered around him towards the stern. "I guessed as much. How exciting!"

Exciting? "Are you not concerned?"

"Should I be? Mr Sessions is still in charge—I assume he'd have called the captain if there was anything to worry about."

She had a point.

"That may change, of course, but for now…" She shrugged, her grin reappearing as she watched the passing waves; it remained undimmed even when a sudden gust threw spray at them. "I enjoy watching the sea, and the way the ship harnesses the power of the wind. Man battling nature and using it for his own ends."

"Nature frequently wins."

"Oh, do not spoil sport, Captain! My cowering below decks will not make the ship any safe—"

She spun around, ducking behind him and hunching her shoulders just as another burst of spray hit them. Jack swore at the shock—it wasn't merely a smattering of water drops, but felt as if someone had thrown a bucketful of icy water at the side of his head. "You might have warned me!"

"I'm sorry—there was no time." But she was laughing, not contrite. She reminded him of his own exhilaration on a fast ride, ignoring rain and flying mud—although that was usually when he had a proper house to return to, with a hot bath and a roaring fire.

Miss Clara was still laughing up at him when he saw the next dousing coming, and he stepped smartly to one side.

"Aah!" She wiped her face with one hand and shivered. "How ungentlemanly of you!"

"Tit for tat, Miss Clara." He waited with interest to see how she would take it. Her brief pout reminded him of Miss Kitty's flirting, then she licked her lips and grinned. She had a very pretty mouth, in a face glowing with fun. Wet strands of hair stuck to her cheeks and neck, and Jack found himself wishing he could lick the salt from her lips for her. Help her mop up the trickles of cold water that must have got inside her coat.

"Captain?" She sounded uncertain, and he wondered if he'd been staring.

Good heavens—what had come over him?

"I'm sorry, Miss Clar— Watch out!" He acted the gentleman this time, managing to turn so his back took the brunt of the spray, and he felt only a small rivulet of cold running down his neck.

Miss Clara was looking behind them, where the horizon was now obscured by a grey sheet of rain. "Exhilarating as this is, Captain, I fear Kitty will not be pleased at the prospect of having my wet clothes hanging in the cabin." She ran her fingers under the collar of her coat. "I should go and change before too much soaks through."

"Very wise." Jack followed her down the companionway—the prospect of spending the rest of the day sitting around the saloon table was now more enticing than it had been, although he should not spend too much time contemplating Miss Clara's mouth.

Jack was sitting at one end of the table with a cup of coffee when Miss Clara finally reappeared. She spread out a set of papers at the other end, near where her mother and sister were quietly talking. Making the fair copy of her father's manuscript that she had mentioned a couple of days ago, Jack supposed. He had to admire her ability to wield a pen as the ship moved, although ink stains on her fingers and a handkerchief with black blotches suggested she might not have mastered the art completely.

He'd brought a book with him, but found himself watching Miss Clara instead of reading. Why did he feel more attracted to her than her sister? Miss Kitty was prettier, by most objective standards.

It wasn't because Miss Kitty had denied any interest in him as a potential husband. Miss Clara was determined not to marry at all. Or was she? It had been Miss Kitty who had stated that her sister did not wish to marry—although Miss Clara had not denied it. Miss Clara did have interesting depths, beyond her liking for storms, but trying to work out why one woman was more appealing than another was a futile exercise.

Leaning back, watching the tiny crease between her brows as she concentrated on her writing, he wondered what she would look like if she dressed her hair more loosely. As he watched, she marked places on text already written, referring back through the pile now and then and copying sections from different pages. She wasn't merely replicating the manuscript—she was editing. But now was not the time to ask her about it.

He opened his book, but after only a couple of pages he realised that his stomach had not settled as much as he'd hoped. If he could not be on deck, the only thing for it was to lie down with his eyes closed until the motion ceased.

CHAPTER 5

$\mathscr{A}$lthough it was still raining the following morning, the *Pegasus* did seem to be moving more smoothly. When the aroma of coffee drifting into his cabin became appealing rather than nauseating, Jack decided to risk breakfast. He'd spent too much of the night remembering Clara licking her lips, and imagining how she might taste, how she might feel in his arms. And when he'd forced his mind away from that, he'd wondered if a woman who enjoyed watching a storm, and had expressed her regrets at not seeing more of the country than Albany, might not mind a life following the drum. Might even relish it...

But such a match was not possible—not without causing a permanent breach with his father. Although Colonel Harper's birth was respectable enough, the earl would not approve of Mrs Harper's connection with trade.

He put that thought from his head as he took an empty seat in the middle of the long table. Jenkins poured a mug of coffee, then brought him ham and eggs. As he ate, the Nolans began to confer over a ledger and, at the far end of the table, Clara was working on her manuscript.

The ship's motion had eased so much that he decided to attempt to read, and managed to concentrate quite well for an hour or so until Jenkins came into the saloon to ask if anyone required refreshments.

As the steward brought in platters with slices of cold meats and pies, and a fresh jug of coffee, Jack saw Nolan eyeing the empty place next to Clara. Jack stood before Nolan could, and moved down the table.

"Do you mind if I join you?"

Clara started as Captain Stanlake spoke—she hadn't noticed him approach. She had done her best this morning to concentrate on Papa's book, but it was difficult with Mama and Kitty sitting close to her, speculating on what would happen when they reached London. And the captain, sitting further down the table, made her feel... Unsettled, that was it. He hadn't been staring at her, but she'd caught his eyes on her once or twice before he started to read his book. Mr Nolan had glanced in her direction a few times as well, but his gaze didn't make her feel the same way.

"Not at all." She gestured to the place beside her and he sat down.

He glanced at Mama and Kitty, still discussing plans, before speaking in a low voice. "I noticed you were editing your father's work, Miss Clara."

"I... er, yes." There was no point in denying it, if he had been observing her closely enough to notice. And why should she deny it?

"Does your father know?"

She tried to read his expression, wondering if he disapproved—but he appeared amused. "Not exactly. He thinks I am making a neat copy, correcting spellings and so on. He has sent a letter to Uncle George, asking him to find an editor." She had offered to edit the manuscript herself, but Papa had declined with an indulgent smile that made her grit her teeth. He was a good and kind father, but persisted in his opinion that most women were like her mother, interested mainly in domestic matters.

"Will you give your edited version to your uncle?"

She had been wondering that herself, but hadn't made up her mind.

"It would seem a shame to waste your efforts," he added, taking a bite of pie.

Clara shrugged. "It's an interesting challenge, even if I have to pass it on to someone else. I... It depends on what kind of man Uncle George is—I was a child when we last saw him."

"From the few moments' conversation I had with your father, I suspect he doesn't share your opinion of the... capabilities of women."

"No, he doesn't. I am having to moderate my views on that topic while working." Papa would read the finished book, and she didn't want to anger him by inserting opinions that were too far from his own.

"Should I volunteer to read it when you have finished?" he asked, his face now serious once more. "You will need a man's opinion to ensure you haven't gone beyond the line of what is acceptable."

Clara stared at him in surprise, almost choking as the coffee in her mouth went down the wrong way. His words were so different from the impression he'd given the day before. Then one side of his mouth lifted, and she noticed the laughter in his eyes.

"My apologies," he said. "I see my attempt at humour was unsuccessful. It cannot be amusing to have your abilities continually disparaged."

She shook her head, still regaining her breath.

"I must also apologise for allowing you to get wet yesterday," he went on. "As you pointed out, it was ungentlemanly of me."

A laugh bubbled up at the memory. "No, sir, do not apologise for that. I should not hope to be treated as an equal in some things while choosing to be helpless in others." She hesitated, recalling the idea that had come to her when he first mentioned fighting alongside Britain's native allies.

"I wonder...That is, Papa has a section about how the natives of the Six Nations assist the British army, and others do the same for the French. But Papa has always been an administrator, and it seems a shame to have those chapters written only from hearsay. I wondered if you would read through those parts and check that he has not misrepresented the way things are."

His brows drew together.

"Only if you don't mind, of course," she added hastily. It was not wrong to ask him that, was it?

"I was only thinking that some of it is not fit for a lady's ears." Then he gave that charming smile of his. "Although I'm reluctant to say such a thing to you—and I imagine you have already read those parts."

"Many would say that Papa's whole book is not suitable for females, and I doubt many would read it."

"If it will help, I am happy to do so. Will you—?"

He broke off just as Clara became aware of someone standing beside her. Mr Nolan.

"May I speak to you for a moment?" he asked.

Clara suppressed a sigh, merely inclining her head.

"I'll see if it is still raining," Captain Stanlake said, pushing his empty mug and plate away and getting to his feet. He gave Mr Nolan a nod before disappearing up the companionway steps.

Opposite, Kitty and Mama had fallen silent. Mr Nolan looked at them and swallowed visibly.

"Do sit down, Mr Nolan," Clara said. "I will get a stiff neck peering up at you."

"Oh. Yes, of course." He sat. "I... I wish to apologise, Miss Harper. And to you, Miss Catherine. I think that you have been avoiding my company, and fear I may have offended you."

He *had* lost that irritating air of superiority. But an apology didn't make her more inclined to spend time with him—he would doubtless say something further that would exasperate her. Unless she explained why she'd been offended?

"Mr Nolan—do you think you would make a good soldier?"

He regarded her blankly, and Clara made an effort to keep her expression one of polite enquiry.

"I...Well, no. That life has never appealed to me."

"A sea captain, perhaps?"

"No."

"But you enjoy being a… a merchant. A trader."

"Why, yes. It is a challenge to make new contacts, negotiate prices, predict what customers will…" He tilted his head to one side. "Are you *really* interested, Miss Harper?"

Good—he wasn't totally impervious. "I am interested in many things. However, my point is that you are not suited to the army. Captain Stanlake is probably not suited to be a merchant, or a barrister. Men have different talents and tastes, do they not? Not to mention different abilities."

'They do, yes." He still looked rather puzzled.

"Yet all women, it would seem, must be content to lead a domestic life, and are all suited only for that."

"I did not say… That is…" He cleared his throat and tugged at his neckcloth. "I never had cause to think about it, but I take your point."

"To be fair, Mr Nolan," Kitty broke in from across the table. "I *will* be perfectly content with a domestic life." Beside Kitty, Mama was smiling.

"Thank you, Miss Catherine." He still appeared ill at ease. "I… I must admit to having more than one reason for befriend… For attempting to befriend you both, besides passing the time at sea in pleasant company. Very pleasant company." He nodded to himself. "When I heard you were related to George Morton I… Well, more joint ventures would be good for our business. I hoped that if I could make myself useful during the voyage, that might facilitate a personal introduction to Mr Morton. The only contact so far has been with my uncle."

Clara looked away, feeling rather guilty at the assumptions she'd made about him. He did have a mercenary objective but, to her mind, hoping for an introduction was a long way from trying to marry purely for money.

"I… I am to be married soon," he went on, going a little red around the ears. "My uncle does not entirely approve of my choice, so assisting in a beneficial business arrangement might… might reconcile him."

"Was he hoping you would marry someone else?" Mama asked.

"Nothing had been discussed, Mrs Harper, but there was another company he hoped to make links with."

That, as much as his apology, made him rise in Clara's estimation. He wasn't being mercenary in his choice of life partner.

"Tell me about your betrothed," Kitty said, and Mr Nolan turned in his seat to face her properly.

Clara murmured an excuse and gathered her things together. Captain Stanlake hadn't returned, so it must not be wet outside. This might be a good time to take the air.

Once in her cabin, she stowed Papa's papers safely in their small trunk and pushed it back under the bottom bunk. She took her coat from its hook on the back of the door, but didn't don it immediately.

It was well done of Mr Nolan to apologise—it would certainly make the remainder of the voyage more pleasant now she didn't feel… pursued. She didn't think her comments would really change his view of women, but at least he might manage to avoid irritating her.

How unlike Captain Stanlake, who hadn't made derogatory remarks of that nature at all. He might merely be more diplomatic than Mr Nolan, but if he did share Mr Nolan's views, he hid it well.

Captain Stanlake, too, was probably only befriending her to pass the time—much as Kitty tended to flirt with young men. She felt flattered that his approach was to take her seriously; that was a greater compliment than any remark about her appearance. There had been that odd expression on his face when they'd been out in the storm, but she should not read too much into that—it was likely due only to cold water trickling down his back.

No, their paths were unlikely to cross again when this voyage was over, so she might as well make the most of his company while they were at sea. When they reached England, he would be off to his father's estate, and she… she would forget him soon enough when she had the sights of London to enjoy and new friends to make. Despite Papa's genteel birth, their families were too far apart in society for them to move in the same circles, even if he were not set to return to the Colonies.

Wishing it might be otherwise was futile.

~

The rain *had* stopped, and Jack leaned against the leeward rail looking out across the waves. The sea was an unappealing mass of heaving grey water and white foam, but he wasn't really seeing it. He was reliving the feeling that Nolan's interruption had caused. Was it jealousy?

Nolan was only talking to Clara, with her mother present. Nor had she seemed to welcome his intrusion. There was no reason to be jealous of Nolan.

No—his feelings were a passing attraction, nothing more, and would wear off when they parted company. His fancies had never lasted more than a few months—which was just as well, given his circumstances. In the meantime, she was a pleasant companion to relieve the tedium of a sea voyage.

The companionway door opened and the subject of his ruminations stepped onto the deck, bundled up warmly in coat and scarf. She turned her head, and the smile that appeared when she saw him made him feel warm inside. Too warm.

"What did Nolan want?" he asked. Not that it was any of his business, but she didn't seem to mind him asking.

"To apologise." As she explained, he tried to be pleased that Nolan was now in her good graces. It would limit the time Jack would be in her company, but that was probably for the best.

There was a long silence after she finished her tale, but a companionable one, as they both gazed out over the waves.

"Did you mean your offer to help me with Papa's manuscript, Captain?" she asked eventually.

"Why should I not?"

"Your... I mean, working below, looking down at words on a page..."

"You are referring to my weak stomach? It is bearing up well at the moment. It should behave itself now, unless we encounter another storm. What aspects of your father's book are you most concerned about?"

She turned her back to the waves, leaning with her elbows on the rail, the wind blowing strands of hair free from its pins. His hand lifted to tuck them behind her ear, then he realised what he was doing and thrust it into a pocket.

"It's not the facts themselves, but the way he has expressed some of his opinions. He talks about the natives tracking people in the forests, as if they have some kind of animal sense."

"As if they are inferior beings?" Jack made himself concentrate on what she was saying, not how she looked with the wind making her face glow and eyes sparkle.

"Yes."

"As young Nolan did before you… informed him of the error of his beliefs?"

She gaped for a moment, her brows drawing together, then nodded. "Indeed, sir. I find it best to let men know what they should think—it saves them the effort of attempting to work it out for themselves." The twinkle in her eyes belied her stern expression.

Jack laughed, and she laughed with him—she seemed to know when he was not being serious, and responded in kind. That was one of the many reasons he liked her.

"Now could be a good time to start, Miss Clara. Unless you wish to remain above decks?"

It seemed the grey scene had as little appeal for her as it did for him, and he followed her back to the saloon.

Clara accepted the pages that Captain Stanlake handed to her the next morning after breakfast. "What did you think of it?"

He sat beside her. "The facts are correct, as far as my knowledge extends, but…"

"Be honest, please, Captain."

"If I were one of our native allies, I would be offended at some of the things said. It is difficult to pin down—a matter of the choice of wording, really."

That was a relief—she'd wondered if she had been reading things into Papa's words that were not there. But this *was* Papa's book, not hers. "Papa...?" How to explain her doubts?

"I suspect you could find a more neutral way of expressing things —one that does not denigrate or praise. The latter would be of no use; readers who already consider the natives as lesser beings will continue to do so, no matter what a book such as this might say."

That was true. Most of the young men she'd met readily accepted the natives as fighting allies, or guides through the forests, but other-wise thought very much as Mr Nolan had. Or as Mr Nolan still did— she suspected he would merely moderate the way he talked about the natives if the subject came up again, rather than her words having fundamentally changed his own beliefs. The captain, though, did appear to respect their allies.

"Did you find it interesting to read?" Once more she felt some trepidation while awaiting his answer—she'd given him one of the sections she had already edited.

"It is a little difficult for me to judge, as I already knew most of what was in there."

That sounded like a diplomatic 'no'. She hoped her disappointment did not show on her face.

"I wonder..." He broke off and shook his head.

"Please, Captain, if you have an idea for improving it, do say so."

"It is not the phrasing and so on that makes it rather... dry, but the information conveyed. All fact, and not much of the people them-selves. I wondered if a few anecdotes to illustrate some of the points made might help. I could write some down, if you wish, although my writing style lends itself more to lists and reports."

"I'm sure the subject matter will make it interesting." His conversa-tion was not boring—far from it.

"Do you only wish to edit, or to write yourself?"

How could he know she wanted more than just to make Papa's work readable? Did he know her so well already? "I... I would love to, but have nothing worth writing about. Only the knowledge Papa gathered."

"That might change."

That warmth was in his gaze again, and she looked away before the answering heat within her rose to her face. But he was wrong—if Mama had her way, nothing would change apart from the identity of the man in whose household she lived. She pushed that thought away. For now, editing the captain's stories would be an enjoyable way to occupy the remaining weeks at sea—however unwise it might be to spend so much time with him.

"If we are to work together, you must call me Clara."

"And you must call me Jack."

CHAPTER 6

almouth, England, September 1760
Despite the strong breeze carrying spits of rain, Clara and Kitty went up on deck to watch as the *Pegasus* approached the shore. Beside them, Jack was a convenient windbreak as well as a guide.

"Pendennis Castle," he said, pointing to a grey stone building on the low headland to their left. "It was built in Henry VIII's time. There's another fort on the opposite shore." As he spoke, Mr Sessions shouted orders and men climbed the masts to take in some of the sails; others hauled the yards around.

"Do you know this place well?" Kitty asked.

"Not really—the last time I left from here we had to wait several days for the wind to change, so I hired a local guide."

As the *Pegasus* rounded the point, the ships moored in Carrick Roads came into view, then the buildings of Falmouth to their left. The wind eased as they sailed into the shelter of the harbour, and boats were being rowed towards them even before the anchor dropped—to collect the mails, Clara supposed. And for the customs men to inspect the ship. Then it would be time to ferry passengers ashore—but they were to wait on board until Jack had confirmed the arrangements Uncle George had made for them.

Footsteps sounded behind her, and she turned to see Jonas Nolan. "We must say farewell, Miss Harper, Miss Kitty. Although I hope it is only temporary."

"As do I, Mr Nolan." Clara thought of him as an acquaintance, rather than a good friend, but once he'd overcome his condescending manner towards her, they had had some interesting conversations. Clara now knew a good deal more about the trade in fabrics, wool, and cotton. Not that she was ever likely to need the information, but learning anything new was interesting, and she could not concentrate on her father's book all the time. Even Kitty and Jack had taken an interest.

"We travel via Bristol, and my uncle is in a hurry," Mr Nolan said. He glanced over his shoulder to a pile of trunks. "We are to leave as soon as possible, and may manage to get as far as Exeter tonight. I think you would not like to travel so fast."

"No, indeed not." She wouldn't mind—she would be glad to be in Uncle George's house, with a proper bedchamber and a desk that did not move—but Mama preferred to take things at a rather slower pace.

"I… That is, if it is acceptable, I will call on Mr Morton in London next week to see if you have arrived safely."

"Please do," Kitty replied.

"Nolan, may I accompany you as far as the town?" Jack said. "Ladies, I will see you later."

Clara turned her gaze to the water as the two men walked away. Jack had offered to escort them to London, without Mama having to even hint at the request—something she would not have expected from his impatient demeanour when they had first met in Boston. She was glad that they would not be parting company with him just yet. The past few weeks had been…

Interesting? Enjoyable? Both of those, but possibly also unwise. She'd found herself too fond of Jack's company as they discussed the notes he'd made on Papa's chapters about fighting alongside the natives, then the rest of the manuscript. At other times their conversations had varied from serious discussions of literature or places the captain had been to the kind of nonsensical banter that she'd heard him exchange with Kitty on that first day. She'd never enjoyed conversations so much before.

But it was the warmth she felt as they worked together that had really drawn her to him, not only the easy sharing of knowledge. A sense that they had some connection that went beyond mere collaboration.

As the boat with Jack and the Nolans pulled away, Jack's red coat was visible even when the oarsmen and the other passengers were indistinguishable. Resolutely, she returned to her cabin. She checked once more that the bottles of ink in her lap desk were tightly stoppered, then put it into the small trunk with the manuscript and fastened the strap. Mary had already packed their other trunks.

It might have been better if the captain had not agreed to escort them. They had to part at some time, and if he made his own way home from Falmouth, she would have the three or four days of the journey to get used to the idea of not seeing him again. She had begun to wonder what it would be like to have his company always, but an earl's son did not marry someone of her class.

Jack slowed his hired horse and let the coach pull ahead as they drew closer to the smoke hanging above London. Tempting though it had been to spend these last few days in Clara's company, he'd chosen to ride rather than share the coach. It was much-needed exercise, after weeks at sea.

He was too used to her company, that was the problem. That would have to end now. The letter he'd sent to Marstone Park from Falmouth would reach there today, if it wasn't there already, and he would be expected tomorrow.

The carriage drew to a halt before a tall townhouse in Cavendish Square. Jack's brows rose—if George Morton owned a house here, he must be wealthy indeed.

A footman rushed out of the house and opened the carriage door, helping Mrs Harper out. She turned to Jack as her two daughters descended.

"Thank you for escorting us, Captain. Will you not come in? I'm sure my brother will wish to thank you in person and give you a bed for the night—you are not intending to ride on this evening?"

"No, I am not." There wasn't enough daylight left, and one more night would not matter. "I would be happy to accept Mr Morton's hospitality."

"Have your trunk sent on tonight," Kitty suggested. "Then you will not be without it tomorrow when you get home. Uncle George's butler can arrange it for you."

Home? Marstone Park hadn't been 'home' for a decade. But Kitty was waiting for an answer. "An excellent idea, thank you." He had a change of clothes in a small bag—that was all he needed to keep.

"Ah, here is my brother now!" Mrs Harper hurried off, Clara and Kitty following her up the steps to the door where they were greeted by a tall, slim man, clad in sober dark blue. His hair was hidden by a short wig, but the lines on his face made Jack think he was some years older than his sister.

He greeted the women, then Mrs Harper made the introductions. As she followed the butler inside, Morton turned to Jack.

"My thanks for accompanying my sister and nieces home, Captain."

"It was my pleasure, sir." And it had been.

"I understand I have invited you to stay the night?" Morton's expression was one of serious enquiry, apart from a crinkling around the eyes.

"You did," Jack couldn't help but smile in reply. "For which, my thanks."

"I will see about the arrangements, Captain, if you wouldn't mind waiting for a few minutes? My footman will show you to the library."

While Morton went to confer with the butler, Jack took in the marble tiles on the floor, the gilded frame of a painting depicting a merchant ship in full sail, and the ornate plasterwork on the ceiling. As the footman led him along the hall, he glimpsed a rich tapestry on a parlour wall, floral carpets, and furniture upholstered in pale silks. Morton, it seemed, was a very successful merchant, and not hesitant in displaying his wealth.

He stopped in surprise as he entered the room the footman ushered him into. It was a library—two walls were lined with book-cases, and a desk stood in one corner. A pair of high-backed chairs flanking the fireplace looked old and worn, but comfortable. A large globe stood on a tiger-skin rug in one corner of the room.

"Mr Morton will join you shortly, sir." The footman bowed and left, and Jack looked at the bookshelves. In addition to bound copies of various journals, there was a wide selection of classical and more recent plays, novels, and poetry. Taking a few down, he saw the pages had been cut—these books were not just for show.

"Do borrow anything that takes your fancy," Morton said as he entered the room and crossed to the tray. "Can I offer you a drink? This brandy is particularly good."

"Thank you, yes."

It was good—far better than that provided on the *Pegasus* or at the inns they'd stayed in on their way to London. Jack glanced around the room again as he sipped it, then turned back to his host.

"Tell me, is this your taste..." He gestured to the worn chairs and the bookshelves. "...or the rooms out there? It is quite a contrast."

Morton sat in one of the chairs by the fire, and Jack took the other. "The tiger is a reminder of my time in India—that hunt confirmed my suspicion that I was not naturally a man of action. I prefer plainer things to the... the *expensive* decor out there. More restful." He regarded Jack with an enquiring lift to one brow.

"A wealthy merchant needs to *show* he's wealthy?" Jack surmised.

"Correct. Your own family do the same, no doubt, but to advertise their status and reinforce their right to rule."

He supposed they did—he'd never really thought about it. Did Morton resent the upper classes? It didn't seem that he was trying to ape them. But how did Morton know of his family?

"My sister wasted no time in informing me of your background, Captain," Morton said, anticipating Jack's question.

"I'm an army officer, nothing more."

Morton sighed. "Anne is still desirous of her daughters marrying up, as she thinks of it. Clara and Kitty have grown into fine young women since I last saw them. I'll have my days full—over-full—once I start accompanying them to dinners and parties. But they deserve a chance to choose husbands for themselves. Within reason, of course. Are you planning on staying in Town long, Captain?"

"No, I must be off to Hertfordshire tomorrow." He explained why he had been summoned back. "I will need to call at Horse Guards when I have been home, to arrange to rejoin my regiment. I hope I may call then, to see how... how Mrs Harper and her daughters are going on."

"Please do. Would you care to join us at the theatre one evening? I have a box at Drury Lane—Garrick is particularly fine in a new comedy."

"Thank you, I would enjoy that." And enjoy discussing it with Clara afterwards, although he knew he shouldn't. But he would have the voyage back to Boston to get over his attraction to her. "The only plays I have seen recently are amateur theatricals—with the youngest ensigns playing the female parts." He took a sip of his brandy. "I'm afraid they turn tragedy into comedy, whether or not that is their intention."

"Ha, I can imagine."

"Oh, this is lovely!" Kitty exclaimed as she followed Clara into the bedchamber they would share. The beds were not grand affairs, but draped in pretty, light fabrics embroidered with swags of flowers and leaves, reflecting the patterns printed on the wallpaper.

Clara should be pleased to be here, with new experiences ahead and new people to meet, but she felt sadly flat.

She was just tired, she told herself. Being jolted in a coach for nearly four days would tire anyone—apart from Kitty, apparently. Her sister bounced on the bed to test it, then opened cupboards and drawers.

Kitty ran her fingers through a bowl of dried flower petals, spreading the scent through the air. "There's a little dressing room here, with…"

Clara got up to answer a knock at the door as Kitty chattered on. A maid stood outside, with an armful of towels, and Clara stood back to let her enter.

"If you please, Miss, there's hot water coming up for a bath, and your maid asked which gowns you want pressing for dinner."

"My yellow robe à l'anglaise," Kitty said, coming back into the room while Clara was still trying to think. "Mary will know which one I mean."

"Where *are* the trunks?" Clara asked. She had only the small bag she'd used on the journey from Falmouth.

"Mama suggested they stay downstairs. She said it will be easier for Mary to press the dresses as she unpacks them, before bringing them back up here."

"Miss, what shall I say about your gown?" The maid had deposited the towels in the dressing room and was waiting for Clara to make up her mind.

"The burgundy one, please." That was her most becoming gown. Kitty was nodding in approval at her choice. It was only polite, after all, to look their best when Uncle George was so kind as to let them live with him. "You have the first bath, Kitty."

"No—you first. Then Mary will have enough time to try a different hairstyle for you—it's time you stopped pulling your hair back like that. I've got some ivory ribbons somewhere that will go well with your gown. I'll go and find them." Kitty followed the maid out without waiting for a reply.

Clara ran her fingers through her hair—it *would* be lovely to soak in a hot bath while she washed it. And Mama would insist that she dress more like Kitty—she might as well start now.

That was the only reason.

. . .

Mary had done well, Clara thought as she regarded herself in the mirror. Her hair was dressed a little higher than Kitty's, and the ribbons woven through it made it look a richer brown than usual. The style reduced the roundness of her face, although her skin showed the signs of too many hours spent on the deck of the *Pegasus*.

Kitty, too, was looking lovely, but then it didn't seem to matter what Kitty wore. Even the sun and wind of the last few weeks had only given her face the lightest of tans.

"Come on, Clara, didn't you hear the dinner bell?" Kitty said. "Mary didn't go to all that effort for you to spend the evening admiring your reflection." She grinned. "Come and show off her efforts to the person for whom it's intended."

"Uncle George," Clara muttered as she followed Kitty down the stairs, ignoring her sister's small snort of laughter.

As they entered the parlour, Mama said something about how nice it was to have all their clothing available again, but Clara wasn't listening. Jack had smiled as Kitty appeared, but his expression changed as his gaze shifted to her. It was still a smile, but there was something more in it—it reminded her of the day of the storm, and how his gaze had made her feel.

She took a deep breath and tried to concentrate on what Mama was saying—something about the theatre, and Uncle George's plans for their entertainment.

Uncle George started the conversation at dinner by asking Jack about his experiences in the army, and Jack kept them entertained for some time with amusing anecdotes of people and places, all adapted to delicate female sensibilities by the omission of any details about battles and injuries. That had to be for Mama's benefit, as he had been more forthcoming when they had talked on the *Pegasus*. She suppressed a sigh as she wondered whether the young men she would soon be meeting would… *edit* everything they said to make it suitable for her feeble female brain.

"…heard much of this before." Jack's words were followed by silence. Clara looked up to find all eyes on her—Mama with a frown,

Jack with an expression of amused apology. "I *was* boring you, was I not, Miss Harper?"

Why had she suddenly returned to being Miss Harper? But Jack's head inclined slightly to Uncle George, and she guessed it was because they were now in a more formal situation again.

"Not at all, Captain. I was merely wishing once again that I had seen more of the land than the country between Boston and Albany. Uncle George, did you not visit India some years ago? Will you not tell us something of that?"

If she could not travel to these places, at least she might hear of them from someone who had been there. She listened with interest, allowing the others to ask questions; she would have plenty of time to talk to her uncle later, when Jack had gone. But Mama looked weary, and even Kitty was beginning to droop in her chair. Clara wasn't surprised when Mama stood and announced that she would leave the men to their port. "We will see you tomorrow, Captain," she added. "I'm afraid I am too tired to enjoy a longer evening. I think the girls are, too."

"I will say farewell now, Mrs Harper," Jack said, rounding the table to bow over her hand. "I will be setting off early in the morning."

So soon?

"It has been a pleasure escorting you all. Miss Kitty." He bent over Kitty's hand.

"I do hope you find your father improving," Clara said, as Jack turned to her.

"Thank you. And I wish you success with your... enterprises."

She dropped her eyes at his intense look, and felt the pressure of his fingers on hers, then Mama was shepherding them out of the room.

Such a brief farewell—but what more was there to say? The only surprising thing, really, was that Mama had not pressed Jack to visit them when he returned to Town. It seemed that even she realised there was no future in their... friendship.

CHAPTER 7

The landmarks along the road from London to Marstone Park were familiar, but rather than welcoming each one that showed he was getting closer to the end of his journey, Jack felt as if they were marking a change to his world. Every trip back was like that, to a degree, but this transition felt different.

Life at Marstone Park was ordered and, to his mind, tedious. The army was little different—in peacetime—but there he had a part to play. His role here as second in line to the earldom had vanished eleven years ago, when his first nephew was born. But today he was leaving behind new friends—for he felt that even George Morton had become a friend, despite their short acquaintance. After the ladies had retired they had talked long into the evening, sharing experiences from their travels that were not suitable for feminine ears. Jack had come away with the impression of a man of education and integrity, who dealt honestly with everyone, and Morton had encouraged him to call next time he was in Town.

And Clara… She had been even more beautiful in that gown, with her hair in curls and entwined ribbons—but her appearance had never been the sole reason he found her attractive. She had seemed subdued, rather than happily anticipating her time in Town as she should be. It was selfish, he knew, but part of him hoped she would be missing him as he was already missing her.

As the gates at Marstone Park came into sight, he tried to turn his thoughts to what lay ahead—to seeing his father and brother again, and his brother's family. The day was warm for September, and he welcomed the dim coolness in the belt of woodland surrounding the Park. Riding along the gravelled drive, he enjoyed the last peace he would have for a while, the silence broken only by the sound of his horse's hooves and the creak of leather.

And rustling in the undergrowth…

Instinctively he reached for his pistol, then forced himself to relax. This was England, and footpads wouldn't lurk here, not within the Park. And it certainly wouldn't be the French or their Indian allies.

There was more rustling, the crack of a stick and what sounded like whispers. He smiled and slid off the horse, smacking it on the rump to encourage it to move on a few paces. Then he crept into the trees and pulled his pistol from his pocket, checking carefully that it was not cocked. A glimmer of white showed that his supposition was correct, and he moved closer.

"Hands up! Surrender!" he shouted, pointing his pistol as he strode towards his nephews. Shrieks were followed by giggles as two small figures emerged from the bushes.

"Uncle Jack! You're home!"

"Hello, Will," Jack said, putting his pistol away. "How are you? And you, Alfred?"

"How did you know we were there?" Will asked.

"You sounded like a herd of cows crashing around in there. Did you know I'd arrive today?"

"No," Alfred said. "We were practising being Indians."

"I think you need to practise a bit more." Jack made his way back to the drive, the two boys following. "How is your grandfather?" That was the main reason he was here, after all.

Will's face fell. "He stays in bed all the time now. Mama says he's very ill."

"He was ill two years ago, but he got better," Jack pointed out.

Alfred shook his head. "That's what I said to Mama, but she said he was worse this time."

"What does your father say?" Jack asked.

"Oh, he's not here. We think he's coming back tomorrow."

"He never talks to us, anyway."

"He went away a few days ago, to London. That's why we're out playing now."

What business did Charles have while Father was ill? It was pointless trying to find out anything more from the boys. Alfred was only eleven, if he remembered correctly, and Will nine. "Well, I'd better get up to the house and see for myself. Are you coming?"

They hesitated—torn between wanting to play and being polite, Jack guessed.

"Never mind. I'll come and see you in the nursery later." He laughed as they scuttled off into the trees, whispering—loudly—to each other to move quietly. He mounted and let the horse amble along the drive, further rustling in the bushes giving away the position of his nephews. Wondering if they were planning on ambushing him, he spurred the horse into a canter. He'd love to play with them, but he really ought to present himself at the house first.

Beyond the trees, he turned into the track that would take him directly to the stables, skirting around the extensive parterre that fronted the house.

"Mr Jack!" The old stable master hobbled towards him, a wide grin on his face.

"Good to see you, Gibbs."

Gibbs took the reins as Jack slung his saddlebags over his shoulder and unstrapped the small bag he'd fastened behind the saddle. "This chap needs to be returned to the Eagle in Hertford."

"Very good, sir."

His greeting indoors was rather more formal. The butler, appointed since Jack left to join the army, didn't have the familiar manner of retainers who'd seen him grow up, and politely informed him that his usual room was prepared, the clothes he'd left had been aired for him and Tindale, his father's valet, would attend him shortly and arrange a bath.

"Is Lady Wingrave in residence?" he asked. The boys had said his brother was away, but it might help to ask his sister-in-law about that before seeing his father.

"I believe she is in the gardens, sir. Shall I inform her of your arrival?"

"Yes, please do. Tell her I will come to her as soon as I've made myself presentable." He ran up the stairs.

Jack found Sarah sitting in a small wooden pavilion in the far corner of the orchard. Her head was bent over a small embroidery frame, her unpowdered hair dressed loosely, and he thought once again what a good wife his father had chosen for Charles. Whether Charles was a good husband for her was a different matter.

The pavilion was new and surrounded by flower beds that resembled a cottage garden crammed with plants in irregular drifts, quite unlike the formal beds in the main gardens. Most of the flowers had gone now, leaving mainly roses and drifts of pink phlox and purple Michaelmas daisies.

"Hiding, my lady?"

She dropped her frame with a gasp, then a smile. "Jack! You're as bad as the boys, creeping up on me like that!"

"Sorry, I didn't mean to startle you." He pulled up another chair and sat beside her as she placed her embroidery and threads on the table.

"Welcome home, although it's a pity it has to be under such circumstances."

"Father really is dying, then?"

"The physicians think so—it's his weak heart, as it was before. Wingrave summoned several men from London to examine him, but he refused to take the potions they prescribed."

"That was probably a good thing." Jack had little faith in men of the medical profession, apart from the army doctors proficient at sewing up wounds or digging out musket balls.

Sarah nodded. "Yes, although I might have tried to encourage him to take his medicine if they'd all suggested the same thing. They did all tell him to rest, though, and he is."

"That's good." He saw a small shake of her head. "Isn't it?"

"I think he rests because he's tired—that's what Tindale says." She leaned forward and patted his arm where it rested on the table. "He will be pleased to see you; I'm glad you came."

"I nearly didn't," Jack admitted. "After last time, when he was fit and well by the time I got back…" He shrugged. "But he—or Charles, I suppose—got someone at Horse Guards to actually order my return."

"Oh? I didn't know that, but then Wingrave doesn't talk to me much. He's been away for a few days, but he's expected back tomorrow." She looked away, seeming to study the flowers surrounding the pavilion, her mouth drooping. Then she turned back to face him. "I know he's your brother, Jack, but you're nothing like him. The less I have to do with him the better. That's part of the reason for this." She waved a hand, taking in the little garden and the pavilion. "It doesn't suit his notion of suitable surroundings for Lord Wingrave, heir to the Earl of Marstone, so he's not likely to come across me here."

"I'm sorry." Although he'd only spent a few months here in total since his brother had married, it hadn't taken him long to realise that Charles wasn't a man who cared about the happiness of his wife.

"Don't be silly, Jack. It's not your fault."

"I met the boys on the way," Jack said, hoping to lighten her mood. "They were playing Indians in the woods. How are they?"

It worked—her face lit up, and Jack listened to descriptions of their progress in their studies, and the clever things they'd said. If it had been anyone else, Jack would have soon found an excuse to escape, but Sarah's love for her children was so evident that he listened with genuine interest.

Charles was a damned fool.

Would Clara be like Sarah? She clearly had affection for her family.

But wondering about that was futile. It might not be his duty to beget an heir, but it was his duty to marry someone within his own class.

Later that afternoon, a footman found Jack in the nursery on the top floor, and requested his presence in Lord Marstone's room. Jack stood, brushed down the knees of his breeches, and carefully stepped over the ranks of toy soldiers arranged beside the line of books that represented the St Lawrence River.

"But you haven't taken Quebec yet," Alfred complained.

"You haven't built Quebec yet," Jack countered. He indicated an area of carpet. "You need to make a flat-topped hill here. We'll attack in the morning—if you're not supposed to be having lessons."

He pulled the nursery door closed behind him, hearing the beginnings of a disagreement about how to build a hill. Had he and Charles bickered like that when children? He didn't remember, but then he didn't recall playing with his brother often, either. He'd spent most of his free time in the stables.

Expecting a sick-room, Jack was surprised to find his father sitting in a chair by the window, a blanket wrapped around his legs and a glass and decanter of water on a small table beside him. The valet bowed and withdrew.

The optimism about his father's health on seeing him out of bed was dispelled as Jack drew close enough to take in the greyish tinge to his skin, the hollow cheeks, and the tremor in the hands resting on the arms of his chair.

"Hello, Father."

"Welcome home, Jack." His voice was reedy, and too quiet. "I'm glad you've come in time."

In time? Jack was about to protest that his father had some years yet, but thought better of it. Father had never been one to dress up the truth in hopeful lies.

"So am I." In spite of the differences they'd had over the years, he meant it.

"How are you?"

"I'm well." Short of money, as usual, but he wasn't going to repeat that complaint.

"That's good." Father turned his head and looked out of the window, towards the parterres lit by the lowering sun, but Jack got the impression he wasn't seeing them. Finally, he took a long, breath.

"I wanted to tell you I'm proud of you, Jack. The career you've made for yourself in the army."

"Thank you." That was all he managed to say, remembering the furious arguments when he had announced his wish to buy a commission.

"I was worried about the succession," his father went on. "Beyond you and Charles, there was only a very distant cousin. That was why I objected twelve years ago. But now Charles has two boys…"

"Fine lads they are, too," Jack said into the silence.

"Yes. Jack, I was wrong to only buy you a commission in a foot regiment. It was obvious you would join the army, whatever I said. I could have bought you higher than a mere lieutenant, and in a cavalry regiment."

"Oh, it suited me well, Father. There's not much use for cavalry, as much of the country there is wooded, and it's been fascinating working with our Indian allies." He'd earned his promotion to captain. Becoming a major would have been good, but if he'd achieved any rank higher than that he'd have ended up spending too much time on paperwork.

They could have had this discussion any time in the years since Alfred and Will had been born. But Father was a proud man, not liking to admit to mistakes. Jack rubbed his forehead—he really must believe he was near the end, to make an apology like this.

"That's good. You will be staying for a while, won't you?"

"Yes, sir."

"Good. Ride anything in the stables you take a fancy to, Jack." He fell silent then, returning his gaze to the gardens.

"I'm tiring you too much," Jack said, when his father hadn't spoken for several minutes. But Father shook his head and waved a hand towards the decanter. Jack poured a glass of water and put it in his father's hand, helping him to hold it to his mouth, then put the glass back on the table.

"I'd like to see you married and settled," Father said, when he eventually spoke. "I still don't like to think of you facing death in battle. Charles—well, Sarah's a lovely woman, but Charles always had a wandering eye, you know. Still, a good marriage to a suitable woman would set you up. There's Wellford's daughter—a pleasant girl, I'm told, although a bit of a bluestocking. That would be a useful political alliance."

Wellford? The Marquess of Wellford? "Why would she want to marry a second son?"

"Come, Jack, don't be modest—you're a war hero…"

No—one mention in dispatches did not make a man a hero, but Father was still speaking and Jack didn't want to argue with him.

"…your appearance is well enough…"

Jack's lips twitched, in spite of the circumstances.

"…and you're still an earl's son. I'll leave you a couple of my northern estates—they're not part of the entail. You'll have income from those, but Wellford will give her a dowry."

A vision of Clara's laughing smile came into Jack's mind, and a sense of unease began to grow. "You've arranged this, Father? Without asking me?"

"No, no, not at all. I only mentioned the idea to Wellford, months ago. But Wellford wants to see her married—he's not as decrepit as me, but he's no youngster either. You needn't think the daughter's too old for you, Jack. He married late, and she's the youngest. She must be about five years younger than you—old enough to have got over any missishness."

The daughter of a marquess would be an attractive proposition for most men—so why wasn't she already married?

"Wellford has a pocket borough," his father continued. "It'd be good for both our families to have a voice in the Commons. And it's as well to have more than two heirs in the next generation." He rested his head against the back of his chair and closed his eyes. "I would like to know you were happily married, Jack. Consider the idea, won't you?"

When his father hadn't moved for some minutes, apart from the laboured rise and fall of his chest, Jack silently got to his feet and crossed to the door.

"I think he's sleeping," he said to the waiting valet. Tindale nodded and slipped into the room as Jack left.

CHAPTER 8

Rather than returning to the nursery, Jack went out into the western gardens. He needed peace to think. It wasn't so much his father's ill-health—he'd been expecting that, and seventy wasn't a bad age to go. No, it was his talk of marriage.

As he strolled between the low, clipped hedges, he thought back to the last time he'd been summoned home, two years ago. Father had said something then about wanting him settled, but hadn't persisted, and there'd been no suggestion of a possible bride. He hoped Father wasn't going to demand a promise to offer for the woman—he didn't even want to consider her, as Father had requested.

He stopped by a fountain, watching the fish swimming in the greenish water, then turned back to look at the house. The building was huge, with classical columns adorning the front and a wide flight of steps up to the main entrance doors. Jack remembered Morton's remark about advertising wealth and status, and realised that this was what the proposed marriage was about, too. And the one Father had arranged for Charles. Jack had no idea whether Charles was happy, but Sarah certainly wasn't. If he were to marry, he wanted to be on amicable terms, at the very least, with his wife.

He made his way into the orchard. The pavilion was empty now, and he wandered on beneath boughs of ripening apples and pears. One day, he might take pleasure in settling down and owning productive orchards like this, and farms and gardens, and all the other rewards and responsibilities of land and property. But that day was not yet—not for many years. He enjoyed the life of a soldier, his sense of purpose, and the camaraderie of his fellow officers.

Clara *likes* seeing new places, an annoying voice in his head said. But although her father was Colonel Harper, son of a baron, her Uncle George was in trade. His father would not approve of that match.

If he ever suggested it.

Could he? Did his father's approval matter?

Father hadn't approved of him joining the army, but had come around—even if a decade too late to be useful.

This was not the time to consider such things, not with his father so ill, and he tried to turn his mind to other matters. But when he returned to his room, he found that his trunks had arrived and the footman currently acting as his valet had unpacked his clothing for him. There was also a small trunk set on the floor near the window.

"That's not mine," he said.

"Beg pardon, sir, but it's got your name on it."

And it had—on a flimsy label that had almost peeled off, and written in a strange hand. Curious, he dismissed the footman and investigated.

The trunk wasn't locked, but held closed with a leather strap. Opening the lid, he found bundles of paper tied up with ribbon, several books, and a lap desk containing pens and stoppered bottles of ink. Clara's desk, that he'd seen so often on the *Pegasus*.

He inspected the trunk and teased off the paper with his name on it, managing to leave enough of the label below to make it obvious that this *was* Clara's trunk, to be sent care of Mr George Morton in Cavendish Square.

Had Clara sent it here?

No—Morton's name and the address were in her hand; the label that had been stuck over it was not. Someone had redirected the trunk here on purpose, and the only people who could have done it were Kitty or Mrs Harper.

Kitty had suggested he send his luggage on—but why would she do this? Clara would be upset when she found her work missing.

He took the bundles of papers out of the trunk and examined them more carefully. They were versions of Colonel Harper's book, but none of them appeared to be the final fair copy that Clara had finished only a few days before they reached Falmouth. She would want them back, but perhaps not urgently. He would write to let her know it was not lost, and take it to London himself in a day or two, to ensure it got there safely.

He had said to Morton that he would call on the family—he should not feel so pleased that he had an excuse to do so.

Clara rubbed her temples as the coach pulled up outside Uncle George's house. The footman let down the step before starting to unload the numerous packages and boxes that were the result of the day's shopping expedition.

She was tired. Tired of traipsing around shops and listening to Mama and Kitty debating the merits of this fabric or that for a dinner gown, whether to buy a hat with feathers or ribbons, which shoes to choose for dancing, for walking. She'd been happy to let Mama and Kitty make many of the decisions for her, as they often did. They had better taste in clothing and colour than she did, and more interest in the matter, too. It was just a pity she'd had to be there while they discussed it all.

It wasn't only that, she thought, as the three of them settled in the parlour with tea and a plate of queen cakes. It was the way Jack had said goodbye last evening—with good wishes, but nothing else.

"Clara? Is something wrong?"

She attempted to smooth the frown from her brow, and shook her head. "I'm just tired, Mama. I will go and lie down before dinner."

"Very well, dear. You do look rather wan. Now, Kitty, what do you think to having a new gown made up from…?"

The parlour door closed on more talk of fashions and furbelows, and Clara made her way upstairs.

What had she expected—or wanted—Jack to say? She'd known from the beginning that nothing could come of their collaboration beyond friendship, and how could a friendship prosper when they were unlikely to meet again?

He had wished her success with getting Papa's book published, though. She would have to discuss that with Uncle George, and it would be well to have the final fair copy ready. Checking that might take her mind off the way she was missing Jack's company.

No-one had brought her small trunk up, so she rang the bell. But the maid, when she arrived, didn't know anything about a small trunk, and nor was it anywhere to be seen when Clara went downstairs to the room where their other trunks were still stored.

She sank onto the lid of her main trunk as a sick feeling settled in her stomach. It must not be lost! Not all Papa's work and her own. But how had it gone astray? She'd had it in her room at the inn the night before they arrived here, and she'd seen the coachman load it yesterday morning. It *must* have arrived in Cavendish Square.

Kitty… Kitty had said something to Jack about his luggage.

She jumped to her feet and hurried to the parlour. Kitty and Mama were still gloating over their day's purchases, and drinking tea.

"Kitty, what did you do with my little trunk?"

Too late, she saw that Uncle George was sitting with them—and was the only one looking surprised. She ploughed on regardless. "Where is it?" She'd thought it odd last night that the trunks had not been brought to their rooms; this must be why. And it meant that Mama was part of the plot. "Kitty, it has Papa's book in it!"

"Don't worry, Clara—I kept back the fair copy. And the captain will return the other papers, I'm sure."

"I need *all* of it, Kitty. Captain Stanlake's things went by carrier—what if it becomes lost?"

"Please do not panic, Clara," Uncle George said, setting his cup down. "It would have been sent with the firm I normally use, and they are very reliable. And I'm sure the captain will ensure it is safely returned." He turned to Kitty and Mama. "Why did you do it?"

"It will give Captain Stanlake an excuse to call," Mama said, with no sign of guilt.

"I asked him to call when he returns to Town, Anne. There was no need for subterfuge."

Mama lifted a shoulder. "We didn't know that when Kitty changed the label. And he would be a good match for Clara."

Uncle George sighed. "A suitor who has to be enticed back isn't worth having."

"He can send the trunk back with a carrier," Clara pointed out, at the same time hoping he would not.

"If he does, you'll know he's not interested and you can stop pining over him," Kitty said.

"I'm not..." She caught Kitty's eye and stopped. That was exactly what she had been doing all day. "Kitty, he's an *earl's* son!"

"Yes, that is Mama's point. But *my* reason for doing it is that you like him, and he likes you."

"The aristocracy don't marry into trade." If only they would... this member of it, at least.

"So that's the only reason you think he won't come back? Not because he doesn't—"

"*Kitty!*"

"This is not the time, or audience, for this, Kitty," Uncle George said firmly. "Clara, if the captain is going to send your trunk back, it should arrive tomorrow or the next day. If it does not, I will send a man to enquire. Will that do? Things are rarely lost in transit, you know—you only hear about the few items that do not arrive, not the hundreds that do."

Clara nodded, her mind in too much turmoil to think.

"Come and talk to me tomorrow about your father's book. Kitty, you will go and get the fair copy you referred to and give it to your sister. I will see both of you at dinner."

Glad to be dismissed, Clara returned to her room. For the first time in her life, she wished she did not have to share a room with Kitty. Having her feelings for Jack discussed in public had forced her to face the fact that she liked him too much for her peace of mind.

~

The next morning—once Quebec had been taken and the boys persuaded to pay attention to their lessons for a few hours—Jack had little to do, so he wandered down to the stables. The sun was shining, and a ride would help to pass the time very nicely.

Gibbs quizzed him about his time in the Colonies, then showed him around the horseflesh currently in residence. Jack duly admired Lady Wingrave's pretty little mare, and the ponies used by the boys. Charles had a fine pair of matched black geldings to pull a phaeton, and several hunters.

"Who is this magnificent beast?" Jack asked, coming to the final stall. The chestnut stallion was well-muscled and large; bigger than any of the hunters. He looked restless, shifting about in his stall.

"Atlas," Gibbs said. "Lord Wingrave bought him for hunting, but he usually uses the others." He jerked a thumb to indicate the animals they'd just inspected. "Poor chap doesn't get taken out often enough. I ride him for exercise more than his lordship does."

Jack reached out and stroked the animal's nose. Atlas snorted and shuffled sideways.

"D'you want to take him out, sir?"

"Why not?" This was a better mount than he'd ever been able to afford.

Gibbs called, and a groom brought a bridle and saddle. When Atlas was ready, Jack led him out into the yard, allowing him to toss his head against the restraint of the reins before gradually bringing him under control. Atlas skittered sideways when Jack mounted, but although strong, he was far from the worst-tempered horse Jack had ridden.

"I may be a few hours," Jack said. "Does the inn at Over Minster still sell a good ale?"

"Aye, that it does. Give him a good run, sir."

Jack nodded, and kept Atlas to a sedate walk until they were beyond the paddocks and out into the parkland. Then he gave the stallion his head for a while, before trying him over some low hedges and then some more challenging obstacles. Atlas tried to go his own way a few times, but soon worked out that Jack was in charge.

An hour later, and after a circuitous route that wound through fields and woods, he dismounted outside the Royal Oak. The ale *was* still as good as he remembered, and three pints later he set off back again, content with life for the present. Good ale, a splendid mount, a sunny afternoon… what more could a man ask?

A woman to warm your bed, that voice said as he rode through the final belt of woodland. One particular woman. An evening of banter with the Harper sisters before taking Clara to…

"Haaah!"

Atlas lurched sideways at the sudden screech, and Jack came abruptly out of his reverie. A small figure danced in front of him, waving a long stick.

"Surrender!" Will shouted, brandishing his spear.

Jack put his hands in the air; Atlas was tired enough to be controlled for a short time with only his legs. "I have no weapons, oh brave and noble warrior." He took hold of the reins and patted his mount. "Well done, Will. You surprised me that time."

Will threw the spear aside with a grin. "I expect you weren't paying attention, sir."

"Possibly," he admitted. "Would the mighty warrior like a ride to the stables?"

"On Atlas?" Will's eyes went round. "Yes, please."

Jack pulled the lad up to sit before him. "Where's Alfred?" he asked, urging his mount into a walk.

"He's doing some extra lessons. Papa says he has to know more because he'll be the earl one day."

"Poor lad."

Will shrugged. "He doesn't think so. He says he's better than me because I'm not going to be Lord anything."

"Hmm. Like me, eh?" He remembered Charles saying something very similar twenty years ago.

Will turned his head. "I'd rather be like you, Uncle Jack."

"Very polite, Will," Jack said with a chuckle, although the lad's smile showed he meant it.

"Do you like Papa's horse?" Will asked, patting the animal's neck. "Papa doesn't take him out very often."

"He's a good ride," Jack said. And wasted on his brother, from what Gibbs had said.

"Papa says he wasn't trained properly."

"He told you that?"

"No. He was angry with Gibbs. I was hiding in the stables and heard him shouting." Will sniggered. "I think Papa had nearly fallen off."

That sounded like Charles. A failure must be the animal's fault, or the servant's—anyone's but his own. He hoped the boys weren't going to take after their father.

"Oh, Mama's there." Will waved happily, and slid off Atlas' back as Jack drew rein in the stable yard.

"Your father's back," Sarah said, ruffling Will's hair. "Go and get cleaned up."

CHAPTER 9

Jack handed the reins to Gibbs and offered Sarah his arm to walk to the house as Will dashed off. She no longer had the carefree air of yesterday, and she set a slow pace as if reluctant to return.

"Wingrave should sell that horse," she said. "But he won't admit that he can't handle it. I hope he didn't see Will up in front of you."

"Why?"

"He told Will the animal was dangerous, so…" She shrugged.

"So he won't be pleased that Will has ridden on him without incident," Jack finished for her.

"He's jealous of you, you know."

"Me? Why? I'm merely a captain in a regiment of foot. He'll have the title and the wealth, and he values those things."

"And you don't?"

"Oh, more money would undoubtedly be useful, but not the responsibility that goes with it. My duty to the regiment and my men is sufficient."

"That's partly it, you know. Your father was so proud when you were mentioned in dispatches, and scours the *Gazette* for news of any actions you might have been involved in."

"He'd do the same if Charles was away for long periods," Jack pointed out.

"Not all feelings are rational."

That was true. "You are very wise."

"It helps to understand what other people are thinking or feeling," she said. "Particularly when their behaviour can have a great effect on me and my sons." She patted his arm with her free hand. "It's a pity he's not more like you."

Startled, Jack stopped and looked into her face, but the droop to her mouth made clear she was not attempting to flirt with him.

There was affection between them, he thought, but that of a brother and sister—not the meeting of minds and friendly teasing in Clara's company that he was already missing. "You're a good mother," he said, at a loss for how to comfort her.

"It's not so bad," she added, releasing his arm as they entered the house. "I do have the boys. He seems happy enough with two sons, and doesn't bother me often now. He finds his own... entertainment... in the village, and his mistress in Town is only half a day's ride away."

Watching her walk away, Jack vowed that he would not marry where there was not mutual liking and esteem, at the very least. And the idea that intimate relations with Cla— with a future wife would be 'bothering' her was anathema to him.

That afternoon, Jack paused outside the door of his father's bedchamber. If Father was asleep, he didn't want to wake him by knocking. He couldn't hear anything when he put his ear to the door, so he lifted the latch quietly and pushed it open a little way. Footsteps sounded, then Tindale appeared and gestured him back out into the hall.

"I'm sorry, sir," the valet said in a low voice, following him out and pulling the door closed behind him. "Your visit yesterday tired him too much, and Lord Wingrave has just been to see him."

"Is he sleeping now?"

"Yes, sir. The physician has been called." Tindale's grave expression suggested that this was not merely normal tiredness.

"Does he normally get out of bed for visitors?"

"No, sir. But he was determined not to greet you lying down." The valet shuffled his feet. "I wanted to send for the physician yesterday, but he wouldn't allow me to."

"You should have come to me, or to Lady Wingrave."

The valet shook his head. "That might have made him worse, sir."

"Being disobeyed?"

The valet nodded. Jack didn't ask what was different now, but it was not good news. His father was either ill enough to know that he needed a physician, or he was so unwell that Tindale had done it without his consent.

"Does my brother know how bad he is?"

"Yes, sir. I… I had to send him out."

Charles wouldn't have liked that—Jack had to admire the valet's care for his master.

"Keep me informed, Tindale. I will stay in the immediate grounds until he… I mean, I will not be far away. Send someone for me if he is well enough to see me."

"I will, sir. Thank you. Er… Before he left, Lord Wingrave said you were to… I mean, he requested that you see him in the library." The valet bowed, then let himself silently back into the earl's bedchamber.

Jack ran a hand through his hair—he could not leave the Park now, not even for a brief visit to London. If he sent a groom with Clara's trunk, she would have it by this evening. He tried to ignore the disappointment he felt at not being able to deliver it in person.

And Tindale had been very diplomatic—Charles had undoubtedly given a command, not a request.

Charles was seated before the fire in the library when Jack arrived. "You got back in time, then," he said, not getting up.

"It's good to see you, too, Charlie," Jack said. "It was just as well I got a direct order to return."

"You doubted my word?"

"Last time I was summoned back, Father was on the mend by the time I arrived," Jack pointed out.

"It was your duty to return; you shouldn't have needed an order from Horse Guards."

Jack wished he hadn't mentioned it. Trying to make allowances for Charles' natural worry about their father's illness, he said nothing more, but poured himself a glass of brandy and sat down. Charles hadn't been particularly friendly last time he was home, but now he seemed actively hostile.

"And Father didn't even thank me," Charles mumbled into his glass. "After all the effort I went to."

He took a long drink, and Jack wondered how much he'd already had. The decanter was less than half full, and surely the butler would have kept it topped up?

"You tired Father too much yesterday, Jack. He hardly managed to speak to me when I got home, and he didn't even thank…" He broke off and shook his head, as if realising he'd already said that. "You should have waited to see him."

"He sent for me," Jack said. He'd been ordered back to England to see his father, and Charles was expecting him not to do so?

"You made him ill!"

Jack pressed his lips together against a retort. He couldn't argue with the fact, but Charles seemed to be implying that he'd done it deliberately.

"And you can leave my horses alone, too," Charles added.

Startled, Jack paused with his glass halfway to his mouth. "Atlas? Father told me I could ride anything in the stables. The animal was in need of some exercise."

"He's my mount."

"All right, if you say so." Charles was angry enough already, without Jack irritating him further. In any case, he'd promised to stay close to the house, so he wouldn't be riding anywhere for a few days. He left his drink unfinished and walked out of the room—he had Clara's trunk to see to.

. . .

Charles' presence suppressed conversation at dinner. The food was as plentiful as on the previous day, but Sarah hardly spoke a word.

"Were you away on business?" Jack asked eventually, feeling the need to break the uncomfortable silence.

"Of course I was!" Charles scowled. "You don't think I'd be away for anything else when Father is so ill?"

Sarah looked up. "I'm sure Jack didn't mean—"

"Really? You know what he's thinking, do you?" Charles turned on his wife. "I've done my best to do what Father wants, and now he's too ill to even talk to me properly. Thanks to Jack exhausting him yesterday." He jabbed a finger in Jack's direction.

"I was attempting to take a brotherly interest, Charlie, that's all," Jack said, trying to deflect his anger from Sarah.

Charles gestured to a waiting footman to refill his glass. "I saw you two walking together. Keep away from my wife, Jack. Some women are silly enough to be attracted to a man in a red coat, but—"

"Don't be ridiculous, Charles. I was talking to my sister-in-law. It would be rude to ignore my hostess."

Sarah was gazing at her plate, her face red and lips pressed together. Charles' accusation was insulting to both of them. He hadn't finished his meal, but with Charles in this mood it would be better for everyone if he were elsewhere. He folded his napkin and placed it beside his plate. "Excuse me, I have some letters to write." He didn't look at either of them as he left. Sarah would understand his apparent rudeness, and he didn't care what Charles thought.

He was still hungry, so he asked a footman to get a tray sent to his room. After that, he would find something to read, but as he ascended the stairs, he heard footsteps and turned to see Charles stalking across the hall towards the library.

Ah, well. It might be time to brush up his skill at billiards while he had access to a decent table.

~

The next morning, Clara chose not to go with Mama and Kitty on another shopping expedition. Instead, she asked for a maid to accompany her while she visited several of the booksellers in Paternoster Row and St Paul's Churchyard. As a result, she spent several pleasant hours browsing the various showrooms, and came away with enough books to keep her occupied for a month. And she hadn't yet explored Uncle George's library.

She had her chance not long after she returned, when a footman asked her to go to her uncle as soon as convenient. On entering the room her attention was caught by the floor to ceiling shelving filled with books, and she only turned towards Uncle George when he cleared his throat.

"A woman after my own heart," he said. He was laughing at her, but kindly. "Make free of the place while you are here, Clara. But I summoned you here because this arrived earlier." He held out a letter, the seal already broken.

Jack's hand—she recognised it instantly, suddenly breathless. It was addressed to her uncle, as was proper, and was brief, stating only that he had her trunk safe and would deliver it in the next few days.

'Deliver it', not 'have it delivered'.

"It seems that Kitty's machinations have worked," Uncle George said. "Do you think it wise to see him again?"

"I… I don't know." Her happiness dissipated. "Probably not."

"But you wish to do so, all the same. Do sit down, my dear."

They sat in the chairs by the fire, Clara with her hands in her lap ready for the lecture she knew was coming. But her uncle surprised her.

"Your father wrote to me about finding an editor and a publisher for his book."

"Yes, he told me he had done so."

"Explain, if you please, why the loss of the original materials would be so upsetting. Kitty assured me this morning, when I questioned her, that you had finished the fair copy."

Did he regard women in the same way that Papa did? And Mama, come to that. Uncle George was Mama's brother.

"Is what you have more than a fair copy, perhaps?" He looked amused, rather than censorious.

"I... Yes, I edited it. Papa is rather... long-winded." Her eyes narrowed. "But I do not find that amusing, Uncle."

"I am not laughing at the idea of you improving the work, my dear, merely at the various... deceptions, shall we say? Deceptions carried out by you and Kitty, for differing reasons."

Kitty had meant well, she supposed, and she felt that her own deception was for a good reason. "Yes, I did deceive Papa, but that was merely letting him assume I would only make a fair copy." But Papa was typical of many men. She made an effort to keep her tone reasonable as she continued. "If men would only recognise that women have brains that are capable of thinking of more than fashion and children, I would not have needed to do that."

He shook his head. "Not all men share those views, Clara. I have become as successful as I have partly by using talent where I find it. A lad born in the gutter, but with intelligence and passion, is more useful to me than some scion of the aristocracy reduced to attempting to earn a living—if he even soils his hands by dabbling in trade."

"And a woman? Would you do business with a woman?" She was happy to find that Uncle George had similar views to her own, but how far did he take them?

"Women are hampered by property laws, as well as the attitudes of many men—and women. However, a number of women run successful shops, for example, or inns and schools."

"But not trading ventures or manufactories."

"Some do, but usually by taking over their husband's business when they are widowed. But I see no reason why they should not start businesses of their own, given sufficient training in matters of finance, and so on. Is that what you want?"

"No." She took a breath and looked away. "I mean, I don't know what I want—and that is because I've never really been given the opportunity to consider anything but marriage and having children."

"You don't want to get married?"

Clara could almost hear 'not even to Captain Stanlake?' running through her uncle's mind. "I do want that—marriage and a family, I mean. If I find the right man." She tried to ignore the thought that she had already done so. "But I enjoyed editing Papa's book, and I was fascinated by what I learned from it, and what Ja— Captain Stanlake told me about his experiences with the natives." She shrugged. "I like learning new things."

"Hmm. I can ask my acquaintance if any of them have a connection to the Blue Stockings Society—although I understand their discussions are limited to literary and artistic matters, rather than other cultures or trading."

Her, a member of the Society? "I'm not sure I have knowledge enough for that." She shouldn't turn down the offer, though, not after the complaints she had just made.

Uncle George waved a hand at the bookshelves. "Work on it, then. I gather that several members publish essays and other works; start by reading those."

"I will, thank you."

"As for your father's book, would you like me to look through his originals and compare it to your edited version? I'm afraid you may need the assistance of a mere male when dealing with publishers, unless your father wishes to pay for copies to be printed." His smile robbed the words of any sting.

"He was hoping to be paid," Clara said. "I… I did have something like that in mind, which was why I was concerned when the original manuscript went astray."

"Very well. We will do that when Captain Stanlake arrives with the trunk." He paused at the sound of voices in the hall. Mama and Kitty had returned, judging by the excited chatter and fragments of instructions about parcels and packages. "I suspect we will be required in the parlour for tea shortly, but do feel free to use this room if you wish to read in peace."

"Thank you, Uncle." But after Jack's note, and Uncle George's understanding, she felt much happier than she had that morning, and was perfectly willing to spend time admiring the latest purchases.

Later in the afternoon, Jonas Nolan paid a call and stayed talking for nearly half an hour. They described their respective journeys from Falmouth, and Kitty and Mama told him of their plans for dinners and visits. He finished by asking if he might introduce his intended to them, and they agreed to meet in the Park the following afternoon for a walk. It wasn't until after dinner that a knock on the front door heralded the arrival of Clara's trunk, accompanied not by Jack but by a groom with a letter.

Clara tried to hide her disappointment, but didn't think she'd succeeded very well.

"He has good reason, I think," Uncle George said, reading the letter and then handing it to her. It said only that his father was very ill, and he could not leave Marstone Park, but he hoped to call when he was able.

"He does," she admitted. The earl must have taken a sudden turn for the worse. Well, Uncle George had suggested several things to do to pass the time, and she had her father's manuscript to check through once more before she took it to a publisher. Those activities might stop her missing Jack's company too much—that was something she should aim for.

CHAPTER 10

*J*ack spent the next few days being where his brother was not. He'd seen his father once in that time—Tindale had come to tell him that Lord Marstone was awake and asking for him. Jack had sat by his bed and talked about his time in the army, not sure whether Father had fallen asleep or was still listening. On his way out, Tindale had whispered that his lordship seemed to be sleeping more easily.

The weather continued fine, the air warm for the time of year, and he'd have liked to take long rides around the countryside. But he'd promised to stay close, so he spent some of his time reading, and the rest with his nephews. When the boys were not doing lessons, they pestered him for more details about battles he'd been in, and eventually he recruited a couple of grooms and the estate carpenter, and they all went off into the woods to build a small fort. The thing was only a few yards across, but they had fun designing it and then working out battle plans for attacking and defending it.

"Captain Stanlake? Sir?" The voice was some way off, but Jack stood up and dusted leaf mould from his breeches. He'd been attempting to creep up on the fort without being spotted.

"Over here," he called.

"Captain, you're wanted back at the house." The footman stopped and gasped for breath. "His lordship…"

"I'm on my way," Jack said. "Alfred, Will, best get yourselves inside and cleaned up. You may be wanted, too."

"Is it Grandpapa?" Alfred asked.

"I expect so." He couldn't think of anything else that would necessitate such an urgent summons. "Quickly, now."

"Tindale says his lordship's taken a turn for the worse, sir," the footman said, as Jack hurried after him. "He's asking for you."

Tindale was waiting by the door to his father's chamber and ushered him straight in. Charles was already there, sitting beside the bed.

"Jack's here now, Father," Charles said, his voice calm but his expression far from welcoming.

Jack sat down at the other side of the bed, in a chair placed ready. "Father," he said, taking the old man's hand.

"I'm glad you came back, Jack," Father said, his voice thin and his words slow. "Promise me you'll marry—I was happy with your mother. I want… I want you to be, too."

"I will, Father." Some day. An image of Clara's face came into his mind. "Soon."

Why did he say that?

"Good, good." Father's voice was weaker still. "Charles?"

"Yes, Father?"

"You're the head of the family, now… We've a proud name. Take care of everyone, my boy."

"I will."

"You'll do well." Father said, after a long silence. He closed his eyes, and his lips curved up slightly. Then his face gradually became slack and his breaths, quiet in the still room, became further and further apart.

"Goodbye, Papa," Jack whispered, using the childhood term. The words almost choked him. He'd seen death aplenty on battlefields, and drowned his sorrow at the loss of good friends with wine and brandy, but this was different. This was the passing of someone who'd always been there, even if half a world away.

Eventually Tindale approached with quiet tread. Jack glanced at him, then placed fingers gently at his father's throat. He could feel no pulse.

"I'll see to him, sir," Tindale said. Charles got to his feet abruptly and went to gaze out of the window. Jack headed for the gardens, in no mood to speak to anyone.

∿

Jack sat up straighter in his chair as the Marstone family solicitor coughed loudly and took a sheaf of papers from his satchel. Everyone in the room stopped talking and an expectant hush descended. It was time for the will to be read.

In the week since his father's death, his two sisters and their husbands had arrived, together with their offspring. The funeral had been held and Father was now entombed with his ancestors in the crypt below the village church.

The week had been tedious, to put it mildly. Charles had supervised all the arrangements himself, but had made it clear that it was not seemly for Jack to ride around the countryside, nor to distract the boys from their lessons. Jack had spent a little time exchanging news with Honora and Aurelia, but he had little in common with his sisters any more, and their husbands were interested only in hunting or gambling.

"The Last Will and Testament of Richard George Stanlake, 7th Earl of Marstone," the solicitor started.

At least the man didn't drone, Jack thought, as he listened to the obvious passing on of the entailed property to Charles, as the new earl.

"...gifts to family members..."

Jack's interest revived a little as his sisters were left sums of money.

"... and to my son, John, I leave the estates at Kirkthwaite and

Nethburn, in Cumberland and Northumberland respectively, to be given into his possession on the occasion of his marriage."

What?

Jack sat up straight, catching a smug glance from Charles. He hadn't expected such a condition, but then he hadn't expected much at all. The requirement would make little difference, other than ensuring he would have enough income to keep a bride when he fulfilled his promise to Father. Luckily, Father had not made him promise *when* he would marry. Or whom.

The solicitor was working his way through a list of servants, each receiving money and a small keepsake as thanks for loyal service. Finally it was over, and the family dispersed to rest or partake of the refreshments laid out in the dining room.

"Come into the library," Charles said, as Jack was about to make his escape. Jack sighed, but did as he was asked. He'd managed to avoid his brother for most of the week, but he ought to let him know that he'd be heading for London the following day. It was time he made arrangements to rejoin his regiment.

"Want one?" Charles asked, pouring himself a brandy and waving the decanter at Jack.

"No, thank you." Jack wondered at his brother's satisfied smile. He seemed remarkably cheerful for a man who'd just buried his father.

"You asked where I'd been on business," Charles started.

"Did I?"

"You did. I'd been to see the Marquess of Wellford, at Father's behest."

Jack didn't like the sound of that.

"I believe Father discussed your marriage?"

"He did, yes." Jack was wary now.

"I've negotiated the contracts with Wellford. They're all ready to sign. It's a pity Father didn't live long enough to see you wed, but he did know at the end that I'd arranged everything the way he wanted it. I've done well for you, Jack."

"Marriage? With Wellford's daughter?"

Charles' smile faded. "Yes, who else would I discuss with Wellford?"

"I'm not marrying a woman I've never seen." Jack tried to push the memory of Clara to one side. The notion of marrying someone he hadn't even met was unthinkable, and he would not have agreed to Charles' proposition even if he hadn't got to know Clara.

"Arranged matches happen all the time."

Yes, and look how yours has turned out.

"You'll have time to get to know her before the wedding." Charles frowned, any hint of satisfaction gone. "And you promised father to wed—I *heard* you. I thought you'd want this."

"I promised to marry. Lord Wellford's daughter wasn't mentioned." Not in that conversation. He knew that was who Father had in mind, but he *had* also said that he wanted Jack to be happy.

"Well, it's all arranged; you can't withdraw now."

"It's not withdrawing if it's something I never agreed to. If you truly thought I wanted the match, then I thank you for your efforts—but you should have consulted me first."

"There wasn't time. Father was dying."

As he'd thought—Charles had arranged it in an attempt to please their father. How strange that both of them had grown up thinking Father favoured the other. "Was that all you wanted to see me about, Charles?"

"Marstone to you, now," Charles spat. "I'm the head of the family, remember? Show some respect."

Jack resisted the impulse to give an exaggerated bow. Coming into the title had really gone to Charles' head.

"It's your duty to marry well, Jack. This will increase our influence, through Wellford's pocket borough. I've done better for you than Father did for me—Sarah's only a viscount's daughter. Besides," he went on, his smug expression returning. "I've just sent a notice of your betrothal to the *Gazette*, and Wellford's expecting you to call to sign the documents."

"You sent—? You did that without even asking me if I was willing?" A gentleman could not call off a wedding once the announcement was public. Jack took a deep breath; shouting at Charles wouldn't help. "What made you think I'd agree?"

Charles gaped at him. "The prestige—the connection to a marquess. And money. She comes with a hefty dowry, and you'll get two of the northern estates when you marry her. It's a shame to split up the family's holdings in the borders, but we'll be gaining from the connection."

"The estates were left to me when I marry. The will did not specify my bride."

"Can you afford good lawyers?"

Of course he couldn't. "You know the answer to that."

Charles' triumphant sneer made him want to plant a fist in his brother's face. That would be no help—other than a momentary relieving of his feelings—so he took himself out of the way of temptation, merely slamming the library door behind him as he left.

Newspaper—Charles had sent a notice to the *Gazette*. Jack didn't have many options, but if the announcement was printed he would have no choice at all.

Charles said he'd sent the notice this morning. Jack sprinted up to his room; whether it had gone by messenger or in the post, he needed to get it back. It didn't take him long to change into riding clothes. Money—he might have to go as far as London. He cursed when he realised how little coin he had, but it would have to do. Saddle bag, pistols, a change of linen, shaving kit, card case—that would be sufficient if he had to be away overnight. He headed down the servants' stairs so he didn't run into Charles on the way.

"Messenger went off half an hour ago, sir," the stable master said, when Jack questioned him. "Was told to take it to London."

"Saddle a horse, now."

"Yes, sir."

"No, wait! I'll do it. You didn't see me." Atlas was the fastest horse in the stables, but Charles was vindictive enough to turn the stable master off if Gibbs saddled the animal for him. This way, Gibbs could deny all knowledge.

Some of Jack's energy must have transferred to Atlas, for the stallion was restive, and Jack wasted a few minutes calming him before he managed to get a saddle on and adjusted properly. Then he was off and galloping down the drive.

Sense returned as he passed through the gates, and he slowed the horse to a canter—even Atlas could not keep up that pace long enough to catch the messenger. The roads were busy with carts and carriages, but Jack had little difficulty passing them. That meant the groom would make good speed, too, unfortunately.

He was nearly at Ponders End before he saw a rider ahead that looked like one of his father's—now Charles'—grooms, dressed in the same dark green as the Marstone Park footmen. Jack slowed Atlas to a trot while he debated what to do. Even if Charles wasn't expecting a written acknowledgement that the notice had been received at the *Gazette*'s offices, he would eventually find out that it had not been delivered.

Waiting until a couple of carriages had passed in the opposite direction, he kicked Atlas into a gallop and called on the rider to stop.

"Captain?" The groom's expression was politely enquiring.

"I need the message you're carrying. There's been a mistake. My… That is, Lord Marstone sent me. The new Lord Marstone."

"I'll take it back to Marstone Park, shall I, sir?"

"No. I'll take it."

The groom held it out. Jack broke the seal and found, as he'd hoped, that there was a separate sheet with the wording of the announcement enclosed. He pulled his notebook and pencil from a coat pocket and scribbled on the back of the covering letter. "Here—if Lord Marstone asks you what happened to the message, show him this." His note might prevent the groom being punished for relinquishing it.

The man took the letter, touched his hat, and set off back the way he'd come. Jack watched him go, debating what to do next.

Lord Wellford. He had to see the marquess, and the sooner the better. Father had spoken of his friend several times, and Jack recalled that his principal seat was somewhere in Yorkshire. But one of the boys had mentioned Charles being in London. Lord Wellford would be at his town house, and it shouldn't be too difficult to find out where that was.

He rode on, pondering duty as he went. Duty to his family, his regiment, his country. And his own happiness. They overlapped, but with Charles' idea of what was due to the family, he could not satisfy them all. Not if it meant tying himself to a woman he'd never met.

And when he wanted someone else.

Did he still have a duty to marry within his class? Charles would have said so. But if he submitted to this demand, his brother would continue to try to order his life. He didn't understand why Charles would want to. He owned the land for tens of miles around Marstone Park, not to mention an estate in Devonshire and several in other parts of the country. And now he had the title, and a voice in the Lords. What more power did a man need?

Jack gave up trying to work it out—he'd never really understood what drove Charles. Was he really jealous, as Sarah had suggested? Of an impecunious captain of foot?

Whatever the reason, he would not live his life at his brother's whim. If he had enough income to support a wife he would ask Clara to marry him—but he didn't.

CHAPTER 11

*I*t was early evening when Jack arrived in Grosvenor Square. Marstone House would be closed up, but Father always kept a skeleton staff, and there might be a butler or footman who knew where Lord Wellford lived when in Town. Failing that, there would be some kind of guidebook in the library.

He didn't bother trying the front door, but rode around to the mews. As expected, the Marstone stables were deserted, but he gave a coin to a groom further down the mews to look after Atlas until the Marstone staff opened the stable, and entered the garden through the back gate.

"Master Jack?" The old footman who answered his knock gaped in surprise, then stood back to allow Jack to enter. "We wasn't expecting anyone, sir; the house is all closed up and Mrs—"

"Don't worry about that… Patterson, isn't it?"

A slow smile spread across the man's face. "Fancy you remembering, sir. Captain, I should say."

"I'm only here for the night. I need to see the Marquess of Wellford, as soon as possible. Do you know where his London house is?"

"It's just across the square, sir. I believe he *is* in residence." Patterson's gaze ran from Jack's head to his boots. "I can open the butler's room for you to use, sir, if you wish to wash before you call. I'll have water put on to heat right away." He eyed the small bag Jack had put on the floor by his feet. "If you let me have your boots, I'll polish them while you change."

"I hope you're good with a clothes brush, too," Jack said. "I've only a clean shirt and neckcloth with me."

Half an hour later, Jack discovered that his efforts to smarten up had been in vain. Lord Wellford's butler was welcoming enough, and appeared to recognise his name, but unfortunately his lordship had gone to his club for the evening and was not expected back until the early hours.

"It is a matter of urgency. What time would be suitable for me to call tomorrow?"

"His lordship should be able to see you at eleven o'clock, sir. I will inform him that you will call then."

Jack lingered in the gardens in the middle of the square rather than returning to Marstone House. It would only take quarter of an hour or so to walk to Cavendish Square, but he should not see Clara until he'd extricated himself from the proposed match with Lord Wellford's daughter. He might find old army comrades in one of the clubs, but he wasn't in the mood to explain why he was here.

He set off eastwards. A meal first, then paying a few shillings for a place in the pit at the Royal Opera House or Drury Lane might help take his mind off things.

Clara sat down beside Uncle George as Kitty went to the front of the box with Miss Templeman, both exclaiming at the size of the theatre and the ornate decorations. Mr Nolan's intended was a pleasant, if rather shy, young woman. Her brother had accompanied them, and stood at the back of the box with Mr Nolan, talking quietly together. Then the play started, and they settled down to watch, seemingly oblivious to the noise and chatter still coming from the people in the pit below.

Clara did her best to concentrate on the performance. Theatres and bookshops had been two of the opportunities that had reconciled her to returning to England, but *The Tempest* had never been one of her favourites amongst Shakespeare's plays. She always wished Miranda would show some spirit, and be treated as something other than… well, a possession to be married off to her father's advantage. Fortunately, she was not in that position, but many women were.

She sighed—she couldn't help thinking that her irritation with the plot would not be nearly so marked if Jack were beside her in the box.

"You seem distracted, Clara." Uncle George kept his voice low. "It is only five days since I saw the notice of the Earl of Marstone's death in the *Gazette*. Captain Stanlake will have duties—there is the funeral, the will to be dealt with, and so on."

Clara sighed. Uncle George was too perceptive. But he was also right—she should not expect to see Jack so soon

By the time the fourth act was coming to a close, Clara had resorted to watching the audience in the galleries and the pit. There were as many people carrying on conversations as there were listening to the actors. Not only conversations, but flirtations and arguments. Then her eyes came to rest on a man in the pit—she could not see his face, but something about the way he stood felt familiar. He appeared to be watching the play, but his head didn't turn as the actors moved across the stage.

He looked like Jack.

Then he turned his head as the people beside him started an argument, arms waving, fingers poking chests.

It *was* Jack.

He was in London, and he had not come to see her. Or had he called in Cavendish Square after they left for the theatre? She should not assume the worst—that he was *not* going to call.

"Is that Captain Stanlake?" Uncle George must have noticed her fixed stare.

"I think so." She did her best to keep emotion out of her voice, but Uncle George was a perceptive man. She hoped Kitty and Mama had not noticed—she didn't want to have to listen to their speculation about why he was in the pit instead of a guest in their box.

"I'm sure there will be a good explanation," her uncle said. "He will probably call tomorrow."

Yes—concentrate on that thought. But even as she made that resolution, he looked up, directly towards her, then immediately turned away and started to push his way through the press of people crowding the pit.

The hope that he was making his way to their box faded when no-one knocked on the door, and had vanished entirely by the time they made their way out to the carriage after the play finished.

Jack was not in the best of moods when he was finally shown into the correct office at Horse Guards the next morning. He'd woken hours before his appointment with the Marquess of Wellford, and decided to start the process of returning to his regiment rather than continue to brood on what Clara must think of him.

He was sure she'd seen him in the theatre last night, and he'd promised to call as soon as he could. But not today, not until he'd seen Lord Wellford. He'd started to write a note to say he had business to deal with before he was free, but she deserved more of an explanation than that.

The clerk rose from his desk as Jack entered. "Captain Stanlake, how may I help you? This office normally only deals with serving officers."

"I *am* a serving officer," Jack protested, as he sat down. Muddled orders were nothing new, especially in the heat of a campaign, but there should not be such difficulties here.

"I have your records here, Captain. They show you resigned your commission two months ago." The clerk opened a folder on his desk and leafed through the documents within it.

"I was in Fort Niagara two months ago," Jack explained,

attempting to be patient with the man. The misunderstanding was not necessarily his doing. "There must be some mistake."

The clerk shook his head. "No, no mistake." He held out a paper. "It was done by proxy."

Jack took the letter, his hand almost shaking with fury. Charles—it had to be. The letter told him little more than the clerk had said; it was not in Charles' hand, but it was his signature—as Lord Wingrave, on behalf of the Earl of Marstone, requesting that the matter be expedited. Charles must have done this at the same time as he'd arranged for Jack to be ordered home.

Jack slapped the letter onto the desk. "I knew nothing of this, and I do not wish to sell out. I came here to make arrangements to rejoin my regiment."

"Oh, dear, this is most irregular." The clerk did look regretful, and Jack reminded himself that the situation was not the man's fault. "I'm afraid that will not be possible, even if you purchase another commission. Your position in your regiment has already been filled—orders to that effect have been sent."

Jack clenched his jaw, trying to control his temper. "The money from the sale of my... my *previous* commission can be used to purchase another."

The clerk consulted another paper in the file. "The orders to accept this sale came from the highest levels, Captain. I'm afraid I do not have the authority to deal with this, even if you were to give me an immediate draft on your bank."

That sounded as if Charles had taken the money. He had not mentioned it, but after his machinations around Jack's proposed marriage, it shouldn't have been surprising.

"Who do I need to see about this matter?"

"Mr Porter, I think, but he is currently in Scotland. He is expected back late next week."

Jack stood abruptly—he was accomplishing nothing here, and he needed a brisk walk to cool his anger before meeting Lord Wellford. Losing his commission might turn out to be the least of his worries. "I will write to make an appointment."

The look of relief on the clerk's face as Jack left the room would have been almost comical in other circumstances.

Lord Wellford's butler showed Jack into a parlour overlooking the gardens behind the mansion. The marquess was, as Father had said, of a similar age, but although the joints in his hands were gnarled and his face lined, his eyes shone bright with intelligence, and there was no sign of a tremor in his limbs as he rose and gestured to Jack to sit facing him.

"I'm pleased to meet you at last, Captain," Lord Wellford said. "My condolences on your recent loss."

"Thank you, my lord." Jack took the seat indicated.

"My daughter will be with us shortly—she did request that she meet you before giving her final agreement to the match. After that, I will have my secretary bring the settlements and so on here for you to look through before you sign them. He will explain the details and make any changes you require. Hopefully not too many; your brother negotiated well on your behalf."

"I…" Jack cleared his throat and started again. "I'm sorry, my lord, but matters are not… not as you think. And it would be better if Lady… if your daughter did not join us at this moment."

Poor woman. Not only to be bargained away like this, before even meeting him, but then to have the arrangements cancelled.

Lord Wellford's brows drew together. "Captain, what is my daughter's name?"

"My brother didn't tell me." He could have asked, but it hadn't seemed relevant as he wasn't going to marry her.

"And you didn't bother to enquire?" Icy didn't come close to describing Lord Wellford's tone. It did, however, indicate that the man had some feeling for his daughter.

"The situation is not—"

"Ring the bell, if you would be so good." It was an order, not a request, and Jack rose to pull the cord next to the fireplace. If he was about to be ejected from the house, his problem would be solved, although he'd hoped to be able to explain himself first.

"Ask Lady Elizabeth to wait until I send for her," the marquess said, when the butler appeared.

The butler bowed and withdrew, and Lord Wellford turned his attention back to Jack. "Your brother assured me that this match would be to the benefit of both our families, in addition to suiting you and my daughter."

Damn Charles.

"My lord, I had no knowledge of the existence of your daughter, let alone the proposed match, until a few days ago."

Lord Wellford glared at him, and Jack felt an unaccustomed impulse to wriggle in his chair. Gradually, the glare turned to puzzlement.

"But how is this? Marstone—your late father, that is—spoke to me about the possibility months ago. I understood your brother was making the arrangements on your behalf while you were still abroad, preparatory to you resigning your commission."

"My father did mention it to me a few days before his death, but only in terms of your... of Lady Elizabeth being someone of whom he would approve. I made no promise about Lady Elizabeth, nor did he ask it of me. I had no idea that Charles was negotiating settlements with you until he informed me of the fact yesterday."

Lord Wellford's gaze pierced him again, then he shook his head. "A bad business, this. It seems that your brother has taken too much upon himself."

That was putting it mildly. "Yes. He also had my commission sold without my knowledge or permission. I have no intention of leaving the army."

"It does seem a trifle... underhand..."

It was downright dishonest, as far as Jack was concerned.

"...but you might still consider the match, Captain. A political alliance between our families would be to the advantage of both."

"I would not do Lady Elizabeth the dishonour of marrying her when I... while my affections are given elsewhere. That would not be fair to either... any of us. It might be a different matter were my affections not already engaged." Even then, he would not have agreed before meeting Lady Elizabeth.

"Hmm. That does rather put a different complexion on things."

"My brother doesn't know that I wish to marry someone else, but he attempted to force my hand anyway." Jack pulled the announcement to the *Gazette* from his pocket and held it out. "I intercepted this before the messenger reached London."

Lord Wellford scowled as he read it. "This would appear to force *my* hand, as well, had I or Elizabeth taken a dislike to you. It was not well done of your brother, to do this before the settlements were signed. Not well done at all, and so I shall tell him when we meet." He handed the paper back. "I take it he only sent the one notice?"

Jack hadn't considered that. Charles would have discovered yesterday that Jack had left Marstone Park—if he suspected what his brother was trying to do, he might well have sent out notices to other papers.

"Ring the bell, Stanlake."

Jack waited until Lord Wellford's secretary had been instructed to contact all the newspaper offices, with instructions to refer any announcements relating to the Wellford family to the marquess before publishing them. Lord Wellford seemed to be in no doubt the various editors would comply.

"Sir, I deeply regret any hurt or distress caused to your daughter. I beg you to believe that my decision is no reflection on her, or you."

"How could it be, Captain, when you had not met either of us? If your brother has spread word of this elsewhere, to my daughter's detriment, he will come to regret it."

Jack let out a silent breath. It seemed the marquess was more angry with Charles than him.

"If you will excuse me, my lord, I have other business I must attend to. Unless you wish me to explain to Lady—"

"No, no. I will explain to Elizabeth myself. Thank you for your honesty, at least, my boy."

Jack bowed and left, thankful to have got off so lightly. Far from gaining beneficial connections, Charles had started his reign as earl by making a powerful enemy.

Jack pondered his next move as he crossed the square. Although he had extricated himself from his arranged marriage—unless Charles had managed to get a notice published elsewhere—he was still in no position to ask for Clara's hand. He had no occupation, and no income—Charles would not continue to pay his allowance after learning that his plans had been thwarted. Not only could he not support a wife, but in his current circumstances he could not support himself, either.

A meeting with Clara could only be to explain, and say farewell. Before doing that, he should see if Charles would concede on anything, slim though the chance was.

He would ride back to Marstone Park before calling on Clara. In all honour, Charles should pass on the money from selling his commission—although it appeared honour was in short supply when it came to his brother.

CHAPTER 12

The carriage stopped at the entrance to the narrow cobbled alley of Paternoster Row. It was only a week since Clara had been here in search of reading material, but this time her uncle was with her.

"Look for a sign with a ship," Uncle George said as they alighted. "That's the place we want."

Clara hadn't taken much notice of the signs hanging above the different booksellers' premises on her previous visit, her interest caught by the books displayed in their windows. This time she found it difficult to take an interest in anything.

They had seen Jack in the theatre two nights ago. On the assumption that if he had time to attend the theatre, he would have time to call on her, she had waited indoors all day yesterday. He had not called. Only a great deal of encouragement from Uncle George had persuaded her to accompany him this morning. He was right, she admitted to herself. Spending the day on tenterhooks waiting for the knocker to sound wasn't doing her any good. She wanted to believe Jack had a good reason for staying away, but that became more and more difficult as time passed. For now, she should try to concentrate on Papa's book.

The sign with a ship in full sail was half-way along the street. Uncle George pushed the door open and ushered her in. "We have an appointment with Mr Longman," he said, as a clerk hurried over. "George Morton, and Miss Harper."

The clerk bowed. "Mr Longman is expecting you. Please step this way, sir, miss."

Mr Longman rose as they entered his office, bowed to Clara, and shook Uncle George's hand. "Welcome, sir. I received your letter describing Colonel Harper's work. It could be a useful addition to our list." He indicated a pair of chairs in front of this desk and they sat.

"This is a fair copy." Uncle George placed the parcel of manuscript on the desk before him. "Courtesy of my niece." He inclined his head towards Clara.

"Thank you." Mr Longman unwrapped the package and scanned the first few pages, then returned to the front sheet. "*Edited* by C. Harper?"

Clara didn't care for the surprise in his voice, but she'd promised to let Uncle George do the talking. He was Papa's official representative.

"My niece improved the work greatly," Uncle George said. "My brother-in-law favours long, complex sentences, and has a tendency to repetition. You may also have the unedited manuscript, if you wish, to assess Miss Harper's modifications."

"I beg your pardon, Miss Harper." Mr Longman had a pleasant smile, now with only the faintest hint of condescension. "I will take your word for it, Mr Morton. Now, you understand that the terms I am about to discuss depend on my acceptance of the work, which I will review later. Nothing is contracted until we have a signed document before us."

"As I would expect from a sensible businessman," Uncle George said, and the two men discussed terms and payments while Clara listened.

"That all went very well," her uncle said, when they were out on the street again. "What would you like to do next? Saint Paul's is just down there, should you wish to see it." He pointed to an alley where the dome of the cathedral loomed in the gap between the buildings. "I could return you to Cavendish Square, or you may accompany me to Wapping. I have business at one of my warehouses."

Clara hesitated. They had already been away from home for a couple of hours. If Jack came and she was not—

"If Captain Stanlake should call while you are out and does not return, you are well rid of him," Uncle George said.

He was right; she must hope her feelings would fade, and one way to do that was to turn her mind to other matters. "The warehouse, if you please."

Uncle George nodded, and handed her into the carriage. She hadn't been this far east in London before, and looked out of the carriage windows with interest as they drove along Cheapside, then past the sinister hulk of the tower of London.

"What do you make of young Nolan?" her uncle asked. "He seems friendly, although why he should be so keen on your, and Kitty's, company when he is already betrothed, I do not know."

"He would like a business connection." Clara related what Mr Nolan had said on the *Pegasus*.

"I suspected something of the sort." He glanced at Clara. "Do not think I am offended, my dear. A man has to make connections somehow, and his betrothed seems a pleasant girl. Kitty has taken to her, and it is good that she has friends of her own age."

"Kitty seems to like Miss Templeman's brother, too."

"Should I investigate his background? It would be best to nip a liking in the bud if Templeman is not suitable husband material."

"I'm not sure Kitty has got that far yet in her affections." Unlike her own feelings about Jack. It was more than ten days since she had seen him—surely she should be missing him less by now?

"I will enquire anyway—it may be relevant if I do business with Nolan. Ah, here we are."

The warehouse was not beside the river, but close enough for the smell of salt and mud to be noticeable. Dozens of masts were visible in the gaps between buildings, and she wished she knew where they had all come from, and where they would be sailing to when they had unloaded their cargoes.

Uncle George told his coachman to return for them in an hour, and then led Clara inside. Instantly, her nostrils were assaulted with more pleasant scents of tea and spices. She looked around, but all she saw were piles of boxes and crates, and shelves full of packages in wood and canvas wrappings, with only the enticing smells to show that this place held anything exotic.

"You may listen to my business, although I warn you it will be nothing but discussion of manifests and shipping dates. Or I will send someone to show you around the warehouse." Her uncle must have seen Clara's doubt in her face, as he laughed. "Do not judge by what you see here—there is a showroom, and you may find some of the packages more interesting than they appear."

Uncle George was correct, naturally, and Clara spent a happy hour with her mind on bolts of embroidered silk, fine muslins, dimities, and calicos hand painted or printed in elaborate patterns. There were shelves with blocks of ebony and sandalwood, ready to be made into marquetry or fine furniture, jars of camphor oil and spices—samples that could be touched and smelled. She only thought of Jack five or six times in the hour.

The day after he'd seen Wellford, Jack rode into Marstone Park via the tradesman's gate. A hired horse on a long rein trotted behind Atlas, ready for his departure later. He'd stopped in Hertford for the night, wanting to be well rested before confronting his brother.

The rough track approached the back of the buildings—out of sight of the main parts of the house, which suited Jack perfectly. There were things he wanted to do before encountering Charles. He dismounted in the stable yard, giving Atlas a final pat on the neck as Gibbs hurried towards him.

"Take him for you, sir?"

Jack handed him the reins, and Gibbs led Atlas into a stall. He wasn't gone long.

"His lordship hasn't found out you took Atlas," the stable master said when he reappeared. "Or if he has, he hasn't said anything about it. I wanted him safely back in his stall as soon as possible."

"Good." Charles was going to be furious enough with him—Jack didn't want his brother taking out his temper on the perfectly innocent staff. He indicated the hired horse. "Take care of this fellow, will you? I'm not sure how long I'll be here."

He took the servants' stairs up to his room. Packing the clothing he'd brought back from the Colonies didn't take long, and there was still space in the trunk. He regarded the closet containing clothes he had left behind when he joined the army—most were well out of fashion, but he selected several suits that didn't seem too dated, and folded them into the trunk, then filled the remaining space with shirts, stockings, and neckcloths. Everything smelled strongly of lavender, but the sachets did seem to have kept the moths away, and the aroma would soon wear off. He would send for the rest of his things later, but if Charles' revenge descended to petty levels, he would have something spare with him.

He rang for a footman to take the trunk down to the stables with an instruction to have it sent to the posting inn in Hertford. Then he considered what to do next. Best to say his goodbyes now, in case Charles was incensed enough to have him escorted from the Park. It was still late morning, and the boys would be in the schoolroom.

A Latin lesson was in progress, and he leaned against the door frame while Will finished reciting the declensions of domus. Quite ironic, Jack thought, given that he was likely to be arguing with Charles shortly about who was master.

"I'd like a few minutes with the boys," Jack said, when Will had finished. The tutor bowed and left the room.

"Is something wrong, Uncle Jack?" Will asked.

"I came to say goodbye. I have to go to London."

Will frowned. "You've just been away. Do you really have to go again?"

"It cannot be helped, I'm afraid. And I may be away for a long time, possibly for years." Whether he rejoined the army or had to find some other occupation, he doubted he'd be welcome here for some time. "Think of me when you play in your new fort."

Alfred's lip stuck out. "I won't have much time to play. Now I'm Lord Wingrave, Papa says I need to spend more time learning about family duty. I will be head of the family one day."

"Of course you will, my lord." Jack made a deep bow. Will smirked, but Alfred didn't appear to notice the irony of his gesture.

"Will you write to us, Uncle Jack?" Will asked.

"If I can. Be good, the pair of you."

He descended to the first floor, but hesitated on the landing. Charles would be downstairs in his study, Sarah most likely in her parlour on this floor, as the wind was too cold for her to be sitting in her orchard pavilion. But Charles had warned him to stay away from her. Although he'd been lucky to have avoided notice so far, the chances were high that someone would see him entering or leaving her parlour, and word would get to his brother. He didn't mind incurring Charles' wrath, but his brother would likely take some of his temper out on Sarah.

No—Sarah would understand why he hadn't spoken to her.

When Jack entered the study, Charles was at his desk dictating letters. He gave a triumphant smirk when he saw Jack, and dismissed his secretary.

"Well, Jack, you crept into the Park quietly! Is all settled?"

It seemed Charles hadn't questioned the groom about delivering the notice to the *Gazette*.

"It is, yes." Jack threw the betrothal announcement on the desk. "Wellford was not pleased to find you'd sent this before Lady Elizabeth had a chance to meet me, or to find you'd lied to him."

That wiped the smirk off Charles' face. "Lied?"

"You told him I'd agreed to the match. I told him I had not."

"You told him…? You… you refused the match?"

"I did, and Wellford accepted my reason for doing so." He was not going to explain that—he could imagine the sneer if Charles found out he'd fallen in love with a woman connected to trade. He glanced at the letters book the secretary had left behind. "I do hope you have not informed anyone else of the proposed marriage. Wellford would be seriously displeased, and I suspect you would not wish to upset him further."

"It was Father's wish that—"

"It was his wish that I marry and be happy—as you well know. Your wife and sons may have to do your bidding, but I do not."

"What will you do, then?" Charles' scowl had smoothed.

"Rejoin my regiment, of course." Or some other regiment; it didn't matter which one.

Now Charles was smiling. "But, my dear brother, you have resigned your commission."

"No, you sold my commission, without my knowledge or consent. But I can buy another, and you owe me the money you got for it." He put his hands on the desk and leaned towards his brother, keeping a tight grip on his temper. Charles hurriedly pushed his chair backwards, as if he thought Jack was going to hit him. "Oh, don't worry, dear brother, I shall not soil my hands with you. But if the money is not in my bank account within two days, I'll spread the story of your fraud far and wide." Charles would have to send a messenger with a draft on his own bank, but it could be managed in the time.

Charles' mouth dropped open. "You would not! That would sully your name as well as mine."

Jack's eyes narrowed at his brother's look of horror. Clearly he wanted the appearance of being an honourable man, even if he did not act as one. "I am merely Captain Stanlake of His Majesty's army, Charles. I do not flaunt my connection to the earldom, and my military record speaks for itself. Whereas you have made false claims to both a powerful marquess and someone influential at Horse Guards. Not paying me will add financial fraud to that list—not the act of a gentleman."

Jack kept his eyes on his brother until Charles nodded, his lips compressed.

"Good, we understand each other. In addition, your actions will significantly affect the time I have to spend in England before I can find a regiment to join—and without any pay. You will also advance me a sum to cover my living costs for that period."

"But you're already getting hundreds of—"

"I will need that money to purchase a new commission," Jack interrupted. "If I have to use it for living expenses, I won't be able to afford a commission, in which case I have nothing to lose by spreading word of your perfidy." He wouldn't do so, for that might eventually harm Alfred and Will, but Charles' resigned expression showed he thought it was possible.

"Oh, very well. But do not show your face here again."

"Two hundred should cover it."

"Two—?" Charles' scowl deepened.

"Family honour, Charlie," Jack said softly. "In my bank, within two days." Then he turned and walked out.

CHAPTER 13

Jack presented himself in Cavendish Square the following morning, the skies and drizzle as grey as his mood. After riding the hired hack into Hertford, he'd taken the stage to London and found a cheap room for the night. He had to eke out his meagre reserves of money until Charles' draft arrived at the bank. If Charles sent it at all.

So here he was, scrubbed and in his least unfashionable suit, about to explain why he hadn't called, and then to say goodbye to the woman he loved and would marry if he could. The easiest course would be to avoid her altogether, so he did not have to remind himself of what he would be losing. But he'd said he would call, and he must. The compulsion to see her one last time was inescapable, no matter the cost.

Perhaps he was imagining his feelings, a logical part of his mind said, but he didn't think so.

The butler showed him into a parlour, saying that he thought the ladies were out but that Mr Morton would see him.

It was for the best, he told himself. Morton was a perceptive man and probably guessed something of how he felt. He would explain his situation and take his leave.

He turned as the door opened—it wasn't Morton, but Clara. He took a step towards her, wanting to take her in his arms, but her expression, as well as his own situation, stopped him. He thought he'd seen a quick smile, but that had now gone and she didn't appear to be as happy to see him as he was to see her. That was probably just as well, for her sake.

"Captain, what brings you here now?" She remained in the doorway.

"I… That is, did your trunk arrive safely?" He didn't care about the trunk, but the words of apology he'd rehearsed depended on her being pleased to see him.

"It did, thank you." She smiled, but it was a stiff, formal thing. "I was sorry to hear about your father. Uncle George saw the notice in the *Gazette*."

"He had a good life," Jack said. "It's never easy, when someone dies."

"I suppose you were kept busy in Hertfordshire?"

"I was, in somewhat unexpected ways. I know… I think you saw me in the theatre. I wanted to call then… I wanted to very much, but there were reasons I could not do so until now. Please, will you let me explain?" He almost held his breath while she considered her answer —it would make no practical difference to their future, but he didn't want to part with her thinking ill of him.

Clara felt the lump of unhappiness inside her begin to dissipate. Something was wrong beyond the loss of his father.

"I am pleased you have come, Jack. I missed our conversations. But what is amiss? What has happened?" She crossed the room to stand before him.

"Clara, I…" He took a deep breath and started again. "My circumstances have changed. I had hoped to ask you to come with me—to ask if you would think about living as a soldier's wife. I know your father is permanently based in Albany, but you must have some idea what life would be like following a regiment. I would often be absent, even if we were both on the same side of the Atlantic."

Clara's breath caught at the beginning of his speech. He did want her as she wanted him! But then she recognised the true meaning of his words—he wasn't asking her to marry him, but wishing he were in a position to do so.

He reached out a hand, as if to touch her face, but then dropped it and moved away. "I shouldn't have spoken. I have even less now than I had before—my brother sold my commission without my knowledge or permission. And he hasn't said so, but he is certain to stop my allowance. Army pay… well, it's barely sufficient for normal expenses, let alone for a wife and family."

The brother he mentioned would be the new Earl of Marstone—a man with rank and power.

"At present, I'm no longer in the army, so with no pay and no allowance either."

Clara listened in growing dismay and then relief as he described the events of the last few days. Financial problems could be addressed, but an unwanted betrothal—there would have been no going back from that if the Marquess of Wellford had not been so understanding.

"Can you not buy another commission?"

"I have an appointment next week at Horse Guards with someone who should be able to deal with it, but…" He shrugged. "My brother can be vindictive."

"If he sold your commission once without your permission, he might do so again, or even prevent you purchasing another now."

"Those were my thoughts, yes." He rubbed his forehead. "I have no other skills, and I am too old to start thinking of taking up the law, or going into the church."

"I cannot imagine you preaching from a pulpit." She should have held her tongue—it sounded as if she were making light of his predicament. But his expression brightened, and he almost laughed.

"It's clear I'm not suited to that, is it not? But what else?"

He had gone from amusement back to dejection—with good

reason—but she did not think giving up so easily was part of his character. And this would be her future, too, now.

"Jack, when battle plans go amiss, what do you do? Surrender?"

"No." He stood up straighter. "Revise the plan, or retreat and regroup so another attack can be made. But if this were a battle, Charles has more troops. If I cannot rejoin the British Army, I suppose there are others who require a soldier's skills."

He sounded as if he were talking to himself, but it gave Clara an idea. She recalled one of the first conversations she'd had with him. "When outnumbered in a strange country, take advice from your native allies."

He frowned. "Native...? I'm not in a strange country."

"You are in the realm of the influence bestowed by wealth and rank, and possibly of legal battles. Those things are strange to you, are they not?"

He began to look interested. "The legal battles, certainly."

"They are not strange to Uncle George—they are a large part of his business. If he cannot assist you, I'm sure he knows other people who can. Would you share your story with him?"

"If you think he can help, yes. But Clara..." His words tailed off, and he suddenly looked uncertain. "What I said before. Would you... I mean, do you... can you return my regard?"

"Yes." The word came out without thought, and she took a step towards him.

Jack stepped away, and put his hands behind his back. "I should not... I mean, not until—"

"Stop talking, Jack." Daringly, she put out a finger and held it across his lips. "You... We... are not going to let your brother spoil our lives, are we? So although we do not yet know how to resolve the situation, we *do* know that we will. Do we not?"

His smile held tenderness... and something else. That expression she'd seen in the storm. She felt suddenly breathless.

"We will resolve it somehow." One hand came up to cup her face and he bent his head until his mouth met hers. It was a strange feeling at first, lovely, but nothing to the warmth that spread through her when her lips parted and the kiss deepened. The hard pressure of his chest against hers, and his hands on her back and in her hair, felt… exciting. Something with the promise of much more.

Jack reluctantly pulled himself away at the sound of a throat being cleared. Loudly. And he felt himself blushing like a schoolboy at the sight of George Morton's raised brows.

"I do hope the two of you have some happy news for me," he said, in a voice that almost sounded stern, but not quite.

"Happy intentions, sir, rather than news. The matter is not straightforward."

"I sense a tale to be told," Morton said. "Best come into the library. Anne and Kitty are likely to return at any moment, and I would rather discuss the matter without their raptures."

Raptures? But Morton had left the room already, Clara behind him, so Jack had to follow.

"A plain tale, if you please," Morton said, when the three of them were seated.

Jack told his story, twice. The second time, at Morton's insistence, he gave all the details of his father's wishes, and the parts of the will pertaining to himself. Morton nodded at intervals.

"Tell me, Captain, would you be offering for Clara if your father were still alive?"

Would he? The question was no longer relevant, but he had been thinking of doing so even before his father died.

"Yes. Why should the two of us be made unhappy to satisfy my father's sense of what is due to the family?" He glanced at Clara, who was looking at her hands folded in her lap. "And now Father has gone, family duty no longer applies. My brother's actions have negated any obligation I might have felt to conform to his wishes."

"And you, Clara. Does the fact that you are likely to be estranged from your husband's family matter?"

Clara shook her head. "You know that a title, or titled relatives, were Mama's ambition, Uncle. Never mine."

"There remains the matter of making a living, sir," Jack said. "As Clara pointed out, my brother could still adversely affect my army career."

"If you were in the King's army, yes."

The prospect of selling his services to some other country did not sit well with him—but what other army was there? Then his eye was caught by the tiger rug.

The East India Company had an army—serving there would still be serving his country, in a way.

"Would someone like my brother have influence in the East India Company's army?"

Morton smiled. "He may or may not, but *I* have a great deal of influence there. I understand they are expanding the army, and a man with your experience would be welcome. You might be able to join as a major, or even higher. Should I make enquiries on your behalf?"

"I..." He was about to accept, but asking Clara to share a life in India with him was very different from returning to the Colonies. Hot and disease-ridden, from what he had heard.

"I would love to see India," she said, as if she had read his mind.

"That is not your only option, Stanlake," Morton said. "You are a landowner, don't forget."

"Charles will not release those estates."

"He will if the law requires it."

"That might take years, and money I do not have," Jack objected.

"Years, yes. But if you had an agent in England, with a power of attorney to deal with the matter on your behalf—what then?"

Could it be as easy as that?

"I would be willing to act in that capacity, if you wish," Morton went on. "I will check the exact terms of the will at Doctor's Commons, but if it is as you say, then I am prepared to take the risk of losing. Call it a joint venture, if you will." He stood. "I will leave the two of you to discuss your options."

· · ·

Clara felt as dazed as Jack looked. "It seems that Uncle George *can* help."

He didn't appear so sure. "How much do you know about India?"

"Not a great deal. Not yet, at least. But I would love to find out." She thought he would tell her it wasn't a suitable place for women, so his next words surprised her.

"We may get there and you—or I, I suppose—find we do not like it after all. Or you may become ill."

She went to stand beside him and put a hand on his arm. "Jack?"

He took her hands. "India looks impressive, doesn't it, in the illustrations you see in books—palatial buildings, exotic clothing... But they don't show the heat and the flies, the diseases, hostile natives. I don't want to risk your health—"

"There were hostile natives aplenty in the Colonies, and disease is everywhere. Besides, what of yourself? I will have to worry about you dying in battle in addition to all those other dangers. It is a foolish thing, falling in love with a soldier, but it is too late for me to think of that now."

His fingers tightened on hers. "You do love me, then?"

How could a man like him appear so uncertain? "Of course I do; did I not say so?" She moved a step closer. "Jack, if India does not agree with us, we will decide together what to do. And whatever we do, your brother will not bother us any longer."

"I will have won in more ways than escaping his influence," he said, with a wry smile. "Not only will he have no power over me, but your uncle will wrest my estates from his grasp."

"And you are marrying against his wishes," she added.

"Your wishes are the important ones here, and mine." And to her great delight, he proceeded to demonstrate again how their wishes for each other would be satisfied.

EPILOGUE

alcutta, India, three years later

Clara stoppered her bottle of ink and left the pages to dry thoroughly, weighted down against the gentle wafting of the ceiling fan. That was her letter to Uncle George ready to be sent on the next merchantman, together with a parcel of fabric samples and carved trinkets. She would enclose Jack's letter to Will with it—Uncle George had worked out a way to get an occasional missive to the lad without the earl finding out. Jack would have liked to write to Alfred as well, but couldn't be sure that he wouldn't tell his father.

She smoothed the fine muslin of her gown—scandalously thin if she were to wear it in public, especially without stays and stockings. But this was her private room, and only her ayah would see her like this. And Jack, of course.

Kitty—now Mrs Templeman—had written that the fabric was proving popular for married ladies, and Clara had laughed at the turn of phrase. She saw the way Jack's eyes lit up when she wore it in the bedchamber, and wondered if Kitty had seen the same expression on her husband's face. Kitty's last letter had carried the news that her husband had at last bought a house in the countryside. Now she could get on with making a rose garden and putting down roots, just in time for the birth of her first child. That missive had been dated four months ago, so Clara was probably already an aunt.

Uncle George's letter had said only that importing the fabric had been very profitable, and would she please concentrate on finding more suppliers of new goods. She was planning a trip with Jack to Dacca when he had some leave—it would be lovely to spend time together, and would also allow her to investigate the production there of muslins, dimities, and calicos. Dacca was reputed to be where the best examples of such fabrics were to be obtained. She would visit the bazaar there, too, in the hope of discovering another craftsman like the one who had carved the ivory elephant on her desk. He now worked with jewels and other rich materials beyond his wildest dreams, and had an increasing number of employees—and Uncle George had an exclusive supplier of ornamental brooches, snuff boxes, and paperweights that were making a tidy profit. Business was so much more interesting than growing roses!

Jack was due back in an hour, so it was time she dressed for the governor's party. She was moving in higher circles than she'd anticipated. On reaching India, Jack hadn't spent long with his initial regiment. He'd shown an aptitude for dealing with native officials and rulers, and had quickly been seconded to the governor's office here in Calcutta. That change had given her the chance to develop her business interests, so both of them were happy at the way things had turned out. She wouldn't be surprised if Jack eventually rose to a high position within the governance of the East India Company.

On her way to her bedchamber Clara looked into the little room they used as a nursery. George was asleep beneath the mosquito netting, one thumb stuck firmly in his mouth. The nursemaid sitting in the corner with some mending bobbed her head—all was well—and Clara crept out quietly. Their son had exceedingly powerful lungs, and she had no desire for him to demonstrate the fact now.

Her ayah was finishing her hair when Jack came into the room. The ayah placed the last pins, then left them.

"You look lovely, as always." Jack stood behind her, his hand playing with one of the ringlets draped over her shoulder.

She slapped his hand away with a laugh and turned to face him. "Don't make Kala have to do my hair again. You're earlier than I expected."

"I am. We have enough time to go via the river, if you are ready? It will be cooler."

"That would be lovely." Cooler, and also more peaceful than travelling the crowded streets in a carriage.

Jack eyed the muslin gown lying across the bed. "You can put that on again when we get home," he said, lifting a fold of the filmy fabric, with a look in his eyes that made her shiver with anticipation.

"I'm sure that can be arranged." Although it was what came after wearing the gown that they were both anticipating.

THE

CUSTOMS AND HABITS

OF THE

WOMEN OF INDIA

with particular notes on the ſtyles
of clothing and coſmetics

by C. STANLAKE

author of
The Caſte Syſtem Explained
Life in a Seraglio
Anecdotes of a Year in Madras
and
The Methods of Manufacture of Indian Muſlins

LONDON

PRINTED FOR THOS. LONGMAN

PATERNOSTER ROW

1778

AFTERWORD

A Question of Duty is a prequel novella for the Marstone series.

Seventeen years after the events in this story, the Earl of Marstone's elder son has died, leaving Will as his heir. The earl is determined that his brother Jack will not inherit the title under any circumstances.

Sauce for the Gander (Book 1 in the *Marstone Series*) is the story of what happens when he attempts to ensure this.

All four full-length novels in the *Marstone Series* are available as a box set.

JAYNE DAVIS

KING GEORGE'S MAN

A GEORGIAN ROMANCE

ACKNOWLEDGMENTS

Copyediting & proofreading: Sue Davison

Cover design: P Johnson

Thanks to my critique partners on Scribophile for comments and suggestions, particularly Leslie and Jim.

Thanks also to Alpha readers Tina, Melissa, Helen N and Cilla, and Beta readers Anu, Barbara, Carole, Claire, Corinne, Doris, Frances, Georgianna, Julie, Kristen, Leigh, Lesley, Margaret, Melanie, Nicky, Patricia, Safina, Sarah M, Sue C, Sue W, and Wendy.

MAP

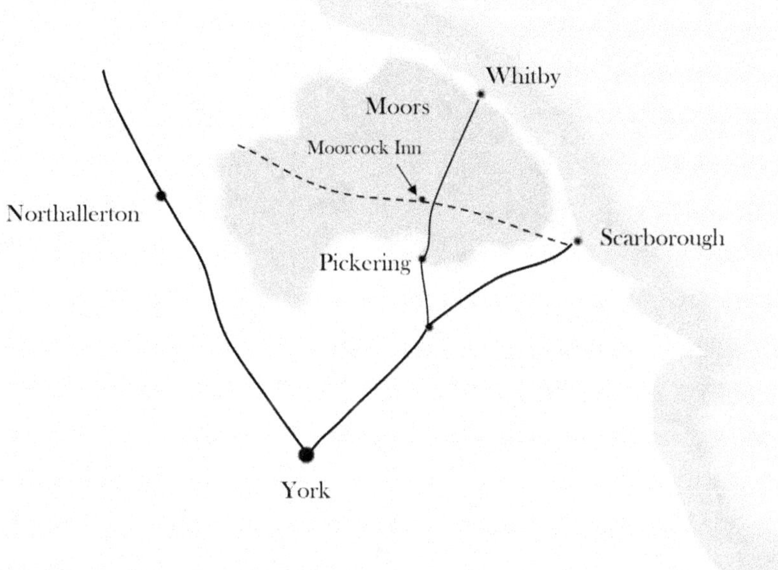

Some of the places and roads mentioned in the story.
The inn is fictional.

CHAPTER 1

The Moorcock Inn, North York Moors, October 1755

Nell Mason arched her back to ease its ache, and settled into the chair by the kitchen fire, grateful that she wasn't expected to clean the public room as well as the kitchen. Her uncle was snoring in his bed upstairs and the inn's customers had staggered off to their homes across the moor; she could be still for a while. Light from the oil lamp glinted off the wet patches on the newly mopped floor. These few moments of peace she spent in the warmth of the fire each night helped her relax before climbing the stairs to her room.

"I don't know why you bother. No-one cares if the floor is clean." Nell's cousin Bett Weaver stood in the doorway, her long hair flowing in glossy black waves down her back and her lips a brighter red than usual.

"A clean floor means fewer rats. I have standards, even if Uncle Silas doesn't."

Bett shrugged. "Much good they do you. You look tired—why don't you go to bed?"

Nell knew better than to think that Bett was being considerate. She wanted Nell out of the way and looked as if she intended to lean on the door jamb until Nell had gone.

"I'll need to bank the fire first." Nell poked the glowing coals to the back of the hearth and slowly shovelled ash onto them, suppressing a smirk when Bett's foot started to tap impatiently. Bett and Uncle Silas never missed an opportunity to mock her, so she relished even the tiniest victories.

Nell lit a tallow candle from the lamp then headed for the door, waiting pointedly until Bett got out of her way. The stairs creaked as she climbed them, and then she was in her tiny room, cold from the draught entering around the ill-fitting casement. Although tired, she put the candle holder on the chair and sat on the bed. She could think here, without the distraction of Bett's presence.

Bett's loose hair and reddened lips suggested she had an assignation with Gentleman Jones. Not a gentleman, despite his name, but called so because he aped the gentry with his elaborate coats and fancy hats—some of them stolen from the people he held up on the King's highways. Without those clothes, and the hard expression in his eyes, he would be unremarkable.

Jones spent many an evening at the Moorcock drinking with the local quarry workers—men who surely could not afford to drink away their meagre wages or buy meals here. The coast was only ten miles to the east, and Nell suspected that her uncle not only bought smuggled brandy and wine, but was also involved in organising the quarrymen to help transport the goods. That would explain why Uncle Silas left several of the guest bedrooms unfurnished, and the fact that he always had enough money for buying food and ale in spite of the few customers that stopped in this remote spot. What need to earn a living honestly when it could be more easily made by other means?

What Bett expected from Jones' visit was obvious—he had been to her room before, but always after an evening in the public room. But why would he come this late if all he wanted was a quick tumble? There must be more to it than that.

Uncle Silas' involvement in smuggling was bad enough, but what if Jones' visit were linked to a highway robbery?

Nell had a home here for as long as she was useful, or until Uncle Silas came to the attention of the law. She had no intention of staying in this place any longer than she had to, but without a character and with only limited cooking skills, she would find it hard to obtain a position elsewhere. There was a little money hidden in her mattress, saved from the occasional coin that came her way from customers, but there was not yet enough to risk leaving here to look for work.

Nell had to find out why Jones was coming. If he only wanted the usual interlude with Bett, she need not worry. But she could be in trouble if he intended to involve them in something criminal. Bett never hesitated to blame her own breakages or spills on Nell, and both she and Silas would surely try to implicate Nell in something more serious if it might reduce the consequences to themselves. She would have to choose between leaving or risking arrest if Jones' plans were discovered. Neither was an attractive option.

She went to the window. The moon was a half circle in the clear sky, and soon to set, but there was light enough to make the track westwards through the heather shine pale. Jones might not come from that direction, of course, but the sound of a horse walking across the cobbles in front of the inn would announce his arrival. Nell pulled the chair close to the window, then blew the candle out and wrapped herself in the blanket from the bed before settling down to watch and wait.

At last she heard the clop of hooves on stone. Throwing the blanket off, she peered out of the window. She could make out only the dark shape of a rider dismounting by the door. There was a faint tap as he knocked with the handle of his whip, then the creak of hinges. A pool of lamplight spilled out of the inn door, glimmering on the rider's silver-trimmed hat as he tied the horse by the door and went inside. It was Gentleman Jones, as Nell had guessed.

Nell crept to the door and along the landing, making her way by feel and stepping over the boards that creaked. Her uncle's snores carried through his bedroom door as she passed. Then she was at the stairs, feeling her way down in the dark with one hand on the wall. She stopped to listen at the bottom.

Bett and Jones had gone into the public room; a sliver of light shining into the passage showed that the door hadn't been latched properly. Nell crept closer. They weren't making an effort to keep their voices down. What need, with Uncle Silas snoring away upstairs and Gibson, the potman, likely in his usual inebriated sleep in his room at the other end of the building?

"...your father in his cups as usual... tell him... important, Bett. Listen, will you?" Jones' voice was sharp, impatient.

"I thought you came to see *me*?" Nell could imagine Bett's pout that would accompany the wheedling tone. "You do want me, don't you?"

His voice was softer this time. "Of course I do, love."

There was silence for a while. Nell was beginning to wonder if Jones really had only come for a tumble, but then Bett spoke again.

"Oh, don't stop, Robbie!"

"Bett, you have to listen." Jones hadn't raised his voice, but there was a note of command in it. "I'll be back in a sennight, if the sky's clear, or the first clear night after that. Tell your father to—"

A yowl and clatter from beyond the shuttered window interrupted him—the stable cat? Nell hurried towards the kitchen, wanting to be out of sight if Jones came into the passage to investigate. She stood behind the kitchen door in silence, hardly breathing, straining her ears.

There was no sound other than the wind moaning softly around the house, so she stepped into the hall again. There was also silence from the front room—it should be safe to listen again.

Jones was speaking. "...what I told you. Make sure he cleans the place himself. No-one else. And he must have everything ready next week. There's a lot depending on this."

Cleaning? Uncle Silas? Nell couldn't imagine it.

"Of course I'll tell him, Robbie. And I'll have my things ready." Then her voice became lower. "Is that all you came for, to tell me?"

"Come here." Jones's voice sounded rough. Nell tiptoed towards the stairs. She was not going to listen to what was about to follow.

A quarter of an hour later, as near as she could guess, Nell heard hoofbeats cross the yard. Through the window, Jones was a mere moving shadow against the pale line of the track leading westwards, then he vanished behind the stand of trees not far from the inn.

Although Nell watched for some time, Jones did not reappear on the part of the track visible beyond the trees. There was enough moonlight, and her eyes were sharp enough to see at that distance, which meant he must have left the track.

A movement closer to the inn caught her eye, but it was brief. It could even have been the cat. With a sigh, she pulled off her cap and unlaced her gown. In the morning, when she wasn't so tired, she'd try to work out what Jones might have told Bett to do.

Nell set the bread to rise, then stood still to listen. Although she'd been up and working for over an hour, no-one else was stirring. Not even Tim, the lad who slept above the stables and who should now be sweeping out the public room and cleaning the tables.

She sighed—it would have been nice to enjoy a little peace before Bett and her uncle were up, but she should go and wake Tim. Uncle Silas wouldn't be happy if he came down and found the cleaning hadn't been done. Not that Silas really cared about cleanliness, but he did demand obedience.

The sun had risen, but the air was still cold as Nell crossed the yard. Dobbin raised his head when she entered the stable, but nothing else stirred.

"Tim!" She waited, then shouted louder. "Tim, wake up. You're late!"

This time there was a muffled response from the loft. Nell waited until she heard movement before hurrying back to the kitchen. There were still no sounds from upstairs, so she laid the fire in the public room and lit it, then collected empty tankards and wiped the tables. Tim would have enough to do getting the room swept before Uncle Silas came down.

She left the tankards in the scullery and began to mix the porridge. As she swung the pot over the fire, footsteps sounded from above, and voices, although Nell could not make out the words. Was Bett passing on Gentleman Jones' orders?

Tim arrived, bleary eyed and with hair sticking out in all directions as usual. Nell handed him a mug of small beer. "You'd best get the public room swept out now."

Silas' voice boomed again, angry, and Nell thought she heard a cry from Bett. Tim winced, gulped the beer down, and took the broom from behind the door. Nell hoped he could finish the job in time. Uncle Silas had brought Tim here from the workhouse two years ago, not long after Nell's mother died. He'd been a scrawny lad; now he was filling out a little even though he was never likely to be tall. He and Gibson were the only friendly people Nell had around her now.

Tim hadn't been gone long when Bett slipped into the kitchen, one side of her scowling face red. She picked up a cloth and took it into the scullery, and the pump squeaked. When she returned, she was holding a wet cloth against her cheek.

"What's got into Uncle Silas?" Nell asked.

"Mind your own bloody business!" Bett spat. "I'll have my breakfast in here today."

Nell carried on cutting yesterday's bread—it would do for breakfast with beef dripping smeared over it.

Bett dragged a chair from the table and slumped into it. "I *said*, I'll have my breakfast here."

Nell raised the knife and pointed it to the shelf above Bett's head. "Bowls." Then to the fire. "Porridge. Help yourself."

"You're getting above yourself again, Nell. You're in *my* house now."

Uncle Silas' inn, not Bett's house. Nell looked pointedly at the cloth Bett still held against her face, but didn't say anything.

Footsteps sounded on the stairs, then there was a stream of curses, echoing clearly along the passage from the public room, and the sound of a table or chair overturning. Nell screwed her eyes shut. Tim was likely getting a beating, but there was nothing she could do about it. Trying to help would only earn her bruises as well.

She finished cutting the bread and set a couple of slices on a plate. When the sounds from the public room stopped, she spooned porridge into a bowl and filled a tankard with small beer.

"Knew you'd see sense." Bett's smile wasn't pleasant.

Nell put the items on a tray. "This is for Uncle Silas. Unless you want me to tell him that you ate his breakfast?" She pushed the door open with her bottom and headed for the public room.

Uncle Silas sat at his usual table near the fireplace and scowled as Nell entered. There was no sign of Tim, and two chairs lay on their sides. Nell set out the breakfast things wordlessly, and slipped out of the room again before Silas could speak.

Bett was eating her breakfast at the kitchen table. Although Nell was hungry, she didn't want to sit across from Bett's sulky face, so she went to inspect the meat hanging in the larder. The side of mutton would be made into stew after she'd eaten breakfast. There was still most of a ham left, and a brace of hares. Not much, but Gibson was due to go for more supplies tomorrow.

Bett had left while Nell was in the pantry. As Nell ladled porridge into her bowl, Gibson passed through the kitchen on his way to the privy. He looked as bleary-eyed as on most mornings, his greying hair, frown lines, and dark shadows beneath his eyes making him look older than his fifty years or so. He took his coat from the hook behind the scullery door and vanished out to the yard.

Nell filled another bowl with porridge and set it on the table ready for Gibson when he returned. The potman drank a great deal in the evenings but, unlike Uncle Silas, he neither became inebriated during the day nor bad-tempered when in his cups.

She sat for a moment staring at her meal, longing for the break-fasts of her childhood. She could almost taste the soft white bread, spread with butter and strawberry jam; feel the delicate china of Mama's teacups. Dinners with fresh fish, or chicken in a creamy sauce, with sweetmeats and fruit to follow. And, more importantly, Mama and Papa with her.

"You all right, Nell?" Gibson asked, when he returned and settled his angular frame on a chair.

"Just remembering how things used to be."

Gibson nodded, and began to eat. He was a man of few words, but those words were usually kind. He had already been working at the inn when Nell came to live here with her mother. She had been four-teen when Papa died and Mama had been forced to ask her brother to assist them. Assistance that had been grudgingly provided. Gibson had helped them learn the tasks that Silas had demanded in return for their keep, and covered up a few mishaps that would have earned her uncle's wrath.

Silas had turned off the woman who used to cook for him and told Mama that it was her job now, and that brat of hers—Nell—could help. It wasn't only grief and work that had worn Mama down, but the jeers at how she'd come down in the world—from a banker's wife to the cook in a moorland inn. Look at her now, he'd said, she who had always thought herself better than Silas because of her fancy clothes and fancy ways. Although Nell couldn't recall Mama ever saying any such thing.

Then, one snow-bound night three years after they'd arrived at the Moorcock, Mrs Mason had not woken up. Nell didn't know if she'd suffered an apoplexy or just decided not to struggle any longer. Nell hadn't been given much time to grieve—at seventeen, she had become the Moorcock's cook. The two years since had felt long indeed. Even when she did escape this place, her life would still be filled with the drudgery of everyday tasks. So different from days spent at her lessons, or talking to Papa about the history and poetry he loved.

Nell picked up her spoon. Best not to think of such things. If she was unhappy, she did at least have enough to eat.

Later, as she chopped and fried mutton and onions, and put them on to simmer, Nell's thoughts turned to what she had overheard.

Cleaning was an odd thing for Jones to demand of her uncle. It could not be anything in the inn—Uncle Silas never did that himself, and Nell couldn't see any reason for Jones to order him to. Had Jones done something criminal nearby and wanted Silas to remove the evidence?

What about the instruction to 'have everything ready'? Nell guessed that was a matter of organising men to move smuggled goods. Such things could be stored nearby, most likely in an abandoned quarry. But Silas wouldn't have been in such a foul mood if the order Bett passed on had been only about moving barrels or crates. And Bett had said she would have her things ready—was she planning to run off with Jones?

Silas was still out of temper when he stormed into the kitchen a little while later, his bulk seeming to fill the room. He didn't stop, but went on out through the back door, leaving a cold draught swirling around her legs. She went to close it, pausing to take in the blue sky above and the moor beyond the stable, the purple of the heather now faded.

He wrenched the outer door open again only a few minutes later, a spade and a brush in his hands, and his face even more thunderous than before. "Where the hell's that bloody boy gone?"

"I haven't seen him since he went to sweep the front room."

To Nell's relief, Silas merely swore and stamped back out into the yard. Careful not to be spotted watching, Nell went into the public room and looked out of the window. Silas set off along the track to the west—the way Jones had gone last night.

What was out there that needed a spade and a brush?

CHAPTER 2

Lieutenant Tobias Bourne stopped his hired horse as he reached the top of the slope. The sun was fully up now, but had no warmth in it yet. The bitter east wind made his eyes water, and he tucked his scarf more securely around his neck. Deep breaths of the chilly air helped to clear his head. The third bottle of wine last night had probably been a mistake, but he hadn't seen his childhood best friend for ten years and they'd had a lot of talking to do.

Well, Toby had done most of the talking. And what a change in William! The two of them had been ripe for all kinds of mischief in their youth, but where Toby had continued the adventurous life in the army, William had settled down with a woman from the village and had recently taken over his father's smithy. A pretty lass, William's wife, and now there were several children as well. There was some attraction in knowing there was a comfortable bed to be had every night, and a woman to warm it, but the idea of staying in one place all his life…? No, that was not for him. He'd fought in Europe, and been lucky enough to earn promotion in the field. Hunting down Jacobites had been less satisfying, but he'd enjoyed the wild loneliness of the highlands. And after this leave, his regiment was to go to the Colonies

—it would be a new land to see, and a new experience to fight alongside Britain's Indian allies.

He kicked his horse into motion again. He had all day to get back to Scarborough, but the air was too cold to linger long. Toby didn't know these moors, but this was the way he'd ridden yesterday on the way to William's house. As long as he kept heading a little south of east, he couldn't go far wrong finding his way back.

Toby's thoughts turned to the delectable Miss Delaney, and the dance she had promised him at tonight's assembly. He had first met her last week, when the breeze off the sea had pulled her parasol from her hand; Toby had been in just the right place to catch it and return it to her. And then to be captivated by her green eyes beneath long lashes; her porcelain skin, only slightly flushed by the breeze. She had accepted his arm for the remainder of her walk, leaving the maid to trail along behind them, and he had basked in her admiring glances and charming laugh.

An hour or so after noon, he began to wonder if his direction-finding was working. He couldn't be far out of his way, but he didn't recognise the dale below him, opening out towards the south. He turned northwards to stick to the high ground around the head of the valley, and rode on. If he met another traveller, he would ask for directions.

He came upon the inn unexpectedly, skirting a stand of trees to find a stone building ahead, its sign creaking to and fro in the wind. The paint on the sign was peeling, but there was enough of it left to make out a crude depiction of a grouse, and the lettering could have been Moorcock. There was no-one about, but a thin plume of smoke rose from the chimney, instantly scattered by the wind.

His stomach was telling him it was time to eat, and the horse would appreciate a rest, so he turned off the track. He headed for the outbuildings behind the inn and dismounted, waiting for someone to come and take the horse.

No-one did, so he opened the door of what he took to be the stable. It was, for there were already three horses inside. The straw on the floor was in need of changing, but a net of fresh hay hung on the wall and a bucket by the door was full of water. A ladder at one end led up to an open hatch in the ceiling. It would do, but he should check that he could get some refreshment here before stabling his horse.

An untidy collection of ale barrels stood outside the back of the building. A door opened as he approached; the woman who came out looked young, perhaps twenty or so, her hair concealed beneath a cap. She clutched a shawl about her shoulders, and a stained apron covered her skirts.

"Can I get a drink here?" he called as he walked towards her. "And food?"

She nodded, a strand of brown hair escaping from her cap. "Main door's round the front. I'm afraid you'll have to see to your horse yourself." The door closed again before he could thank her.

Shrugging, he loosened the saddle girth and allowed the horse to drink a little water, then settled it inside the building. Draughts whistled around the edges of the door, but it was considerably warmer here than outside.

It was warmer still in the inn. The iron-studded front door gave onto a dim passage, but a door to one side opened into a room with tables, chairs, and a blazing fire. A corpulent man with grizzled hair and unshaven chin sat at a table in one corner, a large mug in front of him and a scowl on his face. From the lines on his forehead and around his mouth, it was a habitual expression. The two men at the next table were talking in quiet voices over mugs of ale and used plates.

Toby walked over to the fire and dropped his hat on an empty table near to it. A thin man with greying hair levered himself off a stool by the counter in one corner, and Toby crossed the room to order ale. "I want food, too. What do you have?"

"Bett!" The voice came from the large man across the room, making Toby jump.

The potman shrugged. "Take a seat. Bett'll tell you."

It wasn't the woman he'd seen who responded to the call, but a buxom lass with black hair in a loose arrangement with curls draping over one shoulder. She paused in the doorway, her dark eyes moving from Toby's head to his boots, then her red lips curved into a smile and she swayed towards his table.

"What can I get for you, love?"

"Ale, and something to eat. What's on offer?"

"Mutton stew."

Toby waited for her to list some other choices, but she merely raised one brow and folded her arms.

"I'll have that, then." He was here now; he might as well eat.

Bett nodded and left the room, returning after only a moment to collect two mugs of ale from the potman. She put both on the table, and sat down across from him. "Going far?" She leaned forward, the thin kerchief around her neck doing little to hide the tops of the breasts pushed up by her bodice.

"Scarborough." He drank some ale; it was thin and too bitter, but it did help quench his thirst.

"Have business there, do you?"

Toby merely grunted. The calculating way her eyes lingered on his chest made him wonder if she was assessing the quality of his coat. The large man watched with narrowed eyes.

"We don't get many passing travellers." She sipped from her mug.

"I imagine not." Was she merely flirting, or offering more? There were times when he would have enjoyed finding out, but not today— not with the prospect of Miss Delaney's sweet smiles and delicate blushes to greet him this evening.

She pouted. "Don't say much, do you?"

"No." He took another mouthful of ale, glad when she was distracted by someone behind her. The woman he'd seen earlier rested one corner of a laden tray on the table. Toby pushed his mug out of the way as she put a platter of bread in front of him. She was struggling with the bowl of stew, and Bett made no move to help, so he reached out and took it himself.

"Thank you, ma'am."

The woman looked into his face, brows raised in surprise, then she smiled.

"It smells good." He breathed the savoury aroma of meat and fried onions, and prodded the contents of the bowl with his fork. The whitish lumps were pieces of potato and turnip, not globs of fat as he had first thought.

"Bett!" The call came from the large man. "More ale!"

Bett picked up her mug and flounced across the room.

"Thank goodness." Toby had muttered the words beneath his breath, and was surprised to hear a chuckle. The woman's smile widened, the smooth skin beside her brown eyes crinkling. Her face, shiny with heat from the kitchen, showed genuine amusement—a far more attractive expression than Bett's sultry pout.

"Enjoy your meal," she said. "There's plenty of stew if you want more, but only cheese and some apples to follow." She nodded at his mug. "Bett'll get you more of that if you want it, although I'm told the brandy is much better quality than the ale."

"This will be sufficient, thank you. Am I on the road for Scarborough here?"

"If you're heading east, yes. Keep straight on when you get to the cross. I'm not sure where you turn once the track leaves the moors, but you can ask again." She picked up the tray and crossed to the other occupied tables.

An unusual woman to find here—her speech was more refined than Bett's, with little trace of the local accent . He shrugged, and concentrated on his food.

The stew tasted as good as it smelled, and the bread, although coarse, was fresh enough. He did not linger over his meal. An odd inn, he reflected as he rode away. Only the cook seemed to be doing any real work; there wasn't even a boy in the stables. It surely could not attract much custom from passing travellers, not with such limited fare on offer. Certainly no-one would go out of their way to call. But it wasn't his business, and he still had ten miles or more to cover before darkness fell.

∽

Nell hung her apron on the peg behind the scullery door and donned her cloak. She was worried about Tim; how badly had Uncle Silas hurt him this morning? She hadn't seen him since then, and this was her only chance to look for him.

She had to go now, while the inn was quiet; some of the men from the quarry a few miles away would be arriving soon and she'd be needed to cook.

"Tim?" she called inside the stable, her voice only loud enough for Tim to know that it wasn't Uncle Silas looking for him. When there was no response, she kilted up her skirts and climbed the ladder to the loft. Enough light came through the small window for her to see Tim's blankets folded on his straw pallet, but nothing else. He wasn't there, and neither were his coat or his spare shirt and breeches. Had he finally decided that returning to the workhouse was preferable to staying here?

The sounds of this morning's beating hadn't gone on long, and Tim obviously hadn't been hurt badly enough to prevent him climbing the ladder to get his things, or walking away from the inn. That was a small relief.

Back on the ground, she opened the stable door a little way and checked that no-one was in the yard before creeping out and going around to the front of the inn. If Uncle Silas knew that Tim had run off, he might go after him.

Tim had come from a workhouse to the north of the moors, but the nearest towns were south and east. Nell hoped he'd gone to one of those—if he'd left early this morning, he might reach his destination before nightfall. Walking in any other direction would mean him spending a night on the moor, and that could be dangerous in this cold weather.

Nell strode east along the track, hoping to find some trace of his passage—although what that might be, she didn't know. A footprint in a muddy patch, perhaps. The only people she'd noticed passing the inn today had been on horseback. Perhaps the traveller who hadn't appreciated Bett's attentions might have given him a ride?

She smiled to herself as her brisk pace helped to ease some of the aches from bending over a chopping board and cooking pot for too long. She wasn't used to being thanked, and the stranger's smile had lifted her spirits for a while. So, too, had Bett's sulk at being ignored by an attractive man. For attractive he had been, with hair as black as Bett's, neatly tied back, and a rather weathered face. Many of the men here were unshaven, but on him a day's growth of beard looked appealing rather than unkempt. He was a head taller than her, and broad to match—with muscle, not fat. A pity he was only passing by. A smile and a kind word now and then would help her get through her days.

She stopped at the stone cross—a frequent destination for her when she had a little time to herself. It was half as tall again as she was, the letters carved into it now blurred by wind and time. It reminded her of Papa—he had never been here, but old things like this had always fascinated him.

The sun was nearing the western horizon, painting the sky in pink and orange. It was time to turn back. When she reached the inn, Nell slipped in the back door and hung up her cloak—only to find her uncle sitting at the kitchen table, his mouth turned down and brow creased.

"Where have you been? Your place is here, in the kitchen!" He banged a fist on the table.

Nell winced. "I went for a walk." As she did most days when it wasn't raining, but it was better not to say that.

"Why? Where did you go?"

"Along the track." Nell was taken aback by the suspicion and anger in his voice. "To the cross."

His scowl lightened. "Get me some of that stew. Bring it to the public room."

Nell went to the pot hanging above the fire and ladled out the last of the mutton stew. An unappetising skin had formed on the surface; Nell stirred it in instead of skimming it off. Uncle Silas wouldn't notice.

Back in the kitchen after giving Silas his meal, she started frying more onions for a new batch of stew. Would telling her uncle she'd walked to the west have made him angrier? She was sure now that something was hidden out there. Jones had set off in that direction but turned off the track. If he had been heading for somewhere north or south of here, it was far easier to go east a little way then turn at the cross to take the road that linked Pickering and Whitby. Riding through the heather at night was like to get the horse injured. Jones might be a vicious thief, but he wasn't stupid.

Could Tim's absence be connected to whatever Silas was doing with Jones? If the shadow she'd seen last night had been Tim, then he, too, might have overheard Jones. That could explain why he'd over-slept this morning. She hoped he was safe somewhere.

She wanted to know what was afoot—partly out of curiosity, but mainly so she could escape this place if the law were likely to come down on them. If the chance came, she might look to the west of the inn.

But she must not get caught.

CHAPTER 3

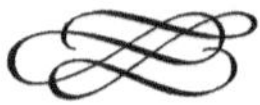

*A*unt Em was waiting for Toby at the bottom of the stairs, inspecting him from his powdered hair to his polished shoes. "You look very fine, Toby!"

Not too bad, he hoped. His one good suit was out of fashion, but he couldn't afford to replace it. His cream waistcoat set off the deep burgundy coat and breeches, and the embroidered trim prevented it from appearing too severe.

"As do you, Auntie." Although he'd been away from home and in the army for ten years, that childhood term had stuck.

Emily Bourne had been a mother to him since his parents had succumbed to the typhus when he was only five. There had been enough money to purchase a commission for Toby, but the Bournes were not wealthy, by any means. Uncle Robert had died not long after Toby joined the army, but although his income had ceased with his death, his uncle had enough put by for Aunt Em to purchase this boarding house. It wasn't in the best part of town, but she kept a clean, respectable establishment and was never short of customers.

Aunt Em's hair was greying beneath the sprinkling of powder, and her face was becoming more lined. She was wearing her best gown for tonight's assembly—a dark green brocade with a paler underskirt the colour of primroses, and lace around the neck and sleeves.

"Shall I fetch a chair for you?" Toby pressed his lips together as he waited for the expected response. But instead of rapping his arm with her fan and telling him that she wasn't yet too old to walk half a mile, she hesitated.

"No, but I might need one on the way back."

"Auntie, are you unwell?" She hadn't shown any sign of it in the week he'd been here, but she'd never been one to coddle herself.

She shook her head. "Just getting old. Come, let us go."

Toby took her cloak from her arm and arranged it on her shoulders, earning a nod of thanks. Then he ushered her through the door and gave her his arm as they set off downhill towards the assembly rooms. The sky was still clear, although the breeze was cold.

"I'm not unwell, Toby, but I am beginning to stiffen up and tire more easily. I have been wondering about taking on another girl to help run the house."

Although relieved that she wasn't ill, Toby didn't like to think of her struggling. "Auntie, if you need me to come home permanently, do say so." He didn't want to give up his army career, such as it was, but Aunt Em had looked after him when he needed it—and willingly, with love.

"Nonsense, Toby, I'm not at my last prayers just yet. And what would you do for a living? I can't see you running a boarding house."

Neither could he.

"Besides, if I need a man about the place, there's always Mr Everidge. I'm thinking he might be looking for a wife."

"What? The old man who always sits by the fire in your parlour?" He must be eighty if he was a day.

She chuckled. "No, silly, I'm not so desperate! His nephew, I mean; he owns the circulating library. I'd never be short of a book again."

He laughed. "That's all right then." But he might call in at the library and see what the younger Everidge was like. He didn't want Aunt Em tied to an unkind or parsimonious man when he would be half a world away and unable to help her.

The strains of a country dance mingled with the cries of seagulls as they mounted the steps to the building. Inside, the dancing was already under way. Toby helped his aunt off with her cloak and escorted her to a group of her friends gossiping in one corner. Aunt Em greeted them and introduced Toby, and they drew her into their circle.

"Go and have fun." She waved towards the dancers—or the refreshment room, he wasn't sure which. The gossip started again as soon as he moved away.

Miss Delaney had promised him a dance but hadn't specified which one, so he should find her before her entire evening was spoken for. He couldn't see her in the rows of dancers moving to and fro, although without knowing what she was wearing it was difficult to be sure. Most of the women wore their hair powdered, and half of them had their backs to him.

He strolled up the room towards the corner dais where the musicians sat, then down the other side. Miss Delaney wasn't dancing, but was part of a group of young men and women. Her green eyes were fixed on a fancily dressed man, one of her delicate hands resting on the pale green of her overskirt, the other toying with the lace at her neck. The man she was watching was around the same height as Toby, and perhaps a few years older, but there the resemblance ended. His coat was edged with a thick band of gold braid, and elaborate embroidery covered his waistcoat—a waistcoat that bulged out over a paunch. Toby edged closer, trying to hear what he was saying.

"...third villain ran off when he saw what had happened to the other two."

"Oh!" One of the younger ladies clasped her hands in front of her chest. "How brave you were, Colonel, to single-handedly deal with three of them!"

Colonel?

"Were the other two dead?" a young man asked.

"Nearly." The colonel looked around his audience, pausing briefly when he met Toby's gaze, then went on. "The one I'd run through was still living. He cursed my aim, and cursed Jones, too, for picking the wrong target."

"They weren't expecting someone like you," Miss Delaney breathed. "But you should not ride alone at night, sir! What if there had been more of them?"

The colonel smiled at her. A condescending smile, Toby thought savagely, but Miss Delaney merely sighed.

"I would have seen them all off, my dear Miss Delaney."

"Was it really Gentleman Jones who got away?"

"Running off like a coward!" another young man said. "I say, well done, sir!"

The colonel's smile froze for a moment. "Er, perhaps he thought I had another pistol. A strategic retreat, I'd say. But we are at an assembly—we should be dancing. Miss Delaney, would you do me the honour?"

"Delighted, Colonel." She took the colonel's hand as Toby stepped forward.

"Good evening, Miss Delaney. May I have the following dance? You granted me the honour when we walked together three days ago."

She looked at him, a small crease briefly forming between her brows, then she smiled and took Toby's breath away. "Lieutenant Bourne, how nice to see you again. You may indeed. I look forward to it." She bowed her head towards him before the colonel led her away.

Toby watched as she took her place in the dance, happy that she had remembered his name and granted the dance. One so lovely would have many admirers. But he should not give her smiles too much importance—however much he admired her, it could be nothing more than a pleasant interlude before he rejoined his regiment. Enticing though the prospect was of having her in his life and in his bed, Miss Delaney was too delicate to follow the drum, and he could not afford to keep her in England in the comfort she deserved. However, there was nothing stopping him enjoying her company while he was in Scarborough.

He had some time to wait for his dance. He could lean on the wall and watch the colonel flirting with Miss Delaney, or he could ensure that Aunt Em was comfortable. To that end, he fetched a glass of orgeat for her and port for himself, and wandered back to the circle of gossips.

"Oh, thank you, Toby," Aunt Em said. She gestured to an empty chair close by. "Why don't you bring that over and join us? Mrs Featherstone was telling us about the robbery."

That again? Would the colonel appear as heroic in someone else's tale? Probably, if they had got it from him. "I've already heard about the colonel's exploits," he said, about to turn away.

"The colonel? Maitland, you mean?"

"If that's the man dancing with Miss Delaney, yes."

Aunt Em peered past him. "Yes, that's Maitland. He has a large house to the north of the town. What has he to do with it?"

Toby pulled the empty chair closer and sat down. Perhaps this wasn't the same incident. "He was telling us how he fought off an attempted robbery on the road last night."

The women all turned to look at the colonel on the dance floor, and a babble of voices broke out.

"Another highwayman?"

"*Attempted* robbery, you say?"

"What happened?"

"I have no idea, madam," Toby said to this last, trying to keep the impatience from his voice. But their interest could be a help. "You should all go and ask him when this dance ends," he added encouragingly.

Beside him, Aunt Em gave a little snort of laughter, but then her expression sobered again. "We were talking of something more serious, Toby. Lord Lanchester's treasure."

That sounded interesting. "Tell me more."

"Lord Lanchester sent silver plate, money, and jewellery to his new manor house in an unmarked coach, with armed guards and two outriders."

Toby nodded. That sounded sensible, but clearly hadn't been effective.

"Yesterday it was going from York to Northallerton, but it didn't arrive. This morning, they found the coach and the bodies of the driver and the guards."

An admirably succinct account, Toby thought. And very different from Maitland's tale of derring-do. "What about the outriders?"

"I don't know."

"Bribed, I should think," another woman suggested. "Someone must have told the robbers about the treasure."

"Or the robbers were just lucky," Aunt Em said. "The outriders would be enough to indicate the travellers had some wealth."

"I'm glad I don't need to travel anywhere," the elderly lady beside Aunt Em said.

Toby stopped listening as the talk turned to ways of keeping safe when travelling. He'd never heard of Lord Lanchester and had no idea where his manor was, but the road from York to Northallerton crossed the flat ground to the west of the moors, thirty miles or more from here. The robbery was unlikely to affect anyone in Scarborough.

The music ended; Toby stood and bowed to the circle of women. "Now is your chance to find out what happened to Colonel Maitland, ladies."

He followed them to where the colonel stood beside Miss Delaney. Several of them started talking at once, leaving the colonel looking bewildered and Miss Delaney distinctly vexed.

"My dance, I believe, Miss Delaney?"

She turned her gaze on him and blinked. "Oh. Lieutenant Bourne." She smiled as she held her hand out, and they took their places as the next set was forming. The colonel sent a venomous glace at Toby before his attention was reclaimed by the gaggle of ladies about him.

"You seem to have made a conquest there," Toby said, while they waited for the music to start. "What regiment does the colonel command?"

"He is in charge of the local militia. They have such splendid uniforms when on duty, do they not?"

"Indeed they do." Plenty of braiding and lace, excellent for strutting around on parade.

"It's a pity he wasn't wearing it when he was waylaid. I'm sure

Gentleman Jones would have thought better of his attack had he known who his victim was."

"I'm sure he would," Toby lied. Militia men might get shot at by smugglers or hit by a stone in a riot, but they never had to face cannon fire or cavalry charges. But it would do no good to say so—and Maitland *might* have the courage and skills of a regular army officer.

"Their uniform would be splendid on you, Lieutenant," Miss Delaney said, her gaze lingering briefly on his shoulders and chest. "Although I expect your usual red coat is well enough."

"You look lovely yourself, Miss Delaney," Toby said, as the music started and he lost any further chance for a conversation. All he could do now was to bask in her smiles, and enjoy holding her hand when the dance brought them together. He should have complimented her on her gown or hair. Or anything, really. It was a shame the October cold prevented a brief tryst beneath the moonlight—for a kiss, if he were lucky—but Miss Delaney was likely to be too much in demand to permit that even had the weather been sufficiently warm.

"I hope to see you again, Miss Delaney," Toby said, bowing as the dance ended. She rewarded him with one last smile, before her hand was claimed by a young sprig wearing a pink coat.

He looked around the ballroom. There were no young ladies obviously in need of a partner, and Aunt Em was still talking away in her group of friends with every sign of enjoyment. He decided to try the punch.

Maitland was in the refreshment room holding forth to a crowd of admiring young men. Toby couldn't avoid overhearing how he and the curious addition of a chance-met companion had fired back, and gritted his teeth at the adoring glances. At least Maitland could not be courting Miss Delaney while he was boasting here.

"Only winged him, sadly." Maitland's voice carried well—too well. "A dead thief would have been better."

"Your punch, sir," the waiter said. Toby took the proffered glass.

"Oh, well done, sir. Hitting a moving target at night is not easy," one of Maitland's acolytes gushed.

Toby turned away, catching the eye of another man waiting for his punch just as Maitland's voice floated across the room again.

"I do my poor best. The other thief rode off."

Toby rolled his eyes and the stranger laughed. He was of an age with Aunt Em—a tall, thin man, finely dressed and bewigged.

"We haven't been introduced," he said, holding out his right hand. "Sir James Troughton."

"Lieutenant Bourne." Toby shook his hand. "Of His Majesty's 23rd Foot."

"Mrs Bourne's nephew, I understand."

"Yes, sir."

"She and my wife are friends. Your aunt speaks highly of you." Sir James looked towards Maitland's group, then back to Toby. "Maitland is quite the hero—by his own account, at least."

"So it would seem."

"Tell me, what did you think of his tale?" Sir James took out a snuff box and offered it.

Toby declined—he'd rather smoke the stuff than sniff it. "I didn't hear all of it, sir. I gather he was accosted on the road by highwaymen."

"A particularly inept bunch, from what I overheard."

There was that dry tone again, and Toby's interest sharpened. "He mentioned a Gentleman Jones."

"Notorious about these parts." Sir James nodded, taking a pinch of snuff. "Not a man to be crossed. If he was part of the group, Maitland is extremely lucky to still be alive."

Toby thought back to what he'd heard earlier. "His tale changes as he tells it, if I heard correctly."

"Becoming more heroic as the night wears on, I suppose."

"On the contrary, sir."

Sir James paused with his hand half-way to his face, then continued and inhaled the snuff. "That *is* interesting. Perhaps we could remove to the ballroom?"

Somewhat mystified, Toby followed him into the ballroom, and they stopped in a secluded spot behind a pillar.

"*Less* heroic, you say?" Sir James prompted. "I should perhaps mention that I am a Justice of the Peace in this area. Maitland has not come to me about this incident, nor have I heard via the local constables."

Toby thought over what he'd overheard. "I only know snippets, sir, so what I tell you may not be correct."

Sir James nodded. "Go on."

"The first time, he single-handedly killed two assailants, and the third one ran off. What I overheard just now was that he and a companion had winged one attacker. I didn't hear any more."

"Hmm." Sir James' eyes narrowed, and he tapped one finger on the lid of his snuff box.

"There was one other thing, though. When he mentioned this Jones, someone said how cowardly Jones was to run off. Maitland looked… taken aback, I suppose. He said it was probably a sensible retreat in case he—Maitland, that is—had another pistol."

Sir James smiled—a satisfied smile, Toby thought. "Did he give any indication of where and when this incident happened?"

"Yesterday evening, but I don't know where, I'm afraid."

"No matter. You have been very helpful, Lieutenant. Thank you." Sir James inclined his head and walked off.

Mystified, Toby watched him go. Then he shrugged and went back to the ballroom to watch the dancing. Maitland's encounter was nothing to do with him.

CHAPTER 4

The following morning, Nell put the porridge over the fire to cook, then started writing a list of provisions she needed to buy. She usually went with Gibson on his weekly trip into Pickering with the cart—it was the only way to ensure the meat and vegetables he brought back were reasonably fresh.

But when Silas came down early for his breakfast, he announced that he would be taking the cart instead of Gibson, and Bett would come with him to buy the supplies. Bett was pleased, too—Nell guessed she would return with new ribbons or lace, and poorer quality provisions than Nell would have chosen.

She would miss her weekly escape from the inn, but she'd much rather stay here than sit beside Uncle Silas all the way. She went upstairs to sweep out the bedrooms, catching sight of the cart against the pale track. It passed the stone cross, but turned left instead of right.

That was odd. The nearest market town in that direction was Whitby, where the moors descended to the coast, and it was half as far again as Pickering to the south. Uncle Silas rode there a few times each month, usually returning the next day with a sore head and his temper even worse than usual, but they rarely went there for marketing. If they were going that far, they wouldn't be back until nearly dusk, so she might have some time to herself this afternoon.

As she wielded her broom, Nell couldn't help wondering again what Jones had been doing, and what orders Bett had passed on to her father. And whether going to Whitby instead of Pickering was part of Jones' plan. She could ask Gibson, but he was unlikely to have seen or heard anything unusual—he never seemed to take much interest in what was going on around him. He'd grumbled at Tim's absence, but only because the task of feeding and mucking out the horse now fell to him.

It couldn't hurt to take a walk, could it? She thought about it as she chopped onions and the last of the mutton. Uncle Silas hadn't forbidden her to go out, nor had he actually said anything about not going west. Could she find some clue about Jones' plans in time to avoid becoming implicated?

By the time the day's stew was over the fire, Nell had made up her mind. Gibson was in the public room, slouched by the fire with a mug of small beer in his hand.

"I'm going for a walk," Nell announced. "If anyone comes, the stew will be ready in an hour."

Gibson looked up and nodded, with a trace of a smile, then returned to contemplating the flames. Nell took her cloak from the peg in the scullery and strode out. Apart from the inn with its nearby stand of trees, and the stone cross to the east, the only things to relieve the monotony of the surroundings were a few scrubby trees in the distance. This place could be beautiful on a sunny day when the heather was in bloom, but now Nell shivered at the bleak loneliness of it all.

She set off westwards. Briskly at first, slowing when she thought she'd gone as far as she'd seen Jones ride in the moonlight. A horse walking through the heather would leave little trace, but she should at least look.

Silas had been told to 'make arrangements', which implied there were goods to be moved. Were those goods already here? She walked for nearly half an hour, not covering much ground but looking carefully at the heather and grass either side of the track. Then she turned back; even Gibson might get suspicious if she stayed out too long, and might mention it to Silas.

It wasn't until she was nearly half-way back that she spotted broken stems in the heather. They could have been damaged by hooves, but when she looked more closely there were other breaks beyond, and another parallel set nearly five feet away.

A cart or wagon had turned into the heather here. There was no trace on the track of a wagon turning, but the ground was hard and stony and it hadn't rained in days. Nell stepped into the heather and picked her way beside the marks. Not far off, the ground sloped gently downward and she could see nothing but heather and a few clumps of grass. She turned back—she didn't have the time to walk further.

Nell paused for a moment when she regained the track; if she did have the time—and the inclination—to find out where the tracks went, would she find this place again? She dared not pile stones to make a marker, but there was another, less precise way.

She counted her paces as she walked, marking the hundreds on her fingers. Almost twelve hundred steps before she reached the Moorcock again. Gibson was still sitting in the public room—Nell wouldn't be surprised if he hadn't moved since she left him.

As she lit a fire in the washhouse for the monthly washing of bed linen, she wondered how she could find out more. Silas was unlikely to leave the inn for a whole day again for some time.

Could she investigate one night?

Toby lay listening to the cries of seagulls as the sky lightened, until the aroma of coffee drifting up from the kitchen stirred him into motion. He should not be lazing in his bed now Aunt Em was up and about. She probably didn't need any assistance with the usual morning tasks, but he could see if there was anything else he could do to help.

Aunt Em accepted his offer, and set the maid to extra cleaning in the bedrooms while Toby took her place fetching the day's milk. Then he was sent to bring sacks of potatoes, turnips, and carrots back from the market, glad as he did so that it was too early for Miss Delaney to be up and about, and see him. A refined young lady like her would look down on men who did that kind of work. He would smarten himself up this afternoon and walk by the shore—he might meet her again there.

Aunt Em kept him busy. He started by carrying coals, oiling squeaky door hinges, and fixing two loose cupboard doors. She was talking about turning out the attic when a boy arrived with a note from Sir James for him. Toby broke the seal and opened it, glad for an excuse to rest.

"Well, what does it say?" Aunt Em looked at it curiously.

"Sir James would be grateful for an hour or two of my time." Toby turned to the boy who'd brought the note. "Tell Sir James I will be with him within the hour."

The boy nodded and ran off.

"What does he want?" Aunt Em asked, as Toby went into the scullery for water. He needed to wash away the dust on his hands and face. "Lady Troughton didn't mention her husband wishing to speak to you."

"He didn't say." He grinned. "It doesn't sound as if I'm in trouble, though. The note did say 'please'."

She regarded him critically as he wiped his face. "You'll do. You've time for a quick bite to eat before you go; it won't take you long to walk there."

Sir James' home was above the town, half a mile or so beyond the houses and with a splendid view of the sea and the castle on its head-land north of the town. The house was old, with sections added by several generations, and at least three times the size of Aunt Em's house.

Toby was shown into the study—a comfortable room with book-cases along one wall, a large desk, and several leather-covered chairs.

Sir James rose from behind the desk. "Thank you for coming so promptly, Lieutenant. Please, take a seat. Brandy?"

"No, thank you, sir. Not at this hour."

Sir James smiled as both men sat. "I understand from what my wife tells me that you attained your current rank by a promotion in the field."

"Yes, sir."

"And that you are on leave. When do you have to report to your regiment?"

"In three weeks, or thereabouts."

"Excellent. Tell me, had you heard of Gentleman Jones before last night?"

"No, sir." Despite the offer of brandy, Toby began to feel that this was not a social call. "Sir, what is this about?"

Sir James toyed with a small bronze statue of Lady Justice on his desk, but his gaze was fixed on Toby's face. Finally he nodded. "I would like your assistance, if you are willing to give it. However, before I explain I must ask for your word that you will not repeat anything I tell you, whether or not you agree to my proposal."

That was an easy enough promise. "You have it, sir."

"Excellent, thank you. The matter is connected with the theft from Lord Lanchester's coach the night before last, and the murder of several men."

Toby sat up straighter in his chair, surprised. Sir James had not mentioned that matter at the assembly. "I heard something of that last night."

"This morning, I had word from the magistrate in the area where the robbery took place. He contacted me because Jones is believed to have associates here. It is fortunate that both this magistrate and the local constable are intelligent men not content to accept initial impressions."

"How so, sir?"

"The constable made a careful examination of the area where the empty coach was found. I say empty, but it contained the bodies of the three guards. Two had been inside, the third on the box."

"No driver?"

"No driver," Sir James confirmed. "But there was also no sign of blood on the ground nearby, or indication that heavy items had been removed to another vehicle. What do you make of that?"

"The robbery happened elsewhere."

Sir James nodded. "Let us assume for now that the thieves knew roughly what was being transported—chests of gold and silver coin, one containing silver plate, and a casket full of jewellery. How would you plan the robbery?"

"I heard last night that the outriders ran off. Is that correct?"

"Apparently so," Sir James confirmed. "Either bribed or cowardly."

Or outnumbered—it would take truly dedicated employees to face down a greater number of highwaymen.

"If the thieves knew the route…?" Toby paused.

"Assume that they did," Sir James said.

"Then they would choose a place to wait where they would not be observed by passers-by, nor seen from too great a distance by the driver and guard." That would be true no matter what pickings they were expecting. But the chests Sir James had described were bulky items, and heavy. "They would need a vehicle to take their booty away," he said, thinking it through as he spoke. "That would be difficult to hide, so why not use the coach itself?"

"Indeed—that is the conclusion the magistrate also came to."

"Where was the coach found?"

"Outside a village a few miles west of the road it was originally travelling. It was not well hidden."

"So the takings have been hidden somewhere, and the coach returned so as not to give an indication where the hiding place is. That doesn't help you track down the robbers or the treasure."

"There is more. The diligent constable took it upon himself to look for the location of the holdup. He found the driver, who was badly injured but not dead."

"Ah. What did he have to say?"

"He fell off the box when he was shot, and managed to crawl into a hedge. He heard the leader of the gang counting the bodies and realising there was one short, but another vehicle was approaching and they had to leave. From what he overheard, he is convinced that the leader was Gentleman Jones."

Toby sat up straighter. "The same Gentleman Jones who held up Colonel Maitland that night?"

Sir James raised a brow. "As far as I know, there is only one Gentleman Jones."

"Did you find out any more about Maitland's encounter, sir?"

"Only that it happened about ten miles north from here, on the road to Whitby. That's around thirty miles from where the robbery took place, with moorland between. The two holdups—if two there were—happened within a couple of hours of each other. It is possible Jones could have got from one place to the other in the time, but very unlikely."

"And that would have left him no time to hide what he stole." There could be more than one explanation for Jones apparently being in two places at once. "He could have left the transport of the chests to his associates," Toby suggested. "The driver could have been mistaken, or Maitland was mistaken." Was it just jealousy of Miss Delaney's favours that made him think it must be the colonel?

"Or Maitland lied. The change in his story you told me of suggests the tale was made from whole cloth. It could, of course, have been a tale told only to show his bravery to the young women at the assembly, but that the supposed hold-up happened on the same day that Lord Lanchester's coach was attacked is surely too much of a coincidence. That is why I would like your help, Lieutenant. Maitland may not be an accomplice of Jones, but I cannot afford to assume that. I cannot trust him, and even if his men are not party to Jones' activities, I cannot use them without involving Maitland himself. It is also possible that Maitland has suborned the regular soldiers stationed in the castle. I need someone to be King George's man in this situation, not one who is looking out for his own interests."

This sounded a more interesting way of spending his leave than helping Aunt Em turn out the attic. "I'm willing, sir, but I don't see what I can do."

"Thank you. I should warn you that the other magistrate is putting it about that the driver was dead when found."

Toby nodded.

"I do have more information. Yesterday I had a visitor. A lad—sixteen or so—came to see me. He'd been badly beaten, and had a tale to tell of happenings at the Moorcock Inn up on the moor."

The Moorcock was largely empty most of the day, for which Nell was grateful. She'd managed to get her undergarments and sheets both washed and dried, and even had the time to make a sweet pudding using the last of the raisins and sugar. It would be stodgy and filling, unlike the pastries and creams she'd loved when she was younger, but filling was what their customers wanted. Now it was simmering in a pot over the fire, next to the evening's stew.

Nell wiped her forehead with the back of her hand and went to the outside door for a breath of cool air. The sun had dipped below a band of cloud on the western horizon, the sky shading from blue to purple. The sharp freshness of the air was welcome after the stifling smells of cooking. Needing to stretch her legs, Nell walked around the inn and headed for the cross. She could see some of the Whitby road from here, but no sign of the cart on it. If her uncle and cousin did not return soon, they would be driving in the dark.

Movement to the east drew her attention—a horseman. As he drew closer, something about him seemed familiar. Closer still, and she recognised the traveller who had thanked her yesterday. He sat his horse well.

He stopped by the cross and doffed his hat. "Good afternoon. I find myself later on my return journey than I intended. Is there a room available for the night?"

"Yes—but not immediately. I'll have to make up the bed." More work—doing that would fall to her even if Bett were not still away. She set off back to the inn.

The stranger replaced his hat, then dismounted and walked beside her. "My name's Bourne." He kept his gaze on her face, one brow raised a little.

"Nell Mason."

He tilted his head. "Miss Mason. I would be quite happy with a blanket and some straw above the stables. I find myself... somewhat embarrassed for funds." His smile was rueful, the twinkle in his eyes friendly.

Miss Mason! It was rare she was called that. "If you wish. There is still no-one to help with your horse, though."

"It is of no matter." He even looked rather pleased. "Brushing him down will warm me."

"You should try spending the day in the kitchen," she muttered. She thought she'd spoken quietly, but he chuckled.

"I can skin a rabbit, Miss Mason, and boil it, but turning meat into a stew as tasty as the one I ate yesterday is beyond me."

"That was mutton."

He grinned, showing white teeth. "I did enjoy your *mutton* stew."

Nell couldn't help smiling in return—he was not amusing himself at her expense. "I'm afraid it is mutton again tonight. Or hare." There were two hanging in the pantry. She didn't like skinning them, but needs must. If she were as forward as Bett, she might have asked Mr Bourne to skin them for her, but she did not want to be under any obligation to a stranger, no matter how friendly.

"You know the way, Mr Bourne," she said when they reached the inn. "There's a pallet in the loft, and blankets." It seemed Tim wasn't coming back, so Mr Bourne might as well use them.

Mr Bourne touched his hat and led the horse into the stable. Nell returned to the kitchen and went into the pantry. Mr Bourne would want breakfast in the morning, and probably more than porridge. There was just enough ham left, if Silas did not return with more this evening. Sounds of talk and raucous laughter came from the public room. Nell sighed, and went to find out if anyone was in want of a meal.

CHAPTER 5

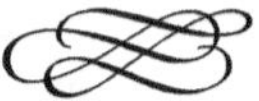

Toby dropped his roll of bedding and spare clothes on the stone flags inside the stable, and unsaddled the horse before going to investigate his sleeping quarters. The loft above the stable was cold, and smelled of horse and damp straw. As Nell Mason had promised, there was a pallet and blankets—both too thin, but he'd slept in worse places. And he had a warm evening and a tasty meal to come, even if the ale here wasn't very good. Outside, the sky still showed pale, but the land was dark. Light spilled from what must be a kitchen window.

A bad-tempered shout from the front of the inn drew his attention, then a horse and cart came into the yard. The buxom Bett sprang down lightly, and the large man from the night before shouted angrily again as he descended. He matched Sir James' description of Silas Weaver—the owner of the place and Nell Mason's uncle.

The potman emerged from the kitchen and began to carry boxes and sacks into the building. Bett picked up a parcel and went indoors, but Weaver caught sight of Toby and staggered towards him.

"What d'you think you're doing in the stable? Who are you?" There was belligerence in his tone, and a strong smell of ale on his breath.

"Passing traveller," Toby said, keeping his voice mild. It was no part of his plan to pick a fight with this man. "The kitchen woman said I could sleep in there."

The landlord swayed backwards on his feet, then put his face close to Toby's. "It'll cost you."

"Naturally." Toby smiled, and eventually the landlord nodded and went indoors after Bett. Toby looked at the cart thoughtfully, then strolled towards it. This might be his chance to look at parts of the inn that patrons never normally saw. "Want some help?" he asked, when the potman reappeared. "They've left you to do all this on your own."

The man spat on the ground. "Stable lad ran off. He'd have helped." He inspected Toby briefly. "Them sacks of veggies go in a room in the cellars."

Toby hefted one onto his shoulder, and picked up another. "Lead on."

"Didn't think you meant it. But thanks. Gibson's the name."

"Bourne." Toby followed him through the scullery into the kitchen, then down a set of stairs lit by a single lantern.

"In there."

Toby set the sacks down. "Must be difficult to get help in a lonely place like this."

Gibson shrugged, leading the way back out to the yard. "It's not too bad. Plenty of ale."

Toby grimaced. "Is there anything better than that swill I drank yesterday?"

A laugh turned into a cough, but Gibson nodded. "There is—I'll see you get some. It's still not *good*, mind." He picked up a small box and headed indoors, and Toby carried the remaining sacks to the store-room. Several doors opened off the cellar passage, but without a lantern there was little he could do beyond trying them. None were locked—anything hidden at the inn was unlikely to be in these cellars.

Nell looked up from the hare she was jointing as Gibson entered with a sack of flour on his shoulder and carried it on through to the pantry. She hadn't heard the cart return.

Bett appeared with a bulky parcel wrapped in cloth under one arm and a satisfied smirk on her face. New clothing, probably—it didn't appear to have much weight. Bett would boast about it, no doubt, but Nell wasn't going to give her the satisfaction of asking, and returned to cutting meat.

"Why's there no coffee?" Bett scowled.

"No-one's asked for it yet." Nell walked around Bett to fetch a pan and mutton fat, and set the pieces of hare to fry above the fire. "Did you buy bacon?" A bit of that would add nicely to the hare stew.

Bett's scowl deepened. "I got all you put on the list. Pa went drinking all day and—"

She broke off as Uncle Silas stumbled through the door. "What're you doing still here, Bett? There's customers and Gibson's busy." He leaned one hand on the end of the table, steadying himself. "Go on, girl, get on with it!"

Bett flounced out of the door, and Silas turned to Nell. "Get me some small beer."

Nell filled a jug from the keg kept in the larder and followed Silas into the public room, where her uncle was now slumped in a chair by the fire.

"More ale here, love!" one of the men at a separate table called.

"Bett'll be here in a moment—can't let the supper burn!" Nell escaped before they could protest.

Back in the kitchen, Gibson brought in the last of the supplies, Mr Bourne following him moments later. "Wash in there," Gibson said, jerking his thumb at the scullery door. Mr Bourne draped his great-coat over the back of a chair and set his hat on one corner of the table before going to the scullery.

"He helped me with the veggie sacks," Gibson explained to Nell.

"Good of him." And unusual. Bett was the only person who ever got help from the customers, and that was generally because they wanted to peer down the top of her gown. "You'd best get to the public room as soon as you've put Dobbin in the stable. They were asking for ale, and I haven't heard Bett come back downstairs yet."

Gibson rolled his eyes and went back to the yard.

By the time Mr Bourne emerged from the scullery, Nell had cubes of bacon and slices of onion frying with the pieces of hare.

Mr Bourne sniffed and smiled. "That smells good. Is that the hare you promised?"

"It is." Nell eyed him warily. Customers didn't normally come into the kitchen, and she was reluctant to be alone with any of them—although the threat of a plate of hot stew 'accidentally' being spilled on them usually deterred unwelcome advances. But Mr Bourne made no move to come closer. "It won't be ready for a while," she added. "Unless you enjoy exercising your jaw."

"Ha, no. Gibson promised me some better ale, though. That will do for now."

"There's mutton stew already hot, or you can have a bit of bread and cheese to tide you over."

"The bread and cheese will do nicely, thank you. But don't disturb yourself, Miss Mason. I can get it if you point me in the right direction."

He could hardly steal much while she was here, so Nell pointed with her spoon. "Pantry's next to the scullery. Bread by the door, butter and cheese on the bottom shelf."

"Do you get much custom here?" he asked, once he was settled at the kitchen table with food and a tankard of ale that Gibson had given him.

"Mostly men from the quarries a mile or two off. A few travellers like yourself."

"It must be bleak in the winter." He leaned back in his chair. "In the summer, too, I should think, in wet weather."

"It's not too bad," Nell said, pouring hot water from the kettle onto the meat and vegetables in the pan, and giving it all a stir. "There's a stream in a wooded valley a little way south—I like to walk there when I have some time to myself." There was pleasure in nature on a fine day, even if only the peace of having no demands on her. Before Papa's death, Mama had enjoyed helping their outdoor man tend the small garden behind their house.

"Lying beside a stream on a hot day," he replied, a little dreamily.

"With nothing to do but think green thoughts in a green shade."

She gazed at him, startled. "Marvell?" His poem about a garden had been one of Papa's favourites, and she often read it when she managed to have a little time away from the inn. A slim volume of poetry was the only one of Papa's books she still had.

"I read poetry now and then," he said. "There's sometimes... When I'm travelling, there's often a long evening to fill." His accent, and his choice of words, sounded far more educated than most of the inn's customers.

"My father enjoyed poetry, amongst other things," she said. "He was interested in antiquities, too."

"What kind of antiquities? Old churches and the like?"

"Not really. He was interested in older things, like stone circles, or the crosses and burial mounds on these moors."

"Are the crosses shrines of some kind? I haven't noticed any others, but then I've only ridden across the moors once or twice."

Nell gave the pan a final stir and sat down at the table. "I don't know. Some are just stones that are most likely put there to mark a way. Papa said that some had a hollow where people left money to help poor travellers. Although if anyone left money on the cross near here, my uncle would have taken it." But Mr Bourne could not want a history lesson. "What takes you across the moors, sir?"

"Oh, this and that," he said easily. "Taking messages, errands." He dabbed up the last crumbs of cheese with one finger. "My thanks for the food, but I should stop pestering you now, Miss Mason. I'll look forward to having some of that hare stew when it's done, if you please." He stood as he spoke, picked up his coat and hat, and headed for the public room.

Nell was sorry to see him go—had her question made him leave? That was the most civilised conversation she'd had since Mama died. She sighed and put that thought aside—it was too depressing to dwell on.

Voices from the passage indicated that more customers had arrived; she stretched her back and went to see if any food was wanted.

~

That night, Toby lay on the straw pallet listening to the wind rattling the loose-fitting casement. This felt an abrupt change from the comfort of Aunt Em's house, where he'd started the day. And a busy day it had been, working out a plan with Sir James, and then riding up here to reconnoitre.

No-one else had arrived to stay the night, and the men in the tavern had all been local workers. Quarrymen, from the snippets of talk he'd overheard. Everything he'd seen so far seemed to confirm what the runaway stable lad had said—the landlord was a drunken lout, his daughter harmless enough but selfish, and Gibson kept himself to himself. Possibly a decent man—the lad hadn't said anything against him.

Nell Mason, though—she was a conundrum. She would be as attractive as Bett if not swathed in a voluminous apron and with her hair hidden by her cap. Kind, the lad had said, and put-upon by her relatives. A well-spoken cook who read poetry; an educated young woman with a father interested in history. Her father must be dead— she'd spoken of him with affection and a tinge of sorrow, and a loving father would not leave his daughter with a man like Silas Weaver. He'd almost asked what had become of her parents, but hadn't wanted to draw too much attention to himself by enquiring, or by spending too long in the kitchen.

But the details of the inn and its usual inhabitants weren't the important parts of the lad's story, and he could find out no more about the rest yet. He'd asked what questions he could without seeming overly inquisitive and raising suspicion, and tomorrow he would ride off to the west. The way Jones had reportedly gone a few nights ago—if the lad had told the truth

Sir James could worry about that—Toby's task was to see what he could find out at this inn, or near it. With the ease of long habit, he cleared his mind of questions and fell asleep.

The eastern sky was beginning to lighten the next morning when Toby let himself into the kitchen to see if anyone else was out of their bed. His luck was in—the fire was stoked, a pot hung above it, and Nell Mason stood at the table kneading dough. She looked up as he entered, a smile quickly replaced by a frown as she wiped her hands on her apron.

"Pray continue, Miss Mason—I did not mean to disturb you. May I use your scullery to wash?" The frigid air outside made using the pump in the yard an unattractive option.

She nodded and returned to her kneading as Toby left. When he returned, she had set the dough aside and the smell of coffee filled the air.

"There's small beer, if you prefer that to coffee," she said. "Do you want breakfast before you leave?"

"Coffee, please, and breakfast, too, if it's no trouble. I'm earlier than your usual customers, I think?"

One corner of her mouth lifted in a wry smile as she took down a mug. "There are few who stay the night, sir. I'll light the fire in the public room if you give me a minute."

He took the coffee. "I'm happy to eat in here, if I will not be in your way." He pulled out the chair he had used the previous evening and sat down without waiting for her reply. Breakfasting in solitary state held little appeal when there was an interesting and attractive woman to talk to.

Nell put one hand on her hip as he settled into the chair. "Please, do have a seat, Mr Bourne."

He must have caught the sharpness in her tone, but merely grinned. "I'll take myself off if you wish. But it's warm in here."

The twinkle of humour in his eyes disarmed her, and she shook her head. "You won't be in the way. I can make the porridge, or there's ham, eggs, bacon—all quick to cook. Yesterday's bread should still be fresh enough."

"Ham and eggs, if you please. And could I have some to take with me as well? I paid your uncle for breakfast when I settled up last night."

Good, that saved her having to think how much to charge him. She cut a generous slice of ham to go with his eggs—something that would earn a reprimand from Uncle Silas if he saw it—and set a pan over the fire to heat while she fetched bread and butter. Mr Bourne seemed content to sit and wait while she cooked, drinking his coffee as he watched her move about the kitchen. His gaze could have felt awkward—threatening, even—but his expression was thoughtful rather than the kind of leer she often saw directed at Bett, and sometimes at her, too.

Once the food was ready, she sliced bread while he ate, and added another thick slice of ham and some cheese. Any hope of more conversation ended when he emptied his plate and stood.

"Excellent, thank you. I'm afraid I must be on my way." He pulled a large handkerchief from a pocket and wrapped the food he was to take, then placed a sixpence on the table.

"You don't need to pay for the bread and ham," Nell said. "Uncle Silas will never know." He was surely owed something for helping Gibson last night.

"Please take it as a token of my appreciation. For this." He raised the wrapped food. "And for the conversation last night." He gave a little bow, and was gone before she could reply.

Nell picked up the coin and gazed at it for a moment before tucking it into the top of her stays. Customers occasionally gave her a penny or two, but never this much—and she was lucky no-one had seen it or her uncle would have had it from her. It would go with the rest of her money in the purse she kept in her mattress.

If only more of their customers were like Mr Bourne, her life would be more pleasant, and it wouldn't take so long to save enough so she could leave.

But wishing for something did not make it happen, and she had porridge to cook.

CHAPTER 6

Late that evening, when the last customer had gone, Gibson came into the kitchen with a handful of empty tankards.

"Is Silas still in the public room?" Nell asked. She needed to wipe the tables, but she'd rather do it after her uncle had gone to his bed.

"Sitting there complaining into his ale."

"What's he saying?" Could Uncle's mood be connected with his orders from Gentleman Jones?

"Don't know." Gibson didn't meet her eyes. "Don't want to know." He left the tankards in the scullery and headed out to the privy in the yard. When he returned, he hesitated before going upstairs. "It's best not to ask, Nell. No good will come of it."

She wasn't going to ask, but she couldn't help wondering.

Not long afterwards, a door slammed, and her uncle's heavy foot-steps trod up the stairs. Nell waited a few minutes, then took a cloth to wipe the tables in the public room. Uncle Silas' bad mood made her think that this was something more than smuggling. A threat from Gentleman Jones, perhaps, or Jones involving Silas in something the law would take more seriously than the loss of customs revenue.

Curiosity warred with caution as she put the mop and bucket away and banked the fire.

Curiosity won. If she could find out what was happening, she might be able to avoid becoming implicated. Tonight could be her best chance—she would go and look.

On her way to her room, she heard Silas' snores reverberating along the narrow upstairs landing; whatever was on his mind hadn't stopped him sleeping. Bett's door was closed, no light showing through the narrow gap beneath it. Gibson was unlikely to come looking, even if he heard anything.

A sennight, Jones had said three nights ago. That meant he would not be back for another three or four days. It would be cold outside, so she pulled on another petticoat.

She trod carefully down the stairs, donned her cloak, and let herself out into the yard. Cloud covered the sky, but it was thin and the moon showed as a bright patch. She lit the stable lantern and closed the shutter—once her eyes had adjusted, the moon would light her way well enough until she was out of sight of the inn.

Twelve hundred paces she'd counted yesterday. She paused to open one side of the lantern after a couple of hundred, aiming the patch of light at the track before her. There was no sign of the marks in the heather when she reached the end of her count, but walking in moonlight, even with the lamp, involved stumbling into unnoticed dips, so her paces might have been shorter than in daylight.

After ten minutes of looking she gave up and set off through the heather anyway. She was in roughly the right place, so she might as well explore what lay beyond the track.

Progress was slow, the heather catching on her skirts, and rocks on the ground beneath almost turning her ankle a few times. More grass and heather; a few rocks large enough to show above it; then a small tree casting a deep shadow far larger than it was.

It wasn't a shadow. Nell crept forward, stopping when the lantern lighting her way shone onto… nothing.

She took another step forward, holding the lantern to illuminate the ground at her feet. No, there *was* something there, but below her;

the glow of lanterns, and the shadowy shapes of men, the sounds of things being moved. She had arrived at the top edge of a quarry.

Jones' men? Who else could it be?

Her hand shook and she dropped the lantern. The flame extinguished; she didn't try to find it but took a cautious step back, then another. She must not be discovered here. She was lucky the lantern-light had not already been seen—she would have to make her way back by moonlight.

She took another step back and turned, but found her way blocked; her arm was taken in a tight grip, then she was spun around and pulled hard against a man, one rough hand covering her mouth.

"If yer scream, I'll stick me knife inter yer."

Nell stiffened even as her heart raced, feeling nauseous at her stupidity in thinking she could do anything to thwart Gentleman Jones. The highwayman was known to be ruthless. Cruel, even. *Why* had she not listened to that voice of caution?

"I'll take me hand away if yer promise not to make a noise." The voice was quiet, but menacing for all that, and the arm holding her felt hard as iron.

She moved her head, the nearest she could manage to a nod, then the hand was gone. He wasn't about to kill her right away, then.

"Follow me and keep yer mouth shut."

The man released her and she swayed on unsteady knees. The idea of attempting to escape was quickly dismissed—she wouldn't get five yards before he caught her, and she was likely to be treated more roughly if she tried.

Her captor must have seen her drop the lantern, for he bent to pick it up. Without looking to see if she followed, he set off parallel to the quarry's edge and then down the slope.

He was moving silently, not even stumbling in the rough heather, but Nell didn't find it so easy. They had nearly reached the level of the quarry floor when she tripped, letting out an involuntary cry as she hit the ground. She lay still as her heart still thumped in her chest, curling into a ball as a futile defence against the promised knifing for making a noise.

Instead, there was a muffled curse, and the sound of footsteps on loose stones approaching.

"Caught 'er at the top looking down, sir," her captor said. "What d'yer want me to do with 'er?"

Light shone and she screwed her eyes against the sudden glare.

"Damn it—why did you let her get so close?"

The newcomer's voice sounded familiar, although she could not say who it was. Nell's fear eased a little as she realised this was *not* Jones. She uncurled, and pushed herself so she was sitting up in the heather. The newcomer stood with his back to the moon, his face in darkness.

"Oh, never mind now. Leave her, and get back on watch—and pay more attention this time. Find a position closer to the track."

"Yessir."

A metallic clank must be her lantern being set down, and the light left her face.

"I'm not going to hurt you, Miss Mason."

Miss Mason? It must be Mr Bourne—what could he be doing here?

"Get up, Miss Mason. We need to talk, but not here."

She pushed herself to her knees, fumbling as her skirts twisted about her legs.

"Are you injured?" He sounded impatient, and she didn't want to anger him further. She was already fortunate that Jones wasn't here. But what if Mr Bourne were just as bad? A kind smile and a liking for poetry did not mean a man was not a criminal.

"No." She answered before he could ask again. She might have a few bruises, but nothing more.

"Good." He gripped one arm, but only to help her to stand, then he picked up her lantern and led the way to an outcrop of boulders out of sight of the quarry. "Sit down."

She obeyed, the sick feeling still in her stomach. "What are you going to do?" Her voice came out on a waver, and she swallowed hard.

"That is a very good question. But first, what are you doing here?"

. . .

Toby set his lantern down and found a smooth rock to sit on. He'd had another long and tiring day—following the stable lad's directions to find this overgrown, disused quarry this morning, then riding on to confer with Mr Hartley, an acquaintance of Sir James in Pickering. Sir James had arranged for Toby to borrow several of Mr Hartley's men to move the chests he had found hidden in the quarry, rather than sending his own men—although he trusted them, he couldn't be certain they hadn't been suborned by Colonel Maitland or might tell what they had been doing when they returned to Scarborough.

This business would have been far easier to manage if Toby had men he knew and trusted working for him. Sir James had written to Toby's colonel, but any soldiers he sent would not be here for a couple of days. *They* wouldn't have let Nell Mason get close enough to see what was happening in the quarry.

She must already know something, or why was she out on the moor at night at all, let alone here?

The men dealing with the chests could finish what they were doing without his supervision, so he had time to discover whether she knew any more about this business than the stable lad did. From what the boy had said, Toby thought it unlikely that she was part of Jones' plot, but it never paid to make assumptions.

He tried to make out her expression, but it was impossible by moonlight, and he didn't want to shine the lantern into her face again. "Why are you here?" he repeated when she didn't answer his question.

He heard her take a deep breath. "I was trying to discover what my uncle is involved in."

Her head was bowed, her voice wavering, and he realised she was still frightened. But if she hadn't believed him when he said he would not hurt her, repeating the statement would not help—and it might work to his advantage if she remained frightened for a little longer. "What kind of thing do you think Weaver is involved in? And why here?"

"Gentleman Jones came to the inn three nights ago—I saw him from my bedroom window. He left along the track in this direction."

She paused, but Toby didn't speak. Allowing someone to fill a silence could be more productive than detailed questioning.

"I saw him on the part of the track closest to the inn, but not on the more distant part. I guessed he had stopped somewhere."

"That answers the 'where' part of my question, Miss Mason, but not why you think your uncle is involved."

He heard a sigh. "I think he is involved in smuggling. And he was very anxious that I not walk the track in this direction."

"Is that all?" he asked, his impatience growing. "Miss Mason, if you think you are protecting Weaver by remaining silent, you are mistaken."

"I… I'm only trying to protect myself."

That could be true, he supposed. "Tell me what you know."

"I overheard some of what Jones said. He came to see Bett, and gave her orders to be passed on to my uncle. He said he would be back in a sennight, if the sky was clear. My uncle had to have everything ready by then."

"What else?"

"Jones told Bett to make sure my uncle cleaned the place himself. He went off somewhere the next day with a spade and brush."

"The place? What did Jones mean by that?"

"I don't know. That's all I heard. 'Clean the place'."

"So tell me how you found this quarry. Did you already know of it?"

"No." She described finding marks in the heather, and how she had made her way back to the same place tonight. Her tale was succinct, without the hesitations someone might make if they were inventing details as they went along. If she were part of Jones' plot, why would she be creeping around the moor at night? Perhaps she *was* innocent, after all.

"Very well. I'm afraid you will have to wait here until we are finished."

"Wait?" She sounded alarmed. "I must get back to the inn."

"No, not now that you have seen me here. I cannot risk Weaver knowing."

"I won't say anything, I promise—just let me go, please! Uncle Silas will know something is wrong if I'm not there in the morning. I give you my word…" Her voice tailed off and she looked up at him. When she spoke again her voice was steadier, less fearful. "If I'm not to tell anyone at the inn, does that mean you're *not* one of Jones' men?"

Was that what she thought? No wonder she had been so frightened. "No, I am not."

"Oh." Her voice was stronger when she spoke again. "If you're not connected with Jones, how came you to know there is something here?"

Now she'd recovered from her fright, it seemed her wits were working well. He could see no harm in telling her. "There was information laid that Jones was here three nights ago."

"By whom?" Her voice was sharp with interest.

"The stable lad that worked for you."

"Tim? Is he all right? Is he safe?"

"I haven't seen him, but he is in the charge of the—" He cut himself short; he should not give away the lad's location. "He is well at the moment, I'm told, other than a few bruises, but his life could be in danger if Jones ever finds out what he has said."

"Well *I'm* not likely to tell him, am I?"

Toby almost laughed at her acerbic tone. No, she wouldn't. She was concerned about the boy's welfare, and he could not believe she had anything to do with Jones and his plans. "I sincerely hope you are never in a position to speak to Jones, let alone pass on such information. But it is essential that no-one else knows what is going on here. Which is why your presence here is a damned nuisance."

He could take her to Aunt Em, he supposed, but as she had said, that would warn Silas Weaver that something was wrong. And his task wasn't just to find the stolen goods—he'd already achieved most of that—but to capture Gentleman Jones. After what Jones had done this time, the authorities didn't really care whether he was dead or alive when Toby handed him over.

"Miss Mason, can you act as if you never left your bed tonight? That you never saw me again after I left the inn this morning?"

"Yes, I can."

She sounded hesitant, and Toby wondered if he would be doing the right thing by letting her go.

"Miss Mason, if you *do* give away anything about our presence here and therefore hinder our plans, you will be considered as guilty as your uncle and others."

CHAPTER 7

*N*ell was certain she could hide her knowledge of this place from Silas and Bett; she was accustomed to concealing her emotions. But should she?

If Silas were arrested—hanged, even—what would happen to her? She had already decided she would escape before becoming implicated in his activities, but at the time the need for that had been only a vague possibility. Now, the idea of leaving to find respectable work in a strange town was frightening. Warning her uncle would give him a chance to escape, but that wouldn't help her; he wasn't likely to take her with him. He might even give her a beating for sticking her nose into his business.

Nell gathered her cloak tighter about her against the cold, tucking her hands in its folds. She would be on her own whatever happened—the choice was whether or not that would be as a criminal herself.

"Miss Mason?"

"I'm thinking," she snapped, then instantly regretted it. She should not be antagonising this man.

To her surprise, he chuckled. "I do beg your pardon, ma'am. I merely wished to ask whether you have anything more to tell me."

Only that Bett was planning on running away with Jones, but what difference could that information make? "No." She shivered.

"You are cold." Mr Bourne stood. "Come, if you've nothing more to say, it's time you went back."

"More like someone walking over my grave." But she *was* cold as well, in spite of her cloak, and would be glad to move. "Can I have my lantern?"

"When you are on the track. Can you make your own way back from there?"

"I'm not a complete fool, Mr Bourne. I would not have come this far had I not been sure I could return."

There was his chuckle again—deep and comforting. She could imagine the easy smile that had first attracted her to him. She'd put herself in danger by coming out here tonight, but the danger was not from him.

"This way." He set off up the slope, and she followed him to the top of the quarry, and then on through the heather. At the track, he said a few words in a low voice to the man who had caught her, then turned to her.

"I will leave you here."

Nell reached for the lantern, but he didn't move.

"Miss Mason, why do you live at that inn? Can you not find a more congenial position?"

"It's the only home I have. My uncle… my uncle took us in and kept a roof over our heads."

"It seems to me you have more than repaid him with your labour." He didn't wait for a reply, but lit her lantern from his own and handed it to her. "Fare well, Miss Mason. Don't take this the wrong way, but I hope I don't have cause to see you again."

Then he was away, blending into the dark of the heather before she could reply.

Nell shuttered the lantern—the moonlight was enough illumination now she was on the track. As she walked, her thoughts returned to her uncle.

Did she owe Silas the chance to escape? As Mr Bourne had just pointed out, he'd had free labour from her to pay for the bed and board. If he'd paid her, she could have earned enough by now to tide her over while she looked for a different position, and she wouldn't have been faced with this choice.

No. Warning Silas would make her a criminal. Regardless of what she might owe him, that was too much.

Toby resisted the impulse to follow Miss Mason to ensure she reached the inn safely. He impressed upon the lookout the need to come and warn him *before* anyone approaching actually reached the quarry, then headed back to see how the others were doing.

Mr Hartley's men knew the southern part of the moors well, which was useful. Both Toby and their employer had emphasised the likelihood of a substantial reward if Lord Lanchester's valuables were recovered, and the certainty of being hunted down and hanged for theft if they were responsible for any of it going astray. They had appeared offended at the very idea, and Toby, used to prevarication from the less trustworthy men in his company, thought they were genuine. But no matter how honest they were, they were not overendowed with wits.

Well, he would have to make do. He headed back into the quarry, unshuttering his own lantern as he approached the chests with their open lids. Lord Lanchester's steward had given him a set of keys to the padlocks. Toby wondered if Jones had a set, too, as the chests showed no signs of an attempt to break into them. Lord Lanchester's keys had not been sent with the coach, but if someone in his employ was working with Jones, they might have made copies. Or Jones might have been in too much of a hurry to look inside the chests when he hid them. Not that it mattered—the chests were full, which meant that little, if anything, had been taken.

"All emptied, sir." The man gestured at the pile of canvas bags at his feet. "Next trip with the pony should be enough to get this lot to safety."

"Very good." He sighed as he regarded the rocks inside the nearest chest. It had not occurred to them that it would be easier to put the empty chests back in their hiding place before adding rocks to hide the fact that they were now empty.

"That's all I can fit in, sir."

Toby closed the lid. "Let's test it." He took hold of the handle at one end and they lifted it between them. It couldn't be as heavy as when filled with coin, but he doubted Jones or his men would recall exactly how heavy the chests had been. He fastened the padlocks and they carried it to the short tunnel hollowed out of the quarry face. They did the same with the other chests, then Toby left the man piling rocks across the tunnel entrance.

Miss Mason's mention of a brush and spade was bothering him. She was intelligent, and would not have mentioned them if Weaver were in the habit of sweeping the yard or the stables. All the stolen chests were here—the only thing missing was a jewellery casket that had been described as small enough to be strapped behind a saddle. Jones must have taken that with him.

They hadn't examined the whole of the quarry when they arrived —the stable lad's description of where Weaver usually hid his contraband had been so accurate, they had gone almost straight to it. Toby suspected the lad had been involved in storing smuggled goods there, but Sir James wasn't interested in convicting such small fry.

A brush implied removing any marks of movement from the sand and gravel on the quarry floor, and a spade suggested hiding or burying something. Not the chests—the piled rocks hid those well enough. The quarry floor was solid rock beneath its thin layer of gravel; Weaver would hardly have dug into that with only a spade, so Toby concentrated on the piles of rubble round the edges.

"Sir?" One of the men came to stand beside him. "I've hidden the place again, if you want to check."

It would do, Toby decided after a quick inspection. "Very good. We'll wait until the man returns with the pony." They were only taking the silver and coin a few miles, to a hut in a wooded valley. Once there, he'd leave the men guarding it while he went to report back and fetch a cart to transport it all to a strongroom in Mr Hartley's house.

"Sir!" The shout came from the edge of the quarry. "Sir, you have to see this!"

Toby went over to the rock pile—one he'd already examined.

"Came over to take a piss, sir," the man said. "Kicked that rock by accident." He indicated a dark shape that looked little different from the rest. "Only it ain't no rock." He kicked it again, with a sound softer than that of a boot on stone.

"Shift some of those rocks, if you please."

The men obeyed, heaving and rolling the stones until they had uncovered what was undoubtedly a human leg clad in a riding boot. The kind that might be worn by outriders working for a wealthy lord.

Weaver's cleaning up had been to hide a body. Or bodies—if this was one of the missing outriders, the other could be here, too. Moving some of the stones littering the quarry floor must have been easier than digging a deep enough hole.

Toby swore. What should he do now? Taking the bodies away would mean an extra trip with the pony, and so more chance of being spotted.

"Uncover enough of him to see what he's wearing, then hide him again. We'll have to come back tomorrow night." Or just leave them there until Jones was either captured or escaped. Sir James or Lord Lanchester could decide that.

Jones must have brought them here to help him unload, and then killed them. Sir James had said Jones was ruthless, but Toby hadn't appreciated just how much of a bastard the man was.

Did Miss Mason know? He hadn't mentioned the latest robbery, or the dead guards and coachmen to her.

And he'd let her return to an inn full of Jones' accomplices.

Nell was exhausted by the time she reached the Moorcock. She let herself into the kitchen as quietly as possible and hung her cloak behind the door. The lantern went into the scullery; she could return it to the stable in the morning. The creaking bottom stair focused her mind, and she managed to avoid the other loose boards as she climbed to her room. Once there, the questions swirling through her mind weren't enough to keep her from sleep.

Those thoughts returned the next morning as she coaxed the kitchen fire into life and put water on to boil. Now she was safely back at the Moorcock—safe for now, at least—her curiosity had been roused. What had Mr Bourne been doing in that little quarry?

They had been moving something, but she hadn't seen what. Probably not smuggled goods; Jones had never been mentioned in connection with smuggling, so they were likely to have been moving stolen goods.

The water boiled and she made coffee, then put oats and more water into the pot. But routine actions like stirring the porridge didn't stop her thinking.

If Mr Bourne had found whatever Jones had left there and the men were merely taking it away, it wouldn't matter if Silas found out about it today. The need for her to pretend nothing had happened suggested that the men might still be there, or were planning to return. Perhaps there was more there than they could move in one night? She'd seen the tracks of whatever vehicle Jones' men had used to deliver it; there had been no sign of a wagon or cart last night, but they could have made two trips with it and she had happened to arrive when it was away. If she went back along the track in daylight, would she see more marks in the heather?

No—be sensible! She was lucky it hadn't been Jones there last night, and that Mr Bourne appeared to be far more of a gentleman than the highwayman.

Or Mr Bourne could be laying a trap for Jones when he returned— which would make just as much sense. More, really, for if Jones had deposited all the spoils of his robbery in one night, it shouldn't take any longer than that for Mr Bourne to remove it.

The porridge was ready. Nell served herself and had eaten most of it in peace before Bett appeared. Unusually, Bett served herself with no pointed comments or sulks.

Nell was instantly suspicious. Now she thought about it, Bett hadn't been as obnoxious as usual for the last few days. As Nell watched, she fingered a ribbon around her neck with a smug smile. Not just a ribbon—the way it hung, and the way Bett fiddled with it, looked as if she had something hanging on it beneath her gown. Then Bett saw Nell gazing at her and her normal scowl returned.

"What are you staring at?"

"Nothing." Nell took her bowl and spoon into the scullery before Bett's mood could sour further—she didn't want to start the day with an argument. She found enough to do there to keep her occupied until Bett had finished her porridge and gone. Leaving her bowl and spoon on the table, naturally.

While frying onions and chopping meat for that day's stew, Nell returned to the happenings of the previous night. She'd said her absence would alert Silas to something being wrong. However, if she left today or tomorrow as the result of an argument, would that raise suspicion? Starting a dispute shouldn't be difficult. What would be harder was causing one that was bad enough to excuse her running away without earning her a beating from Silas before she left.

And what was safer? Staying here and trusting that Mr Bourne would vouch that she was not in league with Jones and her uncle? Or leaving now to avoid arrest and running the risk of not finding a position before her money ran out?

Neither option was good.

CHAPTER 8

"*A*h, there he is! Wake up, Bourne!"

Toby sat up, rolling his shoulders and rubbing his neck as Sir James' voice dragged him from sleep. Dozing in a chair was never a good idea, but he'd been awake most of the night and had only managed a few hours' sleep after arriving at Mr Hartley's house an hour after dawn. He envied Mr Hartley's men, still in their beds above the stables.

"Have they fed you?" Sir James asked.

"Yes, thank you, but more coffee would be good." He'd eaten a hearty breakfast, then sat down in this anteroom to await Sir James' arrival—and fallen asleep again.

"Already arranged. Come along."

Toby followed Sir James into a book-lined study, where Mr Hartley and Calvert, Lord Lanchester's steward, were waiting. Sir James pointed to a side table where a steaming coffee pot stood. Toby poured a cup and took the remaining chair at the central table.

Mr Hartley had a face full of lines and wrinkles, and hair that was white without powder, but his eyes were alert. The steward was a younger man, not much older than Toby.

"I hear you recovered the contents of the large chests, but not the jewellery," Sir James started.

Toby, his mouth full of coffee, just nodded.

Sir James turned to the steward. "Calvert, was anything missing apart from the jewellery box?"

"No. There has not been time to count the coins, but the correct number of bags have been recovered. Jones cannot have taken much, if anything."

"Excellent. Now, Bourne, give us the details, if you please."

Toby drained his cup and set it on the table. "The place was much as the stable boy described, with the chests in a hollow in the quarry face, hidden by a pile of rocks. The locks were undamaged, so either Jones did not have time to look in them, or he had a set of keys."

The steward frowned at that, but said nothing.

"We had no problems transferring the silver and coin," Toby went on. He looked towards Mr Hartley. "Your men worked well, sir."

Mr Hartley nodded, as if that were to be expected.

"However there were some unexpected incidents. It is possible we have found Lord Lanchester's missing outriders."

There was a short silence, then Mr Hartley spoke. "Dead, I take it, as you did not bring them back here with you."

"Indeed, sir. We found one of them, at least—I assume the other was there, too." Toby explained his reasoning in leaving the body they'd found where it was, then addressed Calvert. "He was wearing a bottle green coat with silver trim."

"Those are the colours of Lord Lanchester's livery," the steward confirmed. "Sir James, it seems your supposition that they were working for Jones might have been correct."

"A fitting reward for treachery," Sir James said. "It makes me wonder if anyone else in his lordship's employ was involved. Oh, not you, Calvert," he added, as the steward stiffened.

Lord Lanchester obviously trusted his steward, but Toby wondered what made Sir James so sure. Toby's military experience had taught him not to take others' opinions on faith alone.

"It may be best to leave them where they are until this operation is concluded," Sir James went on. "Going back tonight risks discovery."

Toby wrinkled his nose at the prospect of moving corpses that would have been dead for a week, but he needn't be involved.

"You said *some* incidents, Bourne," Sir James said.

Toby yawned. "Excuse me, I'll get myself some more coffee." He stood and went over to the side table. Should he tell them about Nell Mason? If Calvert *were* passing information to Jones, would that put her in danger? Jones couldn't kill everyone who now knew about his involvement, so what would be the point in killing Nell?

"Bourne?" Sir James sounded impatient.

He couldn't take the risk. He yawned again as he sat down. "Sorry, sir. I'm a bit short of sleep. What did you say?"

"*Some* incidents, you said."

"Did I? The dead outrider was the only unexpected thing we found." That was almost true. They hadn't found Nell—she had found them.

Mr Hartley looked at the clock on the mantelpiece. "Shall we get on, Troughton?"

Sir James kept his gaze on Toby's face for an uncomfortable moment longer, then shrugged. "Bourne, your colonel has replied to my letter. The men you asked for should arrive tomorrow evening. Hartley, they will come here, with your permission."

Mr Hartley nodded. "By all means. It's about time Jones was dealt with. I just hope this effort is more successful than previous attempts to catch him."

"Jones said he'd be back in a sennight," Sir James said. "According to the stable lad. That is the third night from now, by my reckoning."

"It would be well to have the men in place early," Mr Hartley said. "Jones may have said a sennight as a general term, rather than meaning exactly a week."

"That runs the risk of discovery, does it not?" Sir James asked. "Bourne?"

"We should be able to hide in the heather well enough at night, and leave only a couple of lookouts during the day. We've bivouacked in worse conditions." With any luck he would have caught up with his sleep by then. "It'll be full moon by then, but no-one will see a man lying in the heather."

"Very well." Sir James cast a quick glance at Calvert before returning his gaze to Toby. "Do you return to Scarborough today, or will you await your men here? I can take you in my carriage if you wish."

Toby hadn't yet considered where he would stay, but Sir James made the decision for him.

"Gentlemen, I'm sure you have other things to be doing," Sir James said. "I can discuss the disposition of the troops with Bourne on my way home." He stood as he spoke, and the other men followed suit.

"Until tomorrow, then, Bourne." Mr Hartley nodded, and Toby followed Sir James out to the stables, collecting his saddle bag on the way.

"Now," Sir James said, once the coach was in motion. "What didn't you say back there, and why didn't you say it?"

Toby addressed the second question first. "How sure are you, sir, that Calvert is not also in league with Jones?"

"Lanchester has full confidence in him."

"Lord Lanchester presumably also had full confidence in his outriders."

To Toby's surprise, Sir James chuckled. "Indeed. But his lordship would have had far more contact with Calvert than with a pair of outriders. If you are thinking about the keys to the chests, it is entirely possible that someone could have had copies made without Calvert's knowledge. That is something for Lord Lanchester to investigate. Besides, we cannot assume *everyone* is working for Jones—that way madness lies. However, I applaud your caution, which is why we will discuss the details of your plans here, in private. Now, what had you in mind?"

Toby gave a more detailed description of the quarry and the inn than he had earlier, and they discussed what Toby could do in response to different actions—if any—by Jones.

Sir James nodded when they had agreed on a plan. "I suppose we'll know whether Jones has been warned if he doesn't arrive, or comes with an army of his own. Hartley's men are unlikely to be able to find Jones even if they wished to betray our plans, so Calvert is the only one who could do so."

"Er, not necessarily, sir."

Sir James did not look surprised. "Is this what you would not say before?"

"Yes. Miss Mason—Weaver's niece—came to the quarry while we were there. I had no choice but to let her return to the inn. Her disappearance would have warned Weaver that something was wrong."

"What was she doing there in the middle of the night?" Sir James' voice was sharp.

"She also heard Jones talking to the landlord's daughter, and wanted to know what was happening."

"She's not in league with her uncle, then?"

"I don't think so, no." Toby wondered if he was about to be reprimanded for letting her find them. "I could have posted one of the men on the track so she could be turned back before she saw the quarry," he added. "But he would have been more visible there, and turning her back would have alerted her that something was going on. Although she knew that already—she came straight towards the quarry."

"Well, it cannot be helped now," Sir James said, to Toby's relief. "The stable lad spoke well of her. And yes, I don't know if he can be trusted either, but he does seem to have a strong dislike for Weaver. Besides, as you say, her absence would warn Weaver that something is amiss. We have no option but to trust her not to tell what she knows."

Toby went over the plan again in his head, but despite the jolting of the carriage his lack of sleep caught up with him, and he dozed the rest of the way.

Later that afternoon, Toby escorted Aunt Em on a walk by the sea. They strolled for a while near the beach, amid the cries of gulls wheeling against the overcast sky or squabbling over scraps from the women gutting fish. A few hardy souls were bathing in the sea—the very sight made Toby shiver. That was all well and good on a hot summer's day, but not in October with a bracing breeze coming off the water. He'd been cold and wet plenty of times in his life; there was no need to subject himself to that deliberately.

That reminded him of what would be an uncomfortable night or two to come. "I've to be away again tomorrow, Auntie, for two or three days."

"That's a shame—you won't have much of your leave left by the time Sir James has finished with you."

"It keeps me from getting under your feet." In truth, he wasn't sorry to have something useful to do. And it would be better still if some of Lord Lanchester's offered reward came his way.

"It keeps you from being asked to turn out my attic," she retorted, with mock severity, and she pulled her cloak more tightly about her.

"I should have some time afterwards."

"That's good." Her hand went to her hat as the breeze lifted its brim. "It's a bit too windy for me, Toby. I think I'll go and choose a new book."

"Give my regards to your Mr Everidge."

"He's not *my* Mr Everidge."

Was there a note of regret in her voice? Once this business with Jones was over, he must make time to meet the man. When he was an ocean away in the Colonies, he'd be happier knowing she was settled with a good man to look after her.

"Take a chair back, Auntie. I'll see you later."

He watched as she disappeared into one of the narrow streets leading away from the sea, then strode out along the edge of the water towards the castle looming above the town. He lingered for a while near the shipyards, speculating on what type of vessels the hulls under construction would become, and where they would travel.

His way back took him past the circulating library; he went in to see if Aunt Em was still there. She wasn't, but Miss Delaney was. She stood with her back to the window, a book in one hand and a discontented pout to her lips. Following the direction of her gaze, Toby saw another young lady standing with a finely dressed young man near the counter. They were deep in conversation, to the obvious irritation of the man trying to serve other patrons.

Was the man behind the counter Aunt Em's beau? Toby looked more closely, while trying not to be caught staring. The man was perhaps a few years older than Toby—far too young for Aunt Em.

"Why, Lieutenant Bourne, how nice to see you."

Miss Delaney had come to stand beside him—the pout transformed to her lovely smile. He removed his hat and bowed. "Miss Delaney."

"You did not call after the assembly, Lieutenant."

"My apologies. I had some business to attend to, which took me away." As her smile widened, he wondered why he hadn't thought to send a note of apology. Even a small posy, if any flowers were to be had at this time of year. How could his meeting with Sir James have made him forget her?

"Ah, well, that cannot be helped, then. You are forgiven. Do you go to the recital tomorrow evening, Lieutenant? Will I see you there?"

"I'm afraid not," he said with regret. "I have more pressing matters to deal with." He'd gladly put up with sitting on a hard chair for a couple of hours if he could bask in her regard. "What is being performed?"

"Oh, singing, a string quartet." She waved a hand as if the performance didn't matter. "One has to make the most of the limited events here. If only I could spend some time in London, or even York..." She shrugged. "It seems everyone is otherwise occupied tomorrow night."

"May I escort you home? Or for a walk along the shore?"

She shook her head. "No, I thank you. It is too cold and windy." Her eyes slid to a point behind him, and her lips returned to their pout. "I'm afraid I must go now. Farewell, Lieutenant."

Toby barely had time to reply before she stepped around him and out of the door. Through the window, he saw Colonel Maitland bowing over her raised hand on the street outside.

So much for it being too windy for Miss Delaney. Toby consoled himself with the thought she had seemed sorry to leave him. Perhaps the colonel's attraction might be the possession of a carriage?

"Can I help you, sir?"

Toby turned back to the counter. "No, thank you. I merely came in to see if my aunt was still here. Mrs Bourne."

"She was here, sir, but took a chair home half an hour ago. Do you wish to borrow something? You may have an extra volume on Mrs Bourne's subscription—I'm sure Mr Everidge would not mind."

As he walked back up the hill ten minutes later, a slim book on the antiquities of Yorkshire in his pocket, Toby thought Aunt Em might have set her eye on a good man. One who was generous enough for an employee to offer a favour without having to ask for permission first.

Toby had asked for the book on antiquities as he was interested in the history of the castle, but it also included a chapter on the old crosses on the moor. As he read it that evening, he thought again of Nell Mason—her interest in them, and their talk by moonlight. The memory of her voice was still clear in his mind.

How much did she know about Jones and his plans? He still felt there was something she hadn't told him, but that wasn't his concern at the moment. It was the thought of those two dead bodies only yards from where they had talked, and the murdered guards.

He had to warn her if he could do so without betraying his role in this business to anyone else. He would sleep on it, but he thought he would ride over the moors to meet his men in Pickering tomorrow, instead of taking the shorter route that skirted the southern edge of the high ground.

CHAPTER 9

$\mathcal{R}$un or stay?

That question preoccupied Nell so much that she burned the porridge the following morning and only escaped a beating by getting rid of the evidence before Silas was out of his bed. She made an effort to concentrate after that; fortunately, many of her tasks were simple enough to allow her time to think.

If she did leave, where would she go? Mr Bourne had said Tim was safe, but she didn't know where he was or whether she could also find refuge there.

She looked down at her gown, swathed in a stained apron. It was faded in places, some of the bodice seams worn. It would be difficult to persuade anyone that she was sufficiently respectable and trustworthy to take up a position as a kitchen maid, especially if they discovered she'd been working somewhere as disreputable as the Moorcock for the last five years. So she could use up all her meagre savings on lodgings and food while looking for a position, and find herself destitute.

No, she was better off staying where she was and keeping out of sight as much as she could. Containing her curiosity, and pretending not to notice anything that was out of the ordinary. When this business was over, perhaps then she would plan a proper departure—she could make enquires about possible positions next time she went to Pickering market.

It was only as she was serving the day's stew—beef this time—to a couple of travellers that she remembered there might be no more marketing for her to do. What would happen to the inn if Silas were arrested? Could she and Gibson run the place without him? What if Bett were arrested, too?

Then, as Bett swayed her way towards the travellers with their ale, Nell thought that she probably *could* run the inn for long enough to save more money. Neither Bett nor Silas did much that was useful, and if she and Gibson shared all the takings for a week or two, she would have a good deal more than her current savings.

All she had to do was wait, and stay out of trouble.

Nell thought trouble had come to her that afternoon. She caught a glimpse through the kitchen window of another traveller leaving his horse in the stable. Mr Bourne—what was he doing here?

She leaned against the table, a sick feeling knotting her stomach. Was he working with Jones and her uncle after all? Would he tell Silas about her sneaking out onto the moor? Then sense returned, and she took a deep breath. Why would he have been at the quarry in the night if Silas knew about it?

Bett came into the kitchen. Her brows rose as she took in Nell just standing at the table, but to Nell's surprise, she only said another plate of stew was wanted and took herself off again. Something wasn't normal with Bett, but Nell didn't have time to think about that now.

Nell straightened her skirts and tucked loose hair under her cap before carrying a plate of stew into the public room. Mr Bourne looked up and their eyes met for a moment, then his gaze returned to her tray as if they'd never met and all he wanted was food.

Perhaps that *was* all he wanted. Travellers often stopped here for food and ale.

The other customers were busy with their drinks and a game of dominoes. Silas was staring into the fire as usual, too far away to hear if she spoke quietly. Should she ask Mr Bourne why he was here?

But no—as Nell began to unload the tray, Bett came over with a mug of ale and showed no signs of leaving.

"Enjoy your meal," Nell said as she set the platter of bread down.

"Thank you." Mr Bourne pulled a large, folded handkerchief from his pocket as he spoke. "I need some bread and cheese for my journey. You can wrap it in this." He met her gaze for a second with no change of expression, and as soon as she had taken the handkerchief, he picked up his fork and smiled at Bett.

Nell strode back to the kitchen, annoyed with herself. She should be relieved he'd given no sign of recognition, not disappointed because he seemed to be like all the others, drawn to a low neckline and over-reddened lips. She crushed the handkerchief in her fist before dropping it onto the table and heading for the pantry to get some cheese.

Her steps slowed, then she stopped and turned back. The handkerchief had felt stiff, crackling as she squeezed it. Picking it up, she headed for the pantry again and closed the door behind her, then unfolded the linen square. A piece of paper was tucked inside.

Jones robbed a coach, killing several men. Later, he killed two of his allies as well. I found them in the quarry. Large sum of money taken. Jones likely to kill witnesses. Get away if you can. Sir James Troughton is Scarborough magistrate. He will find you somewhere to stay. Burn this.

The kitchen door opened, and Nell hurriedly thrust the note into the top of her bodice. Her knees felt as if they were about to give way as she carried the cheese to the table, but it was only Gibson on his way to the cellar. Once he'd gone, she thrust the note into the fire, watching until it turned to ash and vanished. Then she collapsed into a chair.

At least five men dead at Jones' hand in the last few days; a greater number if the coach had had more than a driver and a couple of guards. Or dead at Jones' order—it came to the same thing. And some of those were men who'd worked with him. Hiding those bodies must have been what Silas had been doing with his spade and brush. Her uncle was now an accomplice in murder.

Gibson clumped up the cellar stairs, a keg of ale on one shoulder. "You all right, Nell? You look a bit pale."

"I felt a bit faint. I'll be well in a moment." The first was true; she wasn't sure about the second.

"Have a bit of brandy. Always helps me." He nodded and went on his way.

The thought of brandy made Nell feel nauseous, but some water settled her stomach. For now, she must hide her fear and carry on as if everything was normal. She cut bread and cheese and wrapped it in the handkerchief, relieved to see her hands were steady in spite of her feelings. She was tempted to let Bett deliver it to Mr Bourne, but he deserved to know his warning had been found.

It was easier than she had expected. Bett was still with him, now sitting at the table while he ate. Nell placed the package at his elbow. "Just as you ordered, sir."

He looked up and nodded, only a slight narrowing of his eyes acknowledging anything more than thanks for the food. Some time later, she saw Mr Bourne enter the stable, then lead his horse out. She made no attempt to speak to him, but crept out into the yard and around the side of the building in time to see him ride away to the east—towards Scarborough, or the Whitby to Pickering road, not towards the quarry.

Uncle Silas was watching, too. He grabbed her arm and dragged her towards the door. "Get back to the kitchen, girl, now! If I see you beyond the yard, you'll wish you'd never been born."

Nell obeyed—Silas did not make empty threats.

Why had her uncle been observing Mr Bourne leave? She left the door between the kitchen and passage open, watching and waiting for the other two travellers to depart. Silas went outside to check where they went, too. Good—that meant Silas probably did not suspect Mr Bourne of anything.

This morning, she'd decided to stay. What Mr Bourne had just told her made her question that decision, and now she also knew where to go. But it was too late now.

As her uncle was keeping a watch on everyone, she would have no chance to escape during daylight hours. She would be quickly missed and Silas would come after her. With his girth he didn't walk quickly, but even old Dobbin could manage a fast enough pace to catch up with her.

She could leave at night, but how far would she get before daylight? Trying to escape and failing could be even more dangerous than staying here and minding her own business.

Or giving the appearance of doing so, at least.

Toby shifted uncomfortably in the heather at the top of the quarry, wishing that Jones would come for his takings. He'd returned to the moor with his men the day after he'd given Nell the warning note, in uniform this time. They'd arrived in the dusk, and achieved nothing that night other than getting cold and damp. As dawn came, they retreated a few miles to a patch of woodland to the south, to warm themselves by a fire.

Now the thick clouds and drizzle of the night before had cleared, and the full moon shone brightly. Below and behind him, nine of his men sat in a circle, their low voices inaudible from this distance. Some way beyond them, his horse was tethered—saddled, and ready to go if he needed it.

His mind turned to Nell Mason, as it had numerous times since he had first called at the Moorcock. She must have read his note, for it was not in the handkerchief with the bread and cheese she'd given him. He had to trust she had destroyed it. He'd have preferred to talk to her directly, but doing so might have marked her out as an ally of his if their bid to capture Jones failed.

Was she still at the inn?

"Sir!" Sergeant Slater approached through the heather from his post by the track. "Cart on the road, couldn't see how many men."

"Very good. Get the men into position."

"Right, sir."

As Slater went on down to the quarry, Toby wriggled further into the heather. He should be hidden well enough, unless whoever was coming actually tripped over him.

The men, when they came, weren't trying to conceal their presence. Toby first saw two shapes silhouetted against the sky, then heard muffled curses as they stumbled on the rough ground. They were heading straight for the quarry, so they must have been here before, and they passed closely enough for him to make out some of their words.

"…how heavy the stuff…"

"…have to bring the cart… more men…"

"…bloody Weaver, never…"

"…said it would be worth our while this…"

Damn—neither of them was Jones. The simple plan was not going to work.

Toby waited until they were several yards away, then followed them, pleased to see no sign of his men. They stopped in the centre of the quarry floor, looking about them.

"…rocks by the wall…"

"…bloody piles of rocks everywhere…"

"…what's that smell?"

"…wait for him to get here before…"

So they were expecting someone else to come—Jones, possibly, or Weaver. It would be easier to capture whoever else came if these two were already taken care of.

"Get them! No shooting!"

The two men froze, then ran for the quarry entrance—straight into the four soldiers now blocking the way. A short scuffle, then the men stood before him, each held between two of his soldiers. It was almost comical, the way their mouths dropped open as they took in Toby's uniform.

"Slater, send someone up to keep an eye on the track." He turned to the prisoners. "Who are you working for?"

The men looked at each other, then back at Toby. One swore, and spat at Toby's feet, but neither of them answered his question.

He didn't have time for this—Jones could arrive at any moment. He jerked his head towards the pile of rocks that hid the dead outriders. "Take them over there." He waited until they had been dragged across the quarry floor. "Notice the smell? D'you know what it is?"

A muffled curse from one of them told Toby that they had guessed.

"The chests you've been employed to move are the takings from a highway robbery by Gentleman Jones. Two of the men who helped him are under those rocks. Do you want to see them?" He hoped not —disturbing the bodies could only make the smell worse.

"We don't know nothing about Jones," one said, lifting his chin. "Weaver from the Moorcock told us to get the stuff onto our cart and wait for him to tell us where to take it. Just like the—" He stopped talking as his companion elbowed him in the ribs.

Just like the other times they'd transported illicit goods, Toby guessed. "Oh, I'm sure the jury will believe you when you say you are innocent. Arriving at a remote place like this by moonlight, to load stolen goods. Nothing suspicious about that, not at all."

One of the soldiers sniggered. "Nubbing cheat for you two."

"On the other hand," Toby added, "if you turn King's evidence, you might avoid the hangman."

Toby let them mull it over while he considered what to do. They probably had more information, although it might take some time to get it out of them. They had said they were to wait for Weaver—if that were the case, Toby could take some of his men to the Moorcock and question the innkeeper directly—the testimony of these men would be enough to have Weaver arrested.

It was more likely that Jones would be coming as well, though. Both Nell Mason and the stable boy had heard him say he would be returning. In that case, it would be best to have these two out of the way and the cart hidden. He could leave enough men here to capture Jones if he came to the quarry first. And if Jones came here and found no cart waiting for him, he'd go to the Moorcock to find out why Weaver's arrangements hadn't been put in place. The only risk was if Jones arrived while they were on their way to the inn.

"Sergeant, you'll stay here with four men. You know what to do. Send one of them to fetch my horse and bring it to the inn. I'm taking these two and the rest of the men to the Moorcock."

CHAPTER 10

Something was going to happen tonight, Nell was certain. Uncle Silas had been more irritable than usual, coming into the kitchen too often for her liking. He never said much, just went through to the scullery and looked out into the yard. Checking she was still here, Nell guessed, and that there was no-one sneaking around looking for things he didn't want to be seen.

Bett, too, seemed to be anticipating something, repeatedly fingering the ribbon around her neck and casting the odd smug look in Nell's direction. Unlike Uncle Silas, she didn't seem worried by what was to come.

Nell carried on with her usual duties, trying her best to ignore her own feeling of doom. She almost wished Mr Bourne hadn't told her about the dead men.

The day followed its usual course—a few travellers wanting food, a few local quarrymen coming in for ale. When the last customers left several hours after dark, Nell banked the fire before mopping the kitchen floor.

Gibson had already retired for the night, but she hadn't heard Silas or Bett go upstairs. In the passage, a line of light showed under the door of the public room. They must be waiting up for someone to arrive.

For Jones to arrive.

Nell went to her room, where she would be safely away from anything that was about to occur. Out of sight, out of mind, with luck. But she didn't undress—instead, she took her spare pocket from the chest and fastened it beneath her skirts. Then she lifted the end of her mattress and transferred the little leather purse with her savings from its hiding place to the pocket. Best to have it on her person in case she needed to leave quickly. Then she lay on her bed to wait.

She didn't sleep—worry about what was to come prevented that. For some time the only sounds were the usual night-creaks of the building. Then hoof-beats made her sit up and peer out of the window.

A cart turned onto the cobbles, with a single man driving and another on horseback beside it. But what made her breath catch were the four men marching behind the cart—were those muskets? Fear knotted her stomach—Jones had brought well-armed men with him. She might be able to escape Jones, but four armed guards…?

As the rider dismounted by the front door, two of the armed men marched on around the side of the inn, muskets at the ready.

Marched?

They weren't Jones' men, they were soldiers. Nell felt weak with relief. Had Mr Bourne sent them?

The rider banged on the front door. "Open up, in the name of the King!"

It sounded like Mr Bourne himself. What was happening?

As Nell crept down the stairs, Uncle Silas and Bett emerged from the public room and hurried into the kitchen. Nell sat on the top step to await events. There was no need for her to let the soldiers in—Silas and Bett would do that themselves when they attempted to escape through the back yard. Men shouted, Bett screamed insults, then a single soldier strode along the passage from the kitchen. He unlocked the front door.

"Got two of 'em, sir," the soldier said, then Mr Bourne appeared.

He wore a red coat, too. Was he an army officer? Why hadn't he said so before?

"Put them in there," Mr Bourne said, pointing at the door to the public room.

Nell stood and took a step down, but Mr Bourne pulled out a pistol and pointed it at her.

"Come down, and keep your hands where I can see them."

Nell didn't move. "It's me. Nell Mason."

"Oh, sorry." He uncocked the pistol and put it back in his pocket. "Who else is in the building?"

"Only Gibson—the potman."

"Fetch him."

Nell stepped back up to the landing—feeling much less afraid, but also unaccountably irritated. It was bad enough being ordered about by her uncle; for Mr Bourne to do it as well was…

It was sensible, she had to admit to herself as she banged on Gibson's door. Mr Bourne wasn't on a social call. Under the circumstances, expecting a polite enquiry about her health was ridiculous.

She banged again, then went back to her room to fetch the lantern. Gibson was at his door when she returned, his nightgown hanging loosely from his thin frame. He squinted at her and rubbed his face. "What d'you want?" A noise from downstairs seemed to dispel his sleepiness and his gaze ran quickly over her. "What's wrong, Nell? Are you well?"

"Soldiers," Nell said. "They want us in the public room."

He shook his head. "Knew it would come to this one day. I'll put some clothes on."

Nell left him to it. In the public room, Uncle Silas and Bett were sitting at a table near the fire. Silas had his usual scowl and was muttering under his breath. Bett's lips were set in a sullen pout, but her hands were clenched tightly together on the table, the knuckles showing white. The soldier standing a few feet away wasn't pointing his musket at them, but he looked ready to use it.

"Lieutenant Bourne said you was wanted in the kitchen, miss," he said, looking at her briefly before turning his attention back to his captives.

When Toby first entered the inn, Nell Mason had been a possible threat at the top of the stairs, then only a moving shadow. When she entered the kitchen, the lamplight showed a wariness in her expression as her gaze went from him to Beckett and Kearny standing by the back door, awaiting orders.

"Why didn't you leave?" His concern made his question come out more harshly than he'd intended. She was in danger here.

Her brows rose, but she answered readily enough. "My uncle was watching me. Watching everyone. He'd have come after me as soon as he found I was missing."

"Whatever happens, the magistrate in Scarborough will help you." If she could get there. "I have two prisoners—men who arrived at the quarry with a cart. Is there somewhere to lock them up?"

"The tack room in the stable has a bolt on the outside and no window."

No—they could try breaking the door down there and no-one would hear. "Somewhere inside the inn? The cellar?"

She nodded. "There's a room with a lock on the door down there. My uncle has the key."

"Beckett, get the key from the landlord."

Beckett hurried off and Toby turned back to Miss Mason. "Is there an upstairs room with a view along the road?"

"My uncle's room is the best—it has a side window as well. Second door on the right."

"Kearney." Toby jerked his head upwards, and Kearney clomped up the stairs, the sound of his footsteps fading as he marched along the landing.

"Miss Mason, I don't know how long we'll be here. It could be all night if Jones doesn't come. Stay with your uncle and cousin, and the potman—you should be safe in there. I won't be far away."

She nodded. As she left, Beckett returned with a key, and they went out into the yard.

"Well, Hoskins?" Toby said, as one of the soldiers approached.

"Cart wouldn't fit in the stable, sir," Hoskins reported as two of the others took the prisoners inside. "Put it behind the building."

Toby couldn't see it, so Jones was unlikely to. "Very good."

"Both horses are inside. Left yours ready to go, like you said." Hoskins turned and pointed to the clump of trees a little way from the inn. "Reckon one of us could 'ide in them trees, keep an eye on the bit of track beyond, where you can't see from the inn."

"Good idea." Hoskins would make a good corporal. "You take that position. I'll be here, near the stable. Come and tell me if you see anything."

Hoskins saluted and headed for the trees while Toby worked out where to position his remaining two men.

The atmosphere in the public room was tense. The young soldier pointed his musket at Nell as she stepped through the door, but relaxed again when he saw who it was. Gibson had arrived, and was slumped in a chair in one corner—from his lack of reaction to her arrival, Nell guessed he had fallen asleep again.

"Where the hell have you been?" Silas snarled. He pushed down on the table as if about to stand, but the soldier pointed his musket again and Silas subsided. "Why did that officer want to talk to *you*?"

Nell sat down at the table furthest from Silas and Bett. She'd be cold here, far from the fire, but that was better than being within reach of her uncle.

"Well, girl?"

Nell glanced at the soldier, who shrugged. She couldn't see any harm in answering. "He wanted to know where he could lock up two prisoners."

Bett's mouth fell open, then she shook her head. "Can't be Jones, Pa, or—"

Silas slapped her, snapping her head sideways. "You keep your mouth shut, hear? If *he* don't repeat what you say, *she* likely will." His finger jabbed in the direction of the soldier, then Nell.

The soldier's eyes flicked over the other empty tables in the room, then he pointed his musket at Bett. "You, move to a different table."

Bett pouted, but did as she was told, her hips swaying as she moved to a table closer to the soldier. Then she eyed him and licked her lips. "You look a nice young man. Have you got a girl?"

Good heavens, what did Bett think she could achieve by that? The lad's face reddened, but he didn't answer.

Bett played with the ribbon around her neck, running her finger down it to where it disappeared just above her breasts. "What's your name, love?"

The soldier hesitated before answering. "Frampton."

Bett's tongue moistened her lower lip. "I could give you a lovely—"

"I don't need to pay for whores."

Nell almost laughed at the expression on Bett's face, but Frampton's words had the desired effect. Bett stuck her lip out and folded her arms. However, although she stopped talking, she didn't take her eyes off him.

She was plotting something, Nell was sure. But what? She had no hope of overpowering the soldier alone, and Silas was too slow and fat to get close to him before getting shot. And although the musket had only one shot—she knew that much—the bayonet on its muzzle was a fearsome weapon.

Whatever Bett's plan was, there was nothing Nell could do about it.

Why should she? She should be concerned for her own safety—she owed nothing to these soldiers. Or to Silas and Bett. Looking at Silas, Nell wondered that she had hesitated at all about keeping word of Lieutenant Bourne's activities from her uncle. Silas was a vicious unpleasant bully—he'd not let Mama starve, but he'd made her life miserable and was doing the same to Nell.

And Bett? She'd readily copied her father's attitudes, and although she wasn't always unfriendly, it wasn't enough. If Nell had to choose between helping the soldiers or helping Silas, there was no question that she was on the side of the law.

Would she have come to the same decision if Lieutenant Bourne didn't have such a friendly smile? She hoped so. It wasn't just his smile that had attracted her, though, nor his brown eyes or broad shoulders. He'd talked to *her;* the Nell who enjoyed reading poetry or history—or reading anything she could lay her hands on. The Nell who had wishes beyond her next meal, who had ideas and opinions of her own.

Whatever took place this night, she was determined that her life would change. Somehow. But all she could do now was wait.

She had no idea how long they sat there in hostile silence. It seemed like forever. Then boots thumped down the stairs—running.

The soldier upstairs had seen someone coming.

Chair legs scraped on the floor, and Nell turned her head to see Bett spring across the room towards Frampton. He held her off with one hand, but she twisted away and reached for his musket.

The muzzle of the weapon swung her way; Nell quickly slid off her chair and took what shelter she could below the table.

Then the musket fired, and someone cried out in pain.

Kearney burst out of the kitchen door, head turning from side to side.

"Over here." Toby stepped out of the shadows, keeping his voice low—sound would carry far on a still night like this.

"Rider coming on the road from the north, s—" He broke off as a shot sounded.

From *inside* the inn? Toby swore. "Get back upstairs and watch."

As Kearney dashed back inside, another shot sounded—this one louder, off to one side, then another from beyond the inn. As Toby rounded the end of the building, he almost collided with Hoskins coming the other way.

"Shot at 'im, sir, but 'e was galloping away and too far off. Which bloody idiot fired—?"

"Never mind that now." The rider must have been Jones—an innocent man would not gallop away if he had nothing to be afraid of.

"Which way did he go—did you see?" Toby ran towards the stable as he spoke, Hoskins keeping pace.

"North on the road, I think."

"I'll go after him. Get Slater and the others back here, then you take the prisoners and the landlord and his daughter to the magistrate at Scarborough at first light, if I'm not back by then. Sir James Troughton." He led his horse out of the stable and checked the girth was still tight. "Take four men with you—if I don't catch Jones, he might still want to kill witnesses."

"Right, sir."

"Good, now fetch Slater."

Hoskins set off at a run, just as the man who'd been stationed in front of the inn arrived. "I expect you missed him, too," Toby said, mounting the horse.

"Yes, sir. Sorry, sir."

"Go and see if Frampton's all right, then get back on watch outside."

The soldier hurried into the inn as Toby rode around to the front. He stopped near the front door and shouted, "Kearney?"

An upstairs window opened. "North, sir. He's out of sight now."

"Keep watching."

He spurred the horse into a trot, onto the track towards the cross, then northwards. The road ahead was pale in the moonlight, winding on across the moor, dipping out of sight in places. It was a pity there weren't more horses available, but it would have been difficult to conceal more than one.

Was that a rider ahead? The dark speck against the road was too far away to make out any details. He urged his mount faster—if Jones came to a turning before he caught up, Toby wouldn't know which way to go.

He must have covered several miles before he saw that speck again, larger now. And not long afterwards he topped a shallow rise in the road to see a horse several hundred yards away, apparently cropping a patch of grass beside the road. Toby reined in, cursing the moonlight; it was bright enough to light his way, but not to make out details amongst the patches of black shade.

The horse was saddled. Was the rider lying injured by the road somewhere? The ground here was more grass than heather, and Toby could see nothing the size of a man close to the horse, so he rode on cautiously.

The horse jerked its head, looking towards Toby, but didn't move away. It jerked again, as if pulling against reins fastened somewhere below it. Tied up…

Ambush!

A shot rang out as Toby kicked his foot out of the stirrup.

CHAPTER 11

$\mathcal{A}$s the sound of the shot echoed around the room, Nell put her head above the table to see Bett flying backwards. Frampton uncurled his fist and bent to pick up his musket. A shot sounded from outside the building, then another.

Nell stood, cautiously. Bett was in a heap on the floor—groaning, but making no effort to get to her feet. Frampton had his back to the wall, his eyes flicking from Bett to Silas to Gibson while his hands moved to reload his weapon.

"You shot me, you stupid bitch." Silas gripped one arm with the other hand, blood running over his fingers. He looked at Nell. "Get me a bandage."

"No-one's goin' anywhere." Frampton spoke before Nell could reply. He levelled his musket at Silas, and his thumb clicked back a lever on its top. "You move out of that chair and I'll put a bullet in your chest. *I* won't miss."

"Frampton?" a voice called from beyond the door.

"Come in." Frampton didn't take his eyes off Silas and Bett as another soldier entered the room.

"What happened? You all right?"

"She grabbed my musket and fired it." Frampton waved the musket barrel towards Bett. "Shot her father," he added.

"Didn't make a very good job of it."

Frampton sniggered. A voice called from outside, and there was an answering shout from above, then the sound of hooves trotting away.

"I wouldn't laugh too much if I was you," the newcomer said. "The lieutenant ain't goin' ter be pleased when he hears about it."

That wiped the smile off Frampton's face. Nell could sympathise— it had taken only a moment's inattention, and who would have guessed that Bett would go to such lengths to protect her lover? She could have been shot herself.

The second soldier went off again. Frampton stayed where he was, even when Bett moaned again and sat up, cradling one cheek in her hand. Silas was still holding his arm, but it looked to Nell as if the blood was no longer flowing and his face was its normal florid hue. Nell felt no sympathy for him.

"I feel sick," Bett moaned, her face pale. She pulled on the table, almost tipping it over as she got to her feet. "I'll just get some water from—"

"No." Frampton's voice was firm. He looked at Nell. "You go. Just water, mind, and come straight back."

Nell fetched a cup of water from the scullery and took it to Bett. Rather than thanks, she received a scowl. "Why are *you* the trusted one? Making up to that lieutenant, were you?" She drank the water, and her colour began to return. "You'll regret it when Jones comes back for me."

Nell held her hand out for the empty cup, so Bett could not be tempted to throw it. "Why would he come back for you?" For the spoils of the robbery, she could understand, but would a ruthless man like Jones, who'd murdered two of his accomplices, put himself in danger for a woman?

"He *will* come back," Bett said, as she gave Nell the cup. "He gave... He *will* come."

Nell sat down. It seemed there was now no immediate threat from Jones, so why were they still being kept in this room?

More soldiers—that was what the men had been waiting for. Nell heard boots across the yard then voices in the hall. Frampton stood up straighter at the sound and cast a nervous glance at the door.

Two more soldiers entered, one with a sash around his waist and an air of authority. He was old enough to be Nell's father, with a weather-beaten face and creases by his eyes that might have come from smiling. Or might not, as he certainly wasn't smiling now. He examined each person in the room without speaking, then turned to Frampton. "Why did you shoot?"

Frampton pointed at Bett, with his hand this time, not his musket. "She jumped at me and pulled the trigger, sarge."

The sergeant looked at Bett again, a slight curl to his lip. "Flashed her bosom at you, did she? Damned idiot."

Nell wasn't sure if he meant Bett or Frampton.

"It wasn't like that, sarge!"

"Ah, well. The lieutenant can deal with that when he gets back. As for the tart, she'd better go as well as the landlord's daughter."

"She *is* his daughter," Nell said, offended by the idea that Silas might be her father. "I'm Nell Mason, the cook."

"Cook, eh?" the sergeant said. "We could all do with some food before we do anything else."

Glad to escape from the public room, Nell brewed coffee, stirred porridge, and fried ham and eggs. And listened to the talk as the soldiers came in twos and threes to eat. From snatches overheard, Nell gathered this was the second night they'd spent waiting for Jones to arrive.

The sergeant came in last. Nell served him porridge and coffee, waiting until he'd emptied the bowl before venturing a question.

"What will happen now, Sergeant? Is Lieutenant Bourne coming back?"

The sergeant eyed the ham waiting to be sliced, and the empty bowl that had contained eggs.

"I'm afraid your men have eaten all the eggs, but there is plenty of bread and ham, Sergeant...?"

"Slater. I'll have some of that, if you please. And more coffee."

Instead of fetching the bread, Nell sat down.

Slater took the hint. "I've orders to send Weaver and his daughter to the magistrate at Scarborough, along with the men we captured at the quarry last night. You're the one that found us there before, aren't you? I can't imagine the lieutenant letting that other one go."

"It was me, yes," Nell admitted.

"And now the daft bugger's gone chasing that Jones on his own," Slater added. The words were a criticism, but there was a hint of affection in his tone, and worry. That made Nell worry, too, but Lieutenant Bourne must know what he was doing.

"When are you expecting him back?"

"Dunno. I was at the quarry; he gave the orders to Hoskins. Depends if he catches up, or loses him."

"What about me, Sergeant? What is to happen to me? And Gibson —the other man in the public room?"

"Didn't get no orders about that. You can go with them into Scarborough if you want, but we was told to send four men in case Jones tried to kill the witnesses. You might be safer staying here."

Nell frowned. Alone with an inn full of soldiers? That sounded just as risky, although in a different way.

"Miss, the lieutenant'd have their boll— I mean, would discipline any of the men who acted disrespectful to you. I would, too." He eyed the ham again, and this time Nell served him, then sat down to her own breakfast.

The stars were beginning to fade into the dawn sky when everyone had been fed, but the lieutenant still hadn't returned. Sergeant Slater sent two men to ready the cart. He stood outside the kitchen door with another mug of coffee in his hand, then strode across the yard to look in the stable. Nell followed him, curious to see what was happening, and wanting a distraction from worrying about what had happened to Lieutenant Bourne.

"Hoskins!" Slater made her jump with his sudden shout, and one of the soldiers came running. "What, exactly, did the lieutenant say you were to do?"

"Take the prisoners and them two indoors to the magistrate."

"Nothing else?"

"He wasn't 'anging about, sarge."

"Hmm. Get this one ready as well." He jerked his thumb in the direction of the inn's cart. "I don't think it's a good idea to have Weaver tell the others what their story should be." He looked at Nell. "More room for you, if you want to go with them?"

Nell had been thinking whether to stay or go, but any risk from the soldiers would apply whether she went with them or stayed here. The thought of sharing the cart with Bett and Uncle Silas all the way to Scarborough decided her.

"I'll stay."

"Good." Slater grinned and patted his stomach.

She'd still be cooking, then. "Will you bring the cart back?"

"The men'll come back with the one that belongs here." He drained his mug and handed it to her.

Had she made the right decision? Nell washed dishes while she mulled over her situation. Some of the soldiers would be staying here, so her vague plan of running the inn with Gibson for a week or so in Silas' absence wasn't going to work. The presence of the remaining soldiers was likely to deter the kind of men who came here in the evenings. And what would she do for money to buy supplies, assuming the soldiers *did* bring the cart back? She didn't want to use her savings.

It had probably been a foolish idea anyway. If she and Gibson were the only ones here, what was there to stop any passing travellers from just taking what they wanted? Including her virtue, if she were unlucky.

She'd stay for now. If she changed her mind later, Scarborough wasn't too far to walk.

Two soldiers brought the prisoners up from the cellar and took them out into the yard, their hands bound in front of them. Two more came in carrying a length of cord and went on into the public room, followed by Sergeant Slater. Nell's lips compressed; no matter how her relatives had treated her, she didn't take any pleasure in the fact they were to be carried off to gaol.

"You can't take me away like this!" Bett's shriek easily reached the kitchen. "I need to go to my room."

"If you want a piss, we'll leave you in here for a few minutes." That was Slater's voice. Nell went closer to listen, stopping in the open doorway.

"I need my clothes. I can't stay in these things for days."

"You can take them if you want, but they'll get stolen in gaol."

Bett's mouth dropped open, then she seemed to collect herself. "I need my clothes."

"Frampton, go and get her stuff." Slater caught sight of Nell standing in the doorway. "Miss Mason'll show you which room."

Bett's shoulders slumped. "Don't bother. I'm not having him looking through my things. Nor *her* either."

"Up to you, miss," Slater said. "Put her in the cart, lads."

"I need to use the chamber pot."

Slater swore beneath his breath. "Be quick." He jerked his head towards Silas, and the two soldiers bound his hands and led him away —sullen, but not protesting. Nell followed Slater into the passage.

Bett emerged a few minutes later, still complaining, and was escorted outside, casting a vicious look at Nell as she went.

Nell stood in the kitchen doorway, watching as Bett settled herself in the cart. Then she frowned as the two carts moved off. There had been something different about Bett—a small thing. A change she had made while she was alone for a few minutes.

The ribbon, that was it.

Bett had worn that ribbon around her neck, and whatever hung on it, since Jones' midnight visit, but she'd removed it while she'd been alone in the public room. Whatever had been hanging on it must now be concealed beneath her skirts. Something Jones had given her, Nell guessed.

But that didn't explain why Bett hadn't wanted anyone else going into her room. Not even Nell, who often went in there to change the sheets or leave washed shifts and petticoats. Had Jones given her some of his pickings to hide?

"You all right, miss?" Slater said, coming towards her.

"Just tired, Sergeant. May I go to my room?"

"Of course."

The first place to look was Bett's room. It was larger than Nell's—naturally—but the potential hiding places were similar. It would be easiest to start with the clothespress; if Bett had hidden something inside her mattress, as Nell had, why would it matter if someone went into her room?

It didn't take long. A long, flat leather-covered box was concealed beneath the undergarments stowed in the bottom drawer—a safe enough place in normal circumstances. It was nearly two feet long and a foot wide. The leather was torn near the lock, the wood beneath splintered, and the lid lifted easily. Nell took it to the window where the light was better, and looked inside. The interior was in two parts, with shallow, velvet-lined trays on each side divided into several small compartments. A few were empty; the others contained jewelled pins, several brooches and fobs, and gold rings, some studded with diamonds and rubies.

Jones could well return for this.

She lifted one tray, her hands stilling as she saw what was beneath. The kind of jewellery she'd only ever seen in prints of royalty or high-ranking ladies. A tiara like a small crown, eardrops, a necklace and a brooch—a matching set, each piece with a large emerald surrounded by smaller diamonds, all set in silver, each in their own, specially shaped compartment. If they were genuine, they must be as valuable as they were beautiful. Nell lifted the tiara out, turning it this way and that in the pale light from the window. A long black hair was caught between two of the diamonds. Of course, Bett had tried them on and admired herself in the mirror.

Hands shaking, she lifted out the other tray. A similar set of jewellery lay beneath that—this one with rubies surrounded by tiny pearls. But there was one empty place—this set had no brooch.

Was that what Bett had hung on a ribbon around her neck? Possibly not, Nell thought. If the missing brooch were of a similar size to the one in the emerald set, it was too big for that. More likely she had one of the smaller pieces missing from the top trays. Nell was surprised Bett hadn't taken more.

If Nell could sell these jewels, she'd be set up for life. She need never be dependent on anyone again.

She should not, but it was tempting.

It would also be stupid. Very stupid. She wouldn't have the first idea how to sell even one of the plainer pins without being found out. And then she'd be transported or hanged for theft. Might there be a reward for finding them? Even a small amount would make her future more secure.

Sounds from below stairs reminded her that she wasn't alone. She hurriedly replaced the trays, closed the box, and put it back where she had found it.

She could tell the soldiers about it, but they might assume she had taken items from the empty compartments in the tray. And if there were to be a reward for finding them, she would rather not share it with anyone else.

If Lieutenant Bourne were here, he would believe that some items had been missing when she found the box. But he hadn't returned. She pushed aside the dismal thought that Jones was not an opponent to take lightly, and the lieutenant might not be the victor in an encounter with him.

No, she would not think about that. There was time yet for him to return, and she had to think what to do next.

She had decided to stay at the inn, but this discovery changed things. If she could tell the magistrate in Scarborough about the jewels, he could have Bett searched. Finding one of the missing pieces of jewellery on Bett would corroborate Nell's story.

Scarborough, then. But the jewels would have to be hidden elsewhere—Bett might have told Jones where she would hide them.

Drawers and clothespresses were too obvious, the spaces beneath beds or behind furniture too easily searched. The cellars, perhaps? There was one room down there that held only broken furniture and some empty kegs. That would have to do.

Sergeant Slater had said that the soldiers would bring the inn's cart back, but she had no idea when that would be, or if Slater would allow her to take the cart and Dobbin to Scarborough. She would set off on foot as soon as she'd hidden the box in the cellar.

CHAPTER 12

Nell paused by the cross to look back at the inn. It had been her home for five years, the monotony of her days relieved only by the weekly marketing trips to Pickering. If all went well, she would never have to live there again. She should be pleased, but that period had been nearly a quarter of her life and it felt strange to think it was over.

She set off eastwards, adjusting the bundle slung over her shoulder. It contained her spare gown and undergarments, and Papa's book of poems, all wrapped in a piece of the oiled cloth that Gibson used to cover the cart. Her meagre savings were still in the pocket beneath her skirt where she'd hidden them—was it only last night? Less than twelve hours ago.

Sergeant Slater had tried to persuade her not to go, in case she was robbed on her way. But her gown and cloak were shabby, and belongings wrapped in cloth were not a sign of wealth. The track across the moor was not known for highway robbery—travellers with something worth stealing were few and far between. She said as much to Slater, who hadn't looked convinced but did not prevent her leaving.

Nell tramped along the stony track, the movement warming her in spite of the chill wind. The clear skies of the night had gone, and grey clouds leached colour from the landscape. Only a brighter strip of sky behind her indicated that better weather might be in the offing.

At first she didn't mind the lack of other travellers, but as she walked on, the moor began to feel lonely. There was nothing to see ahead—only the heather and an occasional scrubby tree. She was but a tiny speck in a vast space.

She *knew* this track led towards the coast, to places where she could ask directions to Scarborough, but she had never been this way before. If she became lost, what then?

"Don't be silly," she told herself. She turned to look behind her again. The inn was out of sight but the cross was just visible against the lighter line of sky. Traces of the road to Whitby showed pale against the grass and heather.

There was a traveller on the road—she was *not* alone. She squinted, trying to make out more detail. It was a horse, but without a rider. Perhaps the traveller had dismounted to relieve himself.

Her way lay in the opposite direction, where the track went uphill. She walked on, but she couldn't resist a final look back from the top of the rise.

The horse was still there, moving slowly. Still without a rider.

Lieutenant Bourne had ridden off along that road last night, and had not returned. Had he fallen off? Or, worse, been killed by Jones and his horse left to wander free?

No, please no.

Not only because he could vouch for her with the magistrate, but because he'd been kind and polite to her. Because he'd talked about poetry and old crosses, and had laughing eyes.

The horse was heading towards the inn. Sergeant Slater had a good head on his shoulders; he'd send men to look for the lieutenant. *If* the horse carried on in that direction and reached the inn while there was still daylight to look.

It was no use—she had to be sure. She could go to Scarborough tomorrow.

· · ·

"It's not the lieutenant's horse," Slater said, when the soldier sent to retrieve the animal led it into the yard. "It's lame, as well."

"Could be Jones' horse," one of the soldiers suggested. Frampton— the one who'd been guarding them last night. "But where's Jones?"

"Lyin' on the moor somewhere, if we're lucky," another said. "And good riddance."

"If it belongs to Jones, where's the lieutenant?" Slater countered.

"Could be takin' Jones on to Whitby," Frampton said. "Makin' him walk, maybe?"

"Why would he do that when he could have brought him here?"

"Perhaps Jones escaped on the lieutenant's horse," Nell suggested, keeping the impatience out of her voice. "Should you go and look?"

"It could be a trap," Slater said. "Frampton, you stay here. If the others come back from Scarborough, keep another two here and send the rest to help. Check you've all got powder and shot."

"Yes, sarge."

"You stay here, Miss Mason. And Gibson. Get him to stable the horse."

Nell nodded. Part of her wanted to help them look, but they would be able to move faster than she could.

Toby swore as he stumbled, and pain shot up his leg again. He was tired, thirsty, and cold. This damned road seemed never-ending. Why did this blasted landscape have no trees, where he might have found a stick to lean on?

He was lucky that Jones' shot had passed through his arm without hitting bone. The deep wound had bled freely, but he'd survived worse. The twisted knee was the result of a bad landing when he fell off the horse. He'd been winded by the fall, too, but managed to shoot at the dark shadow that was Jones, rolling into the heather before Jones could fire again. He'd been well enough hidden in the dark that Jones hadn't managed to find him, and had finally given up and made his escape.

Toby had stopped his arm bleeding by wrapping his neckcloth around it. But when he tried to stand, he discovered that not only had he damaged his knee, but Jones had stolen his horse.

Bastard.

The horse that had been tethered had been set loose, so Toby had no chance of finding and catching it; stumbling around in the dark would most likely end in him making his knee worse. So he'd lain down in a hollow in the heather to give his body time to rest. He'd dozed, wishing for a blanket, and for a woman to curl up with. Oddly, it hadn't been the fair Miss Delaney he'd imagined, but the brown-haired, practical Nell Mason. *She* wouldn't fuss about the cold or the wind.

In spite of his discomfort, he'd fallen asleep, only waking when the sun was above the horizon. His knee still hurt when he put weight on it and his wounded arm didn't want to move. However, needs must, so he began to hobble south along the road.

Hours later, he stopped to rest on a grassy bank beside the track and checked his watch to find that, in reality, only half an hour had passed.

Damn.

How far had he ridden last night before catching up with Jones? Several miles, at least. At this speed, he could still be walking when the sun set.

On top of all of that, he'd lost Jones, and probably the box of jewels with him. Lord Lanchester would be pleased that at least some of his treasure had been recovered, but Sir James had been more interested in ridding the county of the highwayman. After discovering the outriders' bodies, Toby had agreed with him.

He'd failed.

Limping on, he wondered if he should fire his pistol when he was close enough to the inn for the shot to be heard. The soldiers he'd left there might come and investigate. Then they'd take him back, and Nell would sympathise, fetch him something to drink, perhaps bandage his arm.

You're a grown man, you don't need a woman to cosset you.

It would be very pleasant, though, if Nell were the woman in question.

Then he wondered if he'd knocked his head when he fell off his horse, making him hallucinate as well as talk to himself. He hadn't fired a shot yet, but there were shapes on the skyline that looked like soldiers with muskets slung over their shoulders.

They hadn't noticed him. He pulled a pistol from his pocket and fired it, then sat down to wait.

Nell had little to do while the search was under way. The soldier that Slater left behind concealed himself in the stand of trees near the track, so Nell had the inn to herself. Apart from Gibson, of course, but he was sitting in the public room with a glass of brandy, enjoying the place beside the fire usually occupied by Silas.

Needing something to do while she waited, she chopped meat and vegetables to make stew, as she did every morning. Once that was simmering over the fire, she went upstairs to her uncle's room to look along the road. She could see nothing out of the ordinary. Standing there watching wouldn't make things happen any faster, but she remained there for some time all the same.

This was ridiculous. For the last few years, she'd wished for more time alone, more time without Silas or Bett demanding she cook or clean or wash. Now she had a few hours to herself, she didn't know what to do. On a fine day in summer, she might have taken her little book of poems to the wooded stream to the south—but the sky was still grey, the air cold and damp. And she wanted to be here in case there was any news.

In the end, she just brewed a pot of coffee and took a mug out to the soldier keeping watch. He thanked her, then jerked his head towards the east.

"Looks like they found someone, miss."

Nell followed the direction of his gaze. There were five men, not just the four who had gone to search. They were too far off to make out details of uniforms or features, but the soldiers' muskets were slung over their shoulders, and one was limping, leaning heavily on another.

It must be Lieutenant Bourne—and injured, but not too badly. If they'd found Jones, they wouldn't be walking like that.

She felt weak with relief. As if the lieutenant's return would solve all her problems. Which it wouldn't, of course, but at least she could tell him about the jewellery.

"I'll make more coffee." She hurried back into the kitchen. By the time Lieutenant Bourne came in, she had hot water ready with some clean cloths, in case they were needed.

They were. Her breath caught as she took in the dried blood discolouring one sleeve of his red jacket, and his pale face with lines of strain about his mouth and eyes. He pulled a chair closer to the fire and slumped into it.

Nell poured coffee and handed it to him. He took it with a word of thanks.

"What next, sir?" Slater asked, before Nell could say anything. "Should we still keep watch at the quarry?"

Lieutenant Bourne drank some of the coffee before replying. "Yes, send two men there. Put someone upstairs to watch out of that window, and men outside, as well. I doubt Jones will be back in daylight, now he knows we're here, so there's no need to hide—not now, at least."

"Right, sir."

The kitchen emptied of soldiers, and Nell was left alone with Lieutenant Bourne.

"I believe I owe you my thanks," Toby said, eyeing the cloth and bowl of water on the table. He raised his eyes to hers. "For sending my men to look for me. That saved me a couple more hours limping along."

She blushed, and dropped her gaze. But she stepped towards him. "Your arm needs cleaning."

His fatigued imagination had pictured her tending to him, but now he was here, all he could think about was that this place wasn't safe for her. Ignoring her words, he finished the coffee in the mug and held it out for more. He was beginning to feel more alert in spite of his tiredness, the throbbing in his arm, and the ache in his knee. The smells coming from the pot over the fire made his stomach rumble, but his hunger could wait.

He watched as she refilled his mug. She was in danger here. Jones would come back—he still thought the chests in the quarry contained silver and coin, not rocks. "Why didn't you go to Scarborough with the others this morning?"

Her brows rose. "I didn't care to spend hours in the cart with my uncle and cousin. Would you, in my place?"

"No, I suppose not."

"What happened when you chased Jones? Was that his horse?"

"Must be. He probably lamed it by riding too hard, then I came along and provided him with another." The feeling of defeat returned, but to his surprise, she smiled.

"You're still alive, and Jones hasn't got his spoils. You'll get another chance to capture him."

So she did understand why she shouldn't stay here. "Why did you set out to *walk* to Scarborough? You could have been robbed, or worse. I'd have sent someone with you in the cart, when it returns."

She shrugged. "I've nothing worth stealing."

Only her virtue. In spite of the company that frequented this inn, she seemed not to understand the danger a lone woman could face. But she was here now, and hadn't been accosted. He couldn't do anything until the men Slater had sent to Scarborough returned.

"How bad are your injuries?" she asked.

"I haven't looked." He flexed his injured arm—everything still worked, although it hurt like the devil. "Bone's not broken. If you'll help me out of my coat, I'll take a look."

He stood, wincing as he put weight on his damaged knee, and allowed her to ease the coat off his good shoulder first, then the other. It stuck, and he felt something tear as she gingerly pulled the sleeve free. Fresh blood began to show around the dried mess where the ruined shirt stuck to his skin.

Nell face was pale, her gaze fixed on his arm.

"Send one of the men in," he said. "They can deal with it. They've seen it all before."

She swallowed. "I've tended cuts and bruises, when Silas was too free with his fists. And all your men are keeping watch, aren't they?"

They were. "The shirt needs soaking to unstick it. I'll have some of your stew while it's soaking, if I may." Pulling his shirt off was going to hurt whatever he did, but he didn't need to make it worse than it had to be.

Nell dipped the cloth into the bowl, squeezed it and handed it to him. Then she left the room before he could ask for something to hold it in place against his wound. She wasn't gone long, and returned holding a small box and what looked very like a petticoat.

"There's no need to destroy your clothing," he protested, as she made a nick in the hem with a pair of scissors taken from her box. "I'm sure we can find—"

"It's not mine." She pulled, ripping it from top to bottom, then repeated the process to make a long narrow strip. "If Bett hadn't warned Jones, you wouldn't have been shot. It seems only fair she should sacrifice her petticoat."

Toby smothered a laugh, allowing her to bind the damp pad loosely around his arm. She filled a bowl with stew and set it before him. The heat from the fire had eased the chill in his bones, and he moved his chair closer to the table and ate his fill. Then he contemplated removing his shirt—not only the difficulty of getting it off over his head without hurting his arm, but also that Nell might not appreciate having a half-naked man in her kitchen.

"You'd better cut the sleeve off," he said.

She nodded, biting her lip as her scissors snipped around the sleeve, then she teased the stuck linen away. The wound looked deep, and was, now bleeding sluggishly again.

"The surgeon always says it's important to get any bits of clothing out of it," he added.

"I think Bett has some tweezers somewhere." She left, returning this time with tweezers and a lamp. She lit the lamp and set it on the table. "If you turn your chair, Lieutenant, I'll be able to see better."

He did as she suggested, and sat so the light from the lamp fell on his arm. She sat beside him, her head close as she peered at the wound. All he could see was the top of her cap, a few curls of hair escaping from it. But he could feel the tweezers pressing on his torn flesh, little pulls and stabs that made him grit his teeth. Then she straightened her back and reached for the petticoat again, folding a piece into a pad and tying it around his arm with another strip.

"Thank you."

She looked at the remains of his shirt, frowning. "Shall I see if there's a clean shirt in my uncle's room?"

"I'll just put my coat back on, if you'll help me." He might accept that offer later, but for now he didn't want to move his arm more than he had to.

"Sir!" Frampton came clattering down the stairs from his lookout point at an upstairs window. "Cart's comin' back, but there's only one man in it," he reported, then hurried back to his position.

"Damn." He'd been counting on having all his men to help him catch Jones.

CHAPTER 13

"*D*oes it matter?" Nell asked. "That only one of your men has returned with the cart, I mean?"

"It might—I don't know. It depends why Sir James hasn't sent them all back." He gingerly pushed his bandaged arm into the filthy sleeve of the coat Nell was still holding for him. "But it does mean you can go to Scarborough this afternoon in the cart, *with* an escort."

Nell helped him put his good arm into the other sleeve without answering. Now the lieutenant had returned, she should show him the box of jewellery and give it into his safe keeping. But she wanted to be sure that she would get some of whatever reward might be offered—she *needed* it.

"Are you planning to set another trap for Jones?" She was curious to know, but the question was also a way of delaying her decision about what to say.

"Of course. But I'll send you off to safety first. And Gibson, if he wants to leave."

Frampton put his head around the door again before she could answer. "Sir, two men on horseback headin' this way from the road. Just ridin' and talkin' to each other, like."

"Thank you, Frampton. Keep watching." He turned to Nell once the soldier had gone back upstairs. "They may well be travellers in need of refreshment. If I stay close by, can you serve them as if nothing is out of the ordinary?"

Soldiers at the inn were far from ordinary. "They can hardly avoid seeing your men, Lieutenant."

"They already have, most likely. If they ask, tell them we've stopped on our way to Scarborough. That will be less suspicious than saying you're closed. I'll explain later. Where's Gibson, do you know?"

"In the public room."

"Tell him to give the same story." He frowned. "Can he be trusted?"

"He rarely says anything." And stayed away from trouble when he could.

"Very well."

As the men entered the public room, Lieutenant Bourne stationed himself in the passage with a pistol at the ready. He needn't have worried—Nell didn't know the two customers by name, but she did recognise them as having been here before. Nell spoke quietly to Gibson, who nodded and fetched the ale the two customers asked for without speaking. The men showed only a brief interest in the soldiers, and ordered stew.

When she returned to the kitchen after serving them, the lieutenant had put his pistol away and was standing by the back window, looking out.

"Do you want me to carry on as if nothing is happening?" she asked. "If so, I should light the fire in there."

"No, don't encourage them to linger."

He sounded distracted; she crossed the kitchen to see what had his attention. The inn's cart was there, with a soldier unharnessing Dobbin. But there were surely more soldiers in the yard than there should be. As she watched, four of them dragged the cart into the stable and did not reappear.

"What is happening?" she asked.

"I don't know, but I suspect we're about to find out."

The soldier she recognised as Hoskins approached, saluted, and held out a letter. "Sir James sent this, sir."

Lieutenant Bourne took it and broke the seal as he limped back to his chair. As he read, he began to frown, then slammed the letter onto the table with a curse.

"What's wrong?" She couldn't resist asking, even though there was no reason he should tell her what had happened.

"Sir James' men let Maitland talk to—" He pressed his lips together and looked away.

Nell wondered whether she should have apologised for her question, but she *was* involved in this. "I'm on your side, Lieutenant." She drew up a chair. "Who is Maitland?"

Toby considered how much to say to Nell. He shouldn't have mentioned Maitland, but he was furious at Sir James' carelessness. He couldn't see any reason not to tell her—and she did know much of what had already happened.

"Maitland is a colonel in the local militia. Sir James suspects he is either in league with Jones, or accepts money to look the other way or lie for him. That is why I'm here, on what would normally be militia business."

"They sent for the army after the robbery?"

"Not exactly. I was in Scarborough on leave, and Sir James asked me to investigate. When I first came here, I really was just passing by. The second time..." They had talked here in this kitchen—a conversation he'd enjoyed.

"You talked to me to find out about the inn and the people here." There was a flat note to her voice.

"Discussing ancient crosses and poetry was hardly part of my investigations, Nell."

She considered that for a moment, her face lightening, but was not to be distracted. "What did Maitland do?"

"Apparently, he managed to talk to the two carters we arrested. *Not* to your uncle and cousin, as far as Sir James knows."

"You caught those men in the quarry, did you not? So they know you found the chests."

"Exactly." Her intelligence was one of the things that had stirred his interest in her. "I'd hoped that Jones would return for those, and we could try again to apprehend him. But it isn't difficult to guess we would have removed them; there's no reason for him to return now." He indicated the letter. "Sir James suggests Jones may come to check whether we did, in fact, remove the valuables if he thinks there is no-one here. He told Hoskins to conceal the other four men in the cart."

"So Maitland, if he was watching, will think only one man returned."

"Yes—there may also be some of your customers, or people in Scarborough, who will give Jones information. Sir James suggests most of my men can march off tomorrow in full daylight, with you and Gibson, leaving the impression that the inn is closed up and deserted."

"A trap."

"It's a good plan," Toby admitted. "Apart from the fact that Jones wouldn't have lasted so long if he were stupid, and it would be foolish in the extreme to return here when he cannot expect to find anything. We've lost our chance."

"No."

Surprised, Toby waited for her to continue, but instead she looked down at her hands clasped on the table, her brow creased.

"Nell? Do you know something about this that you haven't told me?"

She looked up, her expression still troubled. "My uncle, and Bett, have both helped Jones. Is it certain they will be put on trial?"

"It is very likely. Why?"

"And they'll hang if found guilty, I suppose. They... I..." She swallowed and started again. "I am not trying to excuse them, and will not lie about what they have done. But Uncle Silas *did* give Mama and me a home when my father died."

From what she'd said, and he'd seen, Toby thought Weaver had got by far the better end of that bargain.

"I'd convinced myself that I didn't owe them anything, but I don't want to see them hanged, either. Could your Sir James arrange for them to be transported instead?"

"I can ask him. Or you can, when you get to Scarborough. That's all I can do. Things might go better for them if they agree to give evidence against Jones, but there's probably enough against him already to make sure he hangs when we catch him. They are not in a strong position to bargain."

Nell had been afraid of that, but she'd had to ask. Bett and Silas weren't her only concerns, though. She had still to make a living for herself when she was away from this place.

"What do you know?" He was beginning to sound impatient.

She *had* to tell him, whether or not there was a reward—and she felt he could be trusted not to claim the discovery for himself. "I found a box of jewels that Jones must have given to Bett."

She almost laughed at the astonishment on his face, but before he could speak there was a shout from the public room. "Miss!"

"Damn it. Get rid of them, if you can." Nell stood, but Lieutenant Bourne held out a hand. "No. Wait."

"Miss!" The voice was louder this time.

"They'll come in here looking for me if I don't go, Lieutenant."

"Tell them… tell them your uncle went away and you're going to close up the inn until he returns. Can you do that?"

"Of course."

The men only wanted to pay their reckoning. Nell took their money, and bade them farewell with a warning not to rely on refreshing themselves here on their way back, repeating the reason the lieutenant had given her. Gibson looked at her with more interest than he usually showed in anything, but merely returned to his chair by the fire and his glass of brandy.

Lieutenant Bourne was tapping his fingers on the table when she returned to the kitchen. "Tell me about the jewels."

She told him her suspicions and her finding of the box in a few sentences. "That was why I set out for Scarborough. I was going to tell the magistrate. But I came back when I saw the loose horse."

"Can you fetch the box from the cellar without my men seeing it? If some of them are to return to Scarborough, it's best they don't know."

"Yes. Shall I get it now?" At his nod she went down into the cellars and brought the box back wrapped in a piece of sacking. "There are several empty compartments," she said. "I don't know if they were empty when Bett was given the box; she may have had more items concealed about her person. *I* didn't take anything from it."

"I didn't suppose you had," Lieutenant Bourne said. "I have a list of what should be in it—where can I check in private?"

"There's a room for guests upstairs. I'll tell your men you needed to lie down for a while if they ask where you are." He did look tired.

His lips twisted. "That's not far from the truth."

"What will happen now? Are you still sending me to Scarborough this afternoon?"

He took his watch out of a waistcoat pocket and flicked it open. "It's too late now, I think. I'll send you off first thing in the morning. My men will sleep in the stable, so you will be perfectly safe in here."

That was reassuring. She led the way upstairs. The guest room was sparsely furnished, with only a bed and a chair. And cold, with the chill of a room not heated for months.

Nell put the box on the bed and removed the sacking. Lieutenant Bourne sat next to it and lifted the lid. His brows rose, as hers must have done when she first looked inside.

"The lock was broken when I found it," Nell said.

"I suppose Jones took a few items with him." He lifted the top trays out and gave a low whistle as he gazed at the matched sets of pieces in the bottom of the box. "Worth a pretty penny—if Jones could have sold them for their full worth. Do you have paper and ink? And more coffee would be good."

The sudden change of subject took Nell aback. "Er, somewhere, yes. I'll bring them up."

She would have loved to examine the jewels more closely than she'd had time for when she found them this morning—she was never likely to see things so beautiful again, let alone touch them. With a sigh, she went to find writing materials.

Lieutenant Bourne didn't return to the kitchen. Nell occupied herself making more bread, for the few soldiers left here could be hiding for several days waiting for Jones to return. There was plenty of stew in the pot, and they could make their own easily enough when they needed more—they must do that when on campaign. She laughed at herself as she kneaded the dough—these men didn't need her to look after them. But the appreciative sniff when Sergeant Slater came in pleased her.

"Do we get some of that stew, miss?"

"Help yourself, Sergeant. Or take the pot to the stables with you."

"I will, thank you. But I need to talk to the lieutenant first."

Nell directed him to the guest room. Outside, the sky was fading to dusk—if there were to be any evening customers, they would be here soon. When the dough was rising, fatigue finally overcame her and she slumped into a chair near the fire. She'd had no sleep last night, but her mind was still too busy to let her doze.

Slater clattered down the stairs. "The lieutenant wants you to go up, miss. Looks like he needs more coffee."

With a sigh, she pushed herself out of the chair and picked up the coffee pot. There was no sign of the jewellery box when she knocked and entered the guest room. The lieutenant gestured towards the chair; Nell refilled his mug and sat down.

"I would like your help, Nell, if you are prepared to give it?"

"Of course." She was hardly likely to refuse at this point. "Er... Will it be dangerous?" She hoped not.

To her surprise, he laughed. "Far less so than wandering the moors at night!"

"I suppose that was rather foolish." His laugh hadn't been mocking her, though. "What is the plan?"

"I'm sending you and Gibson to Scarborough tomorrow. Hoskins will be in charge—he's dependable, and there will be five other men with him."

"Will that leave you with enough men here?" Jones might not come alone, if he did come.

"Yes. If I don't send enough men back to Scarborough, anyone watching will know there may still be some of us here at the inn."

That made sense.

"I would like you to take charge of the jewellery," he went on. "But keep it hidden. The box can stay here—can you conceal the jewels beneath your gown? That would be safer than in a bag."

She already had her savings in her pocket. But Bett probably had one or two more that she could use. The jewels would take up far less space than the box when they weren't set out in their individual trays.

"Yes, I can do that."

"Good. I'll give you the box later. Tomorrow, Hoskins will take you to Sir James—I'll give you a letter for him to explain everything, *and* a list of what is currently in the box, so he does not suspect you of stealing any of it on the way. You can stay at my aunt's boarding house until this business is over. I'll write a letter for her as well."

That was helpful, and one less thing for her to worry about. "Is that all I have to do?" It sounded easy enough.

"Not quite." His lips twitched. "Maitland must know I was involved in this business in some way, so if people are to believe the inn is deserted, my absence from Scarborough will have to be explained. It's a simple enough story for all of them to remember—I went galloping off after Jones, and never came back. They had a look, but without horses they could not search far. So when Hoskins returned with no orders, they decided they'd all go to Sir James for instruction."

"And Gibson and I decided to close up the inn as we can't run it ourselves?"

"Precisely."

Nell shook her head. "You have a devious mind, Lieutenant."

He grinned—apparently enjoying all of this. "I surprise myself sometimes. This task is more interesting than marching about the countryside at the behest of generals. Particularly now your discovery has given us another chance to capture Jones."

"What should I do if any more customers arrive?"

"Send them away with the same story as before. You are only here because we've billeted ourselves on you overnight, and you are going to close the place up until your uncle returns. Can you and Gibson manage that? I'll come down shortly and stay in the kitchen, in case you need any help."

"You shouldn't show yourself if your story is to hold."

"I can summon one of my men quickly enough."

Nell thought about his words as she descended the stairs. The events of the last few days were certainly more interesting than her normal tedious life. She wasn't enjoying the situation, as he seemed to be, but she did enjoy his company and wasn't sorry change had come. Particularly now she knew she would be safely out of the way tomorrow. Once away from Silas' demands, her life could take a turn for the better—the chance to see new places, meet new people. And the lieutenant's promise that she could stay with his aunt would give her time to find suitable employment.

Toby finally felt he could relax a little, now he'd decided on a plan. It was tempting to lie down on the bed for a while, but he knew he'd fall asleep. Instead, he pulled the jewellery box from beneath the bed and began to make a list of the items.

He'd known the jewellery casket was still missing—why hadn't he considered that Jones might have left the missing jewellery box in the inn instead of taking it with him? If Jones had been apprehended, finding the jewels on him would have been enough to convict him. Without such evidence, there was only the coachman's testimony to put him at the scene of the crime, and Jones probably thought the man was dead.

In hindsight, it was an obvious plan.

Would he have thought to search the place if Nell hadn't found it? Thank the Lord for her quick wits, and her honesty. At least, he thought she was honest. He'd believed her when she said she hadn't taken any items herself.

He finished the list and hid the box again. There were still letters to Sir James and Aunt Em to be written, but he had promised Nell he'd be nearby in case she had any trouble with customers. He could write the letters later.

And talking to Nell would be a much more pleasant way to spend the evening.

CHAPTER 14

Toby entered the kitchen and found Nell putting bread into the oven. He put his empty mug on the table and pulled out a chair. "Still cooking, Nell?" He sat down, straightening out his injured knee and massaging it.

She stood, arching her back with a wince. "I thought you'd need bread while you're waiting for Jones to return. I assumed your men could cook their own meat."

"We'll manage well enough, yes, but making bread is beyond them. Thank you."

"Should I make more stew for you, Lieutenant? The sergeant took the pot to the stables to feed your men."

"I doubt there'll be any left, in that case. But you've done enough. I'll be content with some of that bread when it's ready, and any cheese or cold meat you have."

"There's bread in the pantry. I'll get it."

"Nell, sit down." It came out as an order. "You look worn to a thread," he added, more softly.

She looked at him in surprise.

"Unless you are getting something for yourself, of course?"

"No. I don't feel like eating."

"Don't worry about tomorrow. My men will see you safely to Scarborough."

"I know." She refilled his mug, and poured herself some coffee. Then she finally sat down at the table, her chair half-turned to face him. "I'm worried about what happens after that. I have a little money, and I hope I will have some reward for finding the jewels, but that will not last for ever. I need to find a position, which will be difficult with no-one to provide a character for me. A recommendation from my uncle wouldn't be helpful, even if he would give me one."

From what he'd seen of Weaver, Toby thought the man wouldn't do anything that didn't benefit himself. This inn was close enough to Scarborough to be known there. Even saying that she'd worked here was likely to make respectable people shun her.

Aunt Em would help if he asked her. "My aunt was considering taking on someone to help in her boarding house. You could work there long enough for her to give you a character when you leave."

"Really?" Her face lightened, and there was the beginning of a smile. "That's kind of you, Lieutenant."

"Toby. My name is Toby." The words came out without thought—but why not? He'd been calling her Nell, and she hadn't objected. And the smile she was giving him now was lovely. His eyes followed her fingers as she tucked a loose strand of hair beneath her cap. A horrid, enveloping thing that gave little clue as to what she'd look like with her hair down, or curled and dressed beneath a stylish hat.

He dragged his attention back to reality. There was more to Nell Mason than a pretty face and comely shape. "You talked about your father before—where did you live?"

"Not far from Derby. My mother's family is from York, and Papa met her when he was there on business."

"What business was he in?"

"He owned a bank." Her lips compressed. "You trust my honesty, Lieutenant. Toby. My father is one reason for that."

"A reputation for honesty is a necessity in a banker, I would imagine."

"Yes, and he brought me up to believe that it is a virtue. But that is not what I meant. His bank failed as a result of a robbery. The victim wasn't my father, though, but someone who had taken out a large loan."

He could guess the rest. "That person defaulted, I suppose, and then there was a run on his bank?"

She nodded. "Papa could have recovered the situation, given enough time, but the investors didn't want to run the risk that he might not. I can hardly blame them, but his business failed, then his heart failed, too. Our house had to be sold, and even then there was not enough to repay everyone. So many people suffered because of that one robbery."

There was sadness in her face, but determination, too. He reached out to touch her arm. "That must have been a horrible time for you. I suppose that is why you and your mother came here?" Realising he still had his hand on her arm, he withdrew it abruptly. "I'll do my best to see you get a better position than you've had here."

He leaned back in his chair. The temptation for her to take something from the jewellery box would have been great in her current situation. "Lord Lanchester appears to be exceedingly rich, and would hardly miss a jewelled pin or two." He regretted the words as soon as he'd spoken them. "I didn't mean to suggest you'd taken anything, Nell, I just meant..." Shaking his head, he stopped talking before he made things worse.

Nell sighed, and rubbed her forehead. She hadn't thought he was accusing her, but she would face the same suspicion from the magistrate—and probably others, too. "You meant that stealing a pin could not have the same effect as that robbery had on my family. That is most likely true, but how could we *know* that? Lord Lanchester would not miss two pins, either, but he would miss the emerald set. Where is the line to be drawn?" She met his eyes for a moment. "I have far more need for funds than his lordship, and I *was* tempted."

"I can imagine. I'm too used to being with the army. Some of my company would never steal from their comrades, but would regard chance findings such as the jewels as fair pickings, considering their owner. Stealing from Lord Lanchester could not hurt him in the same way."

"My wish to be honest was not the only reason," she admitted. "If items are missing—beyond whatever Bett took and would be found on her—I would be an obvious suspect. I am better off hoping for a reward than relying on not being hanged for theft."

"Sensible as well as honest." An approving smile—at least, she thought so. 'Sensible' wasn't the highest of compliments, but it was good to receive any kind of approval.

"I think Aunt Em and you will deal well together," he went on. "You need not worry yet about finding a position, Nell."

Was it wrong to believe him? Not all men were like her uncle.

Her thought was interrupted by a banging on the front door. Toby stood as she did, and followed her, staying just out of sight as she unbarred the door and explained that the inn was closed for a while. This pair were reluctant to take her word for it, but when she suggested calling the soldiers to help persuade them, they cursed and trudged off.

"And tell your friends," Nell shouted after them.

"Lock the door," Toby suggested when she came back in. "I'll have Slater waiting at the back if anyone finds the place shut up and goes to investigate."

Nell fetched bread, cheese, and apples from the pantry while Toby went to give Slater his orders. When he returned, Toby thanked her and filled his plate. Nell took an apple and began to peel it.

"This countryside must have been very strange to you when you came here," Toby said, cutting more cheese. "It's bleak at this time of year."

"Parts of Derbyshire are similar. Papa took us up there sometimes for a day or two—but only in the summer." And they had never ventured onto the expanses of moorland, but kept to the rocky edges and the valleys. "It is very different living permanently in the middle of a moor—although there are fields and woods in the valleys that I have walked to a few times, and the moors have their own beauty on a fine day."

"Less so in the winter," Toby said. "Or when you have to unexpectedly spend the night out there without even a blanket."

Nell laughed at his rueful expression. "You appear to have survived well enough."

He shrugged. "I've slept in worse places."

"Hmm. Well, it wasn't raining. Or snowing."

"Ha, no."

Toby had an attractive laugh, and the lines beside his eyes deepened. He must smile a lot. "Tell me about the places you've seen," she said. "Were you born in Scarborough?"

"No, in Carlisle. My parents died when I was small, and Uncle Robert—my father's brother—took me in. He and Aunt Em lived in a village to the west of the moors."

They were both orphans, then.

"They treated me the same as their daughter—"

"You wore gowns?" Nell made her eyes wide.

He rolled his eyes, but with a smile. "Only until I was breeched. They treated me as if I had been their own son. Jane is married now, and lives in Manchester. Aunt Em moved to Scarborough when my uncle died." He touched her arm again, briefly. "I was luckier in my relatives than you, Nell."

The sympathy in his tone made her swallow hard, and she dropped her gaze. There was no point imagining how things might have been had Papa not died, or had Mama's brother been a nicer person. Her life was about to change, and if all went well, it would be for the better.

"Where did you go in the army?" Better to talk about his life than hers, even if his travels made her envious for opportunities she was unlikely to have.

"Here and there. King George commands, and we obey."

"Over the hills and far away?" Nell recalled her father whistling a tune about soldiers, and occasionally singing it, although he said she was not old enough to see the play from which it had come.

He grinned. "At times, yes. To Flanders, but not Portugal or Spain. And to Scotland, and we're off to the Colonies in a few weeks."

"Did you fight the Jacobites in Scotland? I was young then, but I remember my parents being worried when their army reached Derby."

"Not exactly fight them. We were sent to try to catch the Pretender when he fled after the battle at Culloden, and arrest any sympathisers we found. I was only twenty then, and it didn't feel right to be chasing down people who I might have fought alongside in other circumstances. But the land is impressive." He talked of mountains and lochs, torrential rain and boggy glens, wild coastlines and white beaches with the sun glittering on the sea. Although it sounded a rather uncomfortable country in which to make a living, Nell wished she could see it.

How old was he? Twenty in '46 would make him nine and twenty now. She had the lowering thought that when she reached that age she would have seen or experienced little more than she had now.

Toby had fallen silent, sipping coffee and watching her over the rim of his mug. Then the silence was broken by Hoskins coming in with the stew pot, now containing only the bowls the soldiers had eaten from.

Nell stood. "Leave it by the sink, if you please."

Hoskins deposited it in the scullery. "Good grub, that were, miss," he said, on his way back to the outer door.

"Not so fast, Hoskins," Toby said. "Miss Mason, is there hot water?"

Nell pointed to the pot by the fire. It seemed she needn't do any more work tonight after all. "There is sand and ash for scouring by the sink, if you need it."

Hoskins grimaced, then headed back to the scullery.

"Time for you to retire, if you wish, Nell," Toby said. He looked as though he should be in bed, too, with lines of tiredness on his face. "Sergeant Slater will set a watch and turn away anyone else who comes," he went on. "I doubt Jones will return tonight."

She *was* tired, and feeling less pessimistic about the future than she had for some time. Perhaps tonight she could manage to sleep.

Toby followed her up the stairs, turning to the guest room when she entered her own. She sat on the bed, suddenly feeling too tired even to undress. And that was just as well, as there was a quiet knock on the door.

"Nell?"

No sleep yet, then. "Come in."

Toby had the jewellery box with him. "I'll give you the letters in the morning, but I thought you might want this now. You could leave the box where you found it."

"I will."

"Sleep well." He closed the door quietly behind him.

Nell sighed. She should get the jewels safely stowed now, before she slept. She lifted the jewellery out of the box, spreading the pieces out on her blankets. There was still plenty of fabric left in Bett's ruined petticoat—she could use some of that to wrap each item separately to protect them, and still have enough left over for Toby to change the dressing on his wound.

She found two spare pockets in Bett's clothespress, and took them both. But what had she done with the torn-up petticoat? It was probably still in the kitchen somewhere.

She picked up the lamp and crept down the stairs, not wanting to wake Toby. The torn petticoat wasn't in the kitchen, but hanging behind the scullery door. Nell bundled it under her arm, then paused.

A sound—from inside the inn, not outside where the soldiers were keeping watch. It came again, a scrape of metal on stone. Beneath her, in the cellars.

Her initial panic subsided as she realised no stranger could have got down there with the soldiers about. It must be Gibson. Heart pounding, she opened the cellar door.

"Gibson?"

A strip of light showed as a door opened. "Nell?"

She leaned on the doorframe, gathering herself. Gibson made no move to come up, so she went down to him, in the room where they'd locked the carters. He just stood there as she entered, a spade in his hand. Behind him, a stone slab rested against the wall, and there was a hole in the earth where the slab had been.

"What are you doing?" She sat on an empty crate, her knees still feeling weak from the fright she'd had.

"Leaving." He rubbed a hand through his thinning hair. "You've got that lieutenant to look after you now."

"Look after… What do you mean?"

He sighed, and sat on a box. "I came here years ago because I did something stupid. Broke the law. In this place, people tell no tales." He looked at her face, as if waiting for condemnation.

"Go on."

"Your ma was kind to me, and you reminded me of my daughter. She's ten years or so older than you. She needed money, that's why…" His voice cracked on the words, and he took a deep breath. "When you came here, I'd seen enough of Silas' doings to threaten him with the law if he harmed either of you."

Gibson had been her guardian angel all these years? *Gibson?* Nell put her face in her hands for a moment. However bad her life had been, and Mama's, it would have been so much worse without Gibson's help. "You would have risked being hanged yourself, wouldn't you?"

Gibson shrugged. "I didn't care."

"Thank you. Thank you for what you did."

He shrugged, looking embarrassed.

"What are you doing?" Nell asked after a few moments of silence. She indicated the hole in the floor.

"Getting my savings. There's enough now to pay back what I stole, and to give me a start somewhere else if I don't get taken up for the robbery. But at least I'll see Annie again."

How would he earn money here? Unless… "Did you take it from my uncle?"

He nodded, looking down at his feet. "I know what you and your ma think… thought… about stealing."

Nell couldn't blame him for it. Most of Silas' money was ill-gotten to start with, and he wouldn't have missed what Gibson had taken.

"I heard some of what the lieutenant said about his aunt and her boarding house. You don't need me no more, Nell, and this place'll be closed up when all the soldiers leave in the morning."

"How much did you hear?" Did he know that some soldiers would be staying?

"Enough to know you'll be safe. Nothing that anyone else needs to know."

Nell looked into his eyes; eyes full of sadness. Letting him leave without raising an alarm could put Toby's plan at risk, but she would not try to stop him.

"Are you leaving now?"

"Yes, in case they want me to go with them to Scarborough. They're only watching the road, so I can go out the back and hide in the heather until they've all gone tomorrow."

That was best.

"God speed, Mr Gibson. I hope you find your daughter." She held out her right hand and, after a moment's hesitation, he shook it. When she left the room, he was delving into the earth beneath the floor again.

Back in her room, Nell wrapped the jewellery and stowed it in the spare pockets. They bulged, but should not be too noticeable beneath her skirts. All the while she listened for any sound of Gibson's departure. She heard nothing—not Gibson, or the soldiers. She put the empty box back in Bett's clothespress and closed the door of her cousin's room. For the last time, she hoped.

After all that, sleep did not come immediately when she lay down. The surprise of Gibson's revelations gave way to her thoughts about Toby.

He had come into her room to give her the jewels. Only that. But she had enjoyed her evening talking to him more than anything over the last five years, and she wondered what would have happened had he wanted what most men seemed to.

She would have said no, of course, and he would not have forced her. Mama had described the act of intimacy before she died, and although that had been mainly to warn Nell against doing it outside marriage, she had got the impression that Mama had enjoyed Papa's attentions.

If Toby had wanted her in that way, would she have enjoyed the experience had she been foolish enough to agree?

CHAPTER 15

The next morning, Nell had wondered whether or not to tell Toby of Gibson's departure, but after a quick search of the building, Toby had cursed his absence, then said it should not matter. There had not been time to say much else. Toby had been busy deciding on the best lookout places near the inn while she cooked breakfast and then dowsed the kitchen fire so its smoke could not give away the fact that men were still here.

Finally, Toby helped her into the cart and Hoskins took the reins. She twisted around on the seat as Hoskins drove past the cross. It was less than a day since she'd stopped here on foot, making her solitary way to Scarborough, but it felt far longer than that. Now, she had transport and an escort of redcoats marching behind. She did not know any of these soldiers, but she felt safe knowing they would obey Toby's orders.

The weather was brighter than yesterday, with thin cloud that might yet clear to sunshine. Nell watched the slowly passing scenery. A few patches of late-flowering heather still showed purple, and the rolling moorland gradually softened to rough grass, then fields, as they dropped down to a wider road. Nell made out the glitter of sea in the distance.

Hoskins turned off the road as it began to descend again towards the town clustered around a sandy bay, beneath the old castle. The air smelled of salt. That, and the sounds of seagulls calling, reminded her of her few journeys to Whitby. The cart turned between two low pillars and drew up in front of a large house set in its own grounds. One of the soldiers came forward to help Nell down, and she and Hoskins walked towards the front door. Nell wondered if there was a servants' entrance they should have used, but Hoskins marched up the steps and plied the knocker before she could suggest it.

"Miss Mason to see Sir James," Hoskins announced to the man who opened the door. The butler, from his dress and the way he looked down his nose at the pair of them.

"I have a letter for Sir James," Nell said. "To be given into his hand personally by me," she added, before he could ask for it. She could understand his disdain, given her shabby clothing.

The butler's lips pursed, but he stood aside and waved a hand to usher them inside. "I will inform Sir James that you are here." He turned and stalked off.

"Good for you, miss," Hoskins whispered, tucking his hat beneath one arm. "I'll just find out what 'e wants us to do, then I'll leave you with 'im, if that's all right."

"Yes, thank you."

Nell dropped her bundle on the floor. It was some time before the butler reappeared, but Nell didn't mind standing in the hall—not after sitting on the hard seat of the cart for hours.

"If you will step this way."

They followed him into a book-lined room smelling of leather and beeswax. Nell swallowed a lump in her throat. This room reminded her of Papa's study—the shelves of books, the large desk, and chairs designed for comfort, not for show.

Sir James stood from behind the desk, a welcoming smile on his face. "Miss Mason. Hoskins. I trust your little deception went well, Hoskins?"

"I think so, sir," Hoskins said. "The men stayed 'idden all the way to the Moorcock. Five of them came back 'ere with me."

"So the lieutenant has four?"

"Yessir. Lieutenant Bourne said as you would arrange somewhere for us to stay for a few days. Miss Mason 'as a letter about 'is plan."

"Very good. You may take the cart around to the stables, and wait there with your men until I can make arrangements. You know where that is?"

"Yessir." Hoskins bowed, gave Nell a nod, and left.

"Miss Mason, may I have the letter?"

Nell handed it over. Sir James broke the seal, then looked up. "My housekeeper will provide you with refreshment, Miss Mason."

Nell suppressed her irritation at being treated as merely a messenger. "If you please, sir, I think you may wish me to stay once you have read the letter."

"You know what Bourne said?"

"I believe so, sir."

"Hmm. Well, sit down." He indicated an upright chair, and Nell sat on the edge of the seat, hands folded in her lap. She tried to make out what he was thinking, but his expression hardly changed as he read. Then he put the papers down and looked at Nell—actually smiling now.

"It seems we have much to thank you for, Miss Mason. Bourne said he had a minor injury—how badly was he hurt?"

"A wound to the arm, sir, but the bullet passed through. When I left, he did not appear to be feverish or otherwise unwell." He had hardly been limping this morning, so she did not mention his injured knee.

"That's good. Do the men here know the tale they are to tell about Bourne's fate?"

"Yes, sir."

"Very good. I will have a word with Hoskins before he leaves, just to be sure. Now, Miss Mason, I assume you have the jewels hidden about your person?"

"Yes, sir. Under my skirts." She would be glad to be rid of them; they shifted uncomfortably against her thighs whenever she moved.

"I would prefer no-one else in this house to know they have been found. If I turn my back, could you retrieve them now?"

"Yes, sir."

Sir James stood, turned his chair around and resumed his seat—now hidden completely behind the chair's high back. Nell reached through the slits in her gown and untied the pocket tapes, standing to let them slide to the floor. She placed two of them on the desk, and kept the third on her lap.

"You may turn back now, sir."

He turned his chair, and had picked up one of the pockets before noticing the one she had kept.

"This has only my personal possessions in it."

"Very well." He seemed to have lost his desire for her to leave, and she sat quietly while he emptied the pockets onto his desk, then carefully unwrapped the strips of cloth. He set them out in rows on the polished wood, and began to check them off against the list in Toby's letter. Then he opened a desk drawer and took out another list. Nell leaned forward, trying to see what he was doing.

"You need not worry, Miss Mason—all the items Bourne said you were carrying are present. And he assures me you are too honest to have concealed anything else before giving the box to him."

"I'm glad you believe him, sir." And she was happy Toby had said so in his letter.

"I have little choice at this point but to trust you. Bourne points out that, should he have been mistaken in your character, you have the intelligence to realise that an honestly come-by reward is less risky than a stolen jewel." Sir James tapped the second paper. "You correctly surmised that some items were missing. This is the list Lord Lanchester provided of what was originally in the box."

"I wondered what…" Too late, Nell realised it might be best to say nothing at all about Bett—not if she hoped for some clemency in her cousin's sentence.

"What your cousin had about her neck?" Sir James asked. "Rest assured, Miss Mason, your query has not further incriminated her. Bourne explained what led you to look for the jewels." He returned his attention to the two lists, checking off items again. "In addition to the brooch from the ruby set, there are some jewelled pins missing. Also a matching brooch and ring—both with a central diamond surrounded by seed pearls. A further ring, this one a gold band set with several small diamonds."

"It wouldn't be the pins," she said to herself, and was surprised by a quick snort of laughter from Sir James.

"Most uncomfortable, I imagine, if suspended on a ribbon beneath a bodice."

"That's what I thought, sir." Nell wondered, and was pleased that he was talking to her this way, as if her opinion mattered. He wasn't treating her as an equal, of course, but not as a mere tavern wench, either.

"Which of these do you think she has?, Miss Mason? It makes no difference to Bourne's plan, of course."

"Why don't you search…? Oh—you don't want her to suspect you might have found the box."

"Indeed. She will already have been searched for knives or other weapons, so whatever she has must be fairly well concealed. To search again, more thoroughly, would suggest we know more than she currently thinks, and a gaoler could be bribed to get word to Jones."

Nell considered the missing items. "She probably has one of the rings. From the description, the gold band would be easier to conceal beneath a glove if she chose to wear it."

"I wonder if Jones promised her a ring on her finger?" Sir James said. "More fool her if she thought he'd marry her."

How did Sir James know Bett had been planning on leaving with Jones? Nell didn't think she'd mentioned that to the lieutenant.

Tim! To her shame, she'd forgotten about him. Jones, or Bett, could have easily said something about that when she let him out of the inn that night, and Tim would have heard. "Is Tim still here?"

"Tim? Oh, the stable lad. He's with Bourne's aunt."

"Lieutenant Bourne said I could stay there, too."

Sir James smiled. "That seems sensible. Can I leave it to you to ask her to appear worried about the fate of her nephew?"

Nell nodded, and Sir James leaned back on his chair and tugged on a bellpull. "I'll have someone carry your things and show you the way. Unless you'd prefer a chair?"

"I can walk, thank you, sir."

Sir James rose as she stood. "Thank you for your assistance in this matter, Miss Mason. Pray give my regards to Mrs Bourne."

The butler opened the door in time to hear the last words, and his expression became a little less disdainful as Sir James gave him instructions. She waited beside her bundle until another servant appeared—a man with a far more friendly expression than the butler. He led the way back to the road, and then down the hill into the town. He stopped at a green-painted door and plied the knocker.

"Visitor for Mrs Bourne," he said to the plump maidservant who opened the door, a duster still in one hand. He handed Nell her bundle, then touched his cap and left.

"I have a letter for Mrs Bourne," Nell said, as the maid looked her up and down—with curiosity this time, not the disdain of Sir James' butler. The maid was older than Nell, perhaps thirty or so, with a cheery face.

"This way, miss."

Nell closed the front door behind her, and the maid took her past a couple of closed doors and down some steps into the kitchen. This was a far cry from the dingy room at the Moorcock where Nell had spent so much time. Although the small windows were near the ceiling, the white paint on the walls made the room feel bright and airy. A row of shining copper pots hung from a beam, and shelves held more copper—kettles, pans, and jugs—and stacks of dishes and platters. Baking ingredients were set out on a large, scrubbed table in the middle of the room—a jar labelled flour, a sugar cone, and dishes of raisins and dates. A young maidservant stood with a mixing bowl, her spoon stilled in mid-stir as she took in Nell standing in the doorway.

"Someone to see you, missus," the first maid said, and left.

"Come on in, girl."

Nell's gaze swung to the fire, where a woman sat in a chair. She was a little older than Mama would have been, with a kindly smile.

"My name's Nell Mason, ma'am." Nell stepped further into the room, fumbling in her pocket to pull out the second letter. "Toby… I mean Lieutenant Bourne sent you this. It should explain everything."

"And that?" Mrs Bourne indicated the bundle.

"My things, ma'am. Lieutenant Bourne said I could stay here for a while."

"Did he, indeed?" The words could have been incredulous, but Mrs Bourne was smiling. "Well, sit down while I read this. Mary, you may stop gawping and finish mixing that pudding."

"Yes, ma'am." Mary grinned, and resumed her stirring.

Nell sat down. Mrs Bourne looked surprised and then pleased as she read, but frowned as she turned back to the beginning of the letter and re-read parts of it.

"Am I to understand he gave you this before he went chasing off after…" She looked at the letter again, then her eyes slid briefly to where Mary had paused in her mixing again. "After a highwayman?"

Nell's mouth fell open for a moment, then she nodded. "Yes, ma'am." Toby must have put quite a lot of detail in his letter.

"And he has not returned?"

"Um, he had not when I left the inn."

"You are welcome to stay as long as you wish, of course." She stood. "Come—I was thinking of taking on another maid, and there's a room in the attic already aired. I'll show you, and have fresh sheets sent up. Mary, I expect that pudding to be ready to boil by the time I get back."

As Mary began stirring again, Nell collected her bundle and followed Mrs Bourne. The older woman moved rather stiffly as they climbed three flights of stairs, although there was no awkwardness in her movement once they were walking on the level again.

"Hannah and Mary share that room," Mrs Bourne said, pointing at a closed door. "This will be yours while you are here."

The room was little bigger than her bedroom in the Moorcock, and the view from the small window was only of rooftops—but the walls were as brightly white as in the kitchen, the curtains had a cheerful print of flowers and leaves that matched the quilt on the bed, and a bowl of lavender and other petals scented the air.

"It looks lovely, thank you."

"*Has* Toby returned, Miss Mason?"

"Yes, he has. He was safe and… and well when I left."

Mrs Bourne smiled. "You're not a very good liar, my dear, although good enough to deceive Mary, I think." Her eyes narrowed. "That is, I assume you are telling me the truth now?"

"Yes." Almost.

"Hmm. He didn't say much to me before he left about what he was doing. I assume his little… adventure… is connected with this Gentleman Jones whose recent exploits have made quite a stir in this town?"

"Yes, ma'am." There could be no harm in confirming that, could there? "Mrs Bourne, is Tim here? The stable boy from the inn."

"He will be back later. I gather you and he were friends?"

"Yes. Is he well?"

"He was rather bruised when he arrived, and frightened, but he is improving. He helps about the house, but I give him an hour or two off in the afternoons—he is fascinated by the sea."

Nell could understand that—she had been, too, on the few occasions she had seen it.

Mrs Bourne hadn't finished with her. "What do you have in that bundle? More garments like the one you're wearing?"

"I'm afraid so. Cleaner, though." She should not feel shame at admitting the paucity of her belongings. It was not her fault.

"It was not intended as a criticism, my dear." Mrs Bourne stood back, her head tilted to one side as she inspected Nell. "One of the gowns my daughter left behind when she married may fit you, with a little adjustment. If you do not mind borrowed garments?"

"No, Mrs Bourne. I would be glad of something more… more fitting to this house. That is very kind of you." So kind that she felt tears prick her eyes, and her voice wavered on the last words.

"It is no trouble, my dear. I'll get Hannah to bring some water up, and you may refresh yourself. Then come to my parlour. It is on the floor below this. We will have some refreshment and you can tell me all about yourself. Toby told me only a little in his letter." She smiled—a smile full of warmth and welcome, almost a laugh. "Although probably more than he intended."

She set off down the stairs, leaving Nell wondering what she had meant. But Hannah would be here soon, so she unfastened her bundle. She put Papa's book of poetry on the low clothespress, and her pouch of coins into a drawer. They would be safe enough there. The worst of the creases came out of her other gown with a good shake, and she laid it out on the bed with a clean chemise and cap.

Then she opened the window, despite the cold, and combed out her hair while she breathed in the salty air and listened to the cries of seagulls. She took in all the rooftops with their smoking chimneys—how strange it would feel to be living in a town again, to see people other than the inhabitants of the Moorcock and the passing customers.

Strange, too—in a good way—to live with people who seemed friendly and welcoming.

CHAPTER 16

$\mathcal{N}$ell knocked on the parlour door and opened it when she heard Mrs Bourne call her to enter. The parlour wasn't large but, to Nell's eye, it had all the essentials. Chairs by the fire, a table laid with cups and plates, a steaming pot of chocolate, and a platter with bread and butter.

And a tall bookcase. With books—lots of books. Nearly as many as Papa had owned.

"You may borrow any that you wish to read, my dear. But do have some chocolate first." Mrs Bourne, sitting at the table, was regarding her with amusement.

Had she been staring? Probably. "I'm sorry."

"Don't be. I like a woman who reads. Do pour, will you? Give it a stir, first."

Nell wondered if this was a test—of her manners, perhaps. The delicate blue and white cups and saucers were very different from the coarse crockery at the Moorcock; they reminded her of the time before Papa died. She stirred the mixture, as directed, breathing in the scent of spices, then poured two cups and passed one to Mrs Bourne.

"Thank you. You must be hungry if you've come all that distance today. Do help yourself."

She *was* hungry—and this bread was soft and delicate, the butter plentiful; just as she remembered from her former life. A lump came to her throat again.

"I don't often take chocolate in the middle of the day," Mrs Bourne went on, cradling her cup in her hands. "But I thought it would be a good chance to get to know you better. Hannah is a capable woman, but has no conversation."

Nell bit into the bread, letting out a sigh of pleasure. It tasted as good as it looked.

"And Mary is young, still learning her duties. Once you have settled in, you may help me in the kitchen, and perhaps with serving the meals. Our guests appreciate good food, plainly cooked, and are respectable people. You need have no worries about your safety in this house. Most of them are out during the day, but there is old Mr Everidge who spends his time in the downstairs parlour. He will be glad of a new face to talk to. Then there is…"

Nell was grateful for Mrs Bourne's talk, although she knew she would not recall the half of it later. By the time Mrs Bourne finished describing her current guests, Nell had eaten several slices of bread and butter, and drunk her chocolate. More importantly, she was feeling composed again—less likely to burst into tears of relief, or gratitude.

"Better now?" Mrs Bourne asked. "I do not usually talk so much, you will be pleased to hear."

"Thank you, yes. I… I mean, yes I feel better, not that…" Not that she was pleased Mrs Bourne didn't usually talk so much.

But her hostess was smiling. "I know what you meant, my dear."

"This is just so… so different from what I have been used to these last few years."

"Toby said something of that in his letter. Do tell me how you came to be working in that inn. It hasn't the best of reputations hereabouts."

And so Nell embarked on her life history again, but Mrs Bourne asked for many more details than Nell had told Toby. She found herself recalling things she hadn't thought about for years—happy memories, mostly. At the end of it, she felt drained but oddly light, as if a burden had been lifted from her.

Which it had, of course; she now had a place to stay and prospects for the future. But it wasn't only that—this was the first time she had felt free to talk to someone about her innermost feelings since her mother died. She'd talked to Toby last night, but she'd always been aware that he was there for a purpose, that his main concern was catching Jones, and that his men might walk in and overhear. Talking with Mrs Bourne had been more like talking to Mama, in the days before Uncle Silas' jibes and criticisms made her withdraw into herself.

"Thank you for listening, Mrs Bourne."

Mrs Bourne stood up, and began to put the cups and plates onto a tray. "You are very welcome, my dear. Please, do call me Aunt Em, as Toby does. You may take this downstairs for me while I look out the gown I mentioned."

"Thank you, Aunt Em." It felt strange, calling her that—in a nice way.

Nell carried the tray downstairs, pushing the kitchen door open with one foot.

"Nell!" A chair scraped, then Tim stood before her, a huge grin on his face. "You're here!"

She smiled back as she set the tray on the table and gave him a quick hug. "You're looking well, Tim." Very well indeed. It was just over a week since he'd run off, but already he looked healthier, in spite of the bruise on the side of his face.

"I like it here—the food's good!"

"Better than mine?"

He nodded enthusiastically.

Nell laughed at the dismayed expression that crossed his face as he realised how his response could be taken. "I'm not surprised—Mrs Bourne provides better ingredients."

"Hard worker, he is," Mary put in. She was busy chopping vegetables now, with a pot on the stove that must contain the pudding. "If you put that in the scullery, I'll wash it with the other things later."

As she stacked the used crockery beside the sink, Nell wondered what would become of Tim now. Some of the reward for recovering the stolen goods must go his way, surely. If it hadn't been for him, Sir James wouldn't have known where to send the soldiers. Mrs Bourne might keep him on—this was a far better place to finish his growing than the Moorcock or the poorhouse.

In her parlour, Aunt Em had laid a dark blue open-fronted gown across the back of a chair, together with an underskirt and stomacher in a paler fabric. "This will do nicely for now." She held the skirt against Nell, then nodded. "As I thought, Jane is a little taller than you, but that makes adjustments easier. The lacing in the gown will take up any looseness in the bodice. "You can try it on after supper, and I will ask Hannah to pin the hem—my knees are too old for that these days."

The fabric was serviceable, the style simple—far plainer than the clothing Mama used to wear, but a vast improvement on her current apparel. "Thank you, Mrs Bourne… Aunt Em."

"In the meantime, feel free to read. Tomorrow is soon enough for me to put you to work."

Nell spent the next morning sewing the hem of the underskirt that Hannah had pinned the previous evening, revelling in a genteel task so different from her work over the last years. The kind of thing she might be doing now if Papa's bank had not failed.

She was so lucky to be here. There were fewer servants to help Aunt Em run the house than Mama used to have, but the lodging house was a happy place. The maids worked hard and cheerfully, glad to have Tim's help with sweeping floors and cleaning grates, and happier still at the prospect of another pair of hands in the kitchen. She could be content in this life.

Several backstitches secured the thread on the last length of hem, and Nell shook the skirt out. The gown next—she tried that on, and found that Jane Bourne had longer arms as well as being taller. She began to unpick the hems at the end of the sleeves.

Sewing left her mind free, looking forward to the days ahead. Aunt

Em had said she could have some time off each day, and there was a whole new town to explore, as well as the chance to walk on the beach and gaze out over the waves.

"Very well done, my dear," Aunt Em said later, when Nell tried on the adjusted garments. She sat down at her table. "Nell... This fiction that Toby is missing... is it really necessary?"

"He thinks so—if Gentleman Jones is to be caught."

"In that case, my dear, I think I had better not go out for a few days, until this matter is over. Were he really missing, I would be worried, and I am not a good enough actress to carry that off." She frowned. "Well, I *am* worried, although not as much as if he really were missing. It may seem silly, given that he has been in the army for nigh on ten years, but when he was away, I didn't know what he was doing from day to day. This time, I know he's doing something dangerous."

"It's not so dangerous, Aunt Em. He has some of his men with him." That was true, but Nell couldn't help being anxious, too. Jones was a vicious criminal, and would hang if he were caught. He would have nothing further to lose in killing Toby or his men.

It was too soon to worry, though. The inn had only been supposedly abandoned the day before, and it could take some days for word to reach Jones. She knew that if Toby did not come back, she might not get a share of any reward, but that was only a small part of her concern. She didn't want a friend to be harmed—and she felt he was a friend.

That was all.

Late the following morning, Nell found herself in the circulating library waiting to exchange Aunt Em's book, and eyeing the full shelves behind the counter with anticipation. Papa had not owned nearly so many books, but there had been a couple of cases full and she had been allowed to look at any she wished.

Aunt Em had asked Nell to change her book for her. "Mr Everidge knows the kind of thing I like, dear," she said, handing over the one she'd finished reading.

Tim had come with her and was waiting for her in the sunshine on the street outside, probably becoming as impatient as Nell. The young man behind the counter was talking to another customer—perhaps being too helpful, as the transaction seemed to be taking an age, and there was another young lady waiting who had arrived before Nell.

She was a very fine young lady, clad in an amber velvet cloak over a gown of yellow and white stripes, the ends of her sleeves lavishly trimmed with lace. Nell chided herself for her envy. Terrifying as some of the events of the past days had been, they had led to her working in a much more congenial household and being treated kindly, and Aunt Em was actually going to pay her for her labours.

Shifting from one foot to the other, she squinted to try to read the titles on the books shelved behind the counter. As she took a step forward to try to get a better look, the young lady did something similar and their shoulders collided. The young lady turned to look at Nell, her finely shaped brows rising and her mouth pursed as if she'd smelled something bad.

"Excuse me," Nell said, "I didn't mean to bump into you." She dropped her gaze, and found herself looking at a brooch pinned in the folds of the fichu that filled the neckline of the woman's bodice. A red stone surrounded by tiny pearls. A ruby or a garnet—she wouldn't know. But it must be paste; surely only the aristocracy could afford a real gem of that size?

"What are you staring at?" The woman glared at Nell and covered the brooch with one hand as she turned away and moved to the counter, where the assistant was now free. Nell could almost hear her thought: *You'll never have anything like this.*

Several more customers had entered while Nell had been waiting, and an older man came from a back room and served Nell. He raised one brow and smiled as he took the book Aunt Em had borrowed. He had a friendly face, with laughter lines beside his eyes, and looked to be of a similar age to Aunt Em.

"You must be the young lady staying with Mrs Bourne?"

"Yes, sir. Nell Mason. Mrs Bourne asked me to bring this in, and said you would be able to choose another for her. That is, she said Mr Everidge—"

"I am Mr Everidge, and certainly I will choose." He glanced behind Nell as he spoke, and the bell above the door tinkled as another customer entered. "Do you have any other errands in town, Miss Mason? I would prefer to take the time to make a careful choice, and we are rather busy at the moment."

"I was planning to walk on the beach, sir. I will return in a little while." Perhaps when she returned, she would be able choose a volume for herself as well.

She walked down to the beach with Tim, where they stood gazing out over the glittering waves. They had come here yesterday afternoon, but the weather then had been gloomy, with a biting wind coming off the sea, so they hadn't lingered long. Now, she enjoyed the salty breeze in her face, the boats sailing by, and the cries of gulls.

"Let's go and look at the ships," Tim said, heading for the boats under construction at the end of the beach. Nell listened as he pointed out which would carry coals, which would be used for fishing, and how much each had progressed since he first saw them only a week ago. A lump came to her throat—this enthusiastic and cheerful boy was so different from the cowed lad of the Moorcock. She felt both gratitude that the pair of them had been taken in by someone as good as Mrs Bourne, and anger at her uncle for making their lives a misery.

Tim seemed to have made some friends amongst the shipyard workers, for some of them waved when they saw him. Nell wandered on a few paces as Tim stopped to talk to one of them. Was he too old to be apprenticed to a shipbuilder? She could ask Aunt Em about that.

The castle towered above the shipyards, and now Nell missed her father. He would have had a book about it somewhere on his shelves, and told her how the people had lived and fought there in the past.

Finally Tim had seen enough, and they turned back, walking along the road above the beach rather than across the sand. Many others were taking advantage of the sunshine, and they passed nursemaids with their charges, chattering groups of young ladies, and courting couples.

An amber cloak caught her eye—it was the supercilious young lady from the circulating library, on the arm of a gentleman. A finely dressed man, with braided coat and a fall of lace at his throat. An older woman in servants' garb trailed a few paces behind them.

The young woman stared at her as they approached, and said something to her companion as her hand moved to cover the brooch Nell had admired. The gentleman fixed Nell with a glare, then his lip curled and they walked on. Nell smiled to herself; a snub only hurt when one cared about the opinion of the person delivering it. Then her steps slowed as she recalled her earlier encounter with the young lady.

The brooch—a ruby surrounded by pearls. Why had it taken her this long to make the connection with the items missing from Lord Lanchester's box? Perhaps because she wasn't expecting to see something stolen by Gentleman Jones worn by a fine lady in Scarborough.

Could it really be the missing brooch? Surely such a woman did not consort with highwaymen. Nell could not ask the woman how she had come by it—what possible excuse could she give? If Toby were here, she would tell him, but he was still lying in wait at the Moorcock.

The magistrate—she would have to tell Sir James. He could decide whether or not to ask the young woman about it. He or his wife might even know her. But first, she should try to learn the woman's name.

"Tim, I need to go back to the library, then I'm going to call on the magistrate."

"All right." Tim acknowledged her change of plan without much interest, his attention fixed on a group of young men clad only in drawers and waistcoats wading into the water. Nell shivered in sympathy—if she were to try sea bathing, it would be in July, not October.

Only the young assistant was serving in the circulating library, but this time Nell didn't have long to wait. "How can I help you, miss? Oh, you are Miss Mason. Mr Everidge left this for you." He reached under the counter.

Nell ignored the book he held out. "When I was here earlier, you were serving a young lady wearing an amber-coloured cloak and a gown with yellow and white stripes."

The assistant nodded. "Miss Delaney, yes."

"Thank you." Nell turned to leave, then hesitated. "Do you know where Sir James Troughton lives? Can you direct me?" She knew it was above the town, but wasn't sure of the quickest way to get there from here.

"By all means, miss." He came out from behind the counter and opened the door for her. He pointed up the hill, then to the left. "Go that way, and turn left at the coffee house. That lane leads to Sir James' house." He bowed, and returned to the shop.

Nell set off, her steps slowing as she began to ascend the hill. She stopped to catch her breath as the cobbles turned to a muddy lane, and climbed on until she heard the sound of a vehicle behind her. She stood aside to let a carriage pulled by two horses pass her on the narrow road. As it trundled past, a face stared at her out of the window—the man who'd been walking with Miss Delaney.

The coach stopped just ahead; the door opened and the man stepped out.

"Miss Mason, I believe?" The words were polite enough, but his expression was not friendly.

Nell nodded.

"Allow me to take you to your destination." He stepped towards her as he spoke.

"No, thank you, sir." She could not pass him with the coach in the way, so she turned. Then a hand grasped her arm, bruisingly hard, and swung her around.

"I insist."

Before Nell could try to pull free, he grasped her about the waist with both hands and flung her though the open door of the coach. She landed painfully on her knees, then the door slammed and the coach jolted into motion.

CHAPTER 17

"What are you doing, Colonel?" The voice came from above Nell. A woman.

Nell took a deep breath, waiting for a blow that never came. Cautiously, she got to her knees, to find herself looking into the frowning face of Miss Delaney.

"Why is this person here?" Miss Delaney went on. "You said one of your own maidservants would accompany us, or I would never have sent my own maid away."

"Keep quiet," the colonel snarled from behind Nell. "If you'd kept that brooch hidden as I told you, this need never have happened."

Miss Delaney's eyes widened and her mouth fell open. "Oh!"

Nell scrambled to her feet, her heart racing and a sick feeling developing in her stomach. The movement of the coach unbalanced her, and she fell onto the seat opposite Miss Delaney.

Maitland? It must be—how many colonels could there be in Scarborough?

"But Colonel, what has this—?"

"I told you to keep quiet!" He glared at Miss Delaney until she leaned back in her own corner of the seat, her lower lip trembling and her face pale. Then he turned to Nell.

"Why were you so interested in this?" He held out the brooch Miss Delaney had been wearing.

Nell swallowed hard. "I never saw it before today." That was true, but the wobble in her voice made it sound unconvincing.

"Then why are you on your way to Sir James' house?"

How could he know where she was going?

He must have seen the astonishment on her face, for he went on, "Oh yes, the man in the circulating library was most helpful when we went back there…"

Trying desperately to think, Nell said nothing. The colonel thrust himself towards her, one hand coming to rest on the seat beside her leg, the other on the side of the coach, his face unpleasantly close to hers.

"Miss Mason, there is some talk in the town about the Moorcock and its connection with a recent robbery. You were at the inn when the soldiers were there. There is a box of jewellery missing, and you appeared to take a great interest in the brooch Miss Delaney was wearing. Why?"

Nell could hardly breathe. What would he do if she told the truth?

"There is a reward for the return of the stolen jewellery, Miss Mason, and I intend to have it. If you know anything that might help me find these jewels, you should tell me at once."

Her breath came a little easier. He didn't suspect she knew about his likely involvement with Jones, only that she'd found what Jones had left at the inn. He thought she'd hidden the jewels, so it would be his word against hers about who had actually found them. Who would believe a serving girl against a colonel in the militia?

Sir James would, and so would Toby—but the colonel didn't know that.

"What has the brooch you gave me have to do with missing jewellery?" Miss Delaney asked.

The colonel swore and turned towards her. "If you don't keep quiet, you'll meet the same fate as her."

Fate? Nell dug her fingernails into her palms. "What are you going to do with me?"

Her voice trembled, but that seemed to give Maitland confidence, for he sat back against the squabs opposite with an unpleasant smile on his face.

"If you co-operate, I will let you go. Somewhere far from here, where you cannot make trouble. No-one will miss a drab like you."

Aunt Em would. But Sir James might be persuaded that she had found the missing items and absconded with them. Would Toby worry if she went missing?

Toby.

Toby was still at the inn.

Maitland leaned forwards. "Where are the jewels? Speak, Miss Mason, or I'll find a cliff to throw you off."

"I… I found a box. At the inn."

"Good." He sat back on the opposite bench. "What did you do with it?"

"I hid it at the inn. I didn't want the soldiers to find it." Perhaps her uncle's reputation would help her here—the colonel would assume she was as dishonest as Silas.

The colonel rapped on the roof of the coach with his cane, and stepped down when it came to a halt. Nell couldn't make out what he was saying, and he climbed back in before she could think whether she should try to escape here.

"Where are we going?" Miss Delaney's voice shook. "Colonel, you said you were taking me home!"

"I will, eventually, Miss Delaney. But I have a little errand to run first. One that will enrich our future life together."

Safe for the moment, Nell looked at Miss Delaney. Was she betrothed to Maitland?

"But my reputation?" She pointed at Nell. "If she's a tavern wench, that is no better than us being alone together."

"It matters not, my dear. We are to be wed, after all. Unless, of course, you choose to obstruct me."

Her brow creased as she sank back into her corner. Did the colonel not care that he'd admitted knowledge of the robbery in front of her? Perhaps Miss Delaney hadn't understood.

As the coach trundled towards the moors, Nell's sick feeling of dread began to lessen. The soldiers must still be at the inn—if they had returned to Scarborough, Toby would have come to see his aunt. That meant she would have help. She would not think about what might happen if they *had* left.

What exactly had Miss Delaney said to make the colonel swear and threaten her? "The brooch you gave me," that must have been it. The colonel had effectively admitted he'd given Miss Delaney something he knew was stolen, and he could only have got it from Jones. In payment for services rendered, no doubt.

That sick feeling increased again. Even if he'd only abducted Nell as a means to get the jewellery, he'd now said enough for her testimony to help convict him.

Toby *had* to be at the inn.

Toby paced up and down the kitchen, resisting the impulse to check on Frampton, currently keeping watch from an upstairs window. It was two days since they had bolted the shutters on the ground floor windows and some of the upstairs ones to make the inn look abandoned, but already it seemed like a week. Army life had long spells of tedium, but even on sea voyages one could play cards with fellow officers, or take the air on deck and watch the sailors work the ship.

And today, he didn't even have any hot coffee. They couldn't risk anyone seeing smoke rising from the chimney, or to smell it if someone came close to the inn during the night. Yesterday a blustery wind had been blowing the clouds across the sky and would quickly disperse any plume of smoke, so he'd allowed the men to do some cooking. But with today's calmer weather, they would be eating cold stew again.

They could be here for another week, and Jones still might not come.

"Sir?" The call came from upstairs.

Toby went into the passage. "What is it, Frampton?"

"Coach comin', sir."

"Very well." A coach had gone by yesterday, and several carts. One of the latter had stopped, the driver descending to bang on the door, but he had eventually given up his quest for refreshment and driven on.

Toby went to the back door and signalled to the men in the stable to keep out of sight; Slater, on watch in the trees near the track, would see the coach for himself. Then Toby locked the door.

"It's stoppin', sir!"

Toby waited in the passage. The clop of hooves and grinding of wheels on cobbles penetrated through the ill-fitting door. Then the sounds ceased.

"We barred the door before we left." The words were faint, but clearly a woman.

Nell? What was she doing here?

The door rattled, as if whoever she was talking to hadn't believed her. "There must be a door around the back." A male voice—one that sounded vaguely familiar, but he couldn't place it.

He ran up the stairs into a back bedroom, opening the casement and shutter just enough to see downwards.

Nell appeared, her face pale, with a man walking beside her.

What was Maitland doing here?

The colonel wasn't holding Nell, so was she with him voluntarily? He squashed that momentary doubt—quite apart from it not being her nature to betray him, she knew he and his men were here. Maitland would not be acting as he was if she had told him that.

Maitland tried the back door, then shook it. "Where's the damned key?"

"The soldiers took it when we left." Her voice carried clearly through the open window—she didn't need to talk that loudly for Maitland to hear. "You'll have to break in."

Maitland swore, rattling the door again, then bent to peer at the lock. Toby took a chance and pushed the shutter open a little further, but Nell was watching Maitland and Toby didn't want to risk attracting his attention as well.

Maitland straightened and looked around him. "What's that building?"

"A stable."

"Good, there should be something in there to help me break the door open."

Damn. Maitland was going to find Jones' horse.

Toby hurried back to the kitchen, calling to Frampton to follow him down the stairs. There was no sound outside the back door, so he carefully turned the key in the lock and inched the door open. Maitland was halfway across the yard.

"How many were driving?" he asked Frampton.

"Just one, sir."

"Go out through the front door and make sure he doesn't interfere."

"Yessir."

Toby slipped out of the door and followed Maitland and Nell, treading quietly, then stepped behind one corner of the building as his quarry came to a halt by the stable door.

Where were the soldiers? Nell could see no sign of anyone—no movement, no smell of smoke from the kitchen fire. She tried not to think what Maitland might do when he found there were no jewels at the inn. And the longer it took him to determine that, the worse temper he'd be in.

A sound behind her—a footstep. She turned her head in time to see a flash of red at the corner of the building, and felt weak with relief. Then Maitland flung open the door of the stable and stepped inside—only to release a string of curses and spin around, pulling a pistol from his pocket. "Jones is here. You bitch—you've led me into a trap!" He raised the pistol, pointing it directly at Nell, then his eyes flicked away from her face to something behind her and his mouth dropped open. "You? I thought you were dead!"

"Get him, lads!" The shout came from behind Nell just as someone tugged on her arm. She staggered backwards and stumbled, sprawling onto the cobbles. She made no move to get up—it was Toby who had pulled her away, and he now stood between her and Maitland's pistol. Shielding her.

Another voice shouted from inside the stable. "Drop the pistol. There's two muskets pointed at your back."

Maitland kept his pistol pointing at Toby, his lips compressing as if he were about to fire anyway. But he didn't act quickly enough—Toby flung himself at the colonel and the two men fell to the ground, each gripping the other's pistol hand.

"Stop or I'll blow yer brains out."

The colonel froze as the muzzle of a musket pressed into the side of his head. The other soldier came running from the stable with a length of rope.

"Take him inside," Toby ordered, getting to his feet. "Tie him to a chair. You stay with him, Kearney." The two soldiers grasped Maitland's arms and dragged him off, ignoring his protests.

Toby turned to Nell, crouching beside her. "Are you hurt?"

"No."

She took the hand he extended, his flesh warm against her cold palm as he pulled her to her feet. Her knees almost gave way and he put his arms around her, hugging her briefly. Too briefly. He moved one arm, the other still around her shoulders; she was glad of his strong support even though she was recovering from her fright.

"Come, I'll get you inside," he said. "You can tell me what happened when I've dealt with the driver."

The driver, and Miss Delaney. Even as Nell thought it, Miss Delaney came running around the side of the inn, skirts held up.

"Lieutenant! Oh, Lieutenant Bourne, how pleased I am to see you!"

"What in—?" Toby bit the words off and shook his head, muttering something beneath his breath before inclining his head. "Miss Delaney. I'm afraid your escort is under arrest. Please go indoors."

Miss Delaney came to a stop several paces from them, her gaze going from Nell to Toby and back. "Arrest?"

"Inside, if you please," Toby repeated, his voice hard.

He released Nell, but put a hand on her arm to detain her as she took a step to follow Miss Delaney. He turned to her once Miss Delaney had gone through the back door.

"Perhaps you'd better tell me now. Briefly."

The facts *were* brief. "She had a brooch that matched the ruby set. The colonel gave it to her. She told him I'd seen it. He thought I had the rest of the jewels, and dragged me into his coach. I told him I'd hidden them here."

To her surprise he grinned, amusement crinkling his eyes. "Admirably succinct, thank you." Then he became serious again. "I don't like to send you inside with Maitland there, but I don't want to give him the chance to plot with Miss Delaney what to say when I question them. Tell Kearney he's to stay with you all. I need to get the coach away if we are still to have a chance to trap Jones."

Nell nodded.

"I knew I could count on you." He hurried off, leaving Nell warmed by the praise.

In the kitchen, the soldiers were securing Maitland to one of the kitchen chairs, ignoring his threats to have them transported for manhandling an officer. Miss Delaney stood near the door, wringing her hands, and sent a venomous look in Nell's direction.

"Just following orders, sir," Kearney said, wooden-faced. He straightened, looking at Nell.

"Lieutenant Bourne said you are to remain here."

"Right, miss."

The other soldier left, to return a minute later with two muskets. He handed one to Kearney, and went on through the kitchen. Resuming the lookout, Nell guessed, as his boots clumped on the stairs. Kearney took up a position near the back door, well away from the colonel.

Nell sat at the table and, after a moment, Miss Delaney came and sat nearby.

"You won't get away with this," Maitland spluttered. Nell wasn't sure if he was addressing her or Kearney. "Don't you know who I am?"

Nell ignored him.

"You, girl! I'm talking to *you*!"

Nell wished she could just leave the room. In spite of Kearney's presence, and Toby not far away, she could not be easy in the same room as this man who meant her harm. But Toby had asked her to stay. Kearney would overhear anything Maitland and Miss Delaney said to each other, but another witness might be useful.

"How *dare* you ignore me!"

"He's a colonel in the militia," Miss Delaney said, when Nell still did not reply. "There must be some mistake."

"I think you made the mistake," Nell said, "in getting into that coach." She said no more—it would not do to get drawn into conversation in case she gave something away that Toby did not wish them to know.

Miss Delaney said nothing for some time, then glared at Nell. "It's cold in here; why is there no fire? Light one immediately."

Nell glanced at Kearney—he shook his head. But even had Kearney given permission, she was not about to take orders from Miss Delaney.

"Didn't you hear me?" Miss Delaney's voice was becoming shrill.

"I heard. If you want a fire, light it yourself." Watching her try could be amusing.

Kearney coughed, his frown changing to the compressed lips of a hidden smile. Miss Delaney scowled at her, but sensibly did not make the attempt. Nell was almost sorry.

"You won't get him, you know. Lieutenant Bourne, I mean. He was courting me before…" Miss Delaney flicked a glance at Maitland. "He was courting me."

Toby and Miss Delaney?

Why not? She was pretty, like a portrait. Nell discounted the amber cloak and the well-fitting gown—any woman with sufficient funds could obtain those. But Miss Delaney's complexion hadn't suffered from days spent in a steamy kitchen, and her hands would be smooth and white beneath her gloves, unlike Nell's work-roughened ones. Miss Delaney would know how to dance and flirt and how to make herself attractive to men.

But you are betrothed to the colonel. She could think the words, even if she did not say them.

Nell looked away. Did the woman really think that Nell Mason of the Moorcock was trying to attract a man like Toby? Miss Delaney must think that she had some hope of doing so, or why bother to warn her off? The idea gave her a fluttery feeling in her stomach—one she firmly suppressed. Aunt Em's friendship was a bigger improvement in her life than she had expected; to wish for more would only lead to disappointment.

Miss Delaney's mouth pursed into a sullen pout when Nell didn't reply, but she did not speak again.

CHAPTER 18

$\mathcal{T}$oby found the driver holding the horses' heads. He was a thin man of middling years with greying hair. Frampton, standing nearby, had his musket in one hand with the butt resting on the ground.

"He didn't give you any trouble?" Toby asked.

"No, sir."

Toby nodded and walked over to the driver. "What orders did you have from Maitland?"

The driver appeared wary but didn't have the defiance of a man caught doing something wrong. "I'm just his driver, sir. I drive him into Scarborough quite often, and wait for him. Today he told me to stop halfway up the hill, and that other woman got in."

"But you came here instead of going to Maitland's home."

"Yes, sir. A few minutes after the woman got in, he stopped and ordered me to come up here."

"He didn't try to run off, sir," Frampton added.

"What's the colonel done, sir?" the driver asked.

"Broken the law." That was all the driver needed to know at the moment. But what to do with him? Toby couldn't send him back to Scarborough in case he let drop where he'd left Maitland. If he stayed here, he would have to be locked up—partly for his own safety, if Jones did come and there was shooting. That didn't seem fair. There was also the coach to deal with; it was too big to hide in the stable building, nor was there room for two more horses. "Frampton, can you drive a coach like this?"

Frampton shook his head. "Not with two horses, sir. Never driven no more than a cart."

"The others?"

"Don't reckon so, sir. D'you want me to ask?"

Toby sighed. "No. You'll go with this fellow to Mr Hartley in Pickering—I'll give you a letter to explain." He turned back to the driver. "You will have to stay in Pickering for a few days. Mr Hartley may ask you more about Maitland—I recommend you answer truthfully. If you haven't done anything wrong, you have nothing to fear."

The driver grimaced, but nodded. Toby went to sit in the open door of the carriage, taking out his pocketbook and pencil. When he'd described the situation, he tore out the page and folded it before beckoning Frampton closer.

"This is for Mr Hartley. When you've escorted the driver there, come back here if you think you can reach the inn in the dark without being seen."

"Yes, sir."

As Frampton and the driver climbed to the box and set off, Toby stood back and examined the front of the inn. Apart from the open door, it still appeared to be deserted; the partly open shutter in the upstairs room where they were keeping watch was hardly noticeable. Satisfied, he entered the inn and barred the front door behind him, then headed for the kitchen. Kearney came to attention as he entered.

"Go and watch the back," Toby ordered. With only three men available, keeping a good lookout overnight could be difficult. But that was a problem for later. Maitland was securely fastened to his chair, his expression furious. The two women were sitting either side of the table, not looking at each other. Nell glanced his way with a look of relief, and Miss Delaney greeted him with a smile.

"I'm so glad you're here, Lieutenant Bourne." Miss Delaney rubbed her arms. "It is so cold—can we not have a fire? That woman wouldn't light one, even though there are coals ready. She was most insolent."

"No fire."

"But Lieutenant—"

"Miss Delaney, this room is no colder than the coach you were travelling in. Please be silent." He didn't have the patience to pacify her at the moment. It was a shame Nell had been subjected to Miss Delaney's poor manners, but he'd had no choice.

He pulled a chair from the table and set it down halfway between the colonel and Miss Delaney, angled so he could easily see both.

"Maitland, explain why you brought these two ladies here against their will."

"*Two* ladies?" Miss Delaney's words were quiet.

Toby ignored her, suppressing his anger at the insult to Nell.

"You will regret this," the colonel spat. "I have the ear of men in the War Office."

"If you say so." That might change after today's events. "You have still to explain why you were about to break into this inn."

Maitland took a deep breath and squared his shoulders. "I heard about the robbery of a coach on the other side of the moors, as did everyone in Scarborough. It was rumoured the haul included a box of jewellery." He nodded in Nell's direction. "When Miss Delaney told me that this woman seemed to recognise a brooch she had, I suspected it might be one of the missing jewels and that trollop had seen them. She *admitted* to having hidden them from your men. I thought it was worth investigating." He shrugged. "That is all."

Nell was no trollop. Toby's muscles tensed at the wish to plant his fist in Maitland's face, but that would have to wait. The colonel's explanation would be plausible to anyone who didn't know other parts of the story.

"Where is this brooch now?"

Nell broke the silence. "The colonel has it in his pocket. The right hand one, I think."

Toby retrieved it, moving closer to the window to examine it. The design was similar to the other pieces in the ruby set, although he wouldn't swear to it. But Nell had examined the jewels in more detail, and she had thought it was part of Jones' haul.

He resumed his seat, holding the brooch towards Maitland. "How did you come by this?"

"*I* did not. Where Miss Delaney acquired it, I have no idea, but—"

"You *gave* it to me, Colonel!" Miss Delaney's soft voice had become shrill.

Maitland's brows rose. "No. I have never seen it before today. Of what are you accusing me, Bourne? I will not stand for this!"

Miss Delaney's lips began to tremble. "You gave it to me when you asked me to marry you, Colonel."

"My dear Miss Delaney, you were persistent in your pursuit of me —why would I need to gift you such things to gain your hand? There is my word against yours as to how you came by it." He shook his head. "Who do you think the law will believe: an upstanding citizen and colonel in the militia, or a silly young woman who was desperate enough for a husband to get into a coach alone with a man?"

Miss Delaney's face went white and her mouth fell open. Toby had to feel sorry for her, in spite of the way she was being rude to Nell. Maitland's story would have been convincing, too, if Toby hadn't known about the false alibi the colonel had attempted to provide for Jones.

Nell listened to Colonel Maitland with increasing concern—his explanation would sound reasonable to anyone new to the situation. And whatever Miss Delaney's motives for becoming betrothed to the colonel, it couldn't be pleasant to be dismissed like that.

Toby turned to Nell. "Miss Mason, do you have anything to add to this?"

Nell thought for a moment, trying to recall the exact words the colonel had spoken in the coach. "Miss Delaney mentioned that the colonel gave her the brooch, and he did not contradict her. He also said he would let me go if I co-operated, and throw me off a cliff if I did not."

"Fantasy!" Maitland protested.

"He *did* say that," Miss Delaney put in, to Nell's surprise—and Toby's, by the look on his face.

"Absolute nonsense. You cannot treat me like this, Bourne. I have done nothing wrong, no matter what these women say. Summon my coach and I will return Miss Delaney to her home." There was almost a note of pleading beneath Maitland's bluster.

"This isn't a court, Maitland," Toby said. "I was merely asking for information. And your coach is miles away by now."

"What?" Maitland tried to get up, and almost tipped his chair over. His face turned purple, just like Uncle Silas in a temper.

"You'll be staying here for a couple of days, at least," Toby went on. "All of you," he added, at a gasp from Miss Delaney.

"Good luck finding another fool to marry you, Miss Delaney," Maitland spat. "Your reputation will be gone when I tell how you accompanied me."

Toby got to his feet. "I think it's time we found a place for you in the cellar, Maitland. Miss Mason, do you have the key to the room we used for the two carters?"

"I'll find it." Nell was glad to escape from Maitland's malevolent glare. The key was where she'd left it three days ago, when Hoskins took the carters to Scarborough. She went down to the cellars and checked the room—it held only a few pieces of broken furniture, and the remains of rushlights the carters must have been given when they were locked up here. Maitland wouldn't be very comfortable, but she didn't care.

She returned to the kitchen to give the key to Toby.

"Thank you." Toby took out a pistol and pointed it at the colonel. "Nell, could you untie him from the chair? Maitland, don't worry about what might happen to me if I kill you. I'll just drop your body over a cliff."

There was a little gasp from Miss Delaney as Nell went over to Maitland. She unpicked the knots, being careful not to get between Maitland and Toby, then backed away hurriedly as Maitland got to his feet. Toby gestured towards the cellar.

The silence when the two men had gone felt uncomfortable. Miss Delaney's voice shook a little when she finally spoke. "Do you think he meant it? When Lieutenant Bourne said we would have to stay here, I mean."

"Yes."

"Why? Why would he do this?"

"You'll have to ask Lieutenant Bourne." Toby hadn't mentioned Jones in his questioning, and Nell wasn't sure how much she should say.

"But my reputation—people will think I'm like you. I'll never find a suitable husband!"

Nell sighed. She couldn't really blame Miss Delaney for her opinion. It was what most people would think of a young woman who'd worked here. Nell didn't think Toby was going to lock Miss Delaney in a cellar, so she would be in the woman's company for a few days; the time would pass more easily if she could make some peace with her.

She made an effort to speak calmly. "Despite what you think, Miss Delaney, I am not a trollop. When we return to Scarborough, you will be relying on my presence here to avoid any insinuations about your behaviour. It can only do you harm to spread your mistaken opinion of me."

Miss Delaney's eyes widened. "But you worked here?" She waved a hand. "A tavern, frequented by all sorts of low persons."

"I cook, Miss Delaney. This is not a brothel; it is an inn that serves ale and food."

A small crease formed between Miss Delaney's well-shaped brows. "You speak like… Well, like me. Our servants at home do not."

I am not your servant!

Nell felt like shouting it, but did not. One day she might have to be a servant to someone like this woman. She thought she had been resigned to that fate, but Miss Delaney was testing her acceptance. "My father was a prosperous banker until a robbery made the bank fail. This inn is my uncle's—it was the only place my mother and I had to go."

Miss Delaney nodded, the frown disappearing. "I'm sorry that happened to you. But it means you will understand how important it is that my good reputation remains intact. I have a dowry, but it is not large. I need to make a good marriage."

Nell gave up. Not wanting to remain in the kitchen in case she lost her temper with the woman, she went into the pantry. Seeing how much food was left would be a good enough excuse for leaving Miss Delaney alone.

Toby returned to the kitchen. The sun had set while he'd been talking to Maitland, so he closed the shutters and set the lantern on the table. Miss Delaney was sitting there alone, a frown distorting her face. She looked up at him and smiled—the pretty smile that had so enraptured him when he first encountered her. Now, it left him unmoved.

"Where is Miss Mason?" Even as he spoke, a faint chink of crockery came from the pantry.

"She left." Miss Delaney shrugged, the smile fading. "Lieutenant, I don't understand why you are keeping me here, and why you sent Colonel Maitland's coach away. I *cannot* be away from home overnight, surely you can see that?"

Toby sighed and sat down. "You have Miss Mason to vouch for you."

Her nose wrinkled. "Who will believe a... a woman who has worked in a place like this? And what would *I* be doing with such a woman?"

Befriending her, perhaps? Toby looked at Miss Delaney's creased brow and downturned mouth, and thought that would never happen.

"My parents will miss me—they will have noticed my absence hours ago."

"I sent a message with the coach," Toby said. There was no need to tell her that Mr Hartley's note to Sir James was unlikely to arrive before the morning. He'd left it to the magistrate to decide what to tell Miss Delaney's parents.

"I should be grateful, I suppose, to have discovered Colonel Maitland's true nature before I wed him." She sighed, a rueful smile on her face as she looked directly at him. "Such a foolish mistake I made, when I could have chosen a better man." She fluttered her eyelashes. "A much better man."

"Indeed." But it would not be him. He had discovered more about her character today than in all their other encounters put together, and didn't like what he had learned. Besides, he was not about to wed a woman who had flirted with him a week ago, then become affianced to Maitland.

Steps sounded in the passage and Nell returned. "I was seeing how much food you and your men had left, Lieutenant. I take it there will be no fire lit?"

"I cannot risk it, so no cooking, you'll be pleased to know. Are we to go hungry?"

"No cooking?" Miss Delaney interrupted. "Lieutenant, you still have not explained *why* I am to be kept here against my will. And now starved, it seems!"

"You won't starve," Nell put in. "There is plenty of bread and cheese, and Lieutenant Bourne's men did not eat *all* the ham."

Miss Delaney's mouth pursed and she frowned. Toby spoke before she could complain again. "I cannot spare anyone to take you back to Scarborough. We are here to set a trap for Gentleman Jones, who we expect to come to retrieve the jewellery that your betrothed thought was hidden here."

Her eyes widened. "Gentleman Jones? Am I in danger? Lieutenant, you *cannot*—"

"You will be perfectly safe, Miss Delaney, if you do as I say."

"And he is my *former* betrothed."

Toby shrugged. "As you say. Miss Mason, I think it unlikely Jones will appear until full dark, so we may as well have some food now."

"Your men, too?" Nell asked.

"Thank you, yes. I can take them something without being seen now the sun has set."

Nell set out plates and knives, then headed for the pantry again.

"I would like to... to rest, Lieutenant, if that is all right?" Miss

Delaney said. "Will you have Miss Mason prepare a room for me? And send some hot water up?"

"You may have some cold water, Miss Delaney." He filled a bowl from the pump in the scullery, and took her to the room he'd been using to catch a few hours' sleep now and then. He *had* emptied the chamber pot this morning, so she should have all she needed.

"Do not open the curtains, Miss Delaney, and leave the lamp by the door."

She wrinkled her nose at the rumpled bed, but Toby left before she could make any comment.

CHAPTER 19

ell looked up from the stale loaf she was slicing as Toby entered the kitchen, and set the knife down. She was relieved to see Miss Delaney was not with him. "How many men are there to be fed, Lieutenant?"

"Toby." He slumped into a chair. "Only three in addition to myself. I sent one off with the coach."

"To Scarborough?"

"No, to a friend of Sir James at Pickering."

"Aunt Em will be worried. Miss Delaney and the colonel will be missed, too. They were walking by the sands together, and would have been seen there. The colonel also said he'd asked about me in the circulating library."

Toby ran his hand through his hair and suppressed a yawn. "I sent a note with Frampton, asking for a message to be sent on to Scarborough. It might not arrive until morning but, apart from Aunt Em worrying, that might be all to the good. If Jones hears about it, he might think Maitland is here to take the jewels and come to stop him."

"Are you expecting him to come tonight?"

"Hoping, rather than expecting. I don't know how much longer we can stay here without being discovered."

He did look tired. It must be difficult, not to mention tedious, keeping watch without even a mug of hot coffee.

"Nell, if he does come, I want you and Miss Delaney to hide in the cellar. Out of the way of any possible shooting."

She had no objection to that. "Will you let him get inside the inn?"

"I think I have to—none of us knows what he looks like. Unfortunately, we cannot just shoot anyone who happens to arrive in the hope that he's our quarry."

"Very unfortunate," Nell agreed, suppressing a wry smile.

He rubbed his face. "Oh, yes." One side of his mouth turned up in amusement. "Particularly for the poor innocent concerned."

"I know what he looks like." Very ordinary, apart from his fancy clothing—so not an easy man to describe. "I could—"

"No." His tone was surprisingly severe. "No," he repeated, more gently. "Not unless you can guarantee to identify him by moonlight from an upper window."

Of course she couldn't.

"I will not put you in danger, Nell. But there's also the matter of Maitland. So far, we have no firm evidence that he's been paid by Jones—only inference. I know the evidence that you and your relatives, and Miss Delaney, could give strongly implies his guilt, but don't forget he'll be tried by a jury of his peers—wealthy men."

Men who would think she was a slut, along with Bett; that Miss Delaney was a silly young miss, and Uncle Silas was already a criminal deserving of transportation at the very least. There was no question in her mind who they would believe.

"If we can capture Jones alive," Toby went on, "he will doubtless want to bring Maitland down, too."

"Why would they believe Jones any more than they would believe me or my uncle?"

"It's worth trying. Maitland may give himself away if confronted with Jones." He yawned again. "Excuse me."

"Have some food." Nell buttered some bread, added cheese to the plate, and pushed it across the table towards him.

Instead of starting to eat, he stood. "I'll take some to the men outside first."

Nell fetched napkins and wrapped food. "You must all be short of sleep. I could watch for a while, if you trust me to do so?"

He gazed at her without replying, until she wondered if she'd said something wrong. Or stupid. Then he smiled. "Thank you. It will be a great help if you can watch from the window upstairs."

Nell shivered and rubbed her arms. She could close the window, but the cold air was helping to keep her awake. The moon had risen, but this room was on the north side of the building and would be in shadow. The partly open shutter and casement would not be noticed unless a rider came right up to the building.

If Jones ever came. How did soldiers manage to keep alert for hours when on watch? The landscape was a black shadow, with only the pale line of the Whitby road showing against the darkness, and the fainter line of the Scarborough track to the east.

Toby had lent her his spyglass; she pulled out the tubes and peered through it at the pale road. Nothing, just as the previous time she'd looked, and the time before that. She turned the glass towards the place where the routes crossed. Nothing.

Movement outside caught Nell's eye as she put the glass down. Footsteps sounded on the cobbles—one of the soldiers must be running towards the inn.

She picked up the spyglass and hurried out onto the landing, lit only by moonlight coming through the windows and open doors of the rooms at the back of the inn. She flattened herself against the wall as Toby came racing up the stairs. "Someone coming from the west. Into the cellar. Now." He passed her without slowing, and burst into the room where Miss Delaney was sleeping.

In the kitchen, Slater was checking the priming on his musket. A muffled shriek indicated Miss Delaney had woken, and by the time Nell reached the room in the cellar where her uncle kept his barrels of ale, Toby was behind her with Miss Delaney, pulling her by one arm.

"Keep the door closed." He set the lantern on the floor, then he was gone.

Nell picked up the lantern, holding it high to survey the room. The ale casks were too big for her to move, but there were some smaller tubs of brandy. Nell rolled two into the space in the middle of the room, set them on end and sat on one.

"I don't know why Lieutenant Bourne had to drag me downstairs like that." Miss Delaney rubbed her arm where Toby had held it.

"Gentleman Jones has come. Did he not say?" Toby would not have been so urgent if he didn't think it was Jones.

"But I only wanted to put my shoes on, and he pulled me away." She held one foot out. "I have a hole in my stocking now."

Better than a bullet in you. "He wanted to make sure you were safe. Now be quiet, unless you want Jones to find us here."

"Oh."

Surprisingly, she did stop complaining. Nell strained her ears to listen. There was no sound at all for some time, then a shot. To be heard here, it must have been in the kitchen, or near it.

Miss Delaney put her head in her hands as running feet sounded on the floor above, then a more distant shot.

Then silence.

Toby peered through the window in the lookout room. Only a few minutes had passed since Beckett had run in with the news that a rider was approaching from the west. A moving shadow was Beckett returning to his post in the trees. No-one else was about.

What would Jones do? Croston was outside the stable, well hidden in the shadows, and Sergeant Slater in the kitchen was ready to assist upstairs or protect the women in the cellar.

The sound of hooves came through the open casement before he saw movement. It must be Jones, for who else would come here at this hour? He stepped back from the window—it would not do for his quarry to see him now.

The hoofbeats got closer, slower, then stopped. A normal traveller would knock on the door; instead, Toby heard a curse, and, "Stand still, damn you."

After a few moments, Toby risked approaching the window again to listen. A whicker told him the horse was still there, and a rattle could be Jones testing the shutters on the downstairs windows. Then he heard footsteps, fading.

Toby crossed the landing into one of the back rooms and pressed his face against the casement, trying to see down into the yard. There... still testing the shutters. Toby readied himself to run downstairs if Jones went to the stable to look for a ladder, but he didn't. He dragged an empty barrel closer to where the scullery roof stuck out and clambered up onto the tiles. Toby heard a tinkle of glass from the window above the scullery, and a creak as Jones pulled the casement open. Moving back onto the landing, he took his pistols out and cocked them both. Then he waited, his eyes slowly becoming accustomed to the darkness after the brighter moonlight outside.

Footsteps across the room, a shadow in the patch of moonlight coming through the door, then a shape blocking most of the light.

Toby had to act now. "Stand and drop your weapon!"

The figure froze, then spun towards Toby. The man's face was a pale blur; light glinted on metal as he raised one arm. Toby fired and dived sideways, momentarily blinded by the flare of light, and ears ringing from the reports of both pistols echoing in the narrow landing. Where Jones' shot went, he didn't know, but Jones was no longer there.

A shout and two more shots had Toby running down the stairs, his second pistol at the ready. Slater was slumped on the floor by the cellar door, blood darkening his coat and his arms clasped around his body. "Winged the bugger, sir. He went out the back."

Toby sprinted for the open back door, feet sliding momentarily on one of the splashes of blood. Outside, Jones was already nearing the end of the building—limping, but moving fast enough for all that. Toby raised his pistol, hoping to stop Jones before he got to his horse, but the highwayman was out of sight before he could fire.

Toby shouted. "Shoot him!"

Stopping Jones now was more important than capturing him alive. A shot sounded from the direction of the stable, and Toby reached the corner to see Jones on the ground, face down. He moved one of his arms, as if trying to lift himself, then he slumped into stillness.

The silence in the cellar was broken by shouting and banging. Nell's sudden alarm abated when she recognised Maitland's voice, demanding to be let out. But no-one came.

What had happened? The number of shots meant Jones had not been captured easily—someone could be hurt.

Not Toby, please!

She tried not to think of that, and concentrated on what to do now. Was it safe to leave the cellar? It must be—there were four soldiers, including Toby, and only one man against them. Jones could not have killed or wounded all of them—unless he had brought men with him.

Nell had to know. Jones would search the whole inn looking for the jewels, so if the worst *had* happened, they would be found eventually in any case.

"Where are you going?" Miss Delaney asked.

"To see what happened," Nell snapped.

"You can't leave me in the dark!"

Nell ignored her, and Maitland's shouts. She almost tripped over someone lying on the floor—a body that cursed, and she recognised Slater's voice.

"Sergeant? Do you need help?"

"I'll manage for now, miss, if anyone's hurt worse. Go and see what's happening outside."

Behind her, Miss Delaney gasped.

"Stay here," Nell ordered, and went out into the yard. Three men stood near the corner of the building, gathered around a dark shape on the ground. She felt the tension in her release as she recognised Toby's voice.

It wasn't until she got close that she realised the dark shape was mostly blood. A huge pool of blood, with a man's body lying in it. Bile rose to her throat.

"Nell!" Toby turned her away from the gruesome sight. "He won't kill anyone again."

Nell took a deep breath. After what Jones had done, she should think of it as no worse than slaughtering a sheep or pig.

Toby was still holding her, his hands on her upper arms, his head bent towards her. "Nell..."

She swallowed and looked up at him, although the shadows made it difficult to read his expression. "He deserved it." She straightened her shoulders and he released her, taking a small step back.

"Yes. I... I don't like to ask this of you, but could you bear to look at his face? I'd like to be sure it *is* Jones."

"Who else could it be?"

"It's possible, although not likely, that someone else suspected the jewels were still here and came looking. Your uncle or cousin could identify him, of course, but I need to know now."

"Very well."

"Wait a moment." He went back to the body on the ground and said something to his men. One bent to roll the body over as Toby returned and took the lantern from her. He held it so it only illuminated the dead man's face. Jones' eyes were partially open, his features slack.

Nell had seen both her mother and father after they died—their peaceful expressions had helped her to accept their deaths. Jones did not look peaceful at all. She turned away abruptly.

Toby put one arm about her shoulders, and she turned and leaned into him. She was shivering against the chill, and at the sight of such a violent death. Toby's other arm came around to hold her close, and she took comfort from his warmth and his embrace.

"Nell, I'm sorry." She could feel his voice rumbling in his chest, his warm breath on her cheek.

"No, it's all right. It *is* Jones." She shivered again. "Can I light a fire now?"

He laughed, tightening his arms for a moment. "That's my girl. We could all do with something hot to drink, at least."

A sound from the inn made him slacken his hold and they both turned. Miss Delaney stood in the doorway.

Toby swore. "Keep her inside, will you? The last thing we need now is her in a fit of the vapours."

"What about Maitland?"

"Leave him where he is." He gave her shoulders a gentle squeeze and released her. Feeling oddly bereft, Nell ushered Miss Delaney back indoors with the promise of warmth.

CHAPTER 20

Toby's men found a tarpaulin in the stables and wrapped Jones' body in it. They left it at one end of the stable building, then brought Jones' horse inside. The other horse—the one Jones had abandoned on the moor—was still here. Toby would inspect its leg in the morning; the strain had had time to heal, and a second horse could be useful. Two of his men drew buckets of water from the well to swill away the stain on the cobbles.

Then Toby smelled smoke and smiled to himself—Nell had got the fire started. The kitchen was a much more cheerful place when he entered, with several lamps lit. The fire hadn't yet taken the chill from the air, but a pot of water hung above it and Nell was spooning coffee into a pot. She looked up as he entered, and her brief smile warmed his heart.

Then she frowned, her gaze shifting slightly. "You're hurt?"

He put a hand to the side of his face, feeling the roughness of dried blood. "Splinters from Jones' first shot, most likely." He hadn't noticed at the time. "There's probably a bullet hole in a door upstairs."

"There's a bullet hole in Sergeant Slater, too. He's in the scullery, along with another petticoat. Another one of my cousin's." She gave a wry smile.

He couldn't help smiling in return, in spite of all he had on his mind. "How seriously is he wounded?"

"Not too badly, I think. Miss Delaney went to put her shoes on."

He'd rather hoped Miss Delaney had retired to bed again, although if anyone needed their rest it was Nell. "You don't need to stay up, Nell—you haven't slept at all."

"I'll retire when I've made the coffee. Will you get one of your men to bank the fire when you leave the kitchen?"

"Of course." He rubbed his face as she turned away to take mugs from a shelf. He'd be grateful for the coffee, but he shouldn't have asked her to make it. His men were perfectly capable of that.

In the scullery, Slater was bathing a gash in his side. "Hurts like hell, sir," he said, when Toby asked. "But the bullet went through. Banged my head when I jumped out of the way."

"Daft bugger," Toby muttered.

Slater grinned. "Yessir. I hear one of the others got him."

"Yes."

"Don't suppose your Miss Mason could help me?"

His Miss Mason?

"I think you can manage," Toby said, trying to ignore Slater's assumption. No woman was 'his', and wasn't likely to be, not with his chosen profession. Unfortunately.

The next morning, Toby asked Nell to take breakfast to Miss Delaney, to keep the woman out of his way while he dealt with Maitland. He descended to the cellars and unlocked the door.

"About damned time." Maitland stalked past Toby and up the stairs. "You could have let me out last night."

"I didn't trust you not to run off," Toby said. "Count your blessings I had a pallet taken down for you. And that we got Jones, or you'd be here for another day."

Maitland scowled, but made no further protest as he poured himself coffee from the jug on the kitchen table. "I want breakfast. Where's the slut that—"

Toby's fist met Maitland's jaw, and he staggered backwards, the coffee splashing onto his neckcloth and coat. "You will speak politely about Miss Mason, or you'll walk to Scarborough." Toby rubbed his knuckles. It might have been unwise to hit the colonel, but it felt good.

Maitland's look was murderous, but he made no attempt to retaliate. "You have no authority to detain me here," he protested, rubbing his jaw. "Or to make me walk to Scarborough. Why should I walk? You've got Jones' horse in the stable."

"Recognised it, did you?" Toby enjoyed the momentary confusion on Maitland's face, but the colonel recovered quickly.

"You said you'd got Jones. He must have arrived on a horse."

A good enough excuse, unfortunately. Toby had spent some time the previous evening thinking over what Maitland had said. There was no proof Maitland had assisted Jones, and only the word of the two women that he had abducted them. Toby was certain Nell had told him the truth, but had concluded that Maitland was probably correct about who a jury of landed gentlemen would choose to believe. It pained him to admit it, but Maitland might well escape from this matter with little worse than a bit of gossip.

"You have no authority," Maitland repeated, his voice rising.

"My men with muskets are sufficient authority. You have a choice, Maitland. You can give me your word to wait here until Sir James sends a carriage, causing no further trouble. Or you can walk to Scarborough at gunpoint."

Maitland scowled, but capitulated when Toby said nothing more. "Oh, very well. I will wait here for a carriage."

A carriage accompanied by armed soldiers, if Toby had his way. He and his men were tired after watching for so long, and he didn't want to risk Maitland getting away before Sir James could question him. He would be easier to guard inside a closed carriage.

Maitland's temper did not improve when Nell returned and offered him a choice of porridge or bread and cheese. After a warning glance from Toby, he chose bread and cheese, and ate in silence.

Toby drew Nell into the parlour. "I want to send you and Miss Delancy to Scarborough this morning. You can take a letter to Sir

James with you. Any damage to your reputations will be harder to mend the longer you are away."

Their reputations? It was sweet of Toby to think Nell had a reputation to lose in the way that Miss Delaney had.

"Can you ride?" he asked. "It's best you get back to Scarborough as soon as possible, but I need the cart to take Jones. I don't imagine you'd care to share it."

Nell shivered, shaking her head. "No, indeed! I never learned to ride, although I can probably manage to stay on a horse if someone leads it."

"That might do. If you are happy to make the attempt, I should be able to persuade Miss Delaney that she will be safe enough riding behind Beckett."

Half an hour later, Nell was mounted on the more docile of the two horses, her skirts bunched uncomfortably around her legs and showing rather more ankle than she was used to. Miss Delaney looked no more at ease than Nell, but at least she had Beckett to hold on to.

Nell gripped the front of the saddle as Beckett pulled on the reins and the horse began to move.

Toby chuckled. "Try to relax, Nell, and move with the horse."

He walked beside her for a little way while she became used to the motion. "I will see you at Aunt Em's, tonight or tomorrow, most likely." He touched his hat as she nodded, then set off back to the inn.

As she had done before, Nell turned to look back as they passed the cross. This was the third time she'd thought it would be her last view of the inn; perhaps, on this occasion, she would be right?

They were some way beyond the cross when a carriage came into sight on the track ahead, coming towards them. Even from a distance, the musket held by the man sitting beside the driver was obvious, and there were two more armed men on the step at the back.

"I can't be seen like this!" Miss Delaney complained. "You—Beckett, isn't it? Move off the track, and make sure her horse is between me and the carriage."

Beckett grimaced, and looked at Nell with a shrug before he complied. Nell expected the carriage to pass them without stopping, but it slowed. Then the window slid down and Aunt Em put her head out. "Nell!"

Nell didn't wait for Beckett's help, but managed to dismount without falling. "Aunt Em—how do you come to be here?" She helped Aunt Em to open the door, standing back as one of the men on the coach descended and let down the step.

Aunt Em ignored Nell's question. "Are you well? Unhurt?"

"Yes, both of us. As is Toby."

"Oh, my dear—I was so worried." Aunt Em gave her a quick hug. "Let's get you both back to Sir James' house."

Beckett came over to them. "There's a place a little way back where your driver can turn, ma'am. Do you want me to come on with you, Miss Mason?"

Nell took Toby's letter from her pocket. "I think it might be more useful if you ride on ahead and give this to Sir James. You can see how Jones' horse goes without Miss Delaney up behind you."

Beckett's face lit up with a grin as he took the letter. "Can't argue with that, miss!" He mounted the horse and rode off at a trot.

Miss Delaney came to stand beside them, looking from Aunt Em to Nell. "Are you Lieutenant Bourne's aunt?"

Aunt Em nodded. "Yes. Mrs Bourne."

"I suppose you will do as a chaperone until you take me home." She walked on and allowed the guard to hand her into the carriage.

"She was worried about her reputation," Nell said, unsure why she should attempt to excuse Miss Delaney's rudeness.

Aunt Em smiled. "The petulance of a spoiled miss with no attraction beyond the chance arrangement of her features does not bother me, my dear." Her voice carried clearly—Miss Delaney could not have avoided hearing it. "I suppose she has been rude to you, too?" she went on, more quietly.

Nell nodded, then followed Aunt Em into the coach while the guard tied Nell's horse to the back.

Aunt Em straightened her skirts as the coach started to move. "I will not ask you what happened, as Sir James will want to hear it all as soon—"

"Sir James?" Miss Delaney interrupted. "The magistrate?"

"Of course. Is it your habit to interrupt your elders?" Aunt Em might have been talking to a small child. "You… *suggested…* I could act as your chaperone, Miss Delaney. However, all I have *seen* is a young woman riding astride with her skirts about her knees, clasping a common solider about the waist. Perhaps you should remember that before you try any more of your insolence on me."

Miss Delaney's mouth dropped open. "But I had no choice!"

"No-one will care about that. The truth is always less interesting than salacious assumptions. After all, you assumed the worst of my good friend Miss Mason." Aunt Em paused, then spoke again more gently. "Miss Delaney, you may look down upon me because I keep a boarding house, but I *am* a good friend of Lady Troughton. I am prepared to accept you did not willingly spend the night away from home. However, you *did* leave town with Colonel Maitland of your own volition, did you not?"

Miss Delaney nodded, her lips trembling.

"Your parents have allowed you too much freedom, or you would never have done such a thing. After this, you will need me and Miss Mason as allies if there is not to be damaging gossip about you. Rather than look down on us because you come from a family with more money—through no merit of your own, I may add—you would do well to think up some excuse for your absence and avoid offending those on whom you will depend to corroborate your story. Is that clear?"

The rebuke was all the more devastating for being delivered in a calm voice. Miss Delaney nodded again and turned her gaze to the window, her shoulders hunched.

Aunt Em turned to Nell. "I was worried when you did not return yesterday, and sent Tim to look for you. When he couldn't find you in the town he went to the circulating library, and brought Mr Everidge to see me. We consulted Sir James, and he sent to Colonel Maitland's house to see if you had gone there. His messenger found Miss Delaney's father there, which was when we learned that his daughter was also missing. When Sir James learned early this morning that the colonel was still absent, he thought it might be something to do with the robbery and was about to send mounted men to the Moorcock. I persuaded him you two would benefit from a female to look after you if you had come to harm, and he sent me in his carriage instead."

"Thank you, Aunt Em."

"It was little enough." She paused a moment. "You said Toby was well, too. Has something happened?"

"Jones is dead. Toby's sergeant was injured, but not badly."

"Oh, I'm happy that business is over." Aunt Em smiled. "Although not nearly as happy as you, I dare say."

Aunt Em's sympathetic look made Nell want to cry, which was foolish—she *was* safe now, and had no need to worry about what Jones might do. She nodded, taking a deep breath, and turned to watch the passing scenery.

CHAPTER 21

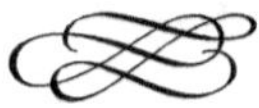

Beckett was waiting on the gravelled drive at Sir James' house when the coach drew up in front of the door. "I'm off back to the Moorcock with the coach, miss," he said, as he handed her down. "Sir James' orders." He nodded, and went to speak with the driver.

The butler showed them all into a parlour, his manner considerably more polite than the first time Nell had come here. "Mrs Bourne, Miss Delaney, and Miss Mason, my lady."

The woman who greeted them was of a similar age to Aunt Em, but more finely dressed. Aunt Em introduced Nell to the magistrate's wife.

"I am happy you are safe, my dear," Lady Troughton said to Nell. "And you, Miss Delaney. Please, be seated. I have sent for refreshments."

Nell sat, admiring the rich fabric of the curtains and upholstery, the patterned wallpaper, and the framed watercolours depicting country scenes and seascapes. She did not have long to gaze at them, for the butler entered.

"Miss Mason, Sir James requests your presence in his study."

Nell rose and followed him. To her surprise, Sir James stood as she entered his study, then resumed his seat and tapped a paper on his desk. "I am pleased you are safe, Miss Mason. Bourne's letter gave me a brief description of what happened yesterday, but I would like to hear your part in it. In detail, if you please."

Nell marshalled her thoughts while Sir James unstoppered a bottle of ink and took a blank sheet of paper from a drawer.

"I was in the circulating library yesterday…" As she told her story, Sir James stopped her frequently to ask for more detail, or to check the exact words said by Maitland and Miss Delaney. When she finished, Sir James read through his notes before looking back at her.

"Directing the colonel to the inn might have jeopardised Bourne's chances of catching Jones, but it did no harm in the end." He smiled. "That is not intended as a criticism, Miss Mason—it was a sensible decision in the circumstances, and has confirmed my suspicions about Maitland's untrustworthiness."

"What will happen to him, sir? And to my uncle and cousin?"

"I cannot say until I have spoken to everyone else concerned. I may need to question you again, and I'm afraid I may also need to ask you to formally identify Jones' body."

Nell grimaced, but nodded. An unpleasant necessity. She wasn't looking forward to meeting her uncle and cousin again, either; they would try to implicate her in Jones' plot if they thought it might help their own situations.

"Thank you, Miss Mason."

Sir James stood again as Nell left the room. The butler, waiting outside the door, ushered her back into the parlour. Empty teacups and plates showed she was too late for the promised refreshments.

"Do sit down, Miss Mason," Lady Troughton said. "I will ring for more."

Nell smiled, although the idea of having to sit and be polite to Miss Delaney was not one she relished. Something must have shown in her face, for Aunt Em spoke up.

"Would you rather return home, my dear? You must be tired."

Home. The idea that Aunt Em's house was her home, even if just for a few months, was comforting. Nell glanced at Lady Troughton, wondering whether their hostess would be offended if she wished to leave, but she smiled.

"I would prefer to go home, my lady."

"Very well. Ring the bell, if you please, and I will order the chairs."

"I'm happy to walk, my lady," Nell said as she pulled on the tasselled cord.

Lady Troughton smiled. "Just one for Mrs Bourne, then."

"If you please, Lady Troughton, I cannot walk that far," Miss Delaney said.

"I sent a note to your parents, Miss Delaney. You will have to await their arrival. In the meantime, my husband wishes to hear your story."

Miss Delaney's mouth opened, but Lady Troughton had already turned her attention to Aunt Em, saying her farewells.

The walk helped to revive Nell, and she told Aunt Em all that had happened over a pot of tea in the parlour. "Is Miss Delaney likely to be in trouble for her part?" she asked, when she came to the end of her story.

"Not with the law, I think—from what you say, she cannot have known that the brooch was stolen. Do not worry about her, my dear. She has parents to look after her." Aunt Em leaned over and patted her hand. "And you have me, for as long as you need me."

Only a fortnight ago, what Aunt Em had just said would have been everything Nell could have wanted. Now, although she felt a great relief that the danger was over and her future secure, there was still a small wish that it had been Toby saying those words. But that was foolish; he would not be here for long before rejoining his regiment.

It was late afternoon when Toby delivered Maitland and Jones' body to the magistrate's house, and later still by the time he had told his tale and listened to Maitland trying to bluster his way out of blame. Finally, Maitland gave his word to remain in his house until Sir James called on him, and left.

"Stay for dinner, Bourne," Sir James suggested. "Mr Delaney said he will call back to see you at seven o'clock, and we haven't quite finished our own discussion."

"Thank you, sir, but…" He looked down at his uniform. It was badly in need of a clean; certainly not fit for dining with a lady. It wouldn't be polite, either, to meet Mr Delaney in all his dirt, even if the man only wanted to thank him.

"Lady Troughton has already dined," Sir James said. He smiled. "I can put up with your appearance a little longer. I will have dinner sent in here."

Sir James let Toby eat in silence until he had assuaged his hunger.

"Is there anything about Maitland that you did not tell me while he was here?"

Toby thought over their earlier discussion. "I don't think so, sir. What are the chances of him being convicted for his hand in the affair?"

"Slim, I'm afraid."

As Toby had thought.

"However, he may well end up in some pecuniary difficulties. My wife has heard he is outspending his income. Miss Delaney's dowry is not large, but it would have helped. Together, no doubt, with whatever Jones paid him for providing an alibi. That is not proven, but I don't think there can be much doubt that Maitland was helping Jones in some way."

Possible pecuniary trouble didn't seem a harsh enough punishment for kidnapping and threatening to kill Nell. At least she was safe now, back with Aunt Em.

"There's nothing to be done, Bourne—not without bandying Miss Delaney's name about. And Miss Mason's. Even then, he may escape punishment. However I will make it clear that he will be under suspicion if either of them comes to any harm. Now, on another matter— you are due to return to your regiment in a week or so, I understand?"

Toby had lost track of the date, and had to think before agreeing.

"With your permission, I will write to your colonel to ask if your time can be extended. I may need to do the same for one or two of your men, if I decide they are needed as witnesses to prosecute

Weaver and his daughter, and the carters. And you have spent a considerable part of your leave on this business—you deserve to have the extra time."

"We are due to sail to the Colonies a week after I return." Although if he did have to stay here longer, he could make sure Nell was settled with Aunt Em, or wherever else she wished to be. He would enjoy spending some time with her, too, now he needn't continually have the business with Jones on his mind.

"I have contacts with some influence at Horse Guards," Sir James said. "Under the circumstances, I think they will arrange for you to follow a few weeks later, if necessary." He smiled. "It will give you time to have the banns read."

Toby dragged his mind back from a picture of walking beside Nell along the beach, or drinking wine together in front of a roaring fire. "Banns, sir?"

"Yes. Unless you wish to go to the expense of purchasing a licence?"

A lump settled in Toby's stomach. Was Sir James talking about Miss Delaney? "Um, you said Mr Delaney would be here to see me, sir?"

"Yes. He thought, under the circumstances, there would be less gossip if it could be put about that Miss Delaney's betrothal to you was announced promptly. And I have to say ..."

No! Toby had admired her when they first met, but his fascination had faded the more he got to know her. Now, every feeling revolted at the thought of being tied to her for life.

"...I think it very honourable of you to—"

"Sir!"

Sir James frowned, but did stop talking.

"Sir, I am not, nor about to be, betrothed to Miss Delaney. I don't recall saying anything that could be misconstrued in that way."

"Good heavens. She did not mention this to me, but to Lady Troughton. I suppose my wife must have misunderstood something Miss Delaney said."

Toby didn't reply. Miss Delaney had hinted he might replace Maitland in her future plans when they talked at the Moorcock, so he doubted Lady Troughton was at fault.

"I don't suppose you would like to, Bourne? She does have a dowry, and is a very well-looking young woman."

"No, sir. Definitely not."

Sir James sighed. "Oh, dear. What a coil."

There was a knock on the door, and the butler opened it. "Mr Delaney, sir."

"Show him in." Sir James turned to Toby and spoke in a quieter voice. "I'm glad we got that cleared up before he arrived."

Mr Delaney was a short man, plump in body and face, and with a beaming smile. "Lieutenant Bourne, I am pleased to meet you. My Catherine told me all about her misadventure, and your gentlemanly promise to—"

Sir James cleared his throat, loudly.

"Oh, I am sorry, Sir James. I should thank you, too, for your help in this matter. We all thought highly of Colonel Maitland when he came to ask for my Catherine's hand. Such a good match, particularly in the limited society here in Scarborough. But it is a good thing, is it not, that she discovered his true nature before it was too late?" He looked from Sir James to Toby, his happy expression fading. "Is something wrong?"

"Please, Mr Delaney, sit down. I am afraid there has been a misunderstanding." Sir James poured port and handed Mr Delaney a glass.

Toby shook his head when offered one; now was not the time to fuddle his brain. He was not going to tie himself to a woman as silly and self-centred as Miss Delaney. But seeing Mr Delaney's crestfallen expression, he chose his words carefully.

"Sir, your daughter is a beautiful young woman, but I am afraid she must have misunderstood." That was better than calling her a liar. "I have no means of supporting a wife in the way to which your daughter is rightfully accustomed. Besides, she is in no need of the protection of my name—she was alone with Colonel Maitland for only a few minutes, and the rest of the time she was accompanied by my aunt's companion."

"Your aunt?"

"Mrs Bourne," Sir James put in. "A good friend of my wife."

"Oh. That will help, I suppose. But how is it you cannot afford a wife, Lieutenant? I understood Lord Lanchester was offering a handsome reward for the recovery of his belongings."

"I have no notion how much that might be, sir," Toby said.

"I believe the promised reward was intended for those who volunteered information," Sir James put in. "Lieutenant Bourne was merely doing his duty. His Majesty's men do not expect extra reward for that."

"Oh, I see. Well, it seems a pity. A great pity." Mr Delaney frowned. "Catherine will be most disappointed."

He looked at Toby, hope in his expression, but Toby made no response.

"Ah, well. There is no help for it—I must go and tell my wife all this."

"Bring your wife and daughter to dinner one night, Delaney," Sir James said. "I will invite Mrs Bourne and her companion, and you may see in what safe hands your daughter has been."

"I will. Thank you, Sir James."

Sir James stood and rang the bell. "My wife will send a note."

"Thank you, sir," Toby said, when the butler had ushered Mr Delaney out.

"Your aunt may not thank me," Sir James said, with a wry smile. "But you dealt kindly with him."

"*Will* I get part of the reward, sir? And will Miss Mason?"

"Yes to both of you, if I have any say in the matter. Your efforts have helped to rid the county of a dangerous criminal."

"Thank you, sir."

Toby took his leave and walked into town, but he didn't go straight to Aunt Em's house. Instead he walked onto the beach, deserted now the sun had set.

The sea was calm, the beach peaceful; noise from the town faded with the distance, leaving only the gentle murmurs of small waves running up the sand. A moment of stillness after the last few days.

There was still the giving of evidence to come, but that was a tedious inconvenience, nothing more.

A time to gather his thoughts.

He could not have been forced to marry Miss Delaney, although there might have been some unpleasantness had news of their supposed betrothal been spread around the town before he could deny it. But the instant revulsion he'd felt at Sir James' statement had helped to clarify his thoughts. It wasn't only that he didn't want to marry Miss Delaney, but he thought he might, very much, enjoy being married to Nell Mason.

He liked her; her courage, intelligence, and honesty. He enjoyed talking to her as well as being drawn to her pretty face and form. When comforting her as she had identified the dead highwayman, she had felt right in his arms. And he worried what might happen to her in the future. No matter what Sir James said, or Aunt Em, there would always be people in Scarborough who knew her as the woman who'd cooked at the Moorcock. An inn that would now be notorious for its connection with Jones. And some of those would make assumptions about her morals.

If she were a married woman, the risk of that would be less. She would have a home with Aunt Em while he was away—as an equal, not as a maid—and he would have the pleasure of her company whenever he could come here on leave. In bed, too—the warm armful he'd dreamed about that night on the moor.

She might not wish to marry him, of course. Aunt Em would employ her for as long as Nell needed the employment, he was sure, and if Lord Lanchester were generous, she would have a well-earned reward. The thought that she might prefer to keep her independence even if she had to work for a living left him feeling dispirited.

He was tired, that was the problem. It was time to get himself clean —and to allow Aunt Em to question him about the last week's doings.

CHAPTER 22

Nell made herself scarce when Toby appeared, despite being pleased to see him again. Too pleased, perhaps, for her own peace of mind. She helped Mary in the kitchen while Toby cleaned himself up and then talked to Aunt Em in her parlour. Aunt Em had suggested that Nell join them, but she could not face hearing about the events of the past day again. That ride in the coach with Maitland had been the most frightening time of the whole experience. Except, perhaps, when she'd been captured near the quarry, but that fear hadn't lasted as long.

She was tired, too, after yesterday's events and keeping watch for part of the night. So she went to bed early, before Toby and Aunt Em emerged from the parlour.

Toby had already left the house the next morning when she joined Aunt Em for breakfast. Aunt Em passed her a folded note. "This is from Lady Troughton. We are invited to dinner tomorrow—you, me, and Toby. Toby should be back by then."

"Where has he gone?"

"Still doing Sir James' bidding—he said something about Pickering."

"He mentioned a friend of Sir James there." She wouldn't see him until tomorrow, then. Not that it should matter—he would be going back to his regiment soon. She looked down at her gown—the one that had belonged to Aunt Em's daughter. Was it suitable for a dinner with the magistrate and his wife? As it had been Aunt Em's gift to her, it felt discourteous to ask.

"Don't worry about your gown, my dear. There is a prettier one of Jane's you can have, and there is enough time to shorten it. You have not forgotten your manners while living at that inn, so we will say you are my companion."

"You don't need a companion, Aunt Em!"

Aunt Em smiled. "Everyone needs some companionship, my dear. Lady Troughton invited us for a reason. It appears Miss Delaney told her that she was to marry Toby, to save her good name."

Oh.

"Toby explained you had been with her all the time, and that as my companion, you were respectable enough to be a chaperone."

Why would he need to do that? "Doesn't he want to marry her?"

"Good heavens, no!"

Nell felt giddy for a moment. That news should not make her feel so relieved.

"She was foolish to trust Maitland," Aunt Em continued. "But she is young and doesn't deserve to suffer from it. Or her parents to be made unhappy, come to that. I know Mrs Delaney a little, and they dote on their daughter. Too much, perhaps, but Lady Troughton's public acceptance of her and her family will go a long way to suppress any gossip about her broken betrothal with Maitland. Now, I'll get the gown, and ask Hannah to help you pin the hem."

Nell spent most of the day making adjustments to the new gown— a pale rose fabric with a pattern of embroidered flowers. She wondered why Aunt Em's daughter had left it behind, until Hannah pointed out a stain around the hem; one that would no longer be visible once it was shortened to fit Nell. When that was done, she helped Mary with some cooking, enjoying making more elaborate sauces and pastries than she had attempted before.

Toby returned partway through the following afternoon, while

Nell was sewing a strip of newly bought lace to the neck of the gown. "Hello, Nell. Is that one of Jane's gowns? It will look well on you."

His smile was approving as well as his words. Nell felt a blush rising to her cheeks; had his gaze lingered longer on her face than on the gown? "Thank you. It is for Lady Troughton's dinner this evening."

"Are you nearly finished? Would you care to go for a walk?"

"I would enjoy that." She hoped the heat in her face did not show as she draped the gown carefully over a chair.

In the kitchen, Toby put her cloak around her shoulders, and offered his arm when they reached the street. They walked down the hill towards the shore. It felt very strange, walking beside him like this. In all their previous encounters, Toby had been a customer at the Moorcock or the man in charge of catching Jones. This felt different. Comfortable, but something more.

"I thought I would let you know what has happened," Toby said when they reached the sands and began to stroll parallel to the water.

Nell's pleasure in the outing faded a little. Although if that had been all he wanted, they could have talked in Aunt Em's parlour.

"Sir James questioned your uncle and cousin this morning, in my presence. Bett had a ring hidden in her petticoat, as you surmised. Lord Lanchester's man identified it as part of the stolen jewellery. That, alone, is sufficient evidence to convict her." He rubbed his forehead. "She appeared to be genuinely distressed when she learned Jones was dead, and insisted on seeing the body."

Nell grimaced at the idea that Bett had really liked such a vicious man, but felt some sympathy, too. How horrible to see your lover like that.

"She identified Jones, which means you do not need to," Toby went on.

"That's good, thank you." The idea of doing so hadn't been worrying her, precisely, but it had been niggling at the back of her mind.

"The two carters were happy enough to state that Weaver had hired them to take some chests and two people to the Whitby area, to meet a boat. It seems Jones was going to flee the country for a while—possibly to sell some of the pieces without them being identified."

Nell nodded, unsure why Toby was telling her all this. She had only seen the two carters for a few minutes, when they'd been locked up in the inn.

"The point being," Toby said, "that you will not be needed as a witness when Weaver and Bett face trial at the next assizes, in the spring. Nor will I."

There would be no reason for him to stay in the country, then. Perhaps that was for the best—the more she saw of him, the more she enjoyed his company.

"You may visit them in gaol, if you wish." He stopped, and turned to face her. "But equally, you need not if you do not wish to. I... I have to tell you that they were not... not complimentary about you."

Nell put her hands to her face. "They blamed me for their arrests, I suppose." That hurt, although it was not unexpected.

"I'm afraid so." He touched her shoulder; gripped it gently. "Nell—you have Aunt Em as family now. She is happy for you to live with her for as long as you wish. And there will be a reward for your part in this, although I don't yet know how much it will be. You need not work again as you have been."

"Thank you." She swallowed. "I know they are my relatives, but I don't want to see them." Best to put that part of her life behind her, if she could, and not think of them again.

He put his arm around her shoulders and gave a short squeeze before letting go.

Toby wondered if he should leave his proposal for later. It could not be easy to be told your only living relatives were hostile towards you; he was glad she had decided not to see them. But her downturned eyes and drooping lips roused his protective instincts and firmed his resolution. During the few moments he'd had to himself today, he'd recalled his thinking on the beach two nights ago, and found no fault with his conclusion. Marriage would give her protection from gossip, and he would have a lovely woman to come home to. One he suspected he would miss very much while he was away.

"There may be gossip, Nell—the Moorcock is notorious in this area. More so, after this business with Jones."

"Will that reflect badly on Aunt Em? I could look for a position—"

"That wasn't what I meant. It may reflect badly on *you*."

She shrugged. "That cannot be helped, can it? I know there is no going back to my former life, but I will be content with Aunt Em." She smiled at him, a somewhat tremulous smile. "I am lucky to have encountered you and your aunt. You have both been so kind to me."

It was easy to be kind to her. It was his pleasure to be so. "Nell, if you were a married woman, there would be less gossip." He took her hands. "Will you allow me to give you the protection of my name?"

Her mouth fell open for a moment, then, instead of the agreement he'd hoped for, a small crease formed between her brows.

He hurried into speech again. "It will help you while I am away. And… and I do enjoy your company, Nell. I would worry whether or not you were safe, otherwise. There is time to call the banns and wed before I have to leave."

Nell pulled her hands away from his, clasping them in front of her. "I do thank you, but it is not necessary. Really, it is not. If gossip does make things uncomfortable here for Aunt Em, she will write a character for me and I will find a position elsewhere." She turned and started to walk along the sand again.

Toby rubbed his forehead, surprised how hurt he felt at her refusal. Had she not understood what he had said, or had he said the wrong thing?

The latter, most likely. He hurried to catch up.

Nell stopped when he put a hand on her arm, but didn't turn to face him. His offer had made her realise how much she'd wanted to hear those words—but not for the reason he gave. If she were still at the Moorcock with little money and no prospects, she might well have accepted to secure her future. But with Aunt Em's friendship and the prospect of some reward money, she had no need to do so. She had hoped to one day have a marriage as loving as the one between Mama and Papa, even if that seemed a remote possibility. A marriage with attraction between the parties, not one made for practical reasons.

Mutual attraction, that was the key. She wanted him—his friendship and his company. And his touch—she was beginning to understand what Mama had meant about intimacy. But she didn't think she could stand being married to someone who did not feel the same way about her.

"Nell, please. I... I didn't express myself clearly. I am not asking this only to protect you. I *want* to marry you."

According to Aunt Em, he had turned down the much prettier Miss Delaney. Perhaps he *did* like her for herself? Was liking enough?

"We have barely known each other for a fortnight," she said. "Less than that, really. We have spent only a few hours in each other's company."

"I see." His voice was flat. "If you feel that way, there is no more to be said. Come, we will walk back."

"No!" Nell spoke without thinking. Had he really given up so easily? Taken her comment as a final answer? She must say more; explain her hesitation. She had nothing to lose. If she made a complete fool of herself—well, there was no-one watching. And she could avoid the embarrassment of having to see him afterwards by keeping out of his way until he returned to the army.

"Toby, I meant that making a decision that will affect the rest of our lives on such short acquaintance is... is taking a big risk. My parents were happy together, but even when I was a child, I knew of married people who were not."

"Nell, you don't believe I would ever mistreat you, do you?" He spoke gently.

"No, of course not." He had been kind to her, but she also felt— knew, even—that he would not. "I need a little time to decide." She had taken more risks recently than ever before, by investigating the quarry and throwing in her lot with the soldiers, but she had considered the consequences first. She should do the same now.

"Sir James has asked my commanding officer to extend my leave," Toby said. "We have a few weeks for you to think about it."

"Thank you." But she could not consider it calmly so close to him. "Shall we return? We are all to go to dinner with Sir James and Lady Troughton."

He held out his arm and she took it. He covered her hand with his own, and they walked close together, their arms touching. It felt good.

Half an hour later, Nell sat on her bed, beside the gown she was to wear that evening. This decision was not like the ones she had made after hearing about Jones' plan. Those had involved her safety, but with Aunt Em's promise of employment and friendship that was no longer a concern.

No, this was about her happiness. But Toby would be returning to his regiment soon, and sailing across the Atlantic. Would she be happy possibly bringing up a babe without its father, other than brief periods of leave? It would be different if Toby's regiment were to be stationed in England, but that might not happen for years. She hoped love might grow between them, but could that happen with Toby away for years at a time, possibly never to return? And if it did, that would make his absences harder to bear. She wouldn't even know if he was well or injured until months after he'd been in a battle.

She took a deep breath and began to unpin her stomacher to change for this evening's dinner. Nothing ventured, nothing gained—she would happily accept Toby's offer, *if* she could persuade him of something first.

Toby knocked on Aunt Em's parlour door. "Your chair is here, Auntie," he said as he entered, then stopped, wordless. Nell had donned the gown she had been sewing earlier. It had a lower neckline than he'd yet seen on her, and it set off her figure well. Her hair was dressed high, with a ringlet over one shoulder, but it was her smile that made his breath catch. A tentative smile, almost shy.

"You look beautiful."

Her cheeks turned a rosy hue and she dropped her eyes.

"Are you sure you want to walk, Nell? It's cold outside."

"I'm sure."

Aunt Em coughed, and Toby dragged his eyes away. "You look very fine, too, Auntie."

"Thank you, my dear. Now you two go on. I will catch you up in the chair shortly."

Toby draped Nell's cloak around her shoulders, carefully drawing up the hood so as not to disturb the arrangement of her hair.

"Tell me about life on campaign," Nell said, as they set out. "Some women follow the army, do they not?"

It seemed an odd question to Toby, but he answered it anyway. "They do, but it can be a hard life. They often have to walk many miles each day when the army is on the move, then set up camp, help to cook, and so on."

"Do you march, too?"

"Officers normally ride. I will need to buy a horse when I get to Boston."

"Do you sleep in a tent?"

This conversation was beginning to feel more like an interrogation. "If I have to, but officers are usually billeted in a house, if possible. Sometimes we're lucky and are very comfortable. At others, particularly on the march, we put up in cold, draughty rooms. It's not a comfortable life."

"No, it is not."

"It's no life for..." Toby shook his head. She hadn't said she could imagine the conditions, or sympathised with him. "Nell, I'm sorry. You must think me unfeeling—that sounds like the way you have been living for the last few years."

She smiled. "Do not apologise. You said you would worry about me when you were away, did you not?"

The abrupt change of subject threw him for a moment. "Er, yes. If we were not wed."

"Do you not think that I will worry about you at the same time?"

"I suppose you would, yes." If she did not worry at all, what would that say about her feelings for him? "But it cannot be helped—I know no business other than soldiering. Nell, I will miss you when I am back with the army, but—"

"No, you won't. Because I will be with you."

Was she accepting him? His heart beat faster at the thought; he had not expected her answer so quickly. But could he agree to her accompanying him? He'd always thought following the drum was no life for a gently bred woman. Nell *was* gently bred, but she was more than that. He looked down at her. "Nell, has this whole conversation been leading up to this?"

She grinned—laughing at him, but also with him. "It has. I know there may be some danger—"

He didn't smile in return—he had to be sure she understood. "We do try to keep womenfolk away from the fighting, Nell, but it is not always possible. There could be considerable danger at times, and sometimes draughty rooms are the least of the discomforts and inconveniences. There may not always be a carriage, or even a horse, available when we are on the move."

"I do understand, Toby. If I were used doing nothing more strenuous than strolling around the town, then what you say would be a problem indeed. I cannot say that I welcome the risks and discomforts, but I would rather have that than worry about what is happening to you when news could take months to reach me." She leaned into him a little as she spoke, squeezing his arm. "And I think there will be compensations, won't there?"

"I hope so." He would certainly do his best to make it so.

Had he agreed? Nell wasn't sure—but he definitely hadn't disagreed. Toby's face looked thoughtful, but the smile he gave her as Sir James' butler opened the door had mischief in it. He said something to the butler that she could not hear.

The butler showed them into a small parlour that Nell had not seen before. It was lit only by the fading daylight outside, and there was no fire in the grate.

"Why are we here, Toby?"

"I thought I might demonstrate one of the compensations. If you agree, that is." He stood before her and lowered the hood of her cloak, then took her shoulders and pulled her close—but gently. He hadn't explained, but the way he was looking at her face, her mouth, made his intention plain. A look that made her stomach flutter.

"What if someone comes in?"

"Then your reputation will be completely compromised and you will have to marry me."

"In that case…" She stepped even closer to him and tilted her face up further. He laughed briefly, then his face became more serious as he cupped her cheeks in his hands and bent his head. Their lips touched briefly, gently. He put one hand on the small of her back and curled the other behind her head as he moved his mouth against hers. He didn't need to pull—as heat spread through her, she moved closer until their bodies were pressed close.

The kiss had to end, and he lifted his head, leaving her flushed. "That will do nicely as a start," she said, when she had recovered her breath. She wanted more, but not here. "So, will I be accompanying you or not?"

"If that is your condition for agreeing, Nell, then yes. I would miss you, too, if I had to leave you in England." He stilled as voices sounded beyond the door.

Nell recognised Miss Delaney's voice, and Lady Troughton greeting her guests. "It would be impolite to continue hiding in here," she said, taking his hand and starting for the door. "As long as you are not going to change your mind?"

"Certainly not!" He unfastened her cloak and threw it onto a chair, then gave her his arm.

It seemed as if dozens of faces were gazing at them as Toby opened the door. He bowed. "Congratulate us, if you please. We are betrothed."

EPILOGUE

Four months later—Boston, February 1756
Nell pulled her cloak more tightly about her against the biting wind. The novelty of watching the waves had worn off after the sixth week of the voyage, but now there was land ahead. And the anticipation of a room in an inn where she could not touch both walls at the same time.

She smiled to herself—the tiny cabin hadn't been all bad. The upper berth had not had much use; once her stomach had become accustomed to the motion of the ship, she and Toby had shared the bottom one.

"Land at last." Toby came to stand behind her, one hand on the rail each side of her, making a shield from the wind. She leaned into the solid warmth of him.

"A new land," Nell said. They had married in Scarborough as soon as the banns had been read, then taken a leisurely journey to Portsmouth. She had seen more of England in those few weeks than in the whole of her life before, and looked forward to more new places and people.

"If my orders allow it, we'll spend a few days here," Toby said, his breath warm on her cheek. "Time to get used to the ground *not* moving beneath our feet." She heard a chuckle. "And get used to a decent sized bed again."

"Do you *ever* think of anything else?" She turned in the circle of his arms, her breath catching at his smile.

"Not when you're near." He pulled her closer. "I love *you*, Nell. All of you, not just what we do in bed together."

He had said so before, but she never tired of hearing it. "I love you, too." She stood on tiptoe and kissed him briefly on the lips before turning back to watch the widening line of grey on the horizon. He chuckled, moving to stand beside her. They watched as the town and harbour gradually grew larger, quays and buildings becoming distinct. They had already packed their belongings into the two small trunks, so they stayed on deck until the ship dropped anchor in the harbour, and small boats rowed out from the quay to collect passengers and cargo.

Toby left Nell soaking in a tub of hot water in the Royal George, and went in search of the army office. It felt good to stretch his legs, although the clutter of people, horses, and vehicles impeded his progress. He found the place without too much difficulty, and waited until the clerk finished dealing with the people ahead of him.

"Your orders, sir," the clerk said at last, handing over a sealed paper. "And a letter. A frigate arrived with mail two days ago."

Toby recognised Aunt Em's handwriting and broke the seal. There was only one sheet but, as usual, Aunt Em had written in tiny letters and crossed her lines. It would take some concentration to read it, but the opening words told him that she was well, so he turned to his orders. He was to report to Fort Frederick.

"How long does it take to get to Albany?" he asked the clerk.

"A sennight, if you're lucky. Twice as long if the weather's against you. Coach or horseback?"

"Coach. I have my wife with me." It still felt a novelty to say that—

and it also felt good. He'd taken Nell riding while they were still in Scarborough, but she wasn't yet confident on horseback. Nor did he want to subject her to the cold of this time of year.

The clerk took a box from a shelf and thumbed through the papers in it. "I may be able to arrange for you to share a coach with the family of another officer travelling that way in three days. Will that suit?"

"Very well, thank you." Toby discreetly placed a coin on the corner of the desk. The clerk wasn't obliged to be so helpful.

"Call back tomorrow, sir." The clerk put the box away, seeming to ignore the coin, but when Toby glanced back from the door it had disappeared.

Rather to his disappointment, Nell was fully dressed when he returned, although her hair was still loose. She sat at the table by the window in their room, reading one of the many books they had brought with them, but set it down when he entered.

"We're bound for Albany." They had examined maps of the Colonies on the ship, and had a good idea of where the various towns and forts were in relation to each other. Albany was a sizeable town, and it would be a good place to leave Nell if he had to—if a baby were to come. He set that thought aside and dropped Aunt Em's letter on the table. "Aunt Em has written. I will let you decipher it."

Nell grimaced when she saw the writing, but made no protest. Toby pulled his boots off and lay back on the bed. "Tell me what it says, Nell. Reading Aunt Em's letters gives me a headache."

"She is well. Tim used some of his reward money to apprentice himself to a Scarborough shipbuilder."

That was good. He didn't know the lad well, but anyone who'd had to work for Weaver deserved some better luck. She read on, frowning at something, then smiling.

"What is it?"

"The magistrate received a note addressed only to 'Nell', saying 'Found her, Forgiven.' Gibson must have found the daughter he left behind years ago."

Mystified, Toby shook his head.

"I told you about Gibson, did I not? He kept me safe. It seems he's happy now." Then her smile broadened even more as she read on. "Aunt Em saved the best news until last."

"Mr Everidge?" Aunt Em's admirer had come for dinner several times while they were in Scarborough. Toby liked him—he was well read and interesting to talk to. But more importantly, he was kind, and seemed to have a genuine affection for his aunt. "Finally decided to get spliced, has he?"

"They will marry in May. Aunt Em will keep the boarding house, but hire a housekeeper to run it for her."

Toby sat up. "That *is* good news. They will deal well together, I think."

"The only other news is that Sir James received information that Maitland was seen conferring with Gentleman Jones a week before the robbery. He sent a constable to bring him in for questioning, but the man arrived to find bailiffs emptying the house and Maitland gone. There's been no sign of him since, but it appears he's now a wanted man and not far from penniless."

"Who cares about Maitland?" There was no news of her relatives, either, but Toby hadn't expected any. They were still awaiting trial—although Sir James had said he thought they were more likely to be transported than hanged.

Toby moved over to the table. "We have an hour or more before dinner. I think you need a rest." He ran his hands through her hair, letting it slip between his fingers.

But he wasn't surprised when she slowly pulled away from his grasp and wound her hair into a knot. "Someone told me once—you, I think—that a good soldier always reconnoitres new surroundings. We should use the time we have to walk around the town. We will only be here for a few days, and I have shopping to do!"

They had invested some of the money Lord Lanchester had given them as a reward, but Nell had kept a portion of hers back to buy herself a new wardrobe. One suitable for the wife of a soon-to-be captain, for Toby had used some of his share to apply for a promotion.

He laughed, and pulled his boots on again. They would look around together, and he might spy a shop where he could buy her a gift. There would be plenty of time for other things after dinner. "The town, then."

From the *Scarborough Advertiser and Record*, 1772

CIRCULATING LIBRARY

George Everidge begs leave to inform his Loyal Cuſtomers and the Public that he is paſſing ownerſhip of his circulating library to Major Bourne, lately returned from the Colonies. Major and Mrs. Bourne have taken new, more commodious premiſes on Princeſs Street which will allow them to further augment the Publications available in every claſs of Literature.

Subſcribers may be aſſured of being liberally ſupplied with the beſt Modern Publications conducive to Information, Amuſement, and uſeful Inſtruction, and the prompt arrival of various Magazines and Periodicals.

The Upper Floor will provide two ſpacious and comfortable Apartments for the ſeparate uſe of Ladies and Gentlemen to whom the buſtle of the warerooms may be an interruption.

For Subſcription Terms or a Catalogue, pleaſe apply in Perſon.

HISTORICAL NOTES

Inspiration

This book was inspired by the Alfred Noyes poem 'The Highwayman', but although I used the general setting and a few incidents, the book does not tell the same story as the poem. I love the rhythms and imagery in 'The Highwayman', but I have never been entirely comfortable with the glorification of a criminal, which is effectively what the poem does. Hence the switch of the highwayman from the supposed tragic hero in the poem to the villain in my story.

You can find the poem on the internet. The Canadian singer Loreena McKennitt has set the poem to music, originally released on her album *The Book of Secrets*.

My thanks to the estate of Alfred Noyes for permission to use incidents from his poem in my story.

Time and place

I set this story in the middle of the 18th century, rather than my normal Regency period, as highwaymen were not at all common by then.

'The Highwayman' is set in a remote inn on an unspecified moor. However, I like to have a good idea of where my story takes place, so I chose the moorland with which I am most familiar—the North York Moors. I have family living near there, so have visited often. The poem is a good fit for these moors, as it refers to the road being visible by moonlight. On the North York Moors the grass and heather is underlain by pale stone, which makes unpaved roads show up clearly in most lighting conditions.

Today, the major roads crossing the moor run north-south; the road between Pickering (to the south of the moors) and Whitby (on the coast to the north) is one of these, and is now the A169. There are no major roads crossing the moors from east to west, although a network of minor roads, bridleways, and footpaths allows an east-west crossing. For the purposes of this story I have imagined a track going east to west, and placed the Moorcock Inn where this crosses the main north-south road.

North York Moors crosses

There are a number of crosses scattered across the North York Moors, in various states of repair, and lots of standing stones and other ancient remains. Many of the crosses date from medieval times, and some have been repaired from time to time. The crosses are such a distinctive feature that the symbol for the National Park depicts one of the most famous ones (Young Ralph Cross – the one I have used as part of the cover image).

Some crosses mark important roads (as does the imagined one in this story), but the purpose of many of them is unknown. They could have marked old coffin routes across the moors (see below), bound-aries between parishes, or land belonging to different owners. A few dating from the 20th century are memorials to well-known local people, and some of the older ones may also have served this purpose. There are various folk tales and legends about the origins of some of the crosses.

Young Ralph Cross is near Castleton, and was known to travellers in the last century for the hollow in its top. Travellers would place money in this, to be used by other passers-by who were too poor to buy food on their journey. This custom was the inspiration for what Nell says about the cross near the inn.

Coffin, or corpse roads, were the routes over which the dead were taken from isolated homes or hamlets to the nearest church where the corpse could be given a proper burial. They occur in the sparsely inhabited parts of Britain, including the North York Moors and Yorkshire Dales.

Quarries and quarrymen

Parts of the North York Moors have been mined for iron and coal, but most of the workings date from the mid-19th century, so well after the time in which this story is set.

Small quarries can be found in various places on the moors. Most are now disused, and were probably dug to obtain stone for a nearby building rather than as a trading enterprise. I didn't want the Moorcock to be busy with passing trade, or it wouldn't have been the kind of inn that would have been run by a man like Silas, or used by a villain such as Gentleman Jones. But an inn does need a certain number of customers to be viable, so I invented some nearby active quarries. And, of course, I needed a disused one as a place for Jones to hide his ill-gotten gains.

The militia and the regular army

The militia regiments were part-time volunteer units organised within each county. They did exist at the time of this story, but were overhauled and given central government funding two years after this story starts (1757). Militia were used for internal matters such as quelling riots and chasing smugglers, and would never have been sent abroad to fight. In fact an irony in *Pride and Prejudice* that many readers miss is that the brave militia men in their red coats whom Lydia and Mrs Bennet swoon over would only have fought another army if the French had invaded Britain.

Over the hills and far away

The song that Toby and Nell refer to in Chapter 14 is 'Over the hills and far away'. This is a traditional British song from the 17th century, although there are several different sets of words for it. Nell is recalling the version by George Farquhar written for the play *The Recruiting Officer* (1706). Part of the first verse is:

Over the hills and o'er the main,
To Flanders, Portugal and Spain,
The queen commands and we'll obey
Over the hills and far away.

Readers who have watched the *Sharpe* TV series (set in the Napoleonic wars) may be familiar with the variation written and sung by John Tams used with the end credits.

Small beer

The text refers to Nell and others drinking small beer with their meals. Small beer is beer with a very low alcohol content (less than 1%), and at the time of this story was a common everyday drink. As boiling water was part of the brewing process, small beer was often safer to drink than water, and also had some nutritional value. As tea became cheaper later in the century, it began to replace small beer as a common drink.

FROM THE AUTHOR

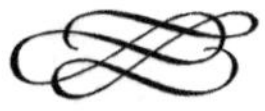

Thank you for reading the stories in this collection; I hope you enjoyed them. If you can spare a few minutes, I'd be very grateful if you could review this volume on Amazon or Goodreads.

You can read more about my books on my website:

www.jaynedavisromance.co.uk

If you want news of special offers or new releases, join my mailing list via the contact page on my website. I won't bombard you with emails, I promise! Alternatively, follow me on Facebook - links are on my website.

ABOUT THE AUTHOR

I wanted to be a writer when I was in my teens, hooked on Jane Austen and Georgette Heyer (and lots of other authors). Real life intervened, and I had several careers, including as a non-fiction author under another name. That wasn't *quite* the writing career I had in mind!

Now I am lucky enough to be able to spend most of my time writing, when I'm not out walking, cycling, or enjoying my garden.

THE MARSTONE SERIES

A duelling viscount, a courageous poor relation and an overbearing lord—just a few of the memorable cast of characters you will meet in *The Marstone Series*. From windswept Devonshire, to Georgian London and revolutionary France, true love is always on the horizon and shady dealings often afoot.

The series is named after Will, who becomes the 9th Earl of Marstone. He appears in all the stories, although often in a minor role.

Each book can be read as a standalone story, but readers of the series will enjoy meeting characters from previous books. They are available as individual novels in ebook and paperback. The full-length novels are also available as a box set in ebook only.

A Question of Duty - Book 0 (Prequel Novella included in this volume)

Sauce for the Gander - Book 1

A Winning Trick - Book 1.5 (Extended epilogue to Book 1)

A Suitable Match - Book 2

Molly's Tale - Book 2.1 (A parallel story to *A Suitable Match*, with the story of the lady's maid's own romance)

Playing with Fire - Book 3

The Fourth Marchioness - Book 4

A duel. An ultimatum. An arranged marriage.

England, 1777

Will, Viscount Wingrave, whiles away his time gambling and bedding married women, thwarted in his wish to serve his country by his controlling father.

News that his errant son has fought a duel with a jealous husband is the last straw for the Earl of Marstone. He decrees that Will must marry. The earl's eye lights upon Connie Charters, whose position as unpaid housekeeper for a poor but socially ambitious father hides her true intelligence.

Connie wants a husband who will love and respect her, not a womaniser and a gambler. When her conniving father forces the match, she has no choice but to agree.

Will and Connie meet for the first time at the altar.

As they settle into their new home on the wild coast of Devonshire, the young couple find they have more in common than they thought. But there are dangerous secrets that threaten both them and the nation.

Can Will and Connie overcome the dark forces that conspire against them and find happiness together?

THE MRS MACKINNONS

England, 1799

Major Matthew Southam returns from India, hoping to put the trauma of war behind him and forget his past. Instead, he finds a derelict estate and a family who wish he'd died abroad.

Charlotte MacKinnon married without love to avoid her father's unpleasant choice of husband. Now a widow with a young son, she lives in a small Cotswold village with only the money she earns by her writing.

Matthew is haunted by his past, and Charlotte is fearful of her father's renewed meddling in her future. After a disastrous first meeting, can they help each other find happiness?

Available from Amazon on Kindle and in paperback. Read free in Kindle Unlimited.

Listen via Audible or AudioBooks.com.

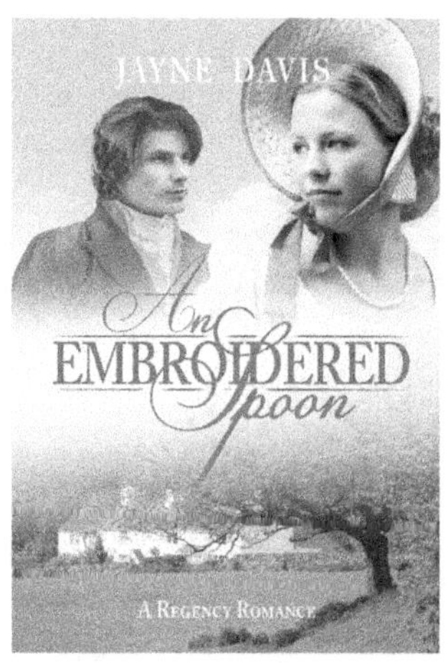

Can love bridge a class divide?

Wales 1817

After refusing every offer of marriage that comes her way, Isolde Farrington is packed off to a spinster aunt in Wales until she comes to her senses.

Rhys Williams, there on business, is turning over his uncle's choice of bride for him, and the last thing he needs is to fall for an impertinent miss like Izzy – who takes Rhys for a yokel. But while a man may choose his wife, he cannot choose who he falls in love with.

Izzy's new surroundings make her look at life, and Rhys, afresh. As she realises her early impressions were mistaken, her feelings about him begin to change.

But when her father, Lord Bedley, discovers the situation in Wales is not what he thought, and that Rhys is in trade, Izzy is hurriedly returned to London. Will a difference in class keep them apart?

Available from Amazon on Kindle and in paperback. Read free in Kindle Unlimited.

Listen via most retailers of audio books.